A GIFT OF NAME

Book 1 of *The Stolen Heir Series*

Val Cates

9/7/19

To Joyce
Thank you for
your support!
Enjoy!

Val Cates

CONTENTS

For Gaven,
who always believed

CHAPTER 1

There is power in a name.

Maybe that's why it's the first thing he takes from us. When you have no name, there is no sense of self, and there's nothing left to lose. I can't remember anything about who I was before I came to Castle Ciar. It's no use. If I, or any of the other nameless slaves here, had a history before we came to these walls, we were forced to forget it. That's the will of Abirad. When he takes your name, you forget who you are.

I'm not certain what my name was, but now I'm just called Boy.

I suppose, in some ways, it is better to forget. I almost prefer it this way. I can't tell you how many times I've watched new slaves being brought to the castle. Their screams echo loudly down the halls as they cry out for their loved ones: their mothers, fathers, children, husbands, wives. The idea that someone could be waiting for me somewhere beyond the walls, that someone could be crying for me and wishing I was home, is an unbearable thought. It's easier to believe I have no one mourning me.

But I guess that's not entirely true. There may be at least one person who misses me. I can't tell anyone about it, not even Wise, who I trust more than anyone, or Old Man, who is my cellmate and mentor. I can't tell Brock, the only other close friend I've ever known. I can't tell any of them that with all the memories Abirad has stolen from me, there is one left intact.

A woman...

She smells of flowers and sunlight. Her hair falls across her shoulders in delicate brown waves, and her eyes are the same stormy grey color as the little boy she holds in the air. I see his reflection in the mirrors that accent the room where they dance. The boy giggles as the woman sweeps him into the air, spinning him around, his chubby cheeks flushed with glee as some distant music plays in the background.

I cling selfishly to the memory, sharing it with no one. I know if Abirad ever found out, he would take this from me, too. I wish for all the world I can know who she is. When I think of her, my heart hammers in my chest, and as much as I fight the idea, I know the boy in the mirror is me, and I know the woman, whoever she is or was, loved me. And from the way my heart aches every time this memory surfaces, I know I loved her, too, even if she is but a bone-deep memory. This memory gives me hope, but it also causes me a dull aching that is painfully difficult to rid myself of, so I lose myself entirely in my work.

It's like a dance, but with more blood, sweat, and tears. I glance down at the bright, crimson liquid that begins to seep from my knuckles. Sweat streams down my face in sharp, stinging rivulets, making me blink my eyes rapidly. The searing sun beats down mercilessly upon my back.

Blood, sweat, and tears.

The only thing I'm missing are the tears, and to be honest, I don't even think I remember how to cry. It's been about six or seven years at my best guess. It's hard to keep track of things here; time is one of the many things I've lost. Knowing the hour or day of the week doesn't matter much in this forsaken place. The only reason I even remember my last encounter with tears is because it was about the time I lost my name, and with it, my hope.

Tears accomplish nothing anyway; they do little more than get the attention of the guards. Attention is not something I want. To be noticed is to feel the swift crack of a whip that tears my shirt to ribbons and leaves deep, gaping wounds upon my back. I've been noticed far more frequently than I like. Even now, I can feel the scars scrape against the thin, threadbare covering that passes as a shirt. It is laughable, scant protection from the oppressive sun.

I glance across the yard and see Brock as he takes out his aggression on the large rock in front of him. In a few minutes, it will be little more than a pile of pebbles. Brock with his towering height, broad shoulders, and muscled arms, he's strong, *really* strong, and one of the best rock breakers we have, hence the name Brock.

I'm not sure if I had a brother before I came here, but Brock has become like one to me. He's the kind of person you want watching your back. Even the guards think twice about tangling with him. While I manage to escape the notice of most people, he has a way of catching everyone's attention, especially the attention of the girls, who always seem to find excuses to linger around his work area. His most recent admirer, Jewel, one of the gem sorters, gives him a long look as she crosses the yard, and he flashes her a brief smile before he bends down to sift through the pile of rocks and gather any precious gems he may find.

We're forced to collect anything that may be of value, but it's the singing stones that are most coveted by Abirad, so much so that anyone who finds one gets a day without labor and an extra set of rations. Brock sees me looking at him and gives a nod in my direction. He hefts his bucket, laden with precious gems, onto his shoulders and lumbers towards the nearest sorting hut. I chance a quick wave before returning to my work.

Brock's days in the yard are numbered. Due to his size and strength, he will surely be sent to the mines soon. That is where they always send the best workers. This will give him an opportunity for a hard cot instead of sleeping on the cold floors of the cells, and he will be able to claim some extra rations, and rumor has it, even an occasional piece of meat. However, there's also a good chance that Wise, Old Man, and

I will never see him again. Many workers die in the mines. It will be hard to see him go, and even now the thought of him leaving gives me a sinking feeling in my stomach.

I grip the pickaxe tighter and cast a brief glance to my right. There's a young boy toiling next to me. His light, blonde hair falls upon his forehead, and his deep, blue eyes are the color of a night sky. I can't help but to admire the look of determination in the kid's face. There's a hint of defiance in his features, and I feel a sharp pang of sadness because I know that one day, not long from now, that look will be replaced by the same hopelessness that masks the faces of all who live here.

I know I've seen the kid before, but never down here in the yards. He's usually surrounded by guards and being hurried from one section of the castle to another. Truth be told, his sudden appearance down here has been a topic of discussion amongst the other slaves. I've seen kids younger than this boy handed pickaxes and sent to rot in the sun, and the sad truth of it is, most of them don't last long. Abirad isn't known for his mercy.

So, what's managed to save this boy from Abirad's anger for so long, and what suddenly changed that he's down here with the rest of us now? He doesn't have the lean look that comes from long hours of work, nor the dead-eyed expression of those who have given in to despair. His hands are still soft, not a single callous in sight. There's a healthy color to his cheeks, and he appears to be fed well enough.

He's been down here for a few hours now, sifting through rocks with his hands. When the guard tosses a pickaxe on the ground near his feet, half of me is genuinely sympathetic, and the other half has to suppress a chuckle at the kid's expression. His jaw drops open, and he is at a loss for words, his lips gaping open then closed like a fish. The kid glares at the guard. If looks could kill, Harding there would be dead. However, he ignores the boy's look of disgust and heads back to his post without a single word. Rare for Harding. Usually, one of his favorite pastimes is to stand upon the ramparts and shout obscenities down at us. He calls it "motivation."

The kid gawks at the tool in his hands, then over to me as I slam my pickaxe into a massive rock to separate bits of mineral from the boulder in front of me. It looks like he's taking mental notes on how to manage this strange, unwieldy thing in his hands. I'm starting to wonder if he even knows what a pickaxe is. He hefts it as best he can, which proves to be quite pitiful. He looks like he's about to fall over from the weight of it, but he manages to muster enough strength to swing the pickaxe forward. I see him wince as the pickaxe hits stone. He staggers a bit but lifts it again, still struggling under the weight of the cumbersome tool.

I toy with the idea of offering the kid some advice, as I've had years to hone the fine art of hard labor, but I make it a point not to speak with those outside of my little circle: Old Man, Brock, and Wise. This little rule has served me well enough. When people befriend others, they tend to organize. Organizing leads to dangerous talk. Dangerous talk inevitably leads to a long, painful death from Abirad's twisted magic. I've seen it happen too many times before. Befriending people makes you let your guard down, or makes you start to think too much about what you could be missing outside these walls.

The kid's still staring at me, but I go back to the dance of blood and sweat. My tears are replaced by pain, and my memories with work. This is the only life I know. I fight the urge to look at the child again, but down comes my pickaxe as I focus on the dance. Even though the long hours of harsh treatment and tough labor make my body ache and hands bleed, I find some small comfort in the sounds of the pickaxe chiming against the rocks.

Up, down, up, down, sift, sift, drop. The pickaxe against the rock. A second time. Sifting through the rubble for gems or precious metals, and when found, dropping them into one of the rusty, metal bins that receive them. I focus on the natural rhythms, on the musical qualities of these sounds. Like a dance.

"HEY! YOU!"

I groan, knowing the voice immediately. Caius, one of the head guards, and arguably, the most heavy-handed. Many times I've been at the wrong end of his whip. Caius loves nothing more than cries and whimpers. Those sounds of despair just make him even more merciless. Maybe that's why I infuriate Caius so much. While others groan and weep, Caius can't manage to get me to make a sound, no matter how hard he hits me.

"You!" He's sounding pretty angry, not at all uncommon of Caius.

I take a deep breath and turn to look at the guard, the man who makes it his daily duty to make my life as miserable as possible. I mentally prepare myself for the thrashing that's sure to follow. However, when I set my eyes upon Caius, I quickly realize that, for once, I'm not Caius's quarry. Rather, he's angrily marching towards the small, blonde child next to me. The child has caught Caius's attention. He, too, will learn that attention is an undesirable thing.

"Just because you're new here you think you don't have to work?" Spittle flies from Caius's mouth as he bends down to scream at the child. "You're working at a dead man's pace!"

The kid drags the back of his hand across his own forehead to rub away the rogue drops of Caius's saliva, then proceeds to frown in disgust. "I'm working as fast as I can."

"Well, work faster!" Caius spins on his heel, preparing to stomp off in the direction of his post.

The kid mutters something under his breath.

"Jerk."

Caius stops abruptly. The kid shouldn't have said that. He's bound to regret it now.

I have no idea what possesses me to do it. I see Caius raise the whip. I see the bent, metal hooks at the ends of the weapon flash in the sun. I see their jagged edges bearing down on the child, preparing to tear his flesh and break his spirit. I see the kid's eyes widen in terror, and I, who make it a point to never meddle in the affairs of others, find myself between the child and Caius's brutal whip.

One jagged talon tears into my cheek, just below my left eye, while another gouges my neck. There is a sharp, biting pain, and as I look down at my chest, I see large torn ribbons of flesh, some of the hooks from the whip still embedded in my body. I hear the startled cry of the kid behind me. I can't turn my head far enough to see him, and even if I could, my eye is swelling fast. Still, I can sense the young, golden-haired boy cowering behind me, and I breathe a sigh of relief knowing the child's cries are of empathy, not pain; I have managed to shield him entirely.

Caius pulls the whip free, sending fresh pain coursing through my entire body. He snarls in disgust. "You! Boy! If you're so eager to pay homage to the whip, perhaps you'd like another taste!" Caius draws back his arm again, preparing to strike me. My arms are still outstretched in an attempt to cover the child behind me. My left eye begins to swell terribly. I can scarcely see through the puffy slit.

A deep, resonating voice fills the air. "That will be enough, Caius."

The voice is commanding, warning. I watch as Caius begins to tremble. There is a firm hand latched onto the guard's wrist, and as I strain my battered eye to see, I recognize the signet ring on the hand of the interference. Abirad.

"Back to your post, Caius," speaks Abirad quietly.

"But-but, sir!" stammers Caius in disbelief. "We do not tolerate such insubordination! This boy got in the way of an appropriate punishment! As such, he must be whipped! The minimum is ten lashes!"

Abirad glowers down at the guard. His emerald green eyes look as if they could incinerate someone with a glance. His long, black hair is tied back. His features are sharp and angular, and his beard short and pointed. I haven't seen him this closely since I was brought here. Despite the years that have passed, he doesn't look any older, while I have grown from a quivering adolescent into a strong, able-bodied young man.

Caius hasn't moved an inch, his hand still poised to deliver another strike. "But... Sir!"

Big mistake, Caius.

Abirad's voice erupts in a roar of pure fury. "I SAID BACK TO YOUR POST!"

I can hear a low hum, followed by a brilliant flash of green light, so bright that it illuminates the entire courtyard. I watch Caius's eyes widen as the guard is violently expelled from view. Caius hurtles backwards, traveling a rather impressive distance, before slamming into a wall. His form slumps, his broken body unmoving as he collapses to the ground in a heap. None of the other guards dare to move to help him in the presence of their irate master. The same men who so often joke with Caius or clap him upon the back turn their eyes away; no one attempts to spare the unconscious guard any further threat of Abirad's wrath. I can't even tell if he's breathing. There's a pool of blood forming on the ground from a wound on the back of his head, and there is bone exposed near his neck.

I notice the other slaves are desperately trying not to look at the proceedings for fear of receiving "attention," too. Their gazes remain downcast, and they throw themselves into their own work and their pursuit of ignorance. I can't blame them; I'd do the same thing.

My legs feel weak and start to buckle. The next thing I know, I'm on my knees, my chest heaving and my wounds feeling as if they have been lit on fire. I feel the cool touch of a small hand upon my shoulder.

In my ear, there is a faint whisper of, "Thank you."

The kid.

Then everything goes black.

CHAPTER 2

Opening my eyes proves to be a far more difficult task than I had hoped. I drift in and out of consciousness for who knows how long. Every now and then, I get a bit of Old Man's smooth, reassuring voice attempting to soothe my feverish dreams. In this place, infection can set in quickly, and in my moments of consciousness, I can hear the sound of Old Man grinding away at a crudely made mortar and pestle. Herbs and other ingredients for salves and poultices are quite difficult to come by as they are scarcely found. Having no currency or means of accounting for debts owed and repaid, we prisoners rely upon a strict barter system. I know these ingredients likely cost Old Man a whole week's worth of the watery gruel that passes for supper.

My left eye is still swollen and my body shudders with pain as Old Man presses a foul-smelling substance into my wounds.

"Stop writhing around then. Let it do its work," speaks Old Man gently.

I manage to relax a little, and after a few moments, I feel the agony gripping my body begin to abate slightly. I push myself up onto my elbows, sending a fresh shock of pain coursing down my chest. I look at the mortar still in Old Man's hands and feel a pang of guilt.

"I'm sorry." I really mean it, too. "That must have been costly, Old Man."

"Typically, yes," agrees Old Man. "But this time, I paid nothing for it."

I shake my head in disbelief. Nothing here is freely given. When there is so little to be had, anything with even a bit of value is coveted. "How?"

Old Man leans back on his heels. "People recognize the rarity of honor, especially in a place such as this. The guards had you brought back here after the incident in the courtyard. I had no sooner set to assessing your wounds when a number of the others appeared at the door of our cell bearing these gifts. I asked how I might repay them, but they would accept nothing."

I can feel the frown forming on my face. "Why should I deserve their kindness?"

"Whether you deserve it or not is not up to you or I to decide. The point is, we have it now, and with a bit of luck, those wounds will heal nicely."

I sit up to inspect the wounds upon my chest, but every time I lower my head, I am accosted by the foul smell of the salve. Moonlight streams through the single, barred window of the cell. From the courtyard, I can hear the sound of a lone pickaxe chiming against rock.

I instantly feel guilty. Injury is not a cause for an evening off. If that were the case, the rate of self-inflicted injuries would rise quickly. Instead, if slaves cannot complete their allotment of labor for the day, others are required to take their places. Since I am temporarily out of commission, some other poor soul is out there bearing the burden of my work.

So, who took my place? My mind instantly drifts to Brock or Wise.

The window is small and high upon the wall. When I was younger, I had never been able to see out of it. Yet, in the time I have been at the castle, I have grown from a small, wiry boy to a tall, lanky young man of around 16, at least at Old Man's best guess. Despite how much I've grown, even now, I have to stand on my tiptoes to see out.

Moonlight glints off the pickaxe and cascades down the small form of the blonde child from the courtyard. His swing has improved since earlier in the day, and that look of determination has not wavered, despite the troubles he has encountered.

"This is senseless." I can't mask my disgust. "Why would they choose him? It will take him four times as long to finish my work than some able-bodied man."

"You misunderstand," says Old Man quietly. "He volunteered. Perhaps your saving him emboldened him. He felt the incident was his fault, and he would let no other stand in his stead. Even Brock couldn't dissuade him from doing so."

The idea of that tiny imp of a kid daring to refuse a request from Brock is almost enough to make me chuckle, if not for the fact I know laughing will probably just succeed in aggravating my injuries further. The kid has spirit, that's for sure.

I can't tear my gaze away from the small child in the courtyard. "Why do you think he was kept in the castle for so long?"

Old Man is thoughtful for several moments. "I know not, Boy. Perhaps you should ask him."

I give a silent nod before seating myself on the damp floor of the cell. I watch as Old Man scrapes what little remnants there are of the salve into a grimy, glass phial. Really, Old Man isn't so old; he's probably in his early fifties. Certainly, there are many far older here, but it is his sage disposition that has earned him his name.

Old Man is the smartest person I've ever met, though by the time Wise is as old as him, she may very well surpass him. In Wise, Old Man has found a rather apt pupil, and he loves nothing more than discussing his readings with her or playing games of chess on the crudely constructed board we have managed to scrape together. He's even been teaching her how to heal, and she has become just as adept as him when it comes to dressing wounds and creating salves. He tried to teach me these things, but I just don't have the mind or the patience to learn it all.

Old Man examines the contents of the phial. His raven

black hair is matted and clumped in some areas, but stuck out at wild, unruly angles at others, giving it the appearance of a hastily constructed bird's nest. His deep, brown eyes are gentle and kind, but every so often light when a particularly clever idea strikes him. He is well-spoken and adept when it comes to problem-solving. Sometimes, he sits in the corner in silence, as if in some trance, for hours at a time. I don't mind the quiet, because afterwards, Old Man prattles on for hours. He had a cellmate shortly before my arrival at the castle, but the other man died. I am of the opinion that Old Man likely talked his previous cellmate to death, but Old Man asserts the guy died of a snakebite he received while working in the yards.

I know what he's doing when he gets like that, when his mouth seems to be moving faster than his mind. He's trying to remember. Every now and then, something will catch his attention. It's usually something unremarkable, like a shiny jewel in a mound of rock and dirt, or one of the creeping vines that attempts to make its way over or through the castle walls. A look of nostalgia will pass over his face and he'll tell me how the shiny jewel is quartz, which can be used as a focus to draw the power of other jewels, or that the creeping vine is marawort, poisonous to ingest, but makes for a decent cure for blisters. However, that's about as far as he's ever gotten. Though such knowledge is plenty useful, it's not what he's looking for. He wants to know who he was, in hopes that will tell him who he is.

"I almost had it today, Boy! Almost! If it were a spider it would have bitten me!" he would say. He'd spend hours at it, sitting in that corner and trying to remember who he was before he was Old Man. But at the end of the day, his knowledge of himself is no greater than when first he started.

Knowledge. It's the one thing Old Man yearns for more than anything. He will do nearly anything to get it. He has a certain charm and charisma that he often turns upon the women who serve our paltry meals. He begs for whatever scraps of paper they can bring to him, regardless of how seemingly useless they might be: a list accounting the number of rocks broken for the day, a sheet of inventory for goods to be brought from the market, small sections from the farmers' almanac regarding possible weather patterns for the season. All of these, he devours.

But even such noble endeavors as the pursuit of knowledge can be dangerous. At least it was for Isabel. She was a soft-hearted, comely serving maid with bright eyes and sunburned cheeks. She was a constant provider for Old Man's want of the written word. She'd bring small parcels wrapped in the folds of her apron, and a huge grin would appear upon her face as she slipped the items through the bars and into Old Man's awaiting hands. His fingers would tremble with excitement.

I remember Isabel's first delivery.

"What is it?" I had asked.

"This, lad, is a book!" exclaimed Old Man with joy apparent upon his face.

Isabel winked at Old Man before disappearing down the corridor.

Daily, Old Man begged Isabel to fetch him more of these delights, but she herself had only three books, all of which Old Man had read voraciously, like a raptor descending upon its prey.

"Don't fret. I may have a way to get you more," assured Isabel.

The steady stream of books continued, and the variety of the topics expanded greatly. There were no more shopping lists or scraps of paper. These were replaced by books on herbalism, geography, histories of the kingdom, and many others. However, Isabel's appearance during these visits took a noticeable turn. Gone was the light from her violet irises and the radiant blush upon her cheeks. Bags appeared under her eyes, her smile all but disappeared completely, and she looked nervous and anxious when she presented Old Man with these tomes.

I figured it out.

One day, I watched as Old Man opened a book, and my eyes fell upon a strangely familiar symbol in the inside cover. It was the same dragon symbol that adorned the banners that hung in the workyards, the very same symbol that was engraved upon Abirad's signet ring.

"These are Abirad's books!" I cried out.

I couldn't believe it! He had to have known! Old Man is many things, but he is no fool. Yet, there had to be some mistake. He wouldn't allow Isabel to put herself in harm's way for the sake of some tomes. But, in my heart I knew the truth. Yes, yes, he would.

"Yes, I know these are Abirad's books, Boy. I have known for some time," replied Old Man without concern. "From his library."

There was a heavy feeling in the pit of my stomach; I felt like I swallowed a stone. "Then she has to stop bringing these or he'll find out! If she's caught, she could be killed, or worse!" I tried to reason with him, but when it comes to books, there's no reasoning with Old Man. He'd sell his soul for any bit of knowledge of the world outside these walls.

"Pshaw!" responded Old Man dismissively.

Yet, my fears would come to pass. One day, Isabel didn't come. I thought she was dead, until several weeks later, across the courtyard, I saw her. She did not remember me... or Old Man.

I wanted to talk to her, to apologize for Old Man's selfishness, but what could I say? How would that sound to this sad, scared new arrival? "Oh, hello! So, I know you don't remember me, or even who you are, but just so you know, my friend there is the reason you're here. And by the way, I didn't do a thing to stop him. Maybe if I'd pressed him a bit harder, you wouldn't be here. Oh well! Let's let bygones be bygones! Enjoy your pickaxe and the threat of floggings."

The worst of it is I don't think it affected Old Man, or if

it did, he never let on about it. He never seemed to show any regret for the hardship his lust for knowledge had caused Isabel. In fact, whenever I'd bring it up, he'd just mutter under his breath.

"For the greater good, Boy... For the greater good."

For the greater good. What's one life when stacked up against another? Are some more valuable than others? That kid out there working my shift, is he more valuable than the rest of us? Is that why he was Abirad's pet for so long?

I watch as the kid lets the pickaxe drop to the ground. His trembling hand moves to brace his back as he attempts to straighten himself. He winces in pain and gingerly begins to make his way towards Harding so he can be taken back to his cell. Harding tilts his head. Maybe it's a trick of the moonlight, but something akin to sympathy crosses over the guard's face. Harding glances around, as if to see if anyone is watching. He doesn't see me peeking through the bars of my window.

He pulls a small roll out of his pocket and presses it in the kid's hand. Harding gestures hurriedly for the kid to hide it in the sleeve of his shirt. I've never known Harding, or any of the guards, to show anyone any kindness. Then again, Harding's weapons have always been his words, unlike Caius who relies so heavily upon brute force. The boy wraps his arms around Harding's waist in a hug, but the guard responds with agitated whispers and more frantic glances around the courtyard. The boy appears embarrassed and quickly pulls away.

In all my years here, I've never seen such strangeness.
Who is this kid?

CHAPTER 3

The next morning, my body feels stiff, and I find it extremely difficult to move. My wounds ache, serving as a throbbing reminder of my actions yesterday.

"Wise passed by this morning. She wishes to speak with you," announces Old Man.

Wise. Wise certainly represents her name well. Old Man enjoys her company, finding her a suitable opponent in his battles of wits. He challenges her with all manner of word games and mental puzzles he's read in his books, and she solves them even faster than Old Man himself. That's how she earned the name "Wise."

She, like Old Man, loves the thrill of learning something new, but she lacks his selfishness for knowledge. I like the look of wonder that affects her features as she pores over Old Man's sparse collection of reading material. Once Isabel was gone, Old Man was left with nothing but a few pamphlets on herbal remedies and a guide on how to identify edible plants and berries in the forest. Yet, Wise treats them as if they are revered documents, handling them ever so carefully, as if within those pages can be found many rare and wonderful treasures.

Wise was the first friend I made here, even before Old Man. She had been Abirad's prisoner years before I arrived, though exactly how long it's been is something she hasn't been able to figure out. Old Man estimates it's been at least a decade, though likely a few years even beyond that. As for Brock, he came along several years after my arrival, at least according to the wall of tally marks that Old Man keeps in a fruitless attempt to mark the passage of time.

A guard opens our cell, and Old Man remains behind. He's a rather slow worker in the yards, regardless of how many times the guards try to motivate him with harsh words or floggings. As a result, he's managed to get himself a rather useful job in the kitchens. Every now and then, he manages to sneak out an extra morsel of food, which he is always willing to share, and we both devour the meager offering like starved beasts.

I make my way down the hall towards Wise's cell, which is separated from our cell by five others. I know I won't have long to chat. Wise and I rarely work the same shifts anymore, but I can chance a few minutes before the guards will be expecting me outside. They will be busy enough with supplying the new slaves that arrived yesterday morning.

Wise works in the yards, too, but she is far too intelligent to be swinging a pickaxe around all day; her talents would be wasted with such labor. While I bust apart rocks all day, Wise's discerning eye can spot a piece of fool's gold from real gold a mile away. She's one of the sorters, tasked with checking through the large buckets of precious gems and stones we collect throughout the day. Sometimes, if a piece is small enough, I watch as she hides it under the folds of her rolled up sleeves.

When I reach Wise, I am heartened by the fact that she isn't in her usual position, sitting on the dirt floor with a bit of stick in her hand. The ground serves as her drawing board for her strange musings and current escape attempts. She doesn't bother to hide them from the guards. She always uses a rather elaborate code to jot down her ideas, a code in which one letter replaces another. Despite her intelligence, she is rather good at feigning stupidity, and she has managed to convince the guards she is not only daft, but illiterate. I've seen them glance down at her work with snorts of laughter. They think she's failing miserably at spelling out words, but I know better.

The fact she's not hunched over on the floor is a good sign. Instead, she faces the window. Even standing on her tip-toes she can't pull herself up enough to see through the bars, but her hand rests above her upon the sill. Maybe it's finally happened. Maybe Wise has finally accepted we will never be free of this place. I don't consider myself a pessimist, but I am a realist, and the fact of it is, we're never getting out of here. Maybe Wise has figured that out, too.

Then my eyes fall upon the carefully written scrawl on the dirt floor. My eyes roll almost involuntarily, and it isn't difficult to summon a sigh. The word before me, RFPNCR, is Wisenease for ESCAPE.

"For heaven's sake, Wise! If this is another one of your—"

Wise turns and gazes at me with her soulful brown eyes. One thing I've learned about her is the easiest way to discern her moods is to look at her eyes. I can see her excitement in them even before I take notice of her smile. It is a smile I have come to both adore and detest. I like the way it causes the dimples to form on her face, but I detest it because I know its hidden meaning: I have a dangerous idea, and I'm going to try to convince you to help me.

"Another one of my *what* exactly, Boy?"

"Nothing, Wise." I sigh heavily, ready to quickly hear her crazy scheme so I can promptly say no and make my way to the yards. "Old Man said you wanted to see me."

Wise is my oldest and dearest friend, and I trust her more than anyone. Truly, I think the world of her. We tend to be of similar opinions on most matters, but her ambitions of escape are the one point we disagree upon.

Other than her ill-conceived notions of acquiring free-dom, Wise has been a voice of reason in this place. While Brock is impulsive and hot-headed, and I am indecisive, and at times, overly cautious, Wise is observant and methodical. She thinks everything through before taking any actions, and one thing I have learned about Wise is that her mind never stops working for even a second.

18

Today, Wise has definitely been thinking harder than usual. There is a small indentation on her bottom lip from where she has been biting it. She always bites her bottom lip when she's deep in thought. Wise spends the majority of the time she is in her cell wholly obsessed with the idea of escape. She is brilliant, but some of her plans border on insane.

She crosses the cell and stops in front of me on the other side of the door. I see she's wearing that thoughtful expression, the one that makes it look like there's a storm brewing in her mind, waiting to unleash itself on the world.

"So, I take it you have another plan, Wise?" I ask wearily.

"Indeed, I do." She grins from ear to ear. Oh, this plan of hers must really be something because she's grinning like a cat that's caught a mouse.

There's a soft noise coming from within the cell, almost like someone's sniffling, trying to will away the tears. This catches my attention. Wise hasn't had a cellmate for weeks. I peek around Wise to see who or what the noise is coming from.

That's when I see him crouched in the corner of the cell. His knees are drawn up to his chest and his elfin chin rests on his forearm. He looks even smaller now than he did in the yards. I can tell from his red-rimmed eyes and the still wet streaks upon his face that he's been crying, but when he sees me, his blue eyes sparkle, and a smile begins to form on his face.

"This is Lark," introduces Wise.

Suddenly, I feel a hard thump on my back, and I nearly fall forward as I let out a yelp of pain.

"Brock!" admonishes Wise. "Be more careful with him! He's still healing!"

Brock's face reddens in embarrassment. "Sorry. I forgot." Brock's gaze shifts to the kid. "Lark?" He smirks at Wise. "You've named him, huh? I suppose you'll be wanting to keep him now."

Brock often jokes that Wise will save every creature in

the world before she remembers to save herself. On closer reflection, this is true. Any stray or injured animal that finds itself within the castle walls becomes one of her "projects" as Brock calls them.

A few years ago, a one-legged chicken showed up in the yard. Brock saw it first and intended on snagging us an extra meal. He picked it up to break its neck and end it quickly, but Wise snatched it out of his hands and marched off leaving Brock staring after her in disbelief.

Brock wasn't happy, but Wise convinced him that a consistent supply of eggs would be more useful than one dead hen. So, "Henrietta" laid eggs for quite some time before her untimely disappearance. I had been under the impression Brock had finally given in and eaten her, especially since she liked to peck at his fingers whenever he'd try to pet her. Wise always joked it was because Henrietta was a good judge of character.

I definitely miss Henrietta's eggs. The extra food was always a blessing. Wise maintained that the hen had started to show her age and likely went off to die peacefully. Even Brock teared up a bit at that.

Wise narrows her eyes at him, but she can't altogether mask the hint of amusement at the corners of her lips. She's commented more than once that Brock is a source of constant entertainment to her. I don't know if it's his blunt honesty, his sarcastic comments, or his general humor, but whatever it is, he always seems to command her attention.

"Still taking in strays, Wise? At least the last one laid eggs. I'm not sure how useful this little runt will be," he jokes, a playful smile playing across his face.

The only time I ever see Brock smile, I mean really smile, not those half-hearted fake smiles he gives to the girls in the yard, is when he's talking to Wise. I suppose her cleverness is entertaining to him as well.

Lark stiffens and raises himself to his full height, which is barely over 4 ft. "I'm plenty useful."

I change the subject. "Why the name Lark?"

Wise shrugs. "He was singing last night... while he was working. It was a song I've never heard before. I liked it."

"So, what were you saying about... you know?" I ask.

It begins as it always does. Wise begins to pace in her cell, back and forth, back and forth, kicking up clouds of dirt as she makes her way across the front of her tiny quarters. "I have a plan."

Brock groans. "This again." He leans heavily against the cell. He must have just finished his shift. He's covered in dirt, and his dark, brown hair is slicked back with sweat. "Wise, when are you going to give it up? We're stuck here."

"It's different this time. I know how we're going to get out of here." Her eyes twinkle with glee.

"So you say... as you did last time... and the time before that... and the time before that..." After about a dozen more times before that, Brock desists in pushing his point.

"I'm serious, Brock. Things have changed and I've figured out something incredible... Something unbelievable! Not only will it get us out of here, but this information has the potential to liberate the entire kingdom!" Wise can barely contain the excitement in her voice.

I relent. I've lost count of how many times Wise has contemplated escape, but this time seems different. Whatever's she's found out, she honestly believes it won't only change our fate, but the fate of everyone in the kingdom.

"Alright. Let's hear it, Wise," I say.

"So, you've heard the stories... Seven years ago, the king's son was taken-"

"Yeah, yeah. Get on with it, Wise. We don't need a history lesson," states Brock, crossing his arms over his broad chest.

Of course we've heard the story. Who hasn't? Ever since Old Man read it in one of his tomes, he had told everyone who had a mind to listen, and it had spread like fire, being passed on from slave to slave, so much so it had become a matter of initiation for new arrivals. True, we might not have any memory of the outside world, but it was something worth knowing, and if knowledge is power, then we at least had something, and that was better than nothing.

"Really, Brock? I swear you irritate me on purpose," mutters Wise.

Brock grins. "Well, not much else to do for fun since betting on mice races was banned."

Despite Brock's interruption, Wise continues her story, perhaps for the benefit of the kid. "Seven years ago, the son of King Ruden, the ruler of Allanon, was taken during the Festival of Mercy."

Old Man had told me about the Festival of Mercy. Every fourth year, an extra day is observed in the calendar. It is meant to commemorate the peace treaty between Allanon and the neighboring kingdom of Blackwood. It was an enduring alliance that lasted for thousands of years. Children born on the Day of Mercy are considered blessed and are foretold to be destined for greatness. Thus, every four years there is a grand celebration in Vericus, the capital city of Allanon.

Well, there used to be anyway. The celebration was suspended when young Prince Trystan disappeared. The prince was one of the blessed, born on the Day of Mercy, and if rumors are true, he was kidnapped by Blackwood spies from his own birthday celebration. Ever since, the kingdoms of Blackwood and Allanon have become bitter enemies.

Wise continues. "Needless to say, the good king was devastated. He had already lost his wife, the benevolent Queen Fiona, mere months before, so the loss of his son and heir plunged him into a deep and inescapable depression. He lost interest in all manner of politics and court."

"This allowed men like Abirad the opportunity to do as they pleased. Without any opposition from the king, Abirad was able to create his own castle, Castle Ciar. However, a large amount of manpower was needed for such a pursuit, and given Abirad's cruelty, no one was about to come willingly. So, he devised a plan. He would enslave citizens of Allanon."

I know the guards will soon notice I haven't stepped out into the workyards, and if I deter my arrival too long, I'm bound to get a good lashing today. "Wise-"

She raises her hand to silence me. "Has it occurred to you that this boy has just now been allowed to join the rest of us? Have you not noticed this child is likely around the same age as the king's son would be now?"

I lean against the cell and peer through the bars to get a better look at the kid. "Why *are* you in the yards now?" I ask him.

"And how exactly did you become so friendly with Abirad? And how did that change?" adds Brock.

Lark slowly rises to his feet. "I don't know what you're talking about. I don't remember anything before yesterday. I remember Abirad shouting at me, saying that I was ungrateful and that I'd learn my lesson. Then he had that guard, Harding, bring me down to the yards."

"That's impossible. You've been here for years..." I shake my head in disbelief. "Why would Abirad wait until yesterday to take your memories?"

"More importantly, why would he let you live in comfort while the rest of us wallow in anguish? What makes you so special?" demands Brock, an edge in his voice.

Lark shrugs. "I'm not... special."

"I disagree," I say quietly. "I saw you last night. I saw Harding give you the bread. He isn't exactly known for his kindness, yet even he is soft towards you. And when Caius was coming at you with that whip, I may have interceded for you, but Abirad never shows himself in the yards. Yet, he spared us... you and me...from more lessons at the end of Caius's whip."

Lark's frustration begins to show, and I feel a pang of guilt for getting him so flustered. "Look! I don't know, all right? I don't remember anything. If the guards or Abirad have at any point shown me more kindness than anyone else, how am I to know what I did to earn it? I don't remember. I don't remember anything!" Lark begins pacing like a caged animal. I can see the tears well in his eyes.

"Isn't it obvious, Boy?" Wise's fingers brush against my forearm and she looks up at me with a certain eagerness in her eyes, as if this piece of information will be the answer to all of our problems. "He's the king's son."

Well, maybe it is.

Wise has said a lot of crazy things, but this is truly the most insane thing I have ever heard her say. "The king's son, Wise? You must be crazy."

"Think about it, Boy! He's the right age. He's got to be about nine or so. And why would Abirad treat him so differently? Why would even a guard such as Harding be kind to him?"

I must be losing my mind, too, because in some strange way, what Wise is saying makes sense. It certainly would explain a lot.

"Look, I've got a plan to get us out of here. You, me, Brock, Lark, and Old Man," states Wise.

"What about Jewel?" asks Brock suddenly. "Maybe we should take her, too."

If looks could kill, Brock would be dead, because the withering look that Wise gives him is enough to make my blood run cold.

Wise ignores his suggestion. "We have to get Lark to King Ruden. Once he sees his son, he will abandon his despair, and we will be able to help him to see reason! We will open his eyes to Abirad's menace, and all the terror he has unleashed on Allanon."

"And what if you're wrong, Wise? What if we've missed the mark? Then we risk our lives, and for what?" I want to believe her, I truly do, but it's a whole lot to take on faith and theory alone.

"Boy..." Wise bites her lip, and I can see the desperation present in her eyes, and the same look of hopelessness and despair that affects all in the walls of Castle Ciar. "What lives?

You call this life? Working day and night under Abirad's commands? Getting whipped and flogged and screamed at for the amusement of the guards? How is this living?"

I make the mistake of glancing at the kid, Lark. His look is pleading, and I don't know why, but I can't force myself to walk away. There's some kind of hunger in that expression, like he truly believes I'm his only chance of getting out of here. I've taken such great pains to shut out the plight of others, and hardened myself to their tears and screams. However, whether I meant to or not, I gave that all up when I put myself in front of Caius's whip.

I take a deep breath to steady my shaking hands. I can't believe I'm actually entertaining this madness. "All right, Wise. I need to get out to the yards. We'll talk about this more tomorrow."

Brock nods in agreement then heads off towards his cell. I turn to make my way out to the courtyard, but behind me I can hear excited whispers between Wise and Lark as the two continue to hatch their plan.

What have we gotten ourselves into?

CHAPTER 4

I can't sleep, no matter how hard I try. My stomach is churning terribly, maybe because of my anxiousness over my discussion with Wise. Or maybe it is the thin, fly-ridden liquid that passed for gruel today. I hear Old Man snoring loudly from the sparse littering of straw that serves as his bed. I thank my lucky stars he's just snoring and not muttering under his breath again. When that happens, he speaks in strange, unrecognizable tongues, some of them odd and guttural. I've tried to use the dirt floor to write down what he says, but when he wakes, and I show it to him, it is nothing familiar to him.

I reach into my pocket and pull out Wise's note again. I don't know how she managed to get it all onto such a small scrap of cloth, likely torn from the bottom of her shirt. I squint my eyes in the dim moonlight and I can just make out the miniscule drawing of the courtyard. Marked on the map is a small storage area behind the sorting room. Wise gave Lark and me impressive pieces of blue stone. She also slipped Brock a considerable piece of rose quartz. We're to "find" them in the dirt and bring them to the sorting room. Once there, Wise will need to place it with others of its kind. She'll ask the guard for the sorting area if she can utilize the laborers, specifically me, Brock, and Lark, to assist her in moving some boxes around in the storage room. She'll say she needs to get to the correct box, which is buried way in the back, and she'd hate to inconvenience someone as important as the guard with such a menial task. Wise can be pretty charming when she tries to be. Meanwhile, Old Man will be bringing the sorters their daily rations. He'll take Wise her food in the storage room. We won't have long, but it's important that the five of us get to speak together, and given our opposite schedules and varied occupations, this seems our best bet.

I close my eyes and try to force myself to sleep. I see the grey-eyed woman and her laughing child, spinning in their dance. If Wise is right, if her crazy plan does work and we manage to get out of here, will I see the woman again? Will she even recognize me? Will she even want me?

I turn over to my side and see that Old Man is shivering on his straw pile. It may be summer, but the nights we spend in these dark, dank cells are still plenty cold. I sit up and peel my shirt off. The sweat has dried, leaving the fabric a bit stiff. It's grimy, and it certainly doesn't smell very pleasant, but it will have to do. I crawl across the floor quietly so that I don't wake Old Man, and I gently drape the shirt over his shoulders. I slowly make my way back to my meager allotment of straw, but a shadow falls over the floor, and I realize that someone is standing outside my cell. I'm afraid to look up, but I know I have to.

I can tell from the once well-made, but now well-worn leather boots, that it is a guard even before I see the face. I sigh deeply, knowing that this will probably mean a few lashes. Once evening has come, we are not allowed to move from our beds.

I lift my eyes, and as they focus on the form outside my cell, I see a guard, Harding, looking down upon me. I watch his hand, expecting to see it resting on the whip at his side, but instead it is clenched in an unmoving fist. He evaluates me in silence, and I notice the expression he gives me is devoid of anger or malice. He says nothing, just simply offers a slight nod before departing.

I crawl the rest of the way to my bed and curl into a fetal position to warm myself. I pick a piece of straw off of my chest and toss it to the side. Old Man was sure to put a fresh dab of salve upon my wounds before he fell asleep. The stuff smells terrible, and everything and anything will stick to it, but it has certainly helped to eliminate some of the discomfort.

My thoughts drift to the nameless people who were kind enough to give him the ingredients for the medicine that helps with my pain. I've never done a thing for them, but they were willing to help me. What if Wise is right? What if her plan does work? Me, Wise, Brock, Lark and Old Man might make it out of here. I know it's unlikely, but let's just say we do. What does that mean for everyone else? An escape attempt will just make things worse for everyone else here. No one has ever been freed from Castle Ciar, and if we somehow manage it, it's a sure bet that no one will ever escape again.

My restlessness results in small bouts of fitful sleep. I pull myself off my straw pile as the sun's distant rays start peeking through the window. I blearily rub my eyes; I find the word exhausted to be an understatement at this point. Whatever comes after what comes after exhausted is about where I am.

My shirt is draped over my shoulders, and I find Old Man's straw pile is already vacant. Near my head is a small hunk of dried cheese. I've no idea how he was able to sneak this past the kitchen guards. Old Man knows how much I love this stuff. Ever since I was a kid, he has always tried to sneak me an extra bit of food, at least as often as he can manage it.

I drag myself to the wash bucket in the corner. I lean over the top, reaching my arms downward to scoop up the sparse amount that's left. Rainwater is all we get for washing, unless we decide to sacrifice some of our water rations for the sake of cleanliness. Most people would rather be caked with mud than go without anything to drink. I dip the tips of my fingers into the cool water. There's not much left. It's been a while since it last rained.

One of the guards unlocks my cell, and I step into the dim hallway. At the next cell over, an older woman and a teenage girl stare blankly at us as we go by. New arrivals. The next three cells offer two workers each, but the only one I know by name is Foul, so named for his rather pungent aroma. At the cell before Wise's, the guard lets out Faint, a boy a little younger than me who has a tendency to pass out in the heat, and Boulder, a monster of a man, who looks like he could crush the boulders in the workyards with his bare hands. Finally, the guard lets out Lark who immediately seeks me out in the growing crowd of people. He hurries to my side and looks up at me with a big, goofy grin on his face.

"Don't look so happy," I whisper to him. "Happy is suspicious."

"Oh. I'm sorry. I didn't know." Lark immediately concentrates on dispelling his smile. It seems a harder task than one would think, but he eventually manages it, and his lips tighten into a thin line.

"What are you grinning like an idiot for anyway?" I ask, only half interested in his answer. I was probably a little older than Lark when I arrived here, and I remember that the stupidest things kept me amused back then. He's probably smirking about the fart that nasty Foul just let out, or maybe the odd expression Boulder makes as he bites his tongue to keep from snapping at Foul.

"Wise told me some stories last night," returns Lark. "Wonderful stories of far off places."

"The most exotic place we'll likely see is the castle's wheatfield," I reply flatly. "That's if we're every lucky enough to get picked to go there. Still tough work, but it beats busting boulders all day."

Boulder turns to look at me, his eyes narrowed.

"I meant *boulders*, not you, Boulder." I quickly explain. "You know. Busting boulders with a pickaxe." I mime breaking a boulder with an imaginary pickaxe just to drive the point home.

Boulder grunts in reply. Not much of a talker that one. To be honest, I don't mind it. In fact, it's probably one of my favorite qualities about Boulder. The times I've worked next to him, he's been a welcome companion. Some people try to fill

29

the air with idle chatter, but he is content to keep to himself.

"Anyway, don't get your hopes up, Lark." As soon as I say it, I regret it. Lark's lip starts to quiver, and I feel like someone's just taken a boot to my stomach. He looks as if he's about to cry, and I feel like an idiot because I know it's my fault.

"Oh, I didn't mean it like that, Lark." I pat him on the shoulder. It feels strange to do so. Other than my little circle, Lark is the first person I've actually made an effort to be openly friendly to. I don't know what it is about the kid. It makes me wonder if the gleeful, grey-eyed child from my memory ever had any little brothers or sisters.

He instantly brightens. It's amazing how fast a child's moods can change. He leans over conspiratorially, beckoning me to lower my ear closer to him. "You think it will work? You know... What Wise is planning?"

"Well, let's hear what she has to say first."

It's not the answer he wanted, so I do one of the things I've always promised myself I'd never do. I lie. Blatantly, outright, bold-face lie. "I'm sure it will work, Lark."

We step out into the courtyard, and I can practically feel my skin sizzle. It's absolutely boiling despite the fact it's so early in the morning. So much for the rest of the rainwater for washing. I guess that it'll probably all be dried up by the time I get back to my cell near dusk. We all move as if we are one mind, heading for our designated areas in the courtyard, but our progress is abruptly stopped. Faint, true to his name, is face down in the dirt in front of us.

I hear one of the guards shout from the watchtower nearby. "Oy! Again! Get that little bugger out of here!"

I almost envy Faint for not having to char in the sun while working. But I also know he won't be getting off easily. Once he comes to, he'll be back in the yards, and depending how long he's out, he just might earn himself a double shift.

We grab our pickaxes from the cart and set to work. Every time I swing the tool in my hand, it feels as if my wounds are on fire. My face is badly bruised, and my eye is still puffy, though the swelling has gone down a bit. The gouges in my chest and on my cheek are no match for the daunting combination of my sweat, the hot sun, and manual labor. After a while, I feel a stinging sensation and find that my shirt is firmly stuck to my chest. Blood mixed with a bit of some yellowish liquid has started to seep from one of the cuts on my chest. The itchy fabric of my shirt certainly isn't helping matters. I pull off my shirt and pour the slightest amount of water onto my chest to dull the pain a bit.

Lark is staring at me, concern evident in his eyes. I wave my hand dismissively to ensure him I'm fine, but he's not buying it. He offers me a bit of water from his canteen, but I refuse to take it. With how hot it is out here, he's going to need every drop of it, or else he'll end up like Faint.

After we've been picking and digging for a few hours, I take a quick look around to make sure no one is watching. Convinced it's safe, I reach into my pocket and pull out the two, blue stones. Lark and I both crouch down and sift through the rubble. Our buckets are full of small shards of clear quartz and a random assortment of gems already. The blue stones are rare, so if we would have "found" them right away, it would have looked awfully suspicious. We add a few more pieces of hematite and agate to our buckets to top them off, then make our way over to the sorting table. On our way there, I catch Boulder staring at me. His eyes are narrowed and firmly locked onto the glinting blue stone in my hand.

We reach the sorting area where we are immediately greeted by Gem, one of Wise's fellow workers.

"Come to dump off, are you? Lot of quartz today, too. Only little pieces, but Abirad will be pleased. He uses a good bit of it. I hear merchants love it, too. Hot enough for you today? I swear, if we don't get some rain soon, I think I'll melt into a puddle!" Gem is yammering away, as Gem so often does.

Luckily, Wise quickly comes to our rescue. "Hello, Boy. Lark. What have you there?"

"We found these." I hold out my right hand and show her

the blue stone. Lark does the same.

Brock comes up beside me. He's got a full bucket balanced on one of his enormous shoulders. He carries it as effortlessly as if it were filled with feathers and not heavy gemstones. I see him glance to the left where Jewel is sorting through another worker's bucket. He catches her eye, and she smiles coyly.

Wise appears mildly annoyed. "Brock. What do you have?"

"A bucket," he answers with a smirk, likely knowing it will annoy her.

Wise gives him a warning look.

He sighs. "A large rose quartz."

"Wow... Those are very rare," chimes in Gem. "Haven't seen those in the longest time! Very hard to come by. Just in time before the shipment goes out, too. A good find like these might even get you a bit of extra gruel."

"Well, let me just take a closer look at these." Wise takes the blue stones out of our hands and takes the rose quartz from Brock a bit more roughly than she needs to.

She proceeds to inspect them for the next ten minutes or so. As far as I'm concerned, she can take all the time she pleases if it stalls me from picking away at boulders. Lark and I watch her examine the stones from every angle. Every now and then she'll throw out a comment like, "Ah, very interesting" or "Hmm... Very unique compared to the other ones we've collected of this kind."

Wise disappears into the storage area, and we hear all manner of racket coming from within. Either she is actually moving heavy boxes around, or she's making a very good show of it. Finally, she pokes her head out and beckons for the guard of the sorting area to come over. Guards are rotated around the perimeter every couple days. I see the tall, muscular form of a guard heading towards us and as he draws closer, I see it's Hollering Harding.

"Great," I mutter under my breath as I recall the peculiarity of my last interaction with him. Perhaps he neglected punishing me then so he could do it now in front of everyone else. Guards like to make a show of beating prisoners; the bigger the audience, the better.

Lark says nothing. His blue eyes are firmly locked on Harding, and the guard doesn't seem to be too comfortable with Lark's staring. Harding lowers his eyes, focusing them squarely on the ground, as if the dust under his feet is the most interesting thing he's ever seen. I know there's something strange going on between Lark and Harding, and for a minute, I wonder if maybe Lark is playing both sides. What if he's a spy that Abirad has sent in here to root out any dissent or plans of mutiny? I glance down at Lark, whose fists are balled at his sides, and I think of his brazen defiance in the courtyard and his red-rimmed eyes in the cell. That quiets any fears I might have about our young companion. Lark might be new down here, but whatever he did to get himself sent to the work-yards, it was obviously some kind of slight against Abirad, which makes Lark all right in my book.

"You three are to help the girl move the boxes in the back," states Harding firmly. He looks back at Wise. "Ten minutes, not a second more. Then they need to be back to picking those rocks." He glances down at Lark, and I watch the guard's face redden considerably before he turns his back to us and begins to walk away.

"Come on." Wise beckons for us to follow her into the storage room. She lowers her voice so only we can hear her. "Old Man should be here at any minute."

The sorting room is a bit of a mess. I wonder if it was like that before Wise wandered back here to search for the box of blue stones. Said box is sitting at eye level on the nearest shelf. She plops the two stones within then hunts down the box for the rose quartz.

A minute feels like a year when you're waiting on something, so it feels like forever when Old Man appears in the storage room. "You're lucky you got any at all, Wise," says Old

Man. "That portly sorter girl, Braids, nearly had me convinced you didn't want it. Then Gem said you were busy, and I could just leave it there. I told her I dare not with Braids licking her lips like a ravenous bird ready to swoop." He passes Wise her small cup of gruel, which she sets upon one of the shelves.

"We can't waste any more time," I whisper urgently. "Out with it, Wise."

"I know how we can get out of here…" Her eyes are gleaming in the dim light of the musty storage area. She pauses to gather her thoughts. "I've managed to get my hands on a map of the castle."

"And how did you do that?" I ask, genuinely curious.

"I gave it to her… some time ago," speaks Old Man, quietly. "I figured it was more useful to her than to me." Something shifts in his expression and he turns his dark eyes to me. "It was in one of the last books Isabel gave me."

Wise reaches into her pocket and produces a well-worn piece of paper. When she opens the map, it's obvious from the jagged edges that it was torn from the book. I hope that it wasn't the reason Isabel ended up down here in the workyards. The creases of the folds are deep and starting to wear thin. Just how many times has Wise pored over this map?

"Look here." Wise grabs a small piece of charcoal off the shelf and circles a section on the map. "This is where we are, in the courtyard. It's located off the back of the castle. The only thing in this section is the cell blocks and the walled in courtyard section here in the middle. As you know, the rocks are shipped from a the mines by cart. There is a guardhouse located at the end of this dirt path. The path leads to this entryway behind us at the sorting station, and the rocks are placed in the courtyard here to be broken apart and sorted."

Wise continues. I see the smirk form in the corners of her lips. She is obviously pleased with our rapt attention, as Old Man, Brock, Lark, and I are hanging on her every word. "The entryway into the courtyard has never been opened while there are slaves working. I've watched, and it only opens at night when the courtyard is cleared. Workers from the mines offload the rocks so they are here for us to break and sort by early morning. Smaller debris from the day's work is gathered up by those miners, placed back in the cart, and moved out of the courtyard."

Wise pauses and the rest of us look at her expectantly. "So, we need to find a way to get into the courtyard at night, when the miners arrive to gather the debris."

Brock laughs to himself. "Oh, so that's it? Just ask one of the guards really nicely to let us out of our cells so we can sneak into the courtyard and hitch a ride out of here? Why didn't I think of that!"

Wise crosses her arms over her chest. "It's not that simple. There is the issue of getting out of our cells. So, there is one more thing..." She reaches into her pocket and carefully produces something about the size of an egg. It has been carefully wrapped in a scrap of cloth, and there is a faint glow emanating from within. As she brings it closer to me, I can hear a faint humming sound.

"Is that-" I can't even complete the sentence.

Brock's mouth is agape in shock as he looks from Wise's face to her hand. "How did you-"

"It wasn't easy," says Wise quietly. "It was a lucky find really. One of the breakers had been rushing to finish his day. He just tossed it in under a pile of other gems. None of the guards saw it, and none of the others sorters took notice. I was back here finalizing the shipment inventory when I came upon it."

"It won't do us any good," says Lark quietly. "We know the stones are powerful, but we don't know how to actually use them."

"Well... *you* don't," speaks Old Man.

Brock shakes his head in disbelief. "And you do? Something you found in one of your books?"

"A bit like that," replies Old Man with a wink. He takes the stone from Wise's outstretched hand. "However, we will need another one. One stone cannot work on its own. The more stones, the more powerful they are. That's why the humming of this one is so faint. It needs a match to truly sing. It may take some time to get another one."

The rest of us just stare at him in shocked silence. He notices our questioning glances.

"I can't explain it, but I remember a bit about them... from my other life," relates Old Man. "I remember the weight of them in my hand, and I remembered the crackle of power that erupted from my palms when I used them. I... I even remember some of the words."

"You... remember..." says Brock slowly, as if the very notion of it is consuming a great deal of his mental effort.

My thoughts shift to the grey-eyed woman, my own treasured memory. If Old Man remembers something, and I remember something, then what about the others? "The rest of you... do you remember anything? Anything at all?" I ask.

If word that his slaves retained some of their memories got to Abirad, he would be sure to do a more thorough job of relieving us of our pasts. It is a risk to even discuss it, but no more than escape would be considered a risk.

Old Man clears his throat. "I remember a tower, so high that it cut into the clouds."

"You mean, like Abirad's tower?" asks Lark. The tower was likely the tallest part of the castle, and the highest part of it seemed to disappear into the clouds.

"Something like that," responds Old Man with a wink.

"Strawberries," says Lark. "I don't know why it's so important, but I remember my hands being full of strawberries."

Brock clears his throat. "A forge... surrounded by weapons. I can almost feel the heat on my face and the soot on my hands."

"Wise?" I ask expectantly.

Wise shakes her head "No... Nothing. Nothing before my years here."

I feel sorry for her. Really sorry.

"Boy? Do you remember anything?" asks Lark.

"No." I lie. I don't know why I lie, but I do. This is the second time today I've lied to the kid, but I guess I'm just not yet ready to share the grey-eyed woman and the child with the same eyes. Part of me worries the moment I give voice to it that it will simply flee from my mind, so I continue to hoard it within me.

"How is it possible" wonders Wise aloud, "to keep something from Abirad?"

Old Man stares at the ground. "Perhaps, some things are far too heavily guarded to be taken, even by Abirad."

Maybe Old Man is right. Maybe there are certain memories that are too powerful to be torn away from us. Maybe it is in these slight glimpses that hope, even in the darkest of times, can be found. True, I might not remember everything about who I was, but it is comforting to know I am not the only one who clings to some distant memory of a stolen past.

CHAPTER 5

The day after our meeting in the sorting hut, I wake in a cold sweat and can't seem to force my body to stop trembling. My brow burns with fever, and I feel absolutely miserable.

"Infection," Old Man says, shaking his head sadly as he examines one of the wounds on my chest. It had likely happened when I reopened some of the cuts while I was working.

Thankfully, Wise and Lark manage to gather the ingredients that Old Man needs for a foul-smelling concoction that he entreats me to drink twice a day. It tastes awful, but it manages to do its job. I still feel a bit weak and uneasy on my feet, but at least I don't shiver as much, and I start to regain some of my strength.

The fever is stubborn and takes nearly three days to break. Brock picks up my shifts, and when I see him pass my cell on the third night, he looks as if he is sleepwalking. His eyes are barely open, and he moves more sluggishly than I have ever seen him.

Once the fever has broken, I return to work. I pass by the cell that Lark shares with Wise. Wise is nowhere to be seen, likely already at the sorting hut. There is a soft snoring sound coming from the corner of the cell where Lark is face down on some damp straw. As I draw closer, my heavy footsteps cause him to stir the slightest bit, and he turns his face in my direction. Even at rest, his expression is one of exhaustion; poor kid looks like he hasn't gotten a decent night's sleep since he showed up in the yard. His hands look raw and blistered, and he has a bandage over one of his palms. I don't want to wake him, but Old Man told me we need to meet again to discuss the plan.

"Lark," I whisper softly. "Lark."

He groggily rolls to his back and rubs his eyes before blearily blinking at me. As his gaze focuses, he grins. "Boy! Hi!" He quickly scrambles to his feet and pats the dust and a few rogue pieces of straw off his stained breeches.

"Come on." I motion for him to follow me out to the yards. He bounces along behind me like some kind of frisky puppy.

I don't know how that kid can always be in such a good mood in a place like this. Maybe it's hope that keeps him going. If that's the case, this plan had better work, because if it falls through, I'm pretty sure it will break his little heart.

Lark and I set to work straight away. Brock is nowhere to be seen. He's probably on the far side of the yard, closer to the sorting hut. That way he can keep making eyes at Jewel. She's pretty enough, and she seems nice.

I'm about twelve buckets in when I remind Lark about the stone in his pocket.

"Oh, right!" he feels around in his pocket and produces the dark blue stone. It's about the size of a robin's egg and is definitely one of the more valuable finds. I have to give it to Wise. Pocketing stones here and there for us to "find" later is one of her more ingenious plans.

Lark scampers away to the sorting hut while I heft a bucket of miscellaneous quartz pieces and a few more precious stones. My "find" for the day is a large, red gem. It's got to be one of the more important ones because I hear they are used in a lot of the jewelry and staffs that Abirad uses.

When I get there, Brock is already standing at the counter. His pickaxe rests across the back of his massive shoulders. Wise is sorting through his bucket. They seem to be joking about something, and both of them are wearing matching smiles of amusement. It's good to see Wise looking a bit more relaxed. The past few days she has been a bundle of nerves. Part of it, I know, was her worry for me. The stress of the plan probably has a lot to do with it, too. Brock says something, and Wise, her smile broadening, shakes her head. Brock always seems to be able to make her smile, even when she's in the worst of moods.

Harding is the guard on duty again for the sorting hut. At first, when Wise asks about additional help resituating the stock room, I worry that he might catch on to our plan. In fact, at the request, his green eyes narrow considerably, as if appraising the idea.

"You already have two to help you. The big one and the half-pint. Shouldn't that be enough?"

Wise reminds him of the rather large inventory currently in their holdings. "Half the quartz section is completely blocked off by a wall of beryl! It's not my fault the workers in the treasury haven't come to pick up the haul for the last two days."

Harding frowns, but he just grumbles that we need to make it quick and not dawdle about all day.

When Brock and I follow Wise into the hut, I see Lark sitting cross-legged on the dirt floor. He's attempting to chew a small bit off a chunk of stale bread. That is a task that is easier said than done, as what passes for bread here is probably harder than most of the rocks we break.

Old Man, lost in thought, is seated upon a wobbly wooden stool.

Wise gets out the map and reviews the specifics of the plan again. There's still the snag of trying to find another singing stone.

Old Man awakes from his reverie for a few short moments. "Don't fret over that. I'll handle it," he assures us.

We start to talk about backup plans in case he is unable to make good on his promise. It's at that point that I see the smallest change in Wise's expression. She doesn't stop talking, but I see her lock eyes with Brock before making a quick glance to the rear of the sorting hut.

Brock instantly picks up on her meaning. He wordlessly rises to his feet, and mere seconds later, we hear a thump followed by Brock's low growl. "What are you doing here?"

The rest of us quickly make our way to the back of the hut, and I see what managed to catch the attention of my friends. It's a slim figure, concealed under a dusty, brown, hooded cloak. It is of such a color that it almost blends into the walls perfectly. I can't make out the person's face, but Brock has his forearm pressed against the person's throat and has succeeded in pinning him or her to the wall.

"Let go of me, rocks for brains!" retorts the figure. It is a feminine voice, and only the slightest bit familiar to me.

"Let her go," speaks Old Man. "She's here upon my request."

Who is *she*?

The figure tosses back the hood of her cloak and reveals lengths of flowing, blood-red hair, and eyes of such a piercing blue that they could freeze a man in his tracks. There's only one person in the whole castle who looks like that.

Scarlet.

Scarlet is a bit of a legend about the castle. Rumor has it she can slip in and out of her cell as she pleases, and the guards are none the wiser of her absence. How she does it so adeptly, especially without getting caught, is a bit of a mystery. They say she can go anywhere she pleases, but she hasn't quite figured how to make it out of the gates. I've heard she lifts things from all over the castle: extra food, flasks of water, blankets, you name it. She hands out most of her pilfered items to the ones who need it most: the old, the young, and the sick, but it's said she has managed to stockpile quite a stash for herself.

"Nice of you to tell us, Old Man," mutters Brock. "I could have killed her."

Old Man laughs. "Not before she would have jammed that pin through your throat."

Brock looks confused, but I quickly realize Old Man's

meaning. Scarlet has a long, thin, metal pin grasped in her right hand, and she looks the part to use it.

Brock frowns and grumbles something under his breath before releasing her.

"Did you bring it?" asks Old Man.

Scarlet nods and reaches in the folds of her chameleon cloak. Her slender fingers emerge seconds later. As she unclutches them, we all intake a sharp breath as she produces the answers to our prayers.

"Another singing stone," breathes Lark, reaching for it.

Scarlet whisks it away from his grasp before placing the stone in Old Man's outstretched hand. "You remember our deal?"

"I do," he replies.

"What deal?" asks Wise.

"Oh. She's coming with us," replies Old Man distractedly. His attention has already been commanded by the stone in his hands.

Brock and Wise exchange a glance, and as usual, it's Brock who gives voice to what they are both thinking "She's *what*? What do you mean she's coming with us?"

"I'm pretty sure he made it clear," snaps Scarlet. "Does he need to speak slower so you actually understand? Are all rock breakers so dumb?"

Brock's face reddens. He's always taken particular exception at being seen as all brawn and no brains.

"Hey!" interjects Wise defensively. "He's not dumb, and if you insult him like that again, that pin is going to end up somewhere very unpleasant for you," she threatens, stepping forward to meet Scarlet's icy gaze.

"Down, girl. I was just joking with your little loverboy," remarks Scarlet.

Wise looks as if she's been slapped. Now it's her turn to redden. "He's not my-"

Seeing the need for a distraction, I decide to speak up. "So, how did you get it? The stone."

Scarlet smiles slyly. "Now, now, Boy. I'm not about to go giving up my secrets. Let's just say that it definitely wasn't an easy task. Hence, why my reward should be sufficient enough to fit my deed. I brought Old Man exactly what he asked for, and with time to spare. It's only fitting he keeps up his part of the bargain and helps me to get out of here, and if that means throwing my lot in with all of you, then so be it."

We all look to Old Man, but he is firmly focused on the singing stone, and we might as all be on another plane of existence entirely as far as he is concerned. Brock and Wise seem to be at a loss for words and do not seem too keen on this idea, but leave it to Lark to break the tension.

He's wearing that dopey grin of his as he bounces up to Scarlet. "Hi, Scarlet. I'm Lark."

Scarlet appears almost amused. "Hi, Lark." She considers him quietly for a moment. "You're the boy from the castle."

Lark bites his lip. "That's what everyone keeps telling me. I don't remember any of that though."

"Huh... Interesting." She tilts her head, her gaze firmly locked on him as if studying him.

"Well, I think we can use all the help we can get," Lark says, turning to the rest of us. "It's just one more person, and if she got that singing stone all on her own, maybe she can help us."

Brock seems to be sulking and nursing his injured pride. "We don't need her help, and I certainly didn't ask for it."

"Fair enough," responds Scarlet stepping forward. "I didn't say I was going to help any of you, did I?"

I instantly recognize the beginnings of a pout on Lark's face, and seeming to notice it as well, Scarlet quickly amends her statement. "Except, maybe you. You- I like."

Lark brightens considerably. "Enough to tell me how you got that stone?"

Scarlet smirks. "I like you, kid, but not a chance." Scarlet turns her attention to Wise. "So... Old Man tells me you're the one planning this whole thing."

"We've all helped," replies Wise quickly. "We all do our part. That's the only way this thing works. We can't risk people just being in it to save their own skins. We look out for each other. You understand?"

Scarlet's lips form a thin line, and she looks around at each of us, appearing to take stock of us. She plops down on an upended bucket. "Noted. Now... Show me this map."

"How do we know we can trust you?" questions Brock suspiciously.

"That's easy. You can't." Scarlet crosses her arms over her chest defiantly. "And I can't trust any of you. However, I've had just about enough of staring at the walls of this place, and I'm ready to take my leave of this castle. I know it better than any of you. If things don't go as planned, I'm your best chance of making it out of here in one piece."

Brock doesn't respond, but he continues to glare at Scarlet. Wise leans over and whispers something in his ear. He seems to relax a bit, but he still doesn't seem completely satisfied.

Brock frowns. "The more people who know, the more the risk of failure goes up. How do we know she won't blab to someone else? She's already said we can't trust her."

"Because it's not in her best interest to tell anyone else. If she could have gotten out of here on her own, she would have by now. She needs us, and Lark is right. She could be very helpful. I'm not asking you to trust her; I'm asking you to trust me. You know that I will always be honest with you, and I'd never do anything to let any of you down. If Old Man thinks this is a good idea, then I support it," reasons Wise.

"As soon as I clear the gates, I'm out of your way," adds Scarlet. "Good chance we will never have to see each other again."

Brock and Wise lock eyes for a moment, and finally, Brock gives a slight nod. Wise brings the map over to Scarlet, who suggests a few useful changes. Apparently the map is at least a few years old, and since then, some rather important changes have been made to the layout of the castle, specifically the addition and redirection of some of the passageways near the cell blocks.

We've already used as much time as we can spare, and we need to head back to the yard before the guards get suspicious. Scarlet, donning her seemingly camouflage cloak, slips out quietly while Old Man makes his way back to the kitchens. Brock heads back to the yards first, and a few minutes later, Lark moves toward the door.

He pauses in the doorway. "Wise?"

She raises her eyes from the map. "Yes, Lark?"

"This will work, right? You really think we can get out of here?" There is pleading in his expression, and a cautious hope in his voice.

Wise smiles gently. "I promise you'll get out of here. I swear it."

Lark grins proudly, heartened by her vow, and disappears through the door.

However, I noticed the careful wording Wise used. "You said *you'll* get out of here. You didn't say *we*," I observe.

Wise nods. "Because I'm not so sure everything will go as planned. Very few things in life ever seem to. However, no matter what happens, we need to make sure Lark gets to Vericus… to King Ruden. It could change everything for everyone."

CHAPTER 6

Our plan progresses well.

That is, until Brock completely loses his mind.

About thirty of us are pulled for an early morning shift; Brock, Wise, and I are among those selected. The sorting huts won't open until dawn, so Wise is working the yard with the rest of us until she is sent there. The three of us labor next to each other in relative silence. It goes on that way for a few hours until Brock tells us something that knocks the wind out of me.

"This is my last week in the yards," he says quietly.

Wise and I both abruptly stop swinging our pickaxes, which makes the closest guard shout at us to resume our work. Wise's tanned face instantly becomes white as a cloud as we exchange looks of alarm.

There's a sinking feeling in the pit of my stomach as I utter the words. "The mines?" I ask.

Brock shakes his head slowly. "No."

He won't make eye contact with either of us, which really gets my pulse racing. It must be bad, but what could be worse than the mines?

I sift through my rock pile and deposit a few gems in my bucket. "Then, what?"

His words come out slowly, as if they must drag themselves the short distance between his mind and his lips. "I've been assigned to a new position. Apparently, a few of the guards took notice of how strong I am. They approached Abirad about me joining their ranks. He agreed."

"Y-you're going to be a guard?" I say a bit too loudly. Thinking better, I lower my voice and repeat the question. "You're going to be a guard? You've got to be joking!"

Brock clears his throat, seemingly more for the extra moment to carefully choose his words than for any discomfort. "This... this isn't easy for me to say, but..."

I look to Wise to see if her face mirrors my own shock, but there's a peculiar expression there, one of almost dread, as Brock utters his next words.

"I'm staying."

I can feel my mouth fall open, and I can't quite seem to find any words for this situation.

Wise looks as if she's been slapped, and for a moment, she is also rendered speechless. When she finally regains control of her voice, it's quavering with barely restrained anger. "You're *what*?"

"I'm staying," he repeats firmly. "Look, you don't have to worry. I'll keep your secret," he promises quickly.

I shake my head in disbelief. "Brock, you can't stay here. Why would you even consider it?" Yet, I think I know his answer even before he gives voice to it.

"Look, there's no guarantee this plan is going to work. If it doesn't, we could all end up dead. I am not into dying, and I'd really prefer that the rest of you stay alive as well," he explains.

But Wise knows him better than that. She can always tell when he's lying, and she doesn't hesitate to call him on it. She shakes her head. "No. No, that's not it. You've never been a coward, Brock. What's really going on? You at least owe it to us to be truthful."

He takes a deep breath. "It's Jewel. She won't go with us."

"What do you mean *won't* go?" demands Wise. "You *told* her? Why would you tell *her*?" I've never seen Wise look so infuriated before. She is typically a paradigm of calm and reason, but she looks as if she'd like to physically beat the sense back into Brock's thick head, and she's strong enough that she could probably do it, too. "What kind of hypocritical nonsense is that, Brock? You didn't want Scarlet to join us because you said it was a danger for too many people to know. At least Scarlet is useful."

"Hey, you don't even know Jewel," snaps Brock in irritation. "You can't say she's not useful." He takes a deep breath. I wonder if it is as hard for him to say all this as it is for us to hear it. "Look, I like her, really like her, and I don't want to leave her behind."

"Brock-" Wise begins, but breaks off abruptly. I can see she's fighting to control her emotions, a combat she is currently losing.

"Besides," continues Brock, apparently trying to convince Wise of his rationale. "You know guards get certain advantages. There's extra rations, and I'd get a cottage on the castle grounds. And guards are allowed to marry."

There is a pained expression on Wise's face. "So, that's it? You're going to stay here and play house with Jewel?"

"So, you want to get married? That's why you want to stay behind?" I ask in confusion.

"What? No! I mean, I don't know," stumbles Brock. "Maybe eventually. She's pretty, and nice, and if not her, there could be someone else..."

"Brock... I... I don't know what to say." I honestly don't. What could anyone say to news like that?

I can practically feel the rage and hurt emanating off of Wise in nearly palpable waves. Nothing else is said for the rest of our shift.

At dawn, Wise prepares to leave for her duties. The three of us heft our buckets and wordlessly make our way to the sorting hut. Brock immediately heads over to the far end of the counter where Jewel eagerly greets him with a smile.

I can see Wise is forcing back tears, and she seems to be trying to will her anger to overpower her sadness.

"It'll be okay, Wise," I assure her. "We can still make the

plan work."

I see her glance over at Brock and Jewel. I see the look of absolute agony in her expression, and then a sudden realization dawns on me, something that I have foolishly overlooked for the longest time. She's not just upset that Brock is staying behind; she's upset that Brock is staying for Jewel.

"Are you going to tell him?" I ask her quietly.

"Tell him what?" mutters Wise.

"Wise, you're the smartest person I know. Playing dumb doesn't suit you," I tease her.

She smiles ever so slightly, but it is a short-lived moment of passing amusement. "Is it that obvious?"

I shake my head. "No. It's taken me this long to figure out. So, will you? Will you tell him?"

Wise sighs heavily. "Why? What good would it do? It would just make things worse. Anyway, the feeling isn't mutual."

"How do you know?"

"I just do."

I guess I should have picked up on it a long time ago. In truth, the signs had been there all along, but somehow, I missed this. My curiosity gets the better of me, and I have to ask. "So, why Brock?"

Wise seems amused by the question. "Why? Plenty of reasons. He's strong and confident. He's smart, way smarter than people give him credit for. In fact, he's one of the smartest people I've ever met. Not in the reads books way... he just... he knows things. He's observant, and he seems to know exactly what I'm thinking and even takes the words right out of my mouth. But..." She pauses for a moment and seems to further consider my question. "I guess the most important thing is that there isn't much to be happy about here, but every time I see him, for just a second, the world isn't so awful."

I can't help but to smirk a bit, wondering what Brock would think if he heard Wise saying all this. I watch as she looks back in Brock's direction, and I hope that one day a girl looks at me the way she looks at Brock.

Wise smiles slightly, but I can tell it's a feat for her to do so; it's obvious that her heart is breaking. "It's all the wonderful things about him, but it's his faults too. I know he's not perfect, and honestly, I don't want him to be. I like him for who he is, and for what he's not. It's everything. Anyway, I'm not the type of girl he would ever be interested in."

Wise is right. Brock has always tended to direct his attention towards slender girls whose chief allure is their physical beauty. As for Wise, she is neither thin nor ample in frame, though she is closer to the latter than the former given her stocky build. She is neither tall nor short, but of average height. People like Brock would find her neither gorgeous nor homely. However, I see the natural beauty she possesses. Her dark brown hair falls just past her shoulders, and when the sun kisses it, it reveals hues of red and chestnut. Her brown eyes are a beautiful, warm color that always seem to bring comfort to those she sets them upon. Brock's admirers tend to be quite pretty, but they lack the intellect and cunning that Wise possesses. They don't have her smile, or her compassion, or her loyalty and love for her friends. When it comes to the heart, she is the most beautiful girl I've ever met.

Had she not been one of my first friends and my closest confidante, I might have fallen in love with her myself. However, our closeness has never borne anything but familial love. She has been a constant in my life, and she has brought me a sense of stability when everything else in the world seems completely out of control. She is always willing to listen to me, even regarding the most trivial matters. When I need to hear hard facts, I go to Old Man, but when I need advice and a sympathetic ear, I have always sought out Wise.

I glance over at Brock, who has a broad smile plastered across his face. Despite the fact he's like a brother to me, I'd like nothing more than to punch him right now for what he's doing to Wise. Then again, I guess I can't really blame him. It's not like he knows. I see Jewel touch his arm, and I see the way Wise frowns as she turns away.

"I thought about telling him... when we left here," says Wise softly. "So much for that."

I don't have any words of comfort for her, so I lightly touch her hand. "It'll be okay, Wise. Everything will work out. I know it will."

The fact is, I don't know any of those things, but it's what she needs to hear right now.

* * *

After my shift is over, I get pulled into the courtyard for laundry detail. As awful as breaking rocks is, it pales in comparison to washing the stains out of the guards' underwear. After that, I'm sent to the fields to help with harvesting, and around nightfall, I finally get to collapse in the corner of my cell.

Old Man is already out like a candle, but despite the fact my body is absolutely exhausted, I can't seem to shut my mind off. All I can think about is Brock's news. I didn't see much of Wise for the rest of the day, other than when I passed her cell before heading to my own. Lark was nestled up next to her for warmth, and she had her arm wrapped around his slender shoulders. She had been wide awake, just staring vacantly into the darkness, biting her lip so hard I was sure she'd draw blood. She was deep in thought, but I think we both know this problem isn't about to be solved. I don't like the idea of leaving this place without him, but Brock is stubborn. When he makes up his mind, that's usually the end of it.

After about an hour or so, I hear a soft tapping on the bars of my cell. I look up and Scarlet is sitting outside my door. She must see the look of panic on my face because she waves a hand dismissively, as if reading my mind.

"Relax," she says. "The guard on duty won't pass through for at least another fifteen minutes."

"What are you doing here?'

Scarlet yawns and rests her hands behind her head. "I needed to stretch my legs. Besides, I nicked some things for our travels... and a couple of these." She tosses me something small and wrapped in a coarse, brown napkin.

It feels warm in my hands, and I quickly unwrap it. It's a small, lemon pastry of some sort. I've never had one before, but I've seen them cooling in the windowsills of the kitchen. The smell makes my mouth instantly water. "Thanks, Scarlet." I cross to my corner of the cell and place it under some straw to hide it.

Scarlet raises an eyebrow as she cocks her head, and I see her ice blue eyes glint in a ray of moonlight that manages to force its way through our sorry excuse for a window. "You aren't going to eat it? It's still warm."

"I'll save it for Lark. He'll love it."

Scarlet just smiles and shakes her head, a hint of amusement present on the corners of her lips. "So... I heard there's going to be one less mouth to feed on our trip. Not having that tree around is definitely going to help make the rations stretch."

"So, you heard about Brock staying?" The words taste sour on my tongue.

"I hate to say it, but... who am I kidding? I love being right. Your friend is an idiot. He really does have rocks for brains."

"I guess love changes people's priorities."

A soft snort escapes Scarlet. "Love is overrated. And anyway, he doesn't love her. Probably loves the way she looks, but that's about it. If he had half a brain, he'd realize..." She gestures with her head in the direction of Wise's cell. "Well, you know, don't you?"

"I'm ashamed to say I didn't... Not until today anyway."

"How is Wise taking it?"

"Not well."

"She can do better, but it's obvious how she feels about him, even if he's too dumb to see it for himself. Any chance he'll change his mind?"

"Unlikely."

"Huh... Well, time marches on. He's made his decision then. I know he's your friend, but try not to dwell on it too much. We'll soon find out for sure if this plan is going to work. See you, Boy." Scarlet disappears as deftly as she had appeared, and I'm left to mull over my thoughts.

I think of Brock, and of Wise, and I think of both the excitement and trepidation that our upcoming attempt at flight brings to my heart and mind. It's hard to believe it, but in a fortnight, during the new moon, we will either be celebrating our freedom or serving as food for worms.

CHAPTER 7

To say that the next few days are wrought with discomfort and general awkwardness would be an understatement. I'm still having trouble accepting the fact that Brock is willingly choosing to stay behind. Wise throws every spare second she can muster into further refining the plan. If she was committed to leaving before, now her need for escape borders on an obsession. I can't blame her. If I were in her position, I'd want to leave in a hurry as well. Anywhere Brock is, Wise is not. He's tried to approach her a few times, but anytime she sees him coming, she immediately changes directions and goes elsewhere.

Lark and I are standing at the sorting hut with our buckets for the day. The contents are exceptionally minimal. It was a pretty poor shipment from the mines, a fact that is sure to put the guards in even fouler tempers than usual. Wise emerges from the back room, and I immediately notice that she looks more exhausted than I have ever seen her.

"Wise?" I know she hears the concern in my voice because she tries to force a faint smile.

"She's not sleeping," announces Lark.

Wise gives him a sharp look.

"What?" asks Lark. "You're not."

"You need to try and get some rest, Wise. We can't expect to make any progress if you're dead on your feet," I reason with her.

"I'm trying. The work here has been more difficult lately." She glances down to the far end of the sorting hut where Jewel is resting her elbows on the counter. "And she's been absolutely useless lately. Now that Brock is becoming a guard, she's decided that she doesn't actually need to do any work anymore." Wise makes a face of disgust. "You want to hear the worst part? She's being transferred next week."

I dump my bucket on the counter so Wise can more easily sift through the contents. "Where's she going?"

"Oh, that's the *best* part." Wise's voice drips with sarcasm. "She got a comfortable new job in the library! The library!" She shakes her head in disbelief. "She doesn't even know how to read! I offered to teach her once. She said, 'Learning is unattractive in a girl, and a pretty smile goes much further.' She then proceeded to offer me tips on how to better fashion my hair. Can you believe that? Ugh! I would have killed to work in the library!"

It's true. It's the one job Wise desired more than any other. I can only imagine the frustration she must be enduring. First, she feels as if she lost Brock to Jewel, and now the girl has managed to take the one job in which Wise might have found some small measure of enjoyment.

I put my hand on hers. "Let her have it, Wise. Soon we'll all be in much better shape than either of them."

Lark raises an eyebrow. "Why are you two holding hands?"

"We are not holding hands!" snaps Wise, just as Brock comes sauntering up to the counter.

"You're holding hands?" questions Brock. A strange expression passes over his face as he locks eyes with Wise.

I quickly pull my hand away. "No. Wise is having a rough day. I'm merely trying to make her feel better."

"By holding her hand," states Lark matter-of-factly.

Now that Brock has arrived, Wise quickly turns to head back to the stockroom.

"Ugh!" Brock groans. As dense as he can be at times, her hasty departures haven't escaped his notice. He's already complained to me about it several times. "Wise! Wait!"

Wise stops in her tracks, but she doesn't immediately turn to face him.

"Why are you ignoring me?" questions Brock. For a moment, there is the slightest hint of hurt in his voice. The two of them have always been close, but now the distance that has so rapidly expanded between them is impossible to ignore.

Wise seems to be battling with her conscience over whether to respond or simply carry on with what she was previously doing. "I'm not ignoring you; I'm *avoiding* you. It's different."

"Fine, then. Why are you *avoiding* me?" Brock presses his massive hands on the counter and leans forward slightly.

For a moment, Wise appears as if she may answer, but Jewel has noticed Brock and begins attempting to escape from a conversation with Gem to make her way towards him.

"It's complicated," Wise mutters. She crosses to the door of the storage room, and her hand rests on the handle.

"Everything in life is complicated," responds Brock. "Now what's going on? Are you mad that I'm staying?"

"I'm not mad at you."

"Disappointed, then?"

"That's part of it." Wise sighs heavily. "It's nothing you need to concern yourself with."

"Obviously, I do. If it wasn't important you wouldn't be avoiding me."

Wise seems unable to point out any flaw in his logic, so she simply dismisses it. "Brock, just let it go."

"Seriously, what's going on? You're obviously mad about something. How am I supposed to fix it if I don't know what it is?"

"You can't fix it," states Wise flatly.

Brock shakes his head in exasperation. "Wise, you're being stupid about this."

Wise freezes as if she's a statue.

"Uh-oh," mumbles Lark. Even at his young age, Lark displays a certain strange maturity. It seems he's already figured out something that Brock hasn't, and even I still struggle with – what you should never say to a girl.

Wise rounds on him. "So, I'm *stupid* now?"

"That's not what I said!" exclaims Brock just as Jewel reaches for his arm. "Wise!"

Wise's gaze falls on Brock's arm, now held by Jewel. "Like I said... it's complicated." She disappears behind the door, leaving the rest of us staring after her.

"What's her problem?" asks Jewel.

Brock shrugs. "I don't know. I wish I did."

* * *

It isn't long before Brock disappears from the yards. He's moved to a room in the barracks. His cell is only vacant for a day before a new slave is placed there. She's an older woman with kind eyes but a broken expression. We take to calling her Hazel on account of the color of her eyes.

I don't see much of Brock anymore, except for the few times he's on duty in the yards. I've seen him at the sorting hut a couple times. He still tries to get Wise to talk to him, but she won't as much as look at him. He spends most of his time following around Harding or another guard named Belas.

As for our escape, everything seems to be going according to Wise's meticulous plans. Scarlet has managed to stockpile some supplies, though there are a few odds and ends she's still working on. Old Man passes most of his time staring vacantly at the wall when he's not intensely studying a small, old, leather-bound book, about the size of my palm. Scarlet had managed to swipe it for him from the library. She said it was way easier than she thought it would be. Apparently, much as Wise anticipated, Jewel is doing a particularly poor job there, so it wasn't difficult for Scarlet to get in and out without being noticed.

Lark is a bundle of nervous energy. The poor kid is practically jumping out of his skin with anticipation. He hasn't been sleeping well, so Wise has taken to telling him bedtime stories, mostly ones she makes up off the top of her head. Her most recent story is about a brilliant librarian who manages to catch the eye of a brave warrior with dark hair and dark eyes. Through her keen intellect, the heroine is able to free the warrior from the clutches of a dreadful enchantress who has a dopey smile and has made it her life's work to destroy every book in the world. I can't help but to think that Wise may be using her own situation as inspiration for that tale.

The time draws nearer for our departure. It had been Old Man's idea to leave during the new moon. Abirad always leaves the castle on the new moon. He is typically gone for a fortnight, sometimes more and sometimes less. Where he goes is a mystery to all of us, but he is fairly consistent on this time of travel.

One morning, there is a particularly fortuitous shipment from the mines that results in a rather large backup at the sorting hut. A few of the slaves, including Old Man, Lark, and I, are pulled in to assist. Fortunately, we end up at Wise's station, and as we organize the stockroom (this time for a legitimate reason) it gives us some time to discuss matters.

"Where do you think Abirad goes?" I ask Old Man.

"The new moon is a popular time for spellcasters to work rituals," he reasons.

"Or perhaps the rumors around the castle may be true, and he is meeting with someone from Blackwood," adds Wise as she dumps some miscellaneous stones into a pile to be discarded.

Old Man nods in agreement. "It would be a clever move on his part. Blackwood would be a strong alliance."

"I still don't understand why King Ruden doesn't do more to intervene," I mutter irritably. "All this madness could be stopped immediately. He controls the entire army of Allanon. Abirad and his forces wouldn't have a chance."

"He's a broken man, Boy. He lost the ones he loves,"

speaks Wise quietly. "When you care for someone that much, everything else seems to pale in comparison. You become blind to all others and deaf to all reason. Love defies logic. It speaks louder than the mind." There is a tightness in her voice and a wetness in her eyes as she speaks, and I know she is thinking of someone else just then. "Whatever his reasons for turning a blind eye to Abirad, we can't count on him magically coming to his senses and getting us out of here. We're on our own."

✳ ✳ ✳

Finally, the time is almost upon us. Three days. It's all that is standing between us and our escape.

I stretch out on my straw pile while Old Man glances at the loose brick in the wall for about the millionth time today. That's where he hides one of the singing stones. It isn't safe to keep them in the same place as they grow stronger when they are together, and their "singing" could draw the attention of the guards, so Wise has the other one. Our cells are far enough apart that we don't have to fear the guards being alerted.

"Rest well, my Boy," murmurs Old Man as he reclines on the ground.

"You as well," I whisper back to him.

I close my eyes and allow the drowsiness to overtake me, and it seems like only a few moments have passed when I am startled awake by a frantic whisper at the door of my cell.

"Boy! Boy! Wake up."

I sit bolt upright and look around in confusion. At first, I see no one, but then a pale, slender hand reaches up to remove the hood of a cloak. Cascades of blood red hair and the gleam of icy blue eyes reveal the figure to be Scarlet.

"Scarlet? What are you-"

She quickly cuts me off, and there is an intense urgency in her voice. "There's no time. Get up. We need to get out of here now. They know!" she hisses.

"They what?"

"The plan. The guards know. Someone told them. They're coming right now."

I feel as if I've been hit with a sledgehammer, and the air leaves my lungs in a strangled gasp. There's no way we can escape now. Still, what other choice do we have? We have to at least try. To simply remain in this cell will result in certain death.

I move to wake Old Man as Scarlet produces a long, thin, metal pin from the folds of her cloak. Old Man stumbles to his feet and immediately grabs the singing stone from its hiding place as Scarlet begins to quietly work the pin into the mechanism of the lock. I have to admit, I'm a bit impressed, and it seems the mystery of how Scarlet manages to escape her cell has been solved.

"Come on," she whispers. "I hid Wise and Lark in the alcove at the end of the hall. We need to move quickly. They'll be here any moment."

Suddenly, a large shadow appears behind Scarlet, and a deep, commanding voice immediately freezes the blood in my veins. "No... We're already here."

CHAPTER 8

I freeze.

My heart sinks so low that I think I might find it in the dirt at my feet.

I know that voice.

Brock, his face ghostly in a faint sliver of moonlight, steps toward the door of my cell. His dark eyes are filled with remorse, and I shake my head in disbelief, rendered speechless by his betrayal. We had been quite careful, but it all made sense now as to how the guards had found out about our plan. Brock. He'd given us up.

"You..." I can barely choke out the word, and I can't begin to assemble any coherent thought.

I can feel Old Man's presence behind me, and he puts a calloused hand on my shoulder in an attempt at comforting me.

Another figure emerges from the shadows. I immediately recognize him as Belas, one of the guards Brock has been training under. His gaze locks on Scarlet, and he immediately lunges forward to reach for her. Scarlet deftly dodges out of his grasp, and it's then that Brock moves faster than I've ever seen him move before. His hand seizes the side of Belas's head, slamming it into the side of the cell with great force. Belas is significantly larger than Brock, but the element of surprise has worked in Brock's favor. Stunned, the guard begins to swear profusely and attempts to reach for Brock's legs, but before he can make contact, Scarlet sweeps toward him, the pin still clutched firmly in her hand. Her hand flashes forward for a split second before returning to her side. When it does, the air grows heavy with the scent of iron, and I see that her fingers are smattered with blood.

Belas's hand clutches at his throat, and a sickening gurgling sound comes from his mouth as he slumps against the cell before falling completely still.

Brock is in shock, his mouth hanging open as he silently gawks at Scarlet.

"You know, that key would speed things up," states Scarlet glancing to the keyring attached to the belt of Belas's motionless form.

Brock bends down, grabs the keys, and tries several before finally selecting the correct one. My cell door slides open, and I quickly step through. Moments later, there is a faint humming sound as Old Man, the singing stone held firmly in his hand, files out behind me.

"Boy, it wasn't me!" Brock protests a bit too loudly, then quickly lowers his voice. "It wasn't me."

"Save it, Brock. We don't have time for this," hisses Scarlet urgently. "We need to get moving. Are you coming with us or not?"

Brock nods numbly.

"Come on. We need to get to Wise and Lark," urges Scarlet.

As we make our way down the hall, the cellblock is a flurry of hushed whispers as there is rarely this much commotion so late at night.

"Boy? Where are you going?" Hazel asks as she presses her face against the bars of her cell.

My stomach knots again. I want to tell Brock to unlock her cell, to unlock all of the cells, or at the very least, I want to assure her that everything will be okay. I want to tell her we'll get help and come back for her, for all of them, but before the words can leave my lips, they sour on my tongue and taste of lies. I don't have it in my heart to be false to her, so coward that I am, I say nothing, not even goodbye.

Scarlet leads us out of the cellblocks and to an alcove off the main corridor where Wise and Lark are waiting. As soon as

Wise lays eyes on Brock she looks as if she's ready to pummel him.

"You!"

Brock's face reddens considerably, and he can't bring himself to make eye contact with her. "Relax, Wise," he mutters. "It wasn't me. It was Jewel. I thought she'd keep it a secret."

Jewel. Of course.

"Idiot!" She punches him in the shoulder, hard enough to make him wince, which is saying something given the fact that it's Brock. "I know it wasn't you. If it was you, you wouldn't have been foolish enough to show your face."

"Then why did you hit me?" asks Brock in confusion.

"Because I told you blabbing to Jewel was a half-witted move!"

"Yeah, yeah. You were right, I was wrong. What's new? I'll make it up to you later," he says with a slight smirk. He's probably just glad she's actually acknowledging he's alive again. "Come on. We need to keep moving."

Brock unsheathes the broadsword at his side and guides us down the corridor. There is a loud commotion up ahead and the thundering of half a dozen sets of boots. Brock freezes in his tracks and rapidly changes directions as he leads us into a narrow hallway off the main corridor. We follow him through several more quick turns to the left and to the right, each time attempting to put more distance between us and the sounds of the guards. Eventually, we reach a dead end, and I notice the look of panic on Brock's face as he frantically searches for another route.

"I-I've never really been in this part of the castle before. I'm not really sure which way we go from here," he confesses. He glances desperately at Scarlet. "You've been out skulking in the hallways before. Do you know where we are?"

"No," growls Scarlet. "I foolishly assumed the guard-in-training might know where he is going."

We backtrack a short way, then Brock stops and looks around in desperation before heading off to the left, and the rest of us follow along behind him. After some time, he abruptly stops and throws up his hands in defeat.

"You have got to be kidding me!" he nearly shouts.

Wise clamps a hand over his mouth, and Scarlet looks as if she's ready to stick that pin of hers right through his neck, too.

"The *guard barracks*, Brock? You led us right to the *guard barracks*?" Scarlet's voice is trembling with quiet rage.

Old Man groans. "Well, this just gets worse and worse, doesn't it?"

Suddenly, a door to our left opens, and a large, cloaked figure, a hood concealing most of its face, emerges from within. The figure has a sword in one hand and a torch in the other. Brock reacts instinctively and immediately whirls around, ready to strike with his broadsword, but the figure parries with its own blade, easily knocking Brock's sword aside.

"Sluggish, as usual." The figure pulls back its hood, revealing a familiar face.

"Harding?" asks Brock, his voice quavering.

Harding grabs him roughly by the shoulder and hauls him inside the room then beckons for the rest of us to follow.

Wise and I exchange uncertain glances, but Lark follows after him without hesitation, and I'm reminded of the unusual kindness that Harding has shown the kid.

Harding quickly maneuvers around the room and lights several more torches. There are armor stands and weapon racks everywhere, revealing the place as a small armory.

"You're fortunate. I was just leaving to see if I could find you before the other guards could," explains Harding.

"Why would you-" I begin to ask, but Harding abruptly cuts me off.

"Quickly! Take what you can," speaks Harding urgently.

I hurriedly scramble around the room and try to find anything that could be helpful in this situation. There are chests filled with armor, helmets, and the like. I find a set of leather armor that looks like it might fit and rapidly don it. Brock approaches me and offers the hilt of a broadsword in his outstretched hand.

"I've never held a weapon in my life," I say.

Brock shrugs. "No better time to start than now. You'll figure it out. Just make sure the pointy end is facing away from you."

I take it from him and curl my fingers around the grip of the weapon. After a few practice swings, I find that I'm comfortable enough with it that I should be able to refrain from accidentally running myself through.

I glance over to Lark. The poor kid is having a terrible time of this; his entire form is trembling with fear. His eyes are as wide as saucers, and I see the tears beginning to form in the corners of his eyes.

His voice quavers as he looks up to Wise for assurance. "Wise... Wise, I'm scared."

It's moments like this that remind me why I care for Wise so much, why she is one of my most treasured friends. Even in the darkest of times, she always manages to keep her calm. I watch as she places her hands on Lark's shoulders and looks him in the eyes.

"It is scary, Lark. You'd be a fool not to be frightened. I'm scared, too. But we'll get through this. You just stay close to me. I won't let anything bad happen to you. I promise." She plunks a too big helmet on his head and throws the lightest leather armor she can find over him.

Harding watches them, his gaze fixed on Lark. He looks as if he wants to say something, but his lips clamp shut in a fine line.

Wise grabs a shield and a handaxe, then pauses as she seems to notice Harding staring at Lark. "Why are you helping us?"

Harding ignores her question and wordlessly crosses to the door before carefully peering out. I glance over to Scarlet who is tucking an alarming amount of daggers into her waistband, the folds of her cloak, and her boots.

"What? It's always good to have a spare... or ten," she says with a smile. Somehow, she's even scarier when she smiles.

There's a clattering sound behind me, and Harding hisses at Old Man. "Quiet down."

Old Man glances up but resumes digging through an unlocked chest in the corner of the room. He finds a bag within it and begins to stuff it with anything that could be useful.

"Wise," he calls softly. "The other stone. Give it to me."

Wise quickly does as he asks, and Old Man places both of the singing stones in a thick, leather pouch before depositing them in the pocket of a long, brown coat he has found. There is a distinct humming sound, but the singing stones are considerably muffled by the thickness of the leather pouch and the added protection provided by his pocket.

Harding swears under his breath then beckons us to the door. "They're coming this way. I have to distract them. Wait until you hear the way is clear then hurry on ahead to the second hallway on the left. Brock knows the way. Just follow him."

Scarlet frowns. "Are you sure about that?"

Brock reddens. "Hey! I've been to the guard barracks before. I—"

Scarlet rolls her eyes. "I don't care. Just know that if you get me killed, I swear I will haunt you for the rest of eternity. I will make you suffer so badly that Abirad killing you would be a more welcome end."

"Brock, you remember what I showed you?" asks Harding.

Brock, his face pale and his dark hair beaded with sweat, gives a simple nod. It occurs to me I've never really seen Brock worried about anything, and somehow his anxiety heightens my own. I always thought he was the bravest among us, but even he looks as if he's on the verge of panic.

Wise glances from Lark to Harding before settling an inquiring gaze on the guard.

Harding takes notice and sighs heavily. "Look, I know you have questions. If I make it out of here, I'll explain everything," he promises. "But there's no time now. You're just going to have to trust me on this." He moves as if to enter the hallway, but Lark abruptly seizes his sleeve. The guard looks down at him, and I swear, Lark appears as if he will start bawling at any moment.

Without warning, Harding pulls Lark into a tight hug and whispers something into his ear. Instantly, Lark freezes, then begins to cry. Harding shushes the weeping boy and beckons for Wise to come soothe him.

Harding, his face contorted with despair, speaks to Wise, but there is a peculiar huskiness in his voice, as if he, too, fights back tears. "No matter what, you must keep him safe. Abirad will not rest until he reclaims him." He takes a last look at Lark before disappearing out the door.

Lark begins to tremble as the tears continue to stream down his face. Wise collects him in a comforting embrace. "It's okay, Lark. It will all be okay."

Outside the door, Harding's voice begins to bellow "This way! This way!"

Dozens of heavy footsteps resound through the hallway as Harding's voice becomes more distant. "They're heading towards the west exit! This way!"

The shouting voices and thundering boots soon dissolve, and Brock takes up his position at the front of our group. "Come on," he whispers.

He follows Harding's directions and takes us down the second hallway on the left... right to another dead end.

"Probably shouldn't have trusted the guard," mutters Old Man.

Scarlet glares daggers at Brock, and I know that in mere moments she just may brandish some very real daggers at him.

"It's okay," assures Brock. "Come on. Follow me." He moves to the left and kneels for a few moments. There is a sound of metal scraping against stone, and as he steps back, I see there's an opening in the floor. Squinting further reveals a rather rickety looking ladder. "There are tunnels under the castle," explains Brock. "Harding told me about them. Said the original inhabitants dug them in the event they had to make a hasty escape. They're not used anymore, and they were sealed some time ago, but it might be our only chance. Harding said the east tunnel leads towards the forest."

Scarlet groans. "It won't do us much good if they're sealed, you know. We'll be trapped like rats down there."

"Don't worry about any seals. I can make short work of those," promises Old Man as he pats the pocket that contains the stones. There's a devilish gleam in his eye, and it unsettles me deeply. It's obvious that he can't wait to put his knowledge of the stones to good use.

"Come on. We have to get moving," urges Wise.

Brock sheathes his sword and peers down the ladder into the darkness below. He grabs a torch from the wall, and holding it in one hand, uses his other to descend the ladder. Wise follows him down and from the bottom whispers encouraging words to Lark as he does the same. Old Man's next, then Scarlet, and finally me. I balance myself at the top of the ladder and pull the metal cover back into place so that hopefully no one will be the wiser of our passing there.

When I reach the bottom of the ladder, it takes my eyes a moment to adjust. The tunnels are pitch black, so much so that I can scarcely see an inch in front of my face, even with Brock holding the torch aloft.

I hear Old Man fumbling in his pocket. There is a dull humming sound that begins to grow louder. He mutters something under his breath, and the next thing I know, the tunnel erupts in light around us. Old Man holds the singing stones, the source of the light, in his outstretched hand.

"How did you-" Brock begins.

"Not important," returns Old Man. "East, you said?"

We trudge through the tunnels, a place so dark and dank that even the rats don't seek refuge there. Even with the light, Lark looks terrified. He holds onto Wise's hand tightly, and she's quick to reassure him when even the slightest noises make him jump. Scarlet falls into step beside me.

"You know, there's a very good chance we won't make it

out of here," she whispers to me.

Unfortunately, she isn't quiet enough, and Lark hears her. He quickly turns to face her, and his eyes widen with fright. Wise shoots Scarlet a withering look.

"I mean- everything will be just fine. We'll definitely escape," she says a little louder.

Lark seems convinced, but when he turns away, Scarlet shakes her head and mouths the words. "No, we won't." She almost seems amused by the situation.

"How do you find this funny?" I ask.

"It's not funny. It's tragic really. We manage to escape, but likely to meet our dooms on the threshold of freedom. I should have stayed in my cell."

"Why didn't you?"

She shrugs. "I guess I needed a bit of adventure in my life."

"Sneaking out under the guards' noses wasn't exciting enough for you?"

"Enh. At first. It loses its luster after a while. Became too easy. I like a challenge." Her blue eyes sparkle with something resembling glee, and when she smiles at me, I feel a strange tightness in my chest.

It feels like hours later when we finally reach the end of the east tunnel. Just as Brock had guessed, the exit is sealed, but there are faint glimmers of dawn forcing their way through the cracks in the rocks, and despite my better judgment, I begin to cling to the hope of the prospect of freedom.

Old Man steps forward, the singing stones in his hand. "You're going to want to step back…"

We quickly clear out of the area. Wise guides Lark to a nearby alcove, and Brock kneels next to them while Scarlet and I do the same on the other side of the tunnel.

"You may want to cover your ears," cautions Old Man.

We don't hesitate in following his orders, all of us eager to see what may happen. Old Man begins to mutter words under his breath, much like when he used the stones to provide light for us. His murmurings are strange to me, as if from another language entirely. The stones begin to hum louder and suddenly there is an enormous blast that seems to suck most of the air out of the room. There is an earsplitting shattering sound as the seal leading to the outside world is violently blown apart, leaving large rocks tumbling to the floor and skittering across the tunnel.

Old Man coughs and swats away a cloud of dust before dragging his long fingers down his face to clear his eyes. "Out we go."

There is light at the end of the tunnel.

CHAPTER 9

Half-exhilarated and half-terrified, we make our way out of the tunnel and into the dawn. The sun is just beginning its ascent over a myriad of trees and spilling its light over the verdant grass below. The countryside seems to stretch on for miles to the left and right as far as the eye can see, but straight ahead is our destination: the forest.

I feel something catch in my throat, like a gasp of awe that can't seem to fight its way to my lips, and it takes me a second or two to realize I'm crying. Scarlet smirks at me, but instead of her usual sass, she reaches into her cloak and offers me a handkerchief.

"I-I've never seen… I can't remember seeing…"

"Grass?" asks Scarlet. "Yeah, there's not much of that in the courtyard or even around the wheat fields."

I nod numbly.

"And sunrises look much different from this side of the walls," comments Old Man quietly. "I had forgotten that. But we shouldn't tarry. If we succeed, then we shall all see many more of these." He claps a hand on my shoulder. "Come, Boy."

We move to cross the expanse separating us from the woods, but our feet have barely cleared the rubble from the tunnel when there is shouting behind us, from far above on the castle walls.

"We've been spotted! Move!" shouts Brock.

We all break into a run as fast as our legs can carry us. Scarlet is a flash of crimson lightning as she speeds forward, leaving me struggling to catch up to her. Old Man's long, twiggy legs are able to cover distance fairly quickly, and Brock barrels forward with haste. It is Lark who is having trouble keeping up.

"Wise!" Lark's panicked cry immediately summons Wise to his side.

"I've got you, Lark. Come on. We have to hurry. Climb on." Wise motions for him to jump on her back and she carries the burden of two with the ease of one. Soon she's a mere few steps behind me, but it's right about then that the arrows begin to rain down upon us.

"TAKE COVER!" bellows Brock, as he shoves me to the ground behind the thick trunk of a tree.

Wise, with Lark still clinging to her back, throws up her shield to absorb the arrows that seek to harm them. There is a dull clinking sound as several of them are deflected by her shield.

"They're reloading! Let's go!" Brock urges us forward, and we continue our mad dash for the tree line of the woods.

However, as we near safety, we realize another obstacle bars our way. Nearly a dozen guards materialize at the edge of the forest; their black surcoats bear the emerald green dragon that is the symbol of Abirad. Their weapons are at the ready, and their gazes are trained on us.

One of the guards calls out to his companions. "Take the child. Kill the rest!"

I draw my weapon and glance directly to my right at Wise. With a protective arm, she shifts the terrified Lark behind her.

"Don't worry, Lark. Just stay behind me, and when I tell you to move, you move."

"Wise." His eyes are wide with fright, and the tears are already starting to stream down his sunburned cheeks.

"It's okay, Lark. We won't let them take you. I promise." Wise looks to me as if to plead for further assurance.

"She's right, Lark. It will be okay." My words sound hollow to me, and I don't know how Lark could possibly find them convincing when even I don't, but it does the job. "Be strong. Stay close to Wise."

The guards begin to advance on us, and Brock immediately closes with the two guards who are nearest to him. The sound of steel on steel seems to spur the rest of the guards into action, and about half of them come barreling towards me and Wise, while the rest are engaged with Brock or Scarlet.

I see glimpses of crimson in beautiful, fluid motion as Scarlet unsheathes her daggers and engages with the guards who are foolish enough to come near her. They signed their death warrants the moment they decided to pursue her, and before I've parried a blow, two of them are already dead at her feet.

Heartened by her success, I rush toward one of the guards. I bring my sword down upon him, but he easily deflects my blow while one of his companions flanks me. I hear a faint whirring in the air, and when I turn, a third guard who had tried to sneak up behind me is lying in a pool of his own blood. He gasps for air as he clutches at the dagger embedded in his throat. I look behind me just in time to see Scarlet give me a wink before bounding off to rain havoc upon another enemy.

Surprisingly, I manage to land a blow against the guard across from me. My blade strikes his sword hand, causing him to drop his weapon and reach for a dagger on his belt with his off-hand.

I suppose desperation can turn anyone into a warrior. While I cannot boast to have the natural skill my companions seem to possess, the weapon in my hand is beginning to feel less like some strange, unwieldy thing and more familiar to me. Perhaps it is because I know that if I cannot use it to the best of my ability, I'll end up hauled back to the castle or dead.

The guard swipes at me with the dagger, but I manage to quickly dodge out of his reach, and a moment later, Brock's sword erupts through the man's chest as my friend has taken the opportunity to drive his blade through the guard's back.

Brock turns his attention to another foe.

The sounds of battle surround me as Wise slams her axe with such power into the side of a guard that the man clutches at his bleeding abdomen before slumping to the ground. I hear Lark whimper as another guard comes towards them, but Wise's axe again strikes true. She embeds it into the guard's thigh before yanking it free.

There's a sharp pain in my shoulder as one of the guards manages to hit me so hard with his sword that it penetrates my armor and slices into my bicep. I cry out in pain, and instantly, Wise is next to me, slamming her shield into the guard's chest and causing him to fall backward. She brings her axe down upon him, giving me time to recover a bit before the next onslaught. Yet another guard swings his weapon towards me in an attempt to take my head off, but Wise isn't about to let that happen. Her axe catches the man in the side of the neck, and yet another guard finds himself dispatched by her hand.

I'm feeling pretty proud of us right then, until I see reinforcements, some on horseback and others on foot, rapidly advancing up the hill towards us. The unit consists of about a dozen more guards.

My sword finds its home in the belly of a guard who had thought I'd be easy prey. While I may not be as intimidating as Brock, I am certainly faster, and the man pays for his mistake with his life. I glance around the area and watch as Scarlet finishes off another guard with one of her innumerable daggers, and Brock pulls his sword free from a fallen foe.

Moments later, Brock, bleeding from a nasty cut on his forehead, is beside me, and Scarlet materializes next to Lark, placing a reassuring hand on his shoulder.

Suddenly, a realization hits me. "Where's Old Man?" I ask Wise. I had lost track of him as soon as the fighting started.

Wise and Brock both shrug, but my question does not go unanswered.

From the tree line, there is an explosive boom, and I

recognize the use of the singing stones once again. The force is great enough to knock four of the guards off their horses, and two additional mounts throw their riders from their backs before hurrying back down the hill.

"Oh sh-" Scarlet nearly finishes her second word, but a stern look from Wise silences her. Yet, I understand her aggravation. More guards can be seen gathering at the base of the hill.

"We have to get to the forest," says Brock firmly. "If we can make it there, it gives us a better chance." He turns to Wise. "Wise. Get Lark out of here."

Wise shakes her head firmly. "If you think I'm leaving you..."

I see the slightest hint of understanding flash across Brock's face.

"You *all*," Wise quickly corrects herself.

Lark grabs Wise's arm, and despite her reluctance, I know Wise will do as Brock says. She'll do what she needs to in order to protect the kid.

"Go on, Wise," urges Brock gently. "We'll cover you two. Try to get to Old Man, wherever he is over there. He can use the stones to keep you all safe."

Wise locks eyes with Brock, and I see an almost pained expression there. She looks as if she wants to say something, but she shakes her head as if dispelling the notion before grabbing Lark by the hand and hurrying towards the tree line.

The first wave of reinforcements, or what's left of them after Old Man's use of the stones, is upon us mere moments later. Two of the guards try to divert and make their way after Wise and Lark, but Brock doesn't give them the chance. He buries his sword into the back of one before tackling the other to the ground and brawling with him for a few moments before knocking the guard unconscious.

Scarlet makes fighting look like some kind of elaborate dance. Her graceful movements carry her from one foe to another, leaving a trail of bloodshed and destruction in her wake. I manage to dispatch two more, and I'm starting to feel more and more comfortable with a blade in my hands. However, fatigue is beginning to catch up to me, and I'm starting to feel a bit lightheaded. We finish off the first wave of reinforcements, but just as we do, the second wave is upon us.

There's another earsplitting boom as the singing stones once again do their job, stopping several of the guards in their tracks. Unfortunately, there are too many guards this time, and I start to feel the pressure as we begin to get overwhelmed.

"Boy!" I hear Brock yell. "There's too many of them! Get out of here! I'll cover you!"

"Not without you," I say firmly. "We can do this together."

"No. We can't," he says with finality. He looks to Scarlet who nods in agreement.

"Boy, you should get moving," concurs Scarlet as she whips another dagger through the air where it hits its mark in the gullet of an advancing guard.

"Why not you? You go. I'll cover you," I say.

Scarlet looks amused and practically laughs at the suggestion. "As I see it, my body count is far higher than yours. Brock and I can handle ourselves. You've lost a lot of blood." She gestures to my arm that had been injured at the beginning of the fight. "If you don't get that tended to soon, you're likely to faint."

I want to argue with her, but I can't. While my spirit is willing to continue, my body is having trouble keeping up, and as I glance at my arm, I see that Scarlet is right. My armor is heavily stained with crimson, and it certainly explains why I'm feeling a bit dizzy.

"I'll see you soon," I say to Brock, as I clap him on the shoulder.

He forces a slight smile, but it occurs to me then that this may very well be the last time I see him. The minute he told me to go to the forest, he had resigned himself to the idea that he could die protecting his friends. The thought both deeply saddens me and makes my heart swell with pride. He truly is a loyal friend, and I only hope that I do see him again.

"Get to the others. Move as far into the forest as you can," urges Brock.

I glance over to Scarlet, but she is locked in combat with another guard, and as soon as I begin to make my way towards the tree line, Brock finds himself surrounded by four more of Abirad's men. I want to rush back to his side and help him, but my failing strength tells me that I wouldn't be of much use, and me being there could be more of a liability to him than a means of assistance. He'd be so busy protecting me that he'd be putting himself at more risk.

I crash through underbrush and head in the direction from which I had heard the singing stones. Wise, her face streaked with blood, both her own and that of the guards, silently stands next to Lark, ready to protect him again should any of our enemies get to the forest. Old Man is muttering under his breath, and moments later, he tells us to cover our ears as he unleashes another blast from the singing stones at Abirad's men.

"Brock says we need to get moving," I tell them.

"Boy! You're pale as a ghost!" Wise reaches into her bag and sets to wrapping my upper arm to slow the bleeding.

"Brock's right," says Old Man quietly. "There are too many of them, and I fear I can't keep this up."

I notice then how pale he is and the rivulets of sweat that pour from his brow. Then, he holds up one of his hands, and I gasp as I see the imprints of the singing stones burned into the flesh of his palm. The skin has already started to blister. His hands look raw, as if he had held them far too close to open flame.

"Magic always comes with a price," he responds to my inquiring gaze. "There are ways to mitigate the damage to myself, I know that much. But unfortunately, I don't recall exactly how to go about doing it." He glances further into the woods. "Well, we best be off." He places the stones in their pouch, and we move to go deeper into the forest.

Old Man takes up a position at the front of our group with Lark right behind him. I glance behind me to see Wise, her gaze fixed in the direction of the hill where Brock and Scarlet are still locked in combat with the guards.

"They need help," she tells me. "I need to go back and help them." She moves as if to leave, but I grab her arm as firmly as I can, which isn't saying much as the blood loss has left me quite weakened.

"Wise, *we* need you. I'm worse for wear, and you saw Old Man's hands. We need you here. We can't properly defend ourselves. And Lark…"

Wise appears conflicted, and I know why.

"He'll be okay," I assure her, even if I don't fully believe it myself.

"You're lying. Your ears always turn red when you lie," she says quietly.

Without another word, she offers me her shoulder to steady me, and we make our way deeper into the forest, farther away from our former prison, yet also farther from our embattled friends.

CHAPTER 10

We proceed at a harried pace for as long as we can manage it. For the first couple hours, we dare not stop for even a moment in fear that we are likely being pursued. Eventually, poor Lark starts tripping over himself from exhaustion, and even I have difficulty maintaining any speed due to the loss of blood from the wound on my arm. We rest for a brief time so Wise can put a fresh layer of bandages on my wound and so Lark can rest his blistered feet.

After this all too short pause, Wise reluctantly gets us up and moving again. Every now and then, I see her cast a worried glance over her shoulder. I know that she is not only watching to see if we are about to be set upon, but also in the hopes that our companions may rejoin us.

Eventually, it gets to be too dark to continue on. We have a couple torches, but they provide only scant light in the thick darkness of the forest, and due to his current injuries, we dissuade Old Man from using the stones to help us to see better. We find an area that has a reasonable amount of natural cover, mostly large rocks and a particularly dense patch of trees, that can obscure us should the need arise.

We can risk only a small fire as we aren't sure if any of Abirad's guards have managed to track us, so Wise, Lark, Old Man, and I huddle around it. Wise had the forethought to grab a couple blankets from the armory, so that helps to take out some of the chill from the crisp, fall, evening air.

Between Wise and Old Man, they manage to tend to my wound. Old Man is able to find some herbs to make a poultice to promote healing and ward off infection, while Wise is able to find me something to help with the pain. She stitches up the wound with a needle and some thread before wrapping it with fresh bandages.

We sit down to eat some dried beef, bread, and cheese that Old Man had nicked from the castle's kitchen. It's then that we hear a faint rustling and the sound of breaking twigs nearby. Wise is instantly on her feet, but suddenly, I hear her give an audible sigh of relief.

"Scarlet!" Lark scrambles to his feet and rushes towards Scarlet, practically knocking her over with the force of his embrace.

At first, she appears startled, but then smiles slightly and pats the back of his head before he reluctantly releases her. He looks behind her, and not seeing what he is searching for, looks around her other side.

An expression resembling sorrow affects Scarlet's pretty features, and she gives Wise a grim, meaningful look. Wise pales and it is as if the air has been forcibly knocked from her lungs. In silence, she struggles to compose herself.

For the next hour or so, Scarlet deflects Lark's questions over Brock's whereabouts until the kid finally passes out, his head on Wise's lap. Wise carefully extricates herself from under him before wrapping a blanket around his sleeping form.

The four of us sit in silence with neither Wise, Old Man, nor I, able to ask Scarlet the questions that need to be asked.

"I don't know for sure that he's dead," says Scarlet quietly. "We were overwhelmed. Brock was hurt. Bad. I tried to get to him, but..."

"It's okay," replies Wise softly. "You tried."

Scarlet stares into the fire, dancing flames reflecting in her ice blue eyes. "I saw him fall to his knees. There was a guard over him with the end of a sword pressed to his throat. That's when things got... weird."

"Weird?" asks Old Man.

"More reinforcements came, but they didn't attack us. They attacked the other guards. Harding was leading them," Scarlet explains.

Wise's mouth drops open in shock, and I'm pretty sure mine does the same.

Scarlet pulls a blanket more tightly around her. "That's around the time I lost sight of Brock. Harding ordered me to get running. I wanted to check on Brock first, but it was absolute chaos. I couldn't find him right away, and by then more guards were heading up the hill."

None of us know what to say. Wise fights back tears, and for the rest of the night, she stares silently into the woods, as if by some answered prayer, Brock will miraculously emerge from the trees. I try to comfort her, but I don't know what to say, because my heart hurts, too, and as much as I care for Brock, I know things are different for her. Whether she admits it or not, she loved him... loves him... and I don't have any experience with that sort of thing.

One by one, we each succumb to our weariness. Old Man is the next one to fall asleep. An hour or so later, Scarlet follows suit. My eyes are beginning to feel heavy, but even though I don't know what to say to Wise, I'm reluctant to leave her alone to her grief. I force myself to stay awake as long as I can; however, despite my best intentions, eventually sleep claims me as well. The last thing I see before I nod off is Wise still staring into the forest, hoping with every speck of faith she can muster, that Brock will come striding into our camp with a victorious smirk on his face, and I think that maybe, just maybe, she might get around to telling him what's in her heart.

CHAPTER 11

Not knowing the outcome of the battle between Harding and his comrades versus the guards still loyal to Abirad, we can't risk resting too long. We have to keep moving.

I wake up after a few hours, and Wise has already set to collecting our belongings and getting everything ready to continue our trek into the forest. Lark is still snoring softly while Old Man echoes this action in a much, much louder fashion. Scarlet, seated upon a fallen log, frowns in annoyance at the abrasive noise and nudges him with her foot so that he'll shift. He does, and the noise becomes at least the slightest bit fainter.

My whole body complains with soreness. My muscles are tight from their use in battle, and my wounded arm is stiff and pained. Wise wordlessly checks my bandages. She doesn't look as if she has gotten any sleep. After tending to me, she gently wakes Lark while Old Man rouses himself from his slumber. We eat in silence, shoulder our meager belongings, and prepare to depart our camp, when in the distance we hear something. It's Wise who picks up on it first, and without a moment's hesitation, she takes off into the woods at a breakneck speed.

"Wise...Boy..."

The voice, faint with pain and exhaustion, is barely audible to the rest of us, but when we realize what's happening, we all run in the direction we had seen Wise disappear.

When we find her, she's kneeling on the ground next to a prone figure.

"Brock!" I rush toward them, but the look on Wise's face tells me that despite the fact Brock is at least with us now, the situation is very dire.

She presses her ear to his chest then glances up at me briefly. "His heart is still beating. He's breathing but barely."

As I look upon him, I see his face is a ghostly pallor. His eyes are closed, and nearly every inch of him is covered in both fresh and dried blood. His body is marked with numerous wounds of varying degrees of severity. The shaft of an arrow, broken in half, is still embedded in his thigh, and there's a serious wound on his left side.

Wise sets to work immediately. She begins to remove his armor and inspects his wounds while she yells to Old Man to find this root and that root.

"Scarlet, start a fire. I've got to stop this bleeding fast. It needs to be cauterized," she says as she evaluates the wound on his side.

Wise is a tangle of emotions. There is relief in her eyes at seeing Brock alive, at least for now. Yet, I can plainly see the grief in her features as she worries over his fate. Despite it all, her voice is calm and collected as she tends to Brock's wounds as quickly as possible.

I've never smelled burning human flesh before, and it's something I hope that I never have to experience again. Wise hurriedly cleans the area around the wound on Brock's side so she can get a better look. Then, she asks for one of Scarlet's daggers and places it into the flames of the small fire Scarlet has started. With a look of grim determination, she presses it against Brock's wound. Brock should be thankful he has passed out, because the pain such a measure would have delivered would have been horrific had he been awake.

"What can I do? Can I help?" asks Lark.

"Yes." Wise reaches into her bag and pulls out a small, dried white flower. "I saw some of these at the edge of our camp. This is Maker's Grace. See the white petals with the blue in the center? They look exactly like this. Gather as many as you can. Don't wander off."

"I won't, Wise," he promises.

"We'll need more allowary root," says Old Man. Lark trots purposefully back towards the camp and Old Man follows after him, leaving Scarlet, Wise, and I with the unconscious Brock.

Scarlet begins to check her belt and proceeds to take inventory of all of her daggers before heading off in the direction from which Brock had come.

"Where are you going?" I ask.

"To make sure he wasn't followed. If any of Abirad's guards are still on our trail, we'll be easy prey here," she replies grimly.

"Good idea," agrees Wise. "We need to make sure Brock is stable before we can risk moving him. Ideally, if we can make camp here for a few days, it may be the difference between life and..." She trails off, unwilling to continue the thought.

Scarlet disappears into the trees, and I kneel on the ground next to my fallen friend. Wise's brow is furrowed in concentration, but the minute the two of us are alone with Brock, the tears begin to well in the corners of her eyes.

"I shouldn't have left him, Boy. I could have helped." Her voice is a pained reflection of her guilt.

"Or, you might have ended up just as bad off as he is... or worse." I glance at the freshly cauterized wound on Brock's side. "Wise... Tell me truly. How bad is it?" I inquire, not sure if I want to know the answer.

She gestures to the wound on his side. "That one was definitely the worst of them. He's lost a lot of blood. If it was even a fraction of an inch over, he would have bled out by now. The rest of the wounds are manageable, though the arrow wound may cause him to limp for a while. If he can just make it through the night, he at least has a chance of getting through this."

* * *

It's several hours later when Scarlet finally reappears. Lark and I have reassembled some of our camp when she emerges so quietly from the trees that Lark gives a yelp of surprise when she plops down beside him.

"You scared me to death, Scarlet!" says Lark clutching his chest.

"Nonsense. You sure look alive to me." She shifts on the ground and comes to sit cross-legged between Lark and me. "I wanted to make sure we are clear. I went a couple hours out and saw no one. It should be safe to remain here a while."

Wise glances up from her ministrations to Brock. "Thank you, Scarlet," she says quietly.

Scarlet gives a slight nod. "Don't mention it. Seriously. Don't. I don't want rocks for brains thinking I actually care."

I expect Wise to bristle at Scarlet's joke, especially given the circumstances, but now that Brock's breathing has returned to normal, and he seems to be resting as comfortably as can be managed, she offers a slight smirk in reply to Scarlet.

Old Man, sitting across from me, applies more salve to his burned hands. Between him and Wise, he may be the more experienced healer, but his wounds have rendered him mildly helpless in this situation, so Wise has shouldered the burden as Brock's primary caretaker.

* * *

For the next two days, Brock slips in and out of consciousness. The entire time, Wise devotedly never leaves his side. When he wakes for the briefest moments, screaming in pain from his many wounds, she pours a few drops of allowary extract into his mouth until the agony subsides. In these moments, she whispers calming words and promises of better days into his ear, and he seems to relax slightly. He constantly reaches out for her hand, wrapping hers tightly in his large fingers. He calls out for her, or for me, and sometimes, a mother he doesn't remember. Yet, also, to Wise's great discomfort, he calls out for Jewel.

When fever sets in and his whimpers of pain begin, Wise wipes his brow with cool cloths, and she sings some song that she picked up from one of her many readings in an attempt to soothe him. She regularly dresses his wounds, and despite pleas from all of us, she refuses to leave him so that she herself may sleep or eat.

Eventually, Old Man is able to talk some sense into her. "Wise, my dear, you're of no use to him if you faint from exhaustion. Eat something, please, and take some rest."

She reluctantly agrees but allows herself only the smallest amount of rest before rising again to tend to him.

On the third afternoon, Lark, Scarlet, and I return with some fresh berries and several, small, silver fish we were able to catch in a nearby stream. Old Man had managed to craft a makeshift net, and it had served its purpose well. As we near our camp, we hear Brock's voice, faint, but present.

Lark and I exchange glances and dash forward while Scarlet continues on at a leisurely pace behind us.

"Brock! Brock!" Lark reaches him first, kneeling beside Wise who is once again dressing his wounds.

Brock, his face still pale and his brown eyes still heavy with exhaustion, offers a weak smile. "Hey, kid."

"You scared us. We weren't sure if you'd make it," I say, and I can't quite mask the twinge of worry in my voice.

"What? And let you have all the fun? I don't think so, Boy," responds Brock, his humor still intact despite his current situation.

Scarlet appears behind me, greeting Brock with a simple nod of her head. He returns the gesture in kind before being the recipient of a barrage of questions by Lark.

"How are you feeling? What happened? How did you escape? How did you find us? What happened to Harding? Where did you last seem him? Was he okay?" asks Lark, and I'm reminded that, of course, he'd want to know what happened to Harding given their unusual relationship.

"Lark," says Wise gently. "I know you have a lot that you want to talk to Brock about, but he needs to rest and regain his strength. Perhaps later?"

"Okay, Wise. Scarlet and I will go cook the fish for us. I caught the biggest one," announces Lark proudly. "But Scarlet caught the most. Boy caught that itty bitty fish. Scarlet said there might be a bite of meat on it."

Scarlet snickers before leading Lark towards the campfire. Old Man, a few pieces of wood under one of his arms, soon joins them.

"I can't tell you how glad I am to have you back with us, Brock," I tell him sincerely.

"I'm glad to be here, Boy."

* * *

Later that night, after Scarlet, Lark, and Old Man have turned in for the evening, I sit alone next to the fire while Wise heaps a few blankets over Brock's large frame.

"It's been getting colder at night. You need to keep warm," she says to him.

He reaches out to clasp her hand. "Thank you, Wise."

"Don't thank me. That's what friends do. We take care of each other."

"Hey... Wise."

"Hm?"

"Since I managed to cheat death, anything you want to get off your chest?" he asks, and I immediately know what he's insinuating.

"I don't know what you mean," she replies simply. I know she does. It's Wise. I'm pretty sure she knows everything.

"Maybe you'd like to tell me why you kept ignoring me for days."

It feels wrong to listen in on such a private conversation, but I can't help myself. I barely breathe as I try to overhear everything that's said. It's around then I notice that Scarlet's eyes are wide open, and she's looking me dead in the eyes, as if we are co-conspirators in eavesdropping.

"I wasn't ignoring you," corrects Wise. "I was avoiding you... and I don't think that's a good idea. Especially right now. You need to rest."

"Wise. I am resting. I'm not going anywhere."

I know Brock's stubborn tone as soon as I hear it. He's not going to let this conversation go until Wise comes clean.

"You won't like what I have to say," replies Wise with certainty.

"How do you know unless you tell me?"

"I just know. You, Boy, and Old Man have been my friends for years... and now Lark, and whether she likes it or not, Scarlet, too"

Scarlet looks shocked by the statement, but she can't help but to smirk slightly at Wise's comment.

"Your friendship means a great deal to me Brock. I won't jeopardize it," responds Wise adamantly.

"Wise..." I watch as Brock gives a gentle squeeze to her hand. "As you said, we're friends. Nothing could ever change that."

Wise sighs heavily. "Fine. But promise me, if you don't like what you hear, our friendship remains intact. We pretend this conversation never happened. Nothing changes between us."

"Fair enough," agrees Brock.

"I..." Wise takes a moment to consider how to voice what's in her head and her heart. "I avoided you because I was jealous."

"Jealous?" asks Brock incredulously. "Of what?"

"Not what. Who."

"Who then?"

Wise seems to be enduring some kind of internal struggle, as if debating whether or not she should continue. Reluctantly, she responds. "Jewel."

"Why?"

"Do you really not know?"

Brock shrugs. "I might have a guess, but I don't like to guess wrong, Wise, so how about you just tell me."

"Brock, I-I have... feelings for you. I've had them for a long time," replies Wise, and I can hear the nervousness in her voice. It must have taken her a lot of courage to finally confess to the way she feels for our mutual friend.

Brock is silent in the wake of Wise's revelation, and finally, it is Wise who must reengage the conversation.

"So... do we pretend this conversation never occurred?" Wise is half joking, hopeful that Brock is simply still processing what she's just said.

"Wise... I think that's for the best," Brock responds curtly.

Scarlet and I exchange sympathetic glances as we are both certain of the hurt Wise is surely feeling. It is even plainer to us when she clears her throat and responds to his statement.

"Very well. That's what we agreed upon." I've known her long enough to be able to tell when she is attempting to keep the prying clutches of sadness at bay.

"Rocks for brains," mutters Scarlet quietly.

"It makes sense now... Why you were so insistent that I leave." There is almost an edge to Brock's tone. "Jewel said she thought you might be interested in me. I told her she was crazy."

"Brock, that wasn't the only reason I insisted that you leave," responds Wise firmly. "You're my friend. I didn't want to leave you behind to be a victim to Abirad's whims. None of us did."

"Even so, I left Jewel behind. And I almost got myself killed. I'm starting to think that maybe I should have stayed."

"Brock, that's foolish."

"Is it? I was happy enough there and bound to be happier due to my promotion. I was certainly in much better health."

Wise's cheeks redden, and when she resumes speaking, there's a slight tremor in her voice. "Well, I'm sorry if you feel you made a mistake. And I told you that I didn't want to tell you anything; I knew it was a bad idea."

Brock sighs. "Well, there's nothing to be done for it now. I'll probably never see Jewel again." He seems to finally notice the forlorn expression on Wise's face. "Look, Wise. I'm not blaming you. I just need you to know that, while I am incredibly grateful for all you have done for me, we are only friends, and that is all we will ever be. I'm sorry."

Wise forces a smile, but it would take a fool to think it's genuine. "It's fine. Don't apologize, Brock." She pulls the blankets over his chest. "Look, I think you've had enough excitement for the day. You need some sleep."

Brock falls asleep quickly, and when he does, Wise sits next to me by the fire. Scarlet sits up and scooches closer to us.

"We heard it all," I admit quietly. "I'm sorry, Wise. I thought he might feel the same way for you."

"It's okay," replies Wise, even though I can hear the slightest traces of disappointment in her voice. "He can't help the way that he feels any more than I can."

We sit in silence for several moments, until Scarlet is the one who breaks it.

"So... we're friends?" she asks Wise, her voice serious.

Wise nods in reply.

"I've never had friends before," comments Scarlet quietly. "I found a pretty friendly chicken once... back at the castle... but I ended up eating it. You know our meals were never filling enough. Would have been a terrible thing to go to waste."

I recall Henrietta's unexplained disappearance, and for a moment, I think Wise may terminate her new friendship with Scarlet right then, but she simply shakes her head in disbelief before settling in for some much needed, and well-deserved, sleep.

CHAPTER 12

It's four more days until Brock has regained enough strength to allow him to continue on our journey. By then, we've fallen into a rhythm in our everyday routine. Every morning, Wise gets up early and monitors Brock's condition then puts together breakfast for the five of us. It usually consists of a few of the dried rations we took from the castle along with some fresh berries and nuts that we've managed to scavenge from around the forest.

Then, Scarlet takes off for a few hours to scout the way behind us to ensure we have not been pursued, then she strikes out on the way ahead to see what lies before us. She's told us there's nothing around for miles except for an abandoned village or two; their inhabitants were likely imprisoned by Abirad or left in haste to avoid his madness. She did manage to find a well-worn travelling road, but she says there aren't fresh tracks there, so it probably hasn't been used too recently. We decide that when it's time to move on, we should head that way as it will give us a better vantage should any of Abirad's men pursue us. Additionally, there are woods on at least one side of the road, which will provide suitable cover should we need to flee.

As for the rest of us, Wise and I work with Brock, helping him to get steady on his feet again. He has a noticeable limp now, but Wise says it should diminish with time. As for Brock, he's simply happy to be alive. I know some of his wounds still bother him, but he doesn't complain about them too much. Instead, he focuses on regaining his strength. He goes to work swinging his sword around, which presents some difficulty as the wound in his side is still healing. The wound in my arm is feeling better every day, and Old Man's hands have just about healed entirely.

Around lunch time, I take Lark fishing, and we sit in comfortable silence (which is truly a feat considering how much Lark likes to ramble), and we bring back whatever we can. By then, Wise is typically scolding Brock about overdoing it, and Scarlet is just getting back from her first round of travels. A few times, I decide to accompany her on these scouting trips, though not too often, as I need to be available in the event that we are attacked at the camp. While Wise can certainly do a fine job of protecting the others should it come down to it, Brock is still not at the point where he could be very helpful, and Old Man spends so much of his time lost in thought that I doubt if he'd even notice if a flaming chariot driven by Abirad himself would tear right through the middle of the camp. He alternates between staring into the distance, his eyes wide open, yet seemingly seeing nothing, and obsessively studying a small book that Scarlet had managed to acquire for him before our hasty departure.

Finally, it's Wise who declares that it's time to move on. "We need to get moving so we can reunite Lark with the king."

Lark shifts uncomfortably, and Wise puts a reassuring hand on his shoulder. "It's okay, Lark. If we're right, and King Ruden really is your father, then he'll be so excited to see you. Being reunited with his son may be the one thing that convinces him to finally move against Abirad. Think how many people it could save."

Lark nods, but the worry in his expression continues to preside whenever the topic of his impending reunion with the man we suspect to be his father is discussed. I don't blame him. Prince Trystan had been taken from Vericus on his second birthday; Lark had practically been a baby and certainly wouldn't remember much, if anything, of his parents. I can only imagine what a difficult situation that would be. Furthermore, the only affection the kid has ever known came from Harding, a point I still find shocking.

On one of our fishing trips, Lark had opened up a bit about the guard. Brock had finally gotten around to answering his questions about what happened to Harding during the escape. The last Brock saw him, he was holding his own against Abirad's loyal guards, and the men who had joined Harding had succeeded in driving some of the sorcerer's forces back towards the castle.

Some questions had been nagging at the back of my mind for quite some time, so I finally decided to just talk to Lark about it. "So, I've got to ask you, Lark... Why did Harding help us to escape? Why did he decide to fight against Abirad after serving him for so long?"

Lark had shrugged and sat in silence for several moments before offering any kind of answer. "I don't think he ever really served the sorcerer. In fact, I don't think he liked him very much at all. I could tell that when Abirad was being cruel to me."

"What do you mean, Lark?"

"It... it's hard to explain because it's all pretty foggy, but I do remember a bit about Harding. He helped to take care of me. I don't remember much about being at the castle, but when I was really little, he used to carry me around. He used to look after me. Whenever Abirad made me cry, which was pretty often from what I can remember, Harding would come and sit next to me and cheer me up. He'd always bring me treats and promise me that things would be better for me someday. I guess he was right about that last part."

"Yes... I suppose this is better than being imprisoned in the castle."

"I remember feeling bad for all of you. Abirad kept me locked in my rooms at all times, but it wasn't so awful really. There were toys there for me to play with. I had a bed that I could sleep in every night. A really nice one. And pillows stuffed with feathers! Sure better than sleeping on sticks and rocks out here. And I don't think I ever really knew what hunger was until I was moved to the cells."

This sparks another question in my mind. "Lark, do you have any idea why you were moved there? You lived in the castle for years, and you were never down in the yards before then."

Lark shook his head sadly. "No. All I remember is that I did something to make Abirad really mad at me. He said I was ungrateful, and that I needed to learn a lesson. Then he sent me to the yards. Even there, Harding tried to protect me. I was mad that he didn't just get me out of there, but he told me to make friends, and that you and Wise were good people who'd probably help look after me. He was right about that. I love Wise. And you Boy. And even grouchy Brock, and Scarlet, and Old Man. I think it must be kind of like having a family."

"Well, there's a good chance the king is your dad, Lark. You'd have a real family. That would make you a prince, too.

Lark appeared confused. "You *are* my real family. We might not have the same blood, but we care about each other, and that makes us family just the same. And I don't care much for the idea of being a prince. For once, I think I'd just like to be a normal kid, whatever that's like. I saw them in my picture books at the castle. They always looked so happy. Laughing and playing. I think I want that."

Sometimes, Lark says things that really make me think. Even though he's just a kid, sometimes he sounds just about as smart as Wise. It's strange really. Sometimes he seems like any other child, but at other times, it's as if there's a much older soul living within him. Perhaps it's his experiences that have aged him prematurely, as I suppose is the case for all of us.

* * *

When we finally leave the camp, we make our way to

the road, which is a slow and laborious process as we are confined to moving at Brock's pace. I can tell he's getting frustrated over not being able to move like he used to, and we have to take frequent breaks so the pain doesn't get to be too much for him. However, everyone is more than supportive. Even Scarlet only jokes at his expense occasionally (usually by likening him to a grandmother turtle).

The first abandoned village we pass through looks as if it's frozen in time. There are still plates and tankards on tables, their contents long since rotted away or eaten by wild animals. The simple homes are overgrown with vegetation, and it looks like the only things living there are squirrels and a few deer who take off into the woods at our approach.

Scarlet reports she's already checked for anything that may be of use or value, but she didn't find anything worth keeping.

The second village yields a nice stock of thick rope. We decide to take some of it because it could be useful. Wise and Old Man also scavenge a few books from the homes as it seems quite certain their former owners won't be back anytime soon. Lark finds a small, careworn, stuffed bear sitting upon a child's cot. There's a jacket there, too. It's dusty, but salvageable, and he seems incredibly pleased with his findings.

We make camp that night in the woods. We don't want to remain directly on the road in the event there are any other travelers, though that seems as if it would be unlikely. We set out again at first light and cover a fair amount of ground on our journey.

That is, until Wise observes that we're going the wrong way.

She glances up at the sun, then back to Old Man. Suddenly, she stops in her tracks as if considering something. "Um... Old Man. I don't think this is the right way. The sun rises in the east and sets in the west. We should be heading west to Vericus, but it looks like we're heading east."

"We are. East, then south," he responds simply.

We all freeze as we're taken aback by his unscheduled change of plans.

"But, we were supposed to get to the capital right away," reminds Lark. "To see the King and try to stop Abirad. Remember?"

Old Man chuckles. "Yes, young man. As if I could forget."

"Then why are we going west?" I ask in confusion.

"We're not going to the capital... not yet anyway," replies Old Man. "There's something I need to get first."

Brock eyes him quizzically. "What do you mean?"

"Before we left, I got my hands on a particular tome," Old Man informs us. "Scarlet snatched it for me... from Abirad's personal study."

The rest of us gawk at Scarlet in silent awe and admiration. I knew she was skilled when it came to getting around the castle, but the idea of her waltzing into Abirad's personal study is something different entirely!

Scarlet, surprised by the sudden attention, takes it upon herself to bow with an exaggerated flourish, and Lark begins to clap loudly in response before Brock shoots him an annoyed glare.

"It helped me to remember something," continues Old Man, ignoring the slight interruption entirely.

"What did you remember?" asks Wise with interest.

Old Man smiles slightly. "Home."

The wind feels as if it has been stolen from my lungs. "Home? You remembered your home? How?"

Old Man seats himself on a fallen log by the side of the road, his long, stork-like legs stretching out before him. "Something in the book. So... on the subject of our memories, here's what I've been able to gather. They've been hidden to us, but not lost forever. The question is, of course, how do we uncover that which is hidden? One of the things I read in that book was the key to our memories. If we see or encounter something from our lives before, it could help us to regain our memories. Such was the case with me and the book."

"How did you remember something through the book?" inquires Wise.

Old Man shakes his head. "The book was written in my own hand."

"You mean, you were the author of it?" I ask. "How is that possible?"

Old Man shrugs. "I don't know, Boy, but I think I'm starting to figure that out. It was strange... When I first saw the book, I somehow knew instantly it was mine. It was as if I held a missing piece to a much larger puzzle. I felt as if I was being flooded by memories. I remembered the feel of the quill in my hand. The stain of ink on my fingers. The gentle breezes through the window rustling the papers on my desk. The more I read in the tome, the more I began to recall."

We are all shocked into silence, and it's Wise who finally voices another question. "What else can you tell us?"

"The stones. They, too, returned something to me," responds Old Man. "A brief glimpse of who I once was, though it makes little sense to me just now. I'm hopeful that, perhaps, more shall return to me."

For the first time in a long time, my soul feels slightly lighter as I realize the depth of what this all means. "And if you are starting to remember, it means we can remember, too."

For the rest of the day, we are all consumed by anxious giddiness. The idea of being able to reclaim, at least partly, who we once were is astounding, and I begin to wonder what it will take for me to learn my past. My mind begins to wander to my most cherished memory: the grey-eyed woman and the giggling boy in her arms. Who was she? Does she still live? That night, as we lay down to sleep, I see her in my dreams, and my heart is filled with hope that I may one day see her again.

CHAPTER 13

It's a few days later when we stumble across Brock's village.

We sleep in a bit more than we intend to and get a bit of a late start. The previous evening, Brock had set off into the woods alone to see if he could find some more roots or berries to supplement our evening meal. Nearly an hour later, he had returned to camp with a considerable-sized deer slung over one of his brawny shoulders. Needless to say, we were all in shock.

"How did you get that?" Lark had asked, his eyes wide with admiration.

Even Scarlet had been impressed, giving Brock a hearty slap on the shoulder, then apologizing when he winced, as some of his wounds still caused him the occasional pain.

Wise, while grateful for the extra sustenance the deer would provide, seemed sad the poor creature had given its life to be food for us.

Brock must have noticed this and said, "It's okay. It didn't suffer."

Honestly, it was the most he had said to her in a couple days. Now that Brock had become more self-sufficient, and Wise didn't have to constantly dress his wounds, he had become a bit more reserved around her.

I had thought things might go back to normal between them and get better once the truth about Wise's feelings came out. However, any affection and all interactions between them had become muted in the wake of Wise's declaration.

They remained civil, but distant, more so on Brock's part than that of Wise. Brock spoke to her only when necessary, and that light banter and laughter between them that I loved so much had disappeared entirely.

I inspected the deer, and oddly enough, I didn't see any obvious sign of a wound that would have resulted in its death. "How did you kill it?" I had inquired.

"It's better if you don't ask," replied Brock with a wink.

I have since become convinced that he killed it with his bare hands.

We ate exceptionally well that night, and we were even able to dry out some of the meat for later use. Needless to say, it was the first time our bellies had truly felt full, at least as far as we could remember.

We all slumbered peacefully and reluctantly woke from our rest. We had intended to get moving at first light, but obviously, we missed the mark on that one.

* * *

After we pack up our camp, we head back to the road and continue on for about half a day's journey. It's then that we come upon a small village, not unlike the others we have passed through, but the moment the place comes into view, Brock is frozen, unable to will his feet forward.

It takes me a few moments to realize he has fallen behind, and when I do, I see that he is standing like a statue, staring at the village in the distance.

"Brock? Are you all right?" I ask, nudging him gently with my elbow.

"I... I don't know." His eyes are wide, and he looks as if he is stuck in some space between alarm and excitement. "Boy... I know that place. I've seen it before," he says, his voice quavering slightly.

Scarlet joins us. She waves her hand in front of Brock's vacant expression. "Brock? Hello, Brock."

"He thinks he remembers that place," I inform her as I point towards the village.

"Then, what are you waiting for? Come on!" Scarlet shoves him forward, and Brock finally seems to recall how to move his feet.

We hurry into the central part of town, and Brock begins to look this way and that, as if searching for something. Finally, we follow a trail to the northern part of town. On the outskirts of the village is a lone building, larger than the rest, with a significant portion of its territory claimed by a rather impressive, though clearly long abandoned, smithy. The sign above the door is weatherworn, and the letters are quite faded, but upon closer examination, it simply reads "Blacksmith."

Brock immediately goes to the opening of the establishment but hesitates, his trembling fingers hovering just inches from the threshold. The door is long gone, and its sparse remnants are little more than large shards of splintered wood upon the floor.

"It looks like it was kicked in," observes Scarlet quietly.

Brock nods numbly. "It was."

"Brock... what do you see?" asks Old Man, his voice a mixture of curiosity and excitement.

"I... I need a minute!" Brock snaps.

Wise pushes her way past me and Scarlet and places a comforting hand on his shoulder. "Brock. Take your time. We're not going anywhere until you're ready."

Brock stares back at her, his expression one of gratitude, and gives a silent nod. It's nearly twenty minutes before Brock finally calms himself enough to step into the building.

I move to follow him, but Wise puts an arm across my chest to stop me.

"Give him a moment, Boy," says Wise softly.

I nod in understanding, and we all wait with bated breath to learn what Brock has discovered. From within, there is a faint sobbing sound. Wise, her face affected with concern and sympathy, goes in alone. I watch as she kneels next to him. He has fallen to his knees, overcome with crashing waves of emotion. His head is bowed, and his face is hidden by his hands. His shoulders tremble as he weeps.

It's the first time I've ever seen Brock cry.

It all seems so surreal. Even in his greatest moments of pain, while he may have yelled out or whimpered in agony, I never once saw him weep. To see such a mighty figure as Brock affected in such a way tears at my heart. After a few more minutes, Wise succeeds in calming him slightly. She stands next to him, her fingers softly stroking his hair as she whispers something soothing to him. Finally, she extends her hand to him, which he gratefully accepts, and she helps him back to his feet.

She gives the rest of us a slight nod, indicating that it is okay to enter.

The inside is an absolute disaster area. Though the passing of time could account for some of the disarray, it is more likely that the entire place was upturned at some point.

"Bandits," guesses Scarlet aloud.

"No," answers Brock, his voice scarcely more than a whisper. "Abirad's men." Brock locks eyes with me, and it is then that I see the depth of sadness that resides there.

"Are you certain?" questions Old Man.

"Yes. I remember them," responds Brock with assurance in his voice. "They... they killed him. Right in front of me."

"Who? The blacksmith?" I ask.

Brock nods. "Yes. My father."

Lark's eyes widen, and he steps closer to Brock. "Your father was a blacksmith? Wow! I wish my father was a blacksmith."

Scarlet shakes her head in amusement. "Lark, your father is a king."

Lark considers this for a moment. "I suppose that's decent enough."

I swear. Sometimes I simply don't understand Lark.

Brock wordlessly crosses the room. "This was where he displayed his work. People came from all over the country for weapons forged by him. Even nobles. That's how grand his blades were." He turns to the left and gestures towards a door. "Back there was the storage room. It's where he kept the surplus weapons. And back there..."

We follow Brock towards another door on the right. "Back here was where we lived." Tentatively, he pushes open the door and we cautiously follow him through.

Therein, we see the remnants of two cots. The one on the left has a small chest for storage at the foot. The other, the one to the right, catches Brock's attention.

"This was mine," he explains. "My father slept over there."

"What about your mother?" asks Lark. "Where did she sleep?"

"Under the earth," responds Brock quietly. "I... I remember she died... some time before my father... before I was taken away."

Brock crosses to the cot on the left and opens the chest. He frowns slightly. "I don't know what I was hoping for... they ransacked everything. Abirad's men."

He stands in silence, lost in thought, then his expression brightens for the briefest of moments. He moves the chest out of the way to expose the floorboards underneath. "Scarlet," he says, "hand me one of your daggers."

She does so without question and Brock begins to pry at the boards with the pointed end of the dagger. After a moment, he grins broadly as the first board comes loose. He uses his hands to pull off two more and unceremoniously tosses them to the side.

He reaches his hand into the floor, and Lark lets out a loud squeak as a small mouse emerges before scuttling off in the direction of the front door. Brock shifts this way and that, reaching his arm down as far as it can go. With a triumphant smile, he pulls something from within. It's long and wrapped in a dusty, brown cloth.

Eagerly, he seats himself on the floor, placing the item on his lap, and almost reverently, he undoes the knot that holds the cloth over the contents. The rest of us watch, transfixed, as he pulls out a broadsword. While I don't know much about blades, it is the most exquisite one I have ever seen, and very likely the most masterfully crafted on earth.

"This was his. My father's. He made it when I was a kid. He didn't make it for me..." Brock frowns as if searching for something. "He was going to make me one like this, but he never got the chance. This one... it was for someone else, but that person was gone. So, he put it away. Kept it. Just in case the person came back."

"Seems like you could have it now... if you wanted it," comments Lark.

Brock considers this for a moment. "I think he'd want me to have it now. It's of no use sitting in a rotting house." He rises and continues to search about the room. Near his old cot, he finds a child's doll, cleverly fashioned from wood, cornhusk, and cloth. Tears well in his eyes, and he gently places the doll in the pocket of his trousers for safekeeping.

We find a few more useful items in the smithing area. There's a finely made dagger that must have been overlooked by Abirad's men and any looters who happened upon the place. Wordlessly, Brock offers the dagger to Scarlet, who gladly takes possession of it.

"We need to make camp for the night. We could stay here. It would keep a roof over our heads and the wind off our backs," suggests Old Man.

"No..." speaks Brock quietly. "I... I can't do that."

"We don't have to. We can find another building or head back into the woods," offers Wise.

"I think I'd prefer the woods." Brock glances around at all of us. "I'm sorry... I don't mean to disappoint you. It's just..."

Wise puts her hand on his arm. "Brock, you don't have to explain. It's fine."

We head towards the forest and make camp. In silence, we have a simple supper of bread, dried deer meat, and a few carrots that we find growing at the edge of the village. After eating, Lark falls asleep almost instantly. Old Man gives a loud yawn, stretches out his spindly limbs, and soon follows suit. Scarlet and I sit next to the fire while Brock and Wise attempt to rest.

When Brock starts crying out in his sleep, Scarlet, startled by the sudden noise, nearly tosses her shiny new dagger at him. Wise instantly sits up, her face marked with concern.

She crosses to the other side of the camp, kneels next to him, and gently shakes his shoulder. "Brock. Brock."

Brock's cries increase in their intensity, but Wise is soon able to rouse him from his slumber, and when she does, the tears flow freely down his cheeks. Wise looks over to me. There's a helpless expression on her face as if she's unsure of how to help him.

"They killed him... they killed him..." Brock suddenly wraps his arms around her waist and holds on to her tightly. "They killed him, and all I did was watch."

Wise lightly caresses the back of his head, gently stroking his hair to soothe him. "Brock, you were a child."

"I was older than Lark. I could have done something. I could have fought them," weeps Brock miserably.

"They would have killed you. You're lucky they didn't," replies Wise gently.

I don't know how long it takes for Brock to cry himself out of tears, but eventually, his sobs begin to subside, and his breathing becomes less ragged and more even. When he's finally calmed, Wise moves to return to the other side of the camp, but Brock holds fast to her.

"Wise..."

He doesn't need to continue his thought. Wise and Brock have always seemed to have a way of communicating without words, as if each knows the other's heart and mind, save for when Wise's affection for him is concerned.

They recline next to each other on the forest floor, and Brock places his head on her shoulder as she wraps her arms around him protectively. She hums some pretty song, and soon, both are asleep, their arms entwined around each other.

Scarlet glances from them to me. "He's going to break her heart. You know that, right?"

I frown, unsure of what to say. "I hope not. I don't think he'd ever mean to."

"She loves him," she remarks quietly.

"I know she cares for him."

"She's a fool. She can do better," states Scarlet matter-of-factly.

"Maybe she doesn't want better. Maybe she just wants what she wants."

"Fair point," she concedes.

"What happened with Brock and his memories... Do you think it will be like that for all of us?" I ask.

Scarlet shrugs in reply. "I'd like to hope I'm not a slobbering, weepy mess like him if it happens."

"Don't worry. You probably won't slobber any more than Old Man does in his sleep." Years of being his cellmate have taught me that difficult lesson.

She laughs, genuinely laughs, and it occurs to me then that it is a rare and wonderful thing. So much of Scarlet's commentary consists of biting wit and sarcastic remarks, punctuated with the occasional eyeroll, groan, or sound of disgust. But to hear her laugh is some kind of magic. That brief moment when her aloof expression is replaced by joy is something to see.

"Do you remember anything, Scarlet... of before?"

Scarlet absentmindedly tugs at the ends of her crimson hair, twirling it around her pale, slender fingers. "A bit... I don't like what I see."

"I'm sorry," I apologize.

"Don't be. We were what we were, and we are what we are."

"What do you mean?"

"I don't remember much. I know that I stole from people.

Sometimes I hurt people. It's not something I'm proud of."

"Perhaps not... But those things did come in handy when we were fleeing the castle."

Scarlet considers this for several moments. "True," she agrees. "In that case, I guess it's not all bad. What about you, Boy? What were you? Some kind of knight-in-training?"

"What?" I laugh. "Why would you say that?"

"You're kind. Chivalrous. Like the knights in the olden tales that Wise tells Lark."

"No. I don't think so. Brock has always been the one that everyone sees as some kind of knight in shining armor."

Scarlet frowns. "He's an idiot in a rusty bucket."

I can't help but to chuckle at her comment, even if it is at my friend's expense. "He's not all bad, you know."

"And he's definitely not all good. I can't say I'm overly fond of him. I mean, I'm glad he didn't die, but I do find him tiresome."

"Well, that's a first. Many girls are fond of him."

"And many girls are poor judges of character. In fact, that and her selflessness may be Wise's only flaws." Scarlet crosses the distance between us and plops down next to me. "What about you, Boy? What do you remember?"

I don't know what compels me to do it, to finally share my memory with someone else, but I tell her about the woman and the grey-eyed boy, sparing no detail of what I have seen.

"She must have been your mother," comments Scarlet.

I nod in agreement. "That's certainly possible. I hope it's not asking too much to see her someday, but if I'd have to forgo that to ensure that Lark gets home safe and Abirad is stopped, I'd give even that memory to see it so."

Scarlet smiles, and again, I feel a tug in my chest as I'm struck by the simple beauty of something as pure as a smile. "See? Chivalrous."

* * *

The next few days pass with relative ease. We continue down the main road on our trek west towards Old Man's home. We manage to cover a considerable distance each day. We also, once again, fall into a comfortable routine. Brock and Scarlet hunt, Lark and I fish, and Wise and Old Man collect herbs we might need and forage for fruit, vegetables, seeds, and nuts.

Things mostly return to normal between Brock and Wise, better than normal in fact, and both seem happier for it. The sound of Brock's jokes and Wise's laughter bring some semblance of peace to the camp. It's wonderful to be able to converse with them again without Wise fleeing or Brock bristling. He doesn't bring up Jewel again, and it seems all the strife between the two of them has been forgotten.

In the evenings, Wise tells Lark stories until he succumbs to slumber. Then, Brock pulls his blanket beside Wise and falls asleep with his arms wrapped firmly around her. One night, I hear Brock whisper something to Wise, and when I glance over at them, I see that they're gazing into each other's eyes, and there's a look of genuine affection that passes between them. I see Brock lean forward, and their lips touch for more than a moment. I see Wise smile, and in my heart, I'm happy for them.

In the days that follow, Brock's vivid dreams begin to decrease, and it seems as if just being near Wise is enough to keep his nightmares at bay, for in the rare instances she rises in the night to do this or that, he soon becomes plagued by painful memories, whimpering slightly in his sleep until she returns to his arms.

Scarlet and I are usually the last to nod off, and we take the opportunity to discuss all manner of things, both trivial and important. Late one evening, after I manage to make her laugh again and again while recounting stories of Old Man's absentmindedness, her fingers graze mine lightly, and something stirs within me. This feeling becomes even greater when she gives me an impish grin and presses a soft kiss on my cheek that lingers long after her lips have left me.

CHAPTER 14

As we progress in our travels, we pass through a few more villages, and each one seems to repeat the same, sad story as the previous ones. The buildings stand vacant and in varying degrees of dilapidation. In most of these small towns, it looks as if the inhabitants simply fled as quickly as possible, grabbing anything of value in their sudden rush to evacuate. Random items are strewn about the floors. Plates and tankards sit where they were left, as if the tables had been set for guests who never arrived. Broken doors forced open by Abirad's soldiers and smashed windows are present in every house or shop we find. Cherished toys lay upon the ground as if dropped by their owners in the heat of flight.

I often find myself staring at the toys that are left behind. While we never see any small skeletons, a fact which we are all immeasurably thankful for, I practically weep over every hastily discarded doll, small stuffed toy, or treasured bauble. These were children whose lives, like our own, were changed forever at the whims of Abirad. Perhaps they were even our fellows at the castle, those we left behind. We don't talk about them, but I see their faces. I see Hazel's hopeful gaze as she realizes I'm leaving. I see Isabel looking at me like a stranger, even though we had once known each other so well. Sometimes, I even see Harding, his expression wrought with pain as he says goodbye to Lark. I often wonder what has become of all of them, but it's too painful to discuss.

The sight of these ghost towns affects all of us, but the worst is when we find remains. Every now and then, we find skeletons proudly displayed in town centers, their remnants likely once intended to warn any who would cross Abirad. Sometimes we find them cowering together in small spaces, such as in closets or under beds. Other times, they are gathered in small groups in public places, such as churches.

While we are accustomed to seeing the occasional wild animal or bird who has claimed areas of the empty villages for their own, the dog surprises us.

We finish looking through a tavern to see if we can find anything of use. Our efforts are awarded with a few candles, a few glass vials, and a handful of leather pouches. Old Man says the last two might be good for protecting the herbs that he and Wise are able to collect. We begin to make our way out of the village when Wise begins to panic.

Her eyes are wild with worry as they search all directions. "Lark! Lark! He was just right here! Lark!"

Her voice echoes through the emptiness that surrounds us. Suddenly, we hear Lark cry out. We exchange fearful glances and make our way towards a small cottage we recently passed. When we arrive, Lark is on his back and a large, scruffy, black shape is pouncing upon him.

Wise dashes forward and Scarlet's dagger is already in her hand when we all realize his cries are of laughter and delight rather than pain.

"He's licking me!" he laughs uproariously, as if it is the funniest thing he's ever seen. "Can I keep him, Wise?"

Brock frowns. "We're already trying to conserve our rations. We shouldn't take on another mouth to feed."

The dog looks as if it hasn't eaten in some time. It is long and lean, its ribs protruding from its sides.

Scarlet pokes the bulge around Brock's belly. "You're eating more than enough. Perhaps he could have some of your share."

Brock gives her a withering look.

"He probably belongs to someone," says Wise. "How else would he have gotten out here?"

"Maybe he's wondering the same thing about us," reasons Lark. "He's probably thinking, 'who are these humans coming through my village? How have they gotten here? Maybe the nice lady one will let the small, fun one keep me.'"

Lark has won this battle. There is no further discussion.

"What are you going to name him?" asks Scarlet as we make our way down the road.

"Dog," responds Lark matter-of-factly. "It's what he is, after all. He's Boy. He's Old Man. He'll be Dog. Do you like it, Scarlet? Do you think he will?" he asks, gesturing to his new friend.

"It's a fine name, Lark, and I'm sure he'll like it. He'll like it more if you give him some of this." She reaches into her pack and hands Lark a small piece of dried deer meat.

Lark grins widely as he takes it from her outstretched hand and offers it to Dog, who eagerly gobbles it up before looking for more. "I don't think he has an owner. If he did, I don't think he'd be so skinny. He seems pretty hungry." He proceeds to feed Dog a few more pieces of deer meat, some cheese, and a hunk of bread. "You can have more at supper, Dog."

Dog seems satisfied with this and happily trots along behind Lark. His tail wags back and forth as he easily keeps pace with our group.

The sun beats down upon us. It's an unseasonably warm day, and around mid-day we decide to seek some shade. We're all sweaty and caked in dirt. Wise's dark, brown hair seems as if it has already grown longer since we left the castle, and she regards it with some annoyance as it keeps falling into her eyes and sticking to the side of her face. She sits down on the ground and attempts to tie her hair back so it's out of her way.

Wordlessly, Brock sits behind her, forming a v-shape with his legs around her. He takes her hair in his hands and deftly begins fashioning it into a long braid.

"How do you know how to do that?" asks Wise curiously.

"I had a little sister," he responds quietly. "She... she

died. Plague. I used to watch my mother do this for her. Eventually, I learned how to do it, too."

This immediately piques Old Man's interest. "You remembered your sister. How?"

Brock reaches into his pocket and produces the small doll he had taken from his home. He holds it up for us to see then carefully replaces it in his pocket. "I have a brother, too... if he's still alive. He wasn't with us when Abirad's men came."

"Older or younger than you?" inquires Lark

"Older," responds Brock simply. "He was big. Bigger than me. And strong. He left home. I don't remember why. The sword... I think it was for him."

Brock finishes the braid, and Wise thanks him before setting to work at preparing us all something to eat. Old Man is intently studying his book. He is so engrossed that he's completely lost to the world around him. Brock makes his way over to where I'm sitting and lowers himself down beside me. Meanwhile, Scarlet approaches Lark as he pours some water into a small, wooden bowl. Dog eagerly laps it up, and Lark refills it for him again.

"Come on, Lark." She hands him one of her many daggers.

"Wow! What's this for?" He quickly scrambles to his feet.

"You're going to learn how to use it."

"I know how to cut my food, Scarlet," responds Lark.

"No, Lark," she chuckles. "I'm going to teach you how to use it to fight."

Wise immediately drops what she's doing to narrow her eyes at Scarlet. "You're going to *what*?"

"He should learn how to defend himself, Wise. What if he finds himself in a situation where one of us isn't there to protect him?" reasons Scarlet.

Wise doesn't seem particularly happy with this situation but can't argue against Scarlet's logic. "Just be careful. If he gets hurt, you'll answer to me."

Scarlet doesn't strike me as the type of person who is afraid of anything. In fact, I'm quite certain she is the definition of the word "fearless." However, even she seems slightly wary of Wise's vague threat.

Scarlet proceeds to teach Lark a few ways to strike with the dagger and how to evade blows in hand-to-hand combat. Brock and I watch, thoroughly entertained with Lark's attempts to mimic Scarlet's moves. While his first few tries are laughable, Scarlet is a good teacher, and he catches on quickly. Every movement Scarlet makes is graceful and fluid. She is quick, but careful, and every strike to the air would be well-placed against an actual foe.

Brock leans over and whispers into my ear. "She's truly beautiful, isn't she? Scarlet. Even more so than Jewel, I think."

"What about Wise?"

Brock shrugs. "What about Wise?"

"Aren't you...?"

He looks at me as if he has no idea what I'm talking about, so I just give a sigh. "Yes, Scarlet is beautiful, but I'm more impressed with her skill. She's an adept fighter. And Lark is learning from her quite well."

"She'd be even prettier if it weren't for her foul temperament. She's bloody terrifying," Brock remarks. "I'd be willing to look past that, though."

I can feel my brow wrinkle in confusion. "What do you mean? There's nothing wrong with her temperament. She's intelligent and quick-witted."

"I'm just saying, she would be more comely if she was a bit kinder."

"She's plenty kind. Just not to you. She finds you obnoxious, and quite frankly, I think I see what she means." I stand and dust off my trousers. "And I think you should spend some more time getting to appreciate her for her virtues and not her form."

I don't realize that Scarlet heard our little exchange until she mouths a silent "thank you" as I walk by her.

After some time, Scarlet decides Lark has enough practice for the day. He happily bounds up to Wise and proudly presents the dagger Scarlet let him keep.

"Look, Wise! I have my first wound! Do you think it'll leave a battle scar? I stabbed myself in the finger." He shows Wise a rather nasty cut on his finger, and Wise's face nearly turns as red as Scarlet's hair. She looks as if she's about to thrash Scarlet when the latter abruptly decides to take the opportunity to scout ahead.

"Come on, Boy." She seizes my hand and pulls me to my feet, practically dragging me further into the woods with her.

We leisurely stroll along and enjoy the peace such a setting provides. The trees grow denser as we move deeper into the forest, and the canopy provides much-needed shade from the brutal sun.

"I'm almost afraid to return to camp. While I think I'm far faster than Wise, she has the protective instinct of a mother bear. I think she'd tear me limb from limb if she thought I harmed her little cub," converses Scarlet.

"She just worries about him. He's just a little boy, and he's been through a lot."

"We all have," replies Scarlet.

"I was about his age when I arrived at the castle."

Scarlet considers this for a few moments. "I think I was slightly older. About 11."

"Wise was very young. Old Man thinks she was probably about 4 when she arrived."

Scarlet's eyes widen in surprise. "4? That means she was there practically her whole life." She shakes her head in disgust. "I remember seeing younger children in the yard, but none as young as that. Why would Abirad want children so young?"

I shrug. It's something Old Man and I have talked about at length. "Old Man thinks he didn't necessarily want to collect children outright. There were never too many of them. Rather, he thinks Abirad did it to intimidate others. Maybe their parents or something of the like. It would be an effective way to get people to fall in line and act according to his whims if he held their children hostage."

"Sadly, that makes sense."

We head towards the road. We don't see much ahead except for open road. There are no more villages within sight. Scarlet stares up at the sky as if studying it. "Looks like rain. Maybe not tonight, but soon."

"You can predict the weather, evade guards, sneak about in plain sight, fight, teach children how to spar. Is there anything you can't do?"

"I'll tell you if I ever figure something out."

We both laugh at her remark and begin to make our way back towards camp.

At night, Lark, exhausted from his training, practically falls asleep while eating. Wise convinces him to turn in early, and within seconds, he is soundly asleep. Dog lies sprawled between his young master and Old Man, who offers the canine the occasional scratch behind his ears.

Wise stretches out in her usual place on the right side of the camp, but surprisingly, Brock does not join her. Instead, he gathers up his blanket and makes his way to the opposite side where Scarlet is getting settled in. He places his blanket near hers as he makes idle conversation about the weather. Wise seems to quickly realize what's going on, and the look on her face nearly breaks my heart.

Scarlet, too, seems to understand what is happening. She rises to her feet, seizes the corner of Brock's blanket, and gives it a hard yank, snatching it out from under him. Wordlessly, she crosses to the edge of the camp to a narrow but deep stream. She tosses it into the cold water before returning to her own blanket.

Wise, who has been watching this event unfold, gives her a look of something resembling gratitude, and I can see the slight smirk on her face as she nestles into her blanket. The look quickly disappears though, being replaced by the same disappointment that had consumed it moments earlier.

Brock sighs, rises to his feet, and makes his way back towards Wise. "May I join you?" he asks.

In reply, Wise picks up her blanket and heads as far away from Brock as possible.

At this point, the heat of the day has been replaced with a biting cold. Brock is sure to have a rather restless night without his blanket to provide him with some measure of comfort against the chill. He gives me a pleading look, and I gesture for him to join me. He lays down next to me and I offer him part of my blanket.

"You're an idiot sometimes. You know that?" I say to him.

He sighs heavily. "I'm beginning to realize that."

My good deed does not go unpunished. I barely get a wink of sleep. Brock's nightmares cause him to thrash about wildly throughout the night. To make matters worse, he drools excessively in his sleep. I can't fathom how Wise could put up with sleeping next to him for so many nights.

Since I can't get to sleep, I sit up and see that Scarlet is staring at me and stifling laughter as Brock, once again, reaches out with a heavy hand and paws at my face.

"Come on, Boy. I'll share my blanket with you," she offers.

I'm tempted to take her up on it, but I very reluctantly reply with a polite refusal. "I'd love to, but I don't want Brock to get the wrong idea."

Scarlet frowns. "When has he ever had a right idea? Besides... would his assumption really be wrong?" A smile plays across her lips, and my heart begins to hammer in my chest.

"I suppose not." I can't help but to grin. "I appreciate the offer, but he's been so boorish lately that I don't really want to chance an argument with him."

I cross to Lark and Dog. The latter raises his head slightly and licks at my hand before settling back in for the evening. I don't want to wake Lark as he seemed absolutely exhausted, so instead I grab a corner of the blanket and quickly fall asleep.

CHAPTER 15

Scarlet was right. The next morning, we awake to a soft drizzle that causes a chilly dampness to cling to the air. It's so cold we can see our breath, and we all huddle closely together around the fire. Brock brings some dry wood to build up the flames a bit more. Meanwhile, Wise sets to checking our inventory of food and says we could do with more nuts or berries.

"I'll see what's around. We should restock whenever we can. The terrain is starting to change a bit. The forest is becoming less dense," remarks Wise. She moves to head away from camp to see what can be foraged.

"I'll come with you," offers Brock quickly.

I can tell this is his way of apologizing. While I doubt he would actually admit to Wise that the situation with Scarlet was wrong on his part, I believe he knows it was a foolish move and wishes to make up for it in some way.

"That's all right. I won't be long," she says quietly. She departs without another word, and Scarlet and I exchange glances.

"I'll go," I volunteer.

I follow behind her, and after a bit of a trek, we happen upon some bushes that are filled with berries. Wise unfolds a large, square cloth and we begin to pile on berries so we can easily transport them back to the camp.

"Are you okay, Wise?" I ask, already knowing the answer. I know she's hurt, but I also know that Wise is one of the strongest people I have ever met, and despite Brock's idiocy, she will reclaim her laughter in time.

She shrugs. "Brock made it very plain to me that we were only friends, and when I comforted him after we came upon his village, I had no delusions that would change. However, after the first night, when he continued to sleep next to me and then... he kissed me. I guess I thought that... well... I thought maybe..." She shakes her head. "It was a foolish notion."

"No. It was a logical assumption. Anyone would have thought it could be something more."

"I don't blame him. I blame myself. I shouldn't have been so naïve."

"He shouldn't have pursued Scarlet so blatantly, especially knowing how you feel about him"

I adore both of my friends, but honestly, I'm a little irritated with Brock currently. It's then that I see the tears beginning to stream down Wise's cheeks. She quickly wipes them away, but they reappear almost instantly.

"I'm sorry, Wise." And I truly am. If I could make Brock see reason, make him see how lucky he is to have someone as wonderful as Wise, I would do anything I could to ease her sadness. Unfortunately, I know there's little I can do in this situation, save offer my shoulder as a place for her to shed her tears in peace.

She places her forehead on my shoulder, and in turn, I wrap one of my arms around her, pulling her close to me. I lean my cheek against the top of her head and give her the time she needs to collect herself.

"I'm sorry, Boy. I shouldn't be blubbering about this. I know it's stupid, and we have far more important things to worry about."

"It's okay, Wise. But I need you to remember something." I place my hands on her shoulders and stare directly into her warm, brown eyes. "Never settle for less than you deserve. You are worth far more than Brock gives you credit for. I love him as a brother, but he's being a fool. You will always have people who care about you. You have me, Lark simply adores you, and even Scarlet speaks highly of you. Old Man sees you as almost a daughter, or at the very least, a favorite apprentice."

It's enough to bring a smile to her face, but it still doesn't capture the degree of regard that I have for her. How many times had I almost let the harshness of my imprisonment consume me, yet it was Wise who brought me back to the light? Even on my darkest days, she has always been there with a kind word and a gentle smile to see me to another morning.

"I promise you, Wise. You will find someone who loves you with his whole heart. While I wish Brock would uncloud his brain and see what's in front of him, that may not happen. But even if it doesn't, I swear, Wise, one day, you will find someone deserving of you. You are the kindest, strongest, most wonderful person I've ever met, and someday, someone will appreciate you for all you are."

She embraces me tightly. "Thank you, Boy. You truly are my greatest friend. You always have been, and you always will be."

I give her hand a gentle squeeze. "Come on, Wise. Let's head back to camp."

When we get back, Lark is still huddled under his blanket, and Scarlet is using her dagger to slice off a few pieces of apple to give to Dog.

"How did it go? Did you find anything?" asks Old Man.

"Plenty. Loads of berries," I say. I glance around the camp and notice that Brock is missing. "Hey, where's Brock?"

Right on cue, Brock comes stalking back into the camp. He pushes past me without making eye contact with either me or Wise and is uncharacteristically surly during breakfast. He doesn't engage in conversation with anyone, and he occasionally shoots a venomous look at me.

After breakfast, Lark is still exhausted, so we agree that there isn't any harm in letting him rest a few minutes longer while the rest of us clean up the camp. Wise helps Old Man to fold his blanket while Scarlet puts out the fire. Brock is next to me as he stuffs his still damp blanket into a pack that he picked up in one of the villages we passed through.

"I saw you," he says quietly. "You and Wise."

"Me and Wise? What do you mean?"

"When you were collecting berries, or should I say looking for an excuse to paw at each other?" There's an edge to his voice that I'm not fond of.

"Brock, what is it that you're implying? She was upset. Because of *you*, might I add. I was merely comforting her."

"Did you comfort her any other way? Maybe let your lips comfort her, too?"

I round on him, aggravated by his ridiculous allegations. "She is my friend. She's been my friend since well before you came around. And she was hurt. Again, by *you*."

Brock appears embarrassed. "You know she had no reason to be upset. I told her before we were just friends."

"And yet, you kissed her."

Brock looks taken aback. "I-I-"

"And here you are carrying on like some kind of jealous lover!"

"I'm not jealous."

"You are, you big oaf!" I can't help but to shout at him, and suddenly, I feel everyone's eyes on the two of us. I grab him by the sleeve of his shirt and drag him away from the camp so we can talk in private. "The fact is she had plenty of reason to be upset. First, she worries herself sick over you, takes care of you, saves your bloody life, and do you even thank her for it? No! You lament that Jewel isn't around for you to ogle and even *blame* her for you leaving and getting injured."

Brock's face reddens in shame, but my blood is boiling, and I'm not done with him yet.

"Then, she comforts you, soothes you when you can't stop weeping-"

"I didn't ask her to do that."

"You didn't have to! That's what friends do for each

other. And Wise did it without a second thought. She didn't expect anything to come of it. But then you decided it would be an intelligent idea to kiss her. Get her thinking you might actually care for her as she cares for you. Then you have the audacity to pursue Scarlet right in front of her."

Brock's eyes are wide, and I know he's likely in a state of shock because in all the time we have been friends, we have never argued before. However, I simply cannot abide his treatment of Wise and the fact he is turning his own issues onto me.

"Now you're upset with me for comforting her when she needed a friend to remind her of her worth!" I continue. "What you saw was me trying to console my friend whose heart is breaking because of *you*. So stop being daft and recognize this nonsense for what it is. You saw us embrace, and that irritation you're feeling, the same awful feeling that poor Wise probably had last night when you decided to try and charm Scarlet, is *jealousy* Brock. The only difference is she's too kind to act like an arse about it!"

Brock drags his hand down his face and shakes his head in frustration. "Look, I- I did kiss her. And when I kissed Wise, it wasn't like when I kissed Jewel, or any other girl for that matter. I felt- I don't know how I feel!"

I can't help but to wonder exactly how many girls Brock has kissed, not to mention, how he would have found the time or opportunity for such things back at the castle. I guess Old Man is right: where there's a will, there's a way. It's not the first time Brock's brought up such things; in fact, he has bragged of his experience on this matter quite a few times before.

"Well, you better figure it out, and until you do, I might advise keeping your lips off of her!" I stalk off, frustrated with my friend, but knowing I need to calm myself before I return to camp. I take a few deep breaths and rejoin the rest of my companions, and moments later, Brock joins us, his face still red and unwilling to make eye contact with anyone.

We continue our journey down the main road. The rain picks up considerably, which makes the path so muddy that our simple shoes begin to get stuck as we trudge along. Within a few hours, the rain transforms into a torrential downpour. Unfortunately, we don't pass any more villages where we can seek shelter until it passes. We consider turning around and heading back to the last town, but that's more than a day's journey in the opposite direction, so we doggedly continue our trek in the hopes that we find something soon.

By nightfall, the rain still hasn't let up, and we still haven't found anywhere to offer us respite from the deluge that follows us like a persistent swarm of mosquitoes.

"We have to try to get some rest," speaks Old Man. "The poor child looks as if he's about to faint from exhaustion." He gestures to Lark, his face pale and his eyes barely open. The kid leans heavily against Dog in an attempt to support his own weary body.

"I've got an idea," offers Wise. "But I'll need all the blankets."

We head into the woods, and Wise hastily ties together some large sticks with the rope we found in one of the villages. After a bit of time, she throws the blankets over the crude frame she has constructed. It is not the sturdiest of tents, and it's exceptionally cramped, but it's better than sleeping outside.

I find myself wedged between Scarlet and Brock, who is still keeping his distance from Wise in the wake of his rather poor decisions. Everyone else has fallen asleep, but Brock incessantly tosses about and can't seem to get comfortable, which in turn, keeps me awake.

"Boy? Are you still awake?" he whispers to me.

"Yes."

"I'm sorry for accusing you earlier," Brock apologizes. "I know it was wrong, and I had no right to behave like such an idiot. And I know I need to find some way to make things right with Wise, but I just feel very confused right now, and I don't know what to do." I can hear in his voice that he's genuine.

"I can't tell you what to do, Brock," I whisper back to

him, "but I will say this. Girls like Wise don't come along every day. She's the only person like her I've ever met, and if she chose you to care about, then you should count yourself lucky. I only hope that one day someone cares for me the way she cares about you."

Next to me, Scarlet shifts, and I feel her long, delicate fingers wrap around my hand. It is a welcome surprise, and when I turn my head to face her, I see that her eyes are still closed, but she's smiling, one of those heart-stopping smiles, that only seem to increase in their vibrance each time I receive one.

* * *

It's on the third day of relentless rain that Lark falls ill. Wise has an exceedingly difficult time rousing him from sleep, and when he merely mumbles under his breath during her repeated attempts to wake him, she becomes concerned. Dog is pressed up against him protectively, and he whimpers slightly as he licks the child's face.

Wise presses her wrist to his forehead. "He's burning up." She looks to Old Man, who immediately kneels by Lark's side. He, too, checks his head, listens to his breathing, and generally inspects him for any other signs of what ails him.

"A fever has definitely taken hold of him. Boy, get into my pack and grab the vial of fever ward," he directs.

I do as he says, and we all watch as he pours a few drops into Lark's mouth.

Lark doesn't wake for more than a few sporadic moments during the rest of the day. When he does, his mumbled words are rambling and incoherent. The rain stops, and we decide to stay put in the hopes that Lark will regain some of his health if he's granted more rest. Unfortunately, the fever still doesn't break.

"We have to get him out of the elements. The chill of the

air can't be helping his condition. He needs more rest and a hot meal," states Old Man.

"I can try to scout ahead and see if I can find a cave or something that could provide us with shelter," offers Scarlet.

"Yeah, and I can see if I can hunt some rabbit for a stew or something," Brock suggests.

"I'll help," I agree.

We all set to our tasks, and a few hours later, around dusk, Scarlet returns from her excursion. An enormous grin is present on her face as she announces that she has found a farm some distance off the main road.

"It looks like there's someone living there," says Scarlet. "I saw candlelight through the windows."

We finish our rabbit stew, clean up our camp, and continue on. Lark is in no condition to walk on his own, so we alternate who carries him. Thankfully, he isn't very heavy. After a few hours of trudging along the mucky road, Scarlet leads us east and down into a small valley.

In the dim light provided by the moon, we see an immense, sprawling farm with a fenced in pasture, large barn, and a plethora of animals milling about. There's a rather large cottage not far from the pasture, and we make our way to the door.

Wise knocks upon the door, calling out, "Hello! Hello! We mean you no harm! We're travelers and we have a sick child with us!"

Brock and I keep our hands on our weapons, just in case whoever lives within is combative when he or she sees us.

"Hello?" calls Wise again. "Please! My friend needs help!"

Finally, we hear heavy footsteps, and the door slowly opens. Before us is a rather large man with broad shoulders and tree trunk arms. He appears to be relatively young, likely in his early twenties. He holds a woodcutter's axe in one hand and a lantern in the other. Upon seeing that we are indeed weary travelers and not bandits or the like, his posture softens, and he places the axe on the ground just inside the door.

He holds the lantern aloft, and when the light illuminates his face, we all can't help but to gasp slightly at the resemblance.

The man's mouth is agape as his gaze settles on Brock.

"Wesley?"

CHAPTER 16

They look so similar that it is immediately evident they are related. They have the same strong, brawny frame, facial features, and complexion. The only difference is while Brock's hair is dark brown, and he has dark eyes, the man in front of us has light brown hair with tints of blonde and strawberry, and eyes of a dark blue that look almost grey in the dim light.

Brock is stunned into silence, but when he regains another of his composure to will his lips to move, his voice comes out in a tremor. "Qu-Quellin?"

The man reaches forward and pulls Brock into a tight embrace, and the two of them immediately start crying. The rest of us are too dumbstruck to say or do anything. After some time, they loosen their grips on each other, and the man, Quellin, holds Brock at an arm's length as he looks him over.

"Wesley... I thought you were dead. I was sure they killed you when they... when they killed our father."

"Brock... Is this your brother?" asks Wise.

Brock nods numbly. "Yes. Yes, he is!" He looks dazed and overwhelmed. "I-I need to sit down. I-I remember everything. All of it! I remember everything!"

Scarlet lets out a loud groan. "Look, I'm really happy for you, but Lark is starting to get heavy."

"Oh! Allow me!" Quellin moves forward and easily scoops Lark up into his strong arms. He carries him into the house as he calls back to us. "Come in! Come in! There's a fire going and some leftover stew from supper. Help yourselves."

We file into the cottage and Scarlet plops down in front of the fireplace. She holds her hands out in front of her to warm them. Old Man eagerly helps himself to a large bowl of stew, and he shares a few hunks of meat with Dog who sits by his side. Wise follows Quellin into an adjoining room. The latter gently places Lark on the bed and sets to bringing in extra blankets and cloths soaked in cool water for his forehead.

I look back towards the door. Brock remains seated on the stoop as he attempts to sort through his emotions. I move back to him and place my hand on his shoulder. "Are you okay?"

He shakes his head in amazement. "I remember everything, Boy. Everything," he repeats. "My father. His name was Titus. He was the greatest smith in all of Allanon. Quellin is my older brother." His hand rests on the sword he recovered from his father's shop. "The sword... the sword was for him. My dad made it for him when he came of age, but he left. They got into an argument, and he left. My mom was dead, and so was my sister, Sarah, so it was just me and my father. I- I need to take a walk. I need to sort this all out in my head."

I grab the lantern off of where Quellin left it on the small, square table in the main room. "Here. Take this with you. It's black as pitch out there."

Brock, or I suppose I should say Wesley, gratefully accepts it and disappears into the darkness. I see the lantern bouncing along as he walks towards the pasture.

With Quellin's help, Wise ensures that Lark is resting comfortably. She manages to get some broth from the stew as well as a cup of cold water into him, and soon he is snoring peacefully. Dog lopes off into the room and hops on the bed, taking up his place at Lark's feet.

Soon, Quellin rejoins us in the main room while Wise remains by Lark's side. Quellin glances around, but frowns when he doesn't see Brock. "Where is he? Where's Wesley?"

"He needed some time to work through everything," I say.

Old Man proceeds to attempt to explain what Brock is going through. He tells Quellin of our imprisonment at the hands of Abirad, being stripped of our memories, and forced to work as slaves. He tells him of our escape, of our journey so far, and encountering the village where Brock and his family had once lived.

"I was the one to bury our father. A few of the villagers managed to escape. The rest were taken by Abirad's men or killed," explains Quellin. "Those who survived passed this way. They told me about what happened, and I set off for the village immediately. I found my father's body, but no one could tell me what happened to Wesley. I searched the village for him, or at least his remains, but I found no trace of him. I thought he might have been taken, but I was never certain."

"So, this is all yours? The farm and all the land here?" I ask.

Quellin nods. "Years of hard work. I left home when I was 14. It was right after our mother died. The doctor said she was sick, but I think it was of a broken heart after our sister perished from plague. Wesley was about 8 then. It was a few years after that when Abirad's men attacked the town, and it's been five more since he disappeared."

"So, how did you end up with all of this?" questions Scarlet as she takes a big swig of cider from a wooden mug.

"I took up an apprenticeship with a local farmer, and when he died with no sons and no wife to take over, he left it to me," explains Quellin.

"As Brock- er- I mean *Wesley* tells it, your father was a master smith. Why didn't you learn from him?" inquires Old Man curiously.

"Because he doesn't believe in living by a sword," answers Brock, appearing in the doorway. "He and father got into a huge row about it before he left. He made this for Quellin." Brock crosses the room places his sword on the table in front of his brother. "It was intended for you. You should keep it."

Quellin shakes his head. "If you truly do remember, then

you know that is not my way. War... Killing... It was never my way."

"No one said it had to be," comments Brock quietly. "Father wanted you to take on the business, not be some front line fighter."

"True, but father forged weapons for warriors, and in the end, that is what got him killed. He lived by the sword, and he died by one." Quellin meets my questioning gaze. "The reason Abirad's men came to the village in the first place was to recruit my father as their smith. When he refused, they killed him. And it's why they took you, Wesley." He pushes the sword back towards his brother. "You should keep it. He would have wanted you to. It would be wasted on me."

My dear friend shifts uncomfortably. "I know- I know that Wesley is my name, but I'm not what I once was. I'll go by Brock, if it's all the same to you."

Quellin shrugs. "Call yourself whatever you wish. No matter your name, you're still my brother, and you and your friends are welcome to stay for as long as you have need to. You may even call this your home, should you wish it, *Brock*." Quellin rises to his feet. "I'm sure you're all exhausted from your travels. I have some extra bedrolls left over from when there were more hands to help at this farm. I'll pull them out for you. Fresh blankets, too. There may be some old clothes I can find for all of you as well. It's not much, and they may be ill-fitting, but it will be warmer than what you have. Brock, I'm sure some of my garments will fit you."

After supper, Quellin fetches and warms water so that we can wash. He promises us proper baths on the morrow when he can see enough to make it to the well. The clean clothes, while a bit big on me, are comfortable enough, and he manages to scrounge up some well-worn boots and even some traveling cloaks.

That night, we enjoy our first truly restful night of sleep in memory. The fire in the hearth spreads warmth throughout the room and dispels the deep chill that has set into our bones.

Later, I see Brock sitting by the fire, his father's sword resting upon his lap. Quellin sits next to him, both of them staring into the flames. The latter places his large hand on his younger brother's shoulder and gives it a gentle squeeze before rising and turning in for the night.

* * *

The next morning, we're awoken by the most delicious smells in creation. Quellin prepares a veritable feast. There's thick cut bacon, sausages, warm, brown bread, freshly churned butter, cold apple cider, eggs laid just that morning, and all manner of accompaniments.

We all eat like kings. I don't know if it's the fact that Lark's fever finally broke, the comforting sounds of friendly conversation, or the mouthwatering smells, but towards the end of our meal, I hear the kid's voice, raspy from lack of use, but there all the same.

"Wise? Wise, where are we?" he croaks out.

"Lark! Thank God!" exclaims Wise in relief. She pulls him into a tight hug, causing him to groan slightly. "I'm sorry, I'm sorry! How do you feel? Are you thirsty? Are you hungry?"

"I'll see to him," offers Quellin, wiping his mouth with a napkin and rising from the table. He prepares Lark a heaping plate, which the boy quickly devours before sheepishly asking for seconds. He eats more than Brock and I combined!

Although we don't want to delay our journey, we decide that Lark should have some time to regain his strength before we continue on our way. We agree to stay for a sennight or so, and Quellin is more than happy to oblige.

After breakfast, Quellin takes us for a stroll around the grounds. Even Lark feels well enough to get some fresh air, though Wise demands that he take it easy, and Brock offers to carry him on his back so he can preserve his strength. The kid complains a bit, but knowing Wise isn't going to budge, he begrudgingly accepts Brock's help.

Quellin tells us his lands are the most fertile for miles, and he has a very healthy stock of just about any farm animal you can imagine. I find myself transfixed by the horses, especially a large, white charger.

"That one is my favorite. The man who owned the farm before me, Sellas, he was a knight in his youth. That one there was bred from his own warhorse's line," recounts Quellin. "Do you ride?"

"Not that I recall," I tell him. "Hard to say for sure."

"How about tomorrow I show you how? I can show all of you, if you'd like," he offers.

The following morning, he makes good on his promise, and we all decide to give it a try, save for Lark, who sleeps in extra late on account of the fact that he is still recovering. Now that he's on the mend, even Wise is more willing to part herself from his side for a few moments.

I'm first to try, and Quellin allows me to ride the white charger, who he says despite his size is quite gentle. I watch how Quellin mounts his own horse, and I nearly fall on my first attempt, but once I'm seated in the saddle, something peculiar happens.

My senses accost me, and even though I'm looking at Quellin, I'm seeing something else, too.

I'm laughing, and as I look down at my hands, they're so much smaller than they should be. I look to my right and the grey-eyed woman is beside me. Her hand is on the small of my back as she helps me balance on top of the small, white pony that I'm riding.

"I'm doing it! I'm doing it!" I know it's my voice, but it sounds so different. It's the voice of a child, even younger than Lark.

The grey-eyed woman smiles at me and places a gentle kiss on my cheek. "You're doing so well, my love. Soon you'll be riding just as well as your father."

"Boy! Boy!" calls Scarlet.

Bewildered by what's just happened to me, I stare at her blankly for some time.

"Boy? Are you all right?" asks Quellin.

"He's remembering," says Brock quietly.

"How do you know?" asks Lark from the grass beside him.

"Because that's how it felt for me. As if I was waking from a dream." Brock gives him a slight smile and ruffles the boy's hair with a large hand.

Quellin is an excellent teacher, and we all manage to quickly pick up on riding, save for Old Man who looks more like a stick doll, his long legs flapping about here and there as he bounces in the saddle.

When it's Wise's turn, Quellin dismounts to help her into the saddle.

"Here," he says, offering her one of his strong, calloused hands. "Let me help you."

Wise smiles back at him. "Thank you. That's very kind of you."

I see Brock frown. He makes eye contact with me, and I give him a warning glance. He simply sighs heavily, but his face quickly contorts with concern as he looks at Wise.

"Wise? Wise!" He rushes forward and hops over the fence. He quickly races to her side, and grabs the reigns of her horse. "Wise, what's wrong?"

Dog starts to bark loudly and proceeds to whine, pressing his cold, wet nose against my leg.

"It's okay, Dog," I assure him. "She's all right."

Tears stream down Wise's face, and she shakes her head in disbelief. "So, this is what it's like. No wonder you felt so overwhelmed, Brock."

"What do you see, my dear?" asks Old Man gently.

"I was on a horse before," she replies. Her voice sounds distant, as if she's in a daze. "I didn't have any control over it though. I was too small. I was on the saddle in front of a man. He was very large, with broad shoulders. He had long, graying hair. And a moustache and beard. He asked me if I wanted to go faster. I laughed and shouted that we should. There's a man with black hair, and a woman with eyes like mine. They're smiling, and they wave to us as we go by."

"It's a memory, Wise," confirms Brock. "Hopefully, the first of many for you. They're not all good. I know mine aren't, but ones like that... those are the best."

We continue our riding lessons without any further excitement, save for Brock nearly getting bucked off a horse. He manages to maintain control and proves himself as a fairly adept rider. However, between all of us, Wise and I seem to be the most natural when it comes to handling mounts, and Quellin even applauds us on our skill.

Quellin unsaddles the horses and we help him to lead them back to the barn. "You know, I was thinking about it, and it certainly wouldn't hurt if you take a horse or two with you on your travels. I can spare a couple, and with a child with you, it might ease the burden of your travels a bit," he offers.

"Quellin, that is far too kind," replies Wise. "We can't thank you enough for your help."

He places a hand on her shoulder. "A bit of kindness after all you've endured is the least I can do. Should you require anything else, please don't hesitate to ask."

* * *

In the afternoon, Quellin asks for volunteers to head to his small, apple orchard to pick apples for a pie. He tells us he's quite skilled at baking but doesn't often get the chance to practice his skills as it is usually just him.

Scarlet pulls a large, red apple from a tree and takes a big bite. A tiny stream of juice trickles down her chin, and her eyes widen with delight. "This is... This is incredible. This is the best apple I've ever tasted. Here." She pulls down another apple and tosses it to me. "Have one."

I bite into it and find that Scarlet isn't exaggerating. It's the perfect balance of sweet and tart. The skin is firm, and the flesh of the apple is fragrant and succulent. "I'm really looking forward to that pie! How many do you think we need?"

Scarlet shrugs. "Let just fill the basket Quellin gave us. It won't hurt to have a few extra just to eat." We immediately set to picking more apples.

"Boy."

"Hm?"

"What was it like for you?"

I tilt my head to the side in confusion. "What do you mean?"

"Getting a memory."

I sigh, already missing the all-encompassing joy the memory brought me. Despite all that we've been through, that moment filled my heart with a hope I've never experienced before. Yet, how can I put that into words? How can I adequately describe it? "It felt like a key had turned in a lock. As if a door were opened, and when it did, I was flooded with the most beautiful feeling. It was peace. True peace." I shrug. "At least that's how it felt for me. Brock said they aren't all like that."

"Most of the time, they haven't been like that for me," confesses Scarlet. "I did get one good one though. Back at the castle, there was a servant who was walking about humming a song. When I heard it, I remembered something." She seats herself on the grass and pats the ground beside her; I sit down next to her.

"It was a red-haired woman. I was sitting in her lap, and she was humming that song. The one the servant was humming. She was beautiful, with shining green eyes and pale skin, and when she smiled at me, my soul felt lighter. I've never known any such happiness before that or since." Her expression changes and becomes one of distress.

"What's wrong, Scarlet?"

"Unfortunately, it wasn't my only memory of her. I remembered that she got sick. She died. I was small, and I remember that I pulled on the sleeve of her dress and begged her to wake up. When she didn't, I held on to her, and I put my head on her chest, but there was no heartbeat, and not even the slightest rise or fall of her chest." She sweeps a rogue tear from the corner of her eye. "Then a man came. He took me by the hand and lead me away. I must have known him, because he didn't seem like a stranger. But he ended up being cruel. He taught me to steal and kill."

We sit together in silence. I don't know how long.

Tentatively, I reach out and take her hand in mine. "I'm sorry, Scarlet."

"Don't be." She stands and pulls me to my feet. "Well, those apples won't pick themselves."

"I am truly sorry that you have so many awful memories, and while I can't promise you won't encounter more sorrow in your life, I believe that you will make better memories, ones that you will look back upon, and they will make you smile. You do have such a beautiful smile."

She stares up at me with those brilliant, blue eyes, and my heart flutters under her gaze. The next thing I know, her lips grace mine. The sun illuminates her bright, red hair, more vibrant in its color than the apples in the trees that surround us.

After several moments, when she finally pulls away, it feels as if the world has shifted somehow, and some part of my story has been rewritten. I'm fairly certain, that for the rest of my life, any time I taste the sweetness of an apple or see the color red kissed by the warm rays of the sun, I'll always think of that particular memory, of Scarlet, and the moment I fell in love with her.

CHAPTER 17

The next morning, I awake to Scarlet's voice. "Come on, Boy. You're not going to sleep the day away, are you?"

I yawn loudly and stretch my arms over my head before propping myself up on my elbows so that I can better see her. "I'm up, I'm up."

"Quellin is going to show us how to set traps and use a bow to catch wild game," mentions Scarlet.

Delicious smells waft from the other side of the room and my stomach grumbles so loudly that Scarlet laughs.

"Okay. Let me just get something to eat first," I say as I toss my blanket aside.

"Here." She tosses something toward me, but I'm feeling rather sluggish, so it just bounces off my chest and into my lap.

I look down and grin at the apple.

She gives me a sly wink and disappears out of the door.

I devour the apple then see what else if available. I shovel in a few mouthfuls of creamy oats flavored with fresh butter and molasses, gulp down some cider, and munch a few pieces of bacon. When I'm done, everyone else is already outside.

Old Man and Lark are tossing a stick for Dog while Brock sits on an old, wooden stool and sharpens his sword with a whetstone. Scarlet is perched upon the fence of the pasture. Her legs swing back and forth as she hums to herself.

Wise and Quellin are just returning from a morning stroll around the grounds. This has become quite common for the two of them. Since our arrival, they've gone out on a walk together once in the morning and once at sunset each day, and the two seem to get on splendidly, having similarly kind and intelligent dispositions. The two of them are laughing merrily as they enjoy the fair weather and each other's company.

When Brock hears them approach, his eyes snap upward at their sounds of amusement. He frowns slightly and returns to his work.

We gather together, and Quellin shows us how to set traps and snares. He manages to catch a rabbit, then he shows us how to kill it and clean it. This part seems to make Wise a bit sad, but even she understands that nuts and berries can't always be found, so killing an animal is often necessary for survival. Surprisingly, Lark shows natural aptitude for this, and we all agree that his traps and snares are the best. Mine are decent enough, as are everyone else's, save for Old Man who doesn't seem to pick up on it very quickly as the animals always manage to dart out of overlooked openings or loose string.

Next, we all try our hands at archery. Brock and Scarlet prove themselves to be the best among us, but Wise also seems to have an aptitude for it.

"Here," speaks Quellin as he steps up behind her. "Your form is decent enough, but if you make some adjustments, you're sure to always hit your mark. Let me show you." He stands behind her so that her back is against his chest, and he assists her in changing her posture and her hold on the bow just the slightest bit.

Wordlessly, Brock tosses his bow upon the ground and stalks off towards the barn while the rest of us look on as Wise effortlessly hits mark after mark with perfect accuracy.

"There! See? You're brilliant at this," encourages Quellin. He gives her shoulder a gentle squeeze then turns towards the rest of us. "What do you say we take a break for a midday meal?" He glances around the area and frowns. "Where's Wesley gone off to?"

I gesture towards the barn.

"I'll go get him." Quellin departs, and the rest of us head back towards the cottage.

Unfortunately, we never make it there as the sounds of loud yelling and things breaking stop us in our tracks. We all exchange worried glances and hurriedly make our way to the barn. I get there first, and as I open the door, I just narrowly avoid being smacked in the head by a flying bucket. Old Man is not so lucky and lets out an "oof!" as it grazes his shoulder before falling to the ground where it can do no further harm.

"It's your fault! You could have helped us! But you had to go running away!" accuses Brock loudly.

"Wesley! I mean- Brock! What could I have done? I would have ended up dead like him or captive like you," reasons Quellin as he dodges another projectile thrown by his younger brother.

"At least you would have died a man and not some coward milking cows and baking apple pies!" shouts Brock angrily.

"Personally, I loved that pie. It was delicious pie," remarks Scarlet from next to me.

"You're being ridiculous!" cries Quellin. "Brock!"

"He tried to fight! He even killed some guards in the process, but they knocked him in the head with his own, bloody, smithing hammer!" Brock's face is crimson, and his entire form is shaking with rage.

"Brock," Quellin says quietly as he raises his hands in front of him to indicate he means no harm.

Brock isn't having it and snatches a pitchfork from a nearby hay bale. He slings it forward and almost skewers poor Quellin! "They dragged him out into the streets in the middle of the night, shackled up like some common criminal!" There are tears streaming down Brock's face, and every word he speaks seethes with anger. "They put him on his knees, he looked up at me once more, and then they took off his head! And where were you, Quellin? Where were you when he bloody needed you? Where were you when I needed you?"

"Brock... I'm truly sorry. I am! But there's nothing I can do to change the past." Quellin is speaking in a calm voice, as if trying to soothe an enraged animal, as he slowly approaches his brother.

"Would you change it if you could?"

"Of course I would!"

"You would have killed those soldiers then? You would have slain them and kept Da and the other villagers safe?"

Quellin's lips are a thin line of controlled anger. "No," he returns firmly. "I wouldn't have killed them. But I would have found a way to make it so they couldn't hurt Da, or you, or anyone else."

Brock unsheathes his sword, and Wise gasps next to me. "Brock!" she calls out.

He looks over to her, and there is a deep, resonating anguish in his eyes. Dolefully, he looks back to his brother. With a growl he throws the sword at Quellin's feet, then stands in silence for a moment, his chest heaving. When he finally reclaims his voice, it comes out with more sorrow than anger. "Sometimes we have to be willing to pick up the sword..." He looks back to the rest of us, his gaze lingering on Wise a bit longer than he intended. "...to protect the people we love."

Brock pushes past Quellin, and the rest of us part around the doorway to allow him to pass through. He stops briefly in front of Wise and looks as if he's going to say something but continues on. I let him go so he can calm himself a bit, but about an hour later when he hasn't returned, I set out to find him.

I trudge through a field and find him sitting on a large rock and staring into the distance. He turns his head when he hears me approach and gestures for me to join him. We sit in silence for some time, neither of us sure of how to broach the subject.

"So... that happened," he finally speaks.

I can't help but to chuckle a bit at the nonchalant way he attempts to regard it. "Yes. That certainly did. Are you okay,

Brock?"

"No. But I will be... someday." He turns to look at me, and I can see that his eyes are red and puffy from weeping. "I'm angry at Quellin for not being there for my father or me when we needed him, but would you like to know why I reacted that way today?"

"Why?"

"Her." His voice is heavy with emotion, and I don't have to inquire as to the *her* he means.

"But why Brock? I told you that you need to tell her how you feel."

He shakes his head. "I want to, but I just can't, Boy."

"Well, you need to before someone else does," I reason.

Brock sighs. "I know."

"You have to do something, or this jealousy is going to consume you."

Brock is thoughtful for a moment. "It wasn't just jealousy, Boy. It was fear. My brother came to me early this morning. Apparently, he's quite taken with Wise. He wants to ask her to stay... with him."

I give him a sympathetic look. "Brock..."

"While I was quite upset with that idea, that's not what drove me so mad. It's that... what if some soldiers show up here one day? How would he protect her, Boy?"

"I don't think Wise needs protecting, Brock," I say with a chuckle. "If anyone needs protecting, it's any fool who thinks Wise is easy prey. She's perfectly capable of standing her own ground. I'd be terrified of her if I were forced to face her in battle, and if anyone is stupid enough to try to hurt someone she cares for, may the Maker help him! She is very capable with her axe and fair with a bow."

"That she is, but my father was a capable fighter, too, and look where that got him when Abirad's men fell upon him. Regardless of Quellin's affection for her, I don't think he'd do enough."

"And you think you would?"

"I know I would," responds Brock firmly, and I can plainly see the seriousness in his eyes. "I'd give my life to keep my friends safe, but... especially her."

"So, what are you going to do about Quellin? Will you tell him how you feel for Wise?"

Brock shakes his head. "I can't even admit to myself how I feel for Wise, much the less to my brother, or especially to her."

I offer him my hand and haul him to his feet. "Come on, Brock."

We head back towards the cottage, both of us unknowing of what is to befall us.

It's only a few days later when Brock's worst fear comes true.

CHAPTER 18

It's two days after Brock confronted his brother about their shared past. Things have mostly returned to normal between the two of them. With Wise's urging, Brock decided to speak with Quellin, and he was able to work through his feelings, at least enough to reclaim some peace between them. To his credit, Quellin's patience with his younger sibling is exceptionally admirable. If I had a brother who nearly killed me with a pitchfork, I don't think I'd be as forgiving.

It's well into the evening when Dog starts barking incessantly, and nothing seems to be able to ease his anxiety. Lark tries scratching him behind the ears and giving him a special treat from the table, but it doesn't help. Finally, he lets Dog outside in the event the beast needs to relieve himself, but once there, Dog arches his back and begins growling menacingly.

"Dog? What's wrong?" asks Lark. He kneels by his furry friend and speaks soothingly to him, but to no avail.

Quellin pushes his chair back from the table and crosses to the door. He frowns slightly and heads outside. We see him make his way towards the rear of the cottage before lumbering towards the very top of the hill. Scarlet and I exchange glances and follow after him.

We find him staring off into the distance in the direction of the main road. His face has gone pale, and there is panic in his blue-grey eyes.

"Get to the barn at once," he says stiffly.

Scarlet and I see them at the same time. Down the road

is a company of over two dozen armored men. More than that, I can't make out.

"Quellin, what's going on?" questions Scarlet.

He doesn't answer and simply makes his way back to the cottage, so we quickly hurry after him.

Brock meets us at the door. "Quellin?"

"Gather everyone up. There's a loft in the barn. It's filled with bales of hay. You can all hide up there," he replies quickly. The fear in his voice is unmistakable.

Brock grabs his brother's arm firmly. "Quellin. What is going on?"

"I didn't know they'd be coming yet." Quellin begins pacing in front of the hearth. "They weren't due for another couple weeks. It must have been your escape. That must be why they're here before they're supposed to be."

"Who?" asks Old Man, rising to his feet.

Quellin's lips form a thin line.

"They're Abirad's men," speaks Scarlet. "I could just make out the dragon symbol on their surcoats."

"What do you mean they 'weren't due for another couple weeks?'" demands Brock angrily. "Quellin! Explain yourself!"

Quellin looks as if he wants to melt into the floor. "They come every month or so. For supplies for the castle."

Brock shakes his head in disbelief, perhaps believing if he does so hard enough he may wake up from some terrible nightmare. "What?"

"I give them goods. Crops. Cattle. Whatever they ask for. In exchange, they leave me in peace," explains Quellin.

Brock snatches him by the front of his shirt. "Abirad's men? The same men who killed our father, destroyed our village, and massacred our friends and neighbors! The same men who helped to imprison me and my friends. You *cooperate* with them?" Brock shoves his brother so hard that Quellin's back slams into the wall. "Do you bake them bloody pies, too?"

"Brock, we don't have time for this," responds Quellin

145

fearfully. "You need to take the others and go hide in the barn. I'll give them what they want and send them on their way. It will be fine."

"My brother isn't only a coward, but he's a traitor, too. They *leave you in peace*! What do you care what they do to the rest of the world if your little piece of heaven is left unscathed!" shouts Brock in disgust.

"Brock! Please!" pleads Quellin, glancing desperately towards the door.

"Come on," Brock gestures for us to follow him, and we do so as quickly as our legs can carry us.

Wise and I help Lark up the ladder and into the loft area. Old Man follows next, then the rest of us.

"What about Dog?" asks Lark. The poor beast starts to whimper as he stares up at us.

"He'll be okay down there, Lark," assures Scarlet.

"But he's all alone down there except for cows and sheep. I bet you he doesn't even speak cow or sheep," states Lark.

"Ugh." Brock groans, but minutes later he manages to hoist Dog up the ladder in one arm while clinging to the rungs with the other.

"Come here, Dog. We have to be really quiet," Lark explains to the creature as if the mutt can actually understand him.

Scarlet and Old Man chance a glance out of one of the small ventilation windows at the top of the barn.

"It's Vortigern," announces Scarlet grimly.

The rest of us know exactly who she's referring to. He's one of Abirad's lieutenants, and one of his most fierce protectors. He is well-known for his brutality, and his bloodlust is said to be second to only one other of Abirad's men, Tarvus Bullgraden, known more commonly as The Bloody Bull. Vortigern makes even heavy-handed guards like Caius look like priests, and the fact that he's here is not a good sign. Where Vortigern goes, death follows.

I move to the window so that I can better see what's going on.

Vortigern and his men are met by Quellin just outside of the cottage. We're too far away to hear their conversation, but from the look of it, it does not seem to be going well. Vortigern appears angry, and despite Quellin's cooperation, the lieutenant doesn't seem to be very pleased. We watch as he draws back his arm and forcefully slams his gauntleted fist into the side of Quellin's head. We see a trickle of something dark on Quellin's forehead, but as strong as he is, he maintains his footing and makes a wide gesture in the air.

"They must be here looking for us," surmises Scarlet.

"You mean *me*," says Lark quietly.

"Lark, don't think like that. They'd be after us if you were here or not. Abirad isn't fond of prisoners escaping him," reassures Wise.

"They're fanning out," speaks Old Man. "We need to be as silent as possible. Some of them are coming this way."

Brock and I stack the haybales a bit higher to further obscure our location from view. We can then do nothing but hide and wait. Scarlet crouches beside me. She has one hand on a dagger, but the other rests on mine, giving it a gentle squeeze. I offer her a weak smile, and I peek around the side of our hay barrier to watch the door.

After a few moments, we hear the door of the barn creak open. At first, I worry that Dog might give our position away by barking, but even he seems to realize how dire the situation is and sits as silently as a statue. We hear footsteps moving this way and that, but none of them seem to come towards the ladder. Either they don't realize it's there, or they just assume the loft is completely full of hay.

Once they're satisfied that the area is clear, they report back to Vortigern, who maintains a position outside of the cottage. A few moments later, more guards, shaking their heads to indicate nothing was found, return from various areas around the farm. Quellin looks relieved, but a moment later, Vortigern orders two of his guards to seize him.

Quellin starts shouting at Vortigern, and Abirad's lieutenant kicks him hard in the stomach, causing him to double over in pain.

That's when we see a large group of guards filing out of the cottage. They are holding torches aloft and begin making their way around the grounds. Two of them light the cottage on fire, and within moments, what started as a small blaze turns into a massive conflagration. Others head to the stables where the horses are whinnying loudly and pawing at the doors of their pens.

"Oh, Maker," breathes Wise.

Old Man shakes his head sadly. "They're penned in. They won't be able to escape."

"No! No! We have to help them," Lark frantically pleads.

Wise pulls him close to her, and he buries his face in her shoulder to muffle his tears. "Shh. We must keep quiet, Lark."

"They're heading this way," observes Brock gravely. "We can't stay here. We'll be burned alive. We have to fight back. If we try to run, they're just going to chase us down. We have to take a stand."

None of us know what to say. Finally, I step forward.

"I agree. We can't just stay in here. Let's head down the ladder. As soon as they draw close enough to the barn, we let them have it." I look to Old Man. "Can you use the stones?"

Old Man nods. "I can, but we must be careful, because if I overdo it, I run the risk of blowing us all up along with Abirad's men."

"Understood," I respond. "Come on."

We head down the ladder, all save for Dog who leaps onto a stack of hay below then hops down to the floor.

I can hear the footsteps of the guards drawing closer, and through one of the windows, I see the orange and yellow flickering of their torches.

"Lark, stay close to the rest of us," warns Wise.

"I will. But if they try to take me, I have my dagger," responds Lark reassuringly.

"Let's hope you don't have to use it," mutters Brock. "Here they come... Now!"

Brock and I push the barn doors open, and in the process we knock over two guards. Brock cuts to the left with Wise and Lark behind him while Scarlet, Old Man, and I head for the right. Immediately, Vortigern orders his men towards the barn. The commotion gives Quellin the opportunity to break free. In the chaos, I see him snatch a club from one of the guards and begin to slam the weapon into anyone foolish enough to come near him.

Brock makes a beeline straight for Vortigern, and my stomach sinks as I see Abirad's lieutenant draw his sword. There is a flash of steel as Brock's weapon clashes with that of Vortigern.

I charge forward with Scarlet right at my heels. We engage with three guards who seem taken aback by the blatant attack. I swing my sword forward with all my might, and it knocks one of the guards off balance. I take advantage of this and bring my sword down upon him again. Scarlet moves so quickly she looks more like a whirring death machine than a human being. She embeds one of her daggers in the throat of a guard, rips in free, then plunges it into the back of another's knee.

Across the way, I see Dog tackle one of the guards to the ground and begin to tear at his exposed flesh with his exceedingly sharp teeth. Then I hear the soft hum of the singing stones as Old Man prepares to unleash their power.

I glance behind me to check on how Wise is faring and see a pile of bodies beginning to form at her feet. She swings her handaxe towards an approaching guard, but he parries it with his shield while one of his fellows attempts to flank her.

Lark darts forward, and I hear Wise shout, but the little guy plunges his dagger into the side of one of the guards. Wise isn't about to let Lark remain in harm's way and buries her axe in the man's back.

"The boy! He's here!" cries one of the guards, and suddenly a large concentration of guards begins to form around Wise and Lark.

Vortigern, still engaged with Brock, hears the call and brings his sword down upon Brock. Brock parries the blow with his sword, but Vortigern kicks forward with his metal boot and sends Brock flying backwards. Brock's head slams against a tree, and he becomes dazed and slumps to the ground. Vortigern begins to head towards the barn as Quellin helps Brock to his feet.

Suddenly, we hear Old Man shout. "Ears!"

We all cover our ears just as one of the guards lunges forward to snatch Lark. Wise intercepts him, and the guard thrusts his sword towards Wise, piercing her through her shoulder. Wise cries out in pain, and suddenly Brock thunders past me. Wise manages to switch her axe to her offhand and brings it down upon the guard who injured her.

"Old Man! Wait! Wise!" I cry out in warning.

Old Man nods in understanding.

Brock appears by Wise's side, and his weapon flashes in the night. His battlecry rings of such fury that its sound sends shivers down even my spine. He places himself between Wise and Lark and an onslaught of guards. One after another of Abirad's men are brought to a halt beneath his sword. His eyes are wild with anger, and his muscles are tense with bloodlust.

Scarlet and I work together to dispatch two more guards as Quellin notices Vortigern attempting to flank Brock. The older brother snatches a woodcutter's axe from a nearby tree stump and barrels forward. He buries the blade deep into the lieutenant's back, and Vortigern falls to his knees. Blood pours out of his mouth, and he collapses forward, dead. Quellin rips the axe free and buries it into the chest of an approaching soldier.

A fresh wave of five guards charges toward us. Again, Old Man gives his warning. There is a bright flash of light, and the guards are violently expelled backwards. When their battered bodies finally hit the ground, they are no longer capable of rejoining the fray.

Though we've managed to dispatch all the enemies around us, there isn't a spare moment for celebration. The fire from the stables has spread and has caught the main barn ablaze. Scarlet and Quellin dash inside to free the frightened animals. Lark kneels on the ground next to Wise as Brock presses his large hand against the awful wound in her shoulder to stop the bleeding. I make my way towards the stables to see if anything can be done for the horses. Of the six that Quellin had, only two, including the white warhorse, remain.

We work through the night. Old Man is able to tend to Wise's wound, and it requires a plentiful amount of stitches to bind the open flesh back together. He gives her allowary extract for the pain, and soon she is resting comfortably, awake, but resting nonetheless.

Scarlet dabs a clean cloth against a gash on my forehead. Though it's painful, I don't even wince. That is a skill acquired from years as a slave in Abirad's castle.

I place my hand over hers, pressing my cheek into her palm. "I'd get injured more often if it meant moments like this."

She playfully swats my shoulder. "You're ridiculous. Keep it up and I just might injure you myself."

I can't help but laugh. Even in such dark times, she is a beacon of light. Despite the horrors this night has brought upon all of us, I feel like being in this place has brought Scarlet and I closer together.

We do our best to help Quellin before our impending departure. Many of the animals fled in the chaos, but Quellin is hopeful that at least some of them will return once they realize it is safe again.

Quellin and Brock set to carrying the bodies of the soldiers to the cottage. This is more likely to get rid of the evidence of the battle than simply burying them. It's a solemn task, and I join them so they are not forced to endure the burden of such a horror alone.

Quellin freezes, his gaze locked on the body of a guard before him. "Is this what you wanted, Brock?" he asks quietly. "Is this what you would have me do- who you would have me be?" He gestures toward the body before him, his axe still buried deep in the guard's chest.

Brock and I peer down at the fallen guard. He is a young man, barely older than Brock and me. In fact, had Brock stayed, it very well could have been him dead this night rather than this unfortunate soul before us.

Brock looks to Wise, still pale from the blood loss brought on by her injury. "Is this what *you* wanted?"

Quellin shakes his head sadly. "I suppose on this matter, we shall have to disagree."

* * *

As the sun rises, we prepare to say our goodbyes. We cannot afford another assault from Abirad's soldiers, and our journey has been put on hold for too long. Brock asks Wise for the millionth time if she won't reconsider resting for a day or two until her wound begins to heal. She assures him she will be fine and won't be dissuaded from departing.

I sit next to her and assist in changing the bandages around her wound. She pulls down the sleeve of her shirt to expose the majority of her shoulder. I pause, thinking we had missed a second wound when dressing her injury, but find that the large, reddish brown, tree-shaped mark on the back of her shoulder appears to be a birthmark.

"Thank you for your help, Boy," says Wise. She sounds exhausted, but then again, we all are.

Quellin is able to scrounge up some supplies and offers one of his two remaining horses to us. "Take the white one," he says to me. "You said you rode a white horse in your youth. It must be a sign."

"We can't do that," I reply. "You've lost so much. Surely you'd want to keep your prized horse."

Quellin shakes his head. "I insist. With Wise injured and Lark so young and prone to tire easily, you could use the assistance."

He extends his hand to me, and I give it a firm shake. He says goodbye to Scarlet, Old Man, Lark, and Dog. When it's time to say goodbye to Brock, he hesitates, and for several moments the brothers just stare at the ground in front of them as if it's the most interesting thing in creation.

"You're always welcome here," speaks Quellin softly. "I know we may disagree on certain matters, but you are my brother, and... and I love you."

Brock smiles slightly. "No. This is your home. This is your way, not mine. I'll find my path someday, but my road doesn't end here."

Quellin pulls Brock into a strong embrace. "Still, the offer stands."

"Thank you, Quellin."

Quellin hands Brock their father's sword. "While I may not be willing to pick up the sword, you certainly are. Keep it. May it help you to protect those you love." Quellin turns his attention to Wise.

"What will you do, Quellin?" she asks.

Despite the circumstances, he offers her a warm smile. "Rebuild. And when I do, I'll make a home worthy of a wife and raising a family." He gives her a meaningful look, and I see the agony on Brock's face. "You could come back and visit, Wise... if you'd like." Quellin shifts nervously on his feet and fidgets with his hands. Somehow, he finds the courage to look into her eyes again. "Maybe you'd even like to make it *your* home."

Brock is next to me, and I can tell that he's holding his breath.

Wise offers Quellin a friendly hug. "That's very kind of you, Quellin. You are a remarkable person, and I'm sure many a woman would be proud to be married to such a gentle and honorable man as you, but as your brother said…" She glances over at Brock, and the two of them lock eyes. "…my path does not end here." She rifles through her bag and pulls out the considerable pouch of gems she was able to smuggle out of Abirad's castle. She takes a large handful and redeposits it in her bag, then offers the rest of the pouch to Quellin.

"I can't take this. What if you need it?" asks Quellin.

"We insist. It's the least we can do for all you have done for us. Use it to help you to rebuild," insists Wise.

Reluctantly, Quellin accepts the pouch from her outstretched hand. "I'll pray for all of you on your journey, in the hopes that you regain what you have lost, as I have gained so much from you being here."

And so, we leave Quellin and his ravaged farm in our wake. He waves to us from in front of the smoldering remnants of his home, and I can't help but wonder if I could endure such tragedy with such optimism. As we walk, Scarlet's hand comes to rest in the crook of my arm, and I start to believe that I could likely endure far worse than this if she were to remain by my side.

CHAPTER 19

We make fair progress on our journey down the main road. Despite Brock's insistence that the injured Wise should ride on the warhorse (whom Lark has taken to calling Horse), she trudges along with the rest of us and lets Lark ride instead.

It's late afternoon when we decide to take a break from our travels. Since the forest has begun to thin out, we simply look for areas of cover not far from the road. There are usually fields of long grass, small outcroppings of rock, or the occasional copse of trees where we can remain relatively unseen while we rest.

Brock asks Old Man for the fifth time since leaving Quellin's to check Wise's injury, and the latter once again reports that she should make a full recovery.

Lark has been uncharacteristically quiet. At first, I think he's just exhausted from the overwhelming nature of battle, but his forlorn expression indicates there may be something troubling him.

"What's wrong, Lark?" I ask him.

"I only wanted to help," he replies glumly.

Old Man raises an eyebrow. "Dear boy, what do you mean?"

Lark sighs heavily. "It's my fault Wise got hurt. I tried to help, but then she had to protect me. That's why she got hurt," he explains guiltily.

Wise shakes her head. "No, Lark. You mustn't feel bad about that. You did well, and I'm very proud of you. But you must promise me that you won't put yourself in harm's way again."

Lark nods obediently. "I won't, Wise. I promise."

Wise places her good arm around his shoulders. "While you only injured that man, taking a life, even in defense, weighs heavily on one's soul. Do you understand?"

Lark nods again. "I understand."

"Don't you feel better now? Why don't you go play with Dog?" I suggest, and he eagerly takes off through the grass. The kid finds a stick and begins tossing it for the excitable creature.

Brock frowns and looks to Wise. "You sound like Quellin."

"No, I recognize there are times in which it's necessary to kill," elaborates Wise. "I wish only to preserve his innocence... for as long as we can. We were all robbed of our childhoods. I won't let him lose his as well."

We watch Lark laugh as Dog gives him a big, slobbery kiss.

"Let him be a child while he can," comments Wise quietly.

* * *

We cover a bit more ground before making camp for the evening. Quellin was kind enough to send us with several saddlebags filled with food. We tuck into a variety of different offerings, though we are careful not to take too much as we don't know if we will encounter lean times ahead.

Wise decides to turn in early, and Brock once again pulls his blanket next to her, though at her questioning gaze, he maintains a respectable distance. She falls asleep first, and I watch him as he holds vigil over her, watching her chest rise and fall rhythmically. She turns slightly, and her blanket shifts. He gingerly reaches over and pulls it back over her shoulders to dispel the evening's chill. Once he's satisfied that she's resting well, he, too, gives in to sleep.

The rest of us gather around our small campfire and prepare our sleeping areas. I put my blanket down on the ground, and Scarlet joins me. She nestles down in her own blanket by my side. Her presence brings a comfortable warmth to the cold evening. Both surprised and delighted by this turn of events, I stretch out on my back, and she places her head on my shoulder.

* * *

I awake to an unusual feeling on my lips and smile slightly, thinking I am the recipient of another of Scarlet's world-altering kisses. However, I certainly don't taste apples, and there is the pungent smell of wet dog.

"Dog!" I sputter, wiping my mouth with the back of my hand.

Scarlet is sitting on a fallen log next to the fire. She laughs so hard she nearly falls off her perch.

Lark, seated across from her, is nibbling on an apple tart. Old Man sits by his side, and Brock and Wise are still asleep. I join my friends around the fire and grab a hunk of bread and a bit of cheese for my breakfast.

"Do you love her?" asks Lark very suddenly.

I almost choke on cheese. "Excuse me?"

"Do you love her?" he repeats. "Scarlet."

"I-uh-er..." I look desperately at Scarlet for some direction, but she simply grins at me with amusement.

Finally, she takes pity on me and responds to Lark's question. "We like each other very much. Why do you ask?"

His next question nearly causes my eyes to pop out of my head.

"Will you get married?" he inquires curiously.

Old Man chuckles at my obvious discomfort with this line of questioning.

Again, Scarlet comes to my rescue. "For now, we are content to simply get through each day. I don't know what the future holds."

Lark takes a big bite of his apple tart. "Brock likes Wise," he says, his mouth full of apple and sugary crust.

"What makes you say that?" I ask. Obviously, he's not wrong; I just wonder how he figured it out.

Lark shrugs. "He gets a funny look when he sees her, and I catch him staring at her when he thinks she isn't looking."

"I see," speaks Old Man. "You're very observant, Lark. That's a very good skill to have."

"Will *they* get married?" he inquires.

Lark is typically very inquisitive, but I feel like he's going somewhere with all these questions. "I don't know, Lark," I answer. "What's on your mind?"

"Do you think Wise could be my mum?" he asks. "I had one once. She smelled like lavender and strawberries. She loved strawberries. She used to give me some."

Old Man rubs his chin thoughtfully. "Ah. You must be remembering the queen."

"Lark," says Scarlet, "why do you want Wise to be your mother? You have a father, and I'm certain he's splendid. You'll see him soon enough."

Lark frowns. "Do you know him?"

"Well, no," admits Scarlet.

"Then how do you know? What if he's not? Some fathers aren't good men," reasons Lark.

"Everyone says King Ruden is a fair and kind man," I offer.

"People can say anything they like," responds Lark. "That doesn't make it true. If he's so kind, why didn't he free us?"

"I don't know. Maybe he was sad for losing you and your mum. Sometimes when people are sad, they don't see important things," I tell him.

"I'm afraid when we get to the castle we'll all be

parted," admits Lark. "I don't want to lose all of you."

"You won't," I assure him. "We can stay on in Vericus for as long as you need us."

"Then you'll have to stay forever because that's how long I'll need you," he replies earnestly. He wraps Scarlet into a big hug, then embraces me, and finally Old Man before bouncing off to play with Dog.

* * *

It's a few days later when Wise learns the fate of her parents.

We continue on the main road east and follow it until it diverges and continues either north or south. Given Old Man's previous estimations on the whereabouts of his home, we head south.

Wise finally relents to Brock's incessant worrying over her and concedes to riding Horse for at least a little while to appease him. Suddenly, I realize Horse's consistent hoofbeats have ceased, and when I turn, I see that Wise has stopped the mount in the middle of the road. She stares straight ahead, as if seeing something the rest of us aren't.

Brock, too, notices and hurries back to her side. "Wise? Wise? Are you all right?"

"Through the trees and down the hill," she says quietly. "We need to go that way."

Brock doesn't question her any further, but simply nods his head and motions for the rest of us to follow.

We make our way along an overgrown path through the trees and emerge on the other side before heading down a small hill.

We see remnants of what used to be a vibrant and flourishing town. It must have been a very large village given the sheer amount of buildings, but every home, shop, barn, or stable is little more than charred rubble buried beneath the obscuring influence of dirt and weeds. While it's impossible to say how long ago the place was razed, it has definitely been ill-treated by the hand of time.

Wise leads us to what used to be the town square. Brock helps her to dismount from Horse, and she wanders to the vestiges of what used to be a large fountain, now little more than a pile of pulverized rock. We see several carts, their horses long escaped or perished, and other miscellaneous trappings hastily discarded by the former inhabitants of the vacant town.

"There was a festival here," says Wise. "A big harvest festival. They held it every year. I remember sitting near this fountain and watching the jugglers and firebreathers with the other children who had come to watch." She points to a crumbling foundation nearby. "That was the inn. The innkeeper was very kind and used to save me the best pumpkin pasties. They were always piping hot and tasted of cinnamon." Her expression becomes sad, and I see her hands begin to tremble slightly. "When they came... Abirad's men, my mother and father told me to go with the other children and some of the women and hide in the inn. They said they'd keep us safe and make sure none of them reached us but..." She can't continue the thought, and the rest of us, save for Lark seem to understand what she implies.

"Well, did they?" he asks, clearly in suspense to hear the answer.

Wise gives him the ghost of a smile. "They tried."

She looks back down the road we had followed into town. "We didn't live in the town. We lived east somewhere, but we used to come visit from time to time. The festival was a grand affair though. My father... he used to live here when he was younger. That's why we were here that day. We had come for the festival."

Wise looks down the central road of the town. She hesitates for a moment, and Brock gently touches her shoulder, speaking softly to her.

"Wise? Are you okay?" he asks.

She stares back at him, and I see an expression of pain in her eyes. "I don't want to go down there, but I know I have to. I just... I feel like I need to." She shakes her head, and I can see that she's fighting to control her emotions.

"Wise," I say as I come to stand by her side. "Take your time. We're all here for you."

Brock nods and wordlessly offers her his hand. At first, Wise hesitates, but eventually she accepts it in her own. She leads us further down the road, and we come upon another small hill. What we see at the base of the hill surprises and appalls us.

Graves, marked only with crossed sticks or large stones, dot the land as far as the eye can see.

"The soldiers flooded the festival. Abirad was with them. I remember hearing something like music, singing stones maybe. They'd sound just before one of the buildings would be lit aflame, and those inside would either run out, straight into the range of the guards' weapons, or be trapped inside and perish."

"My mother and father tried to protect as many of us as they could, but they fell before Abirad's men, and then, when the inn was set ablaze, I was coughing, and I could barely see. I stumbled out of the inn, and one of the soldiers loaded me into a cart that had been fashioned into little more than a giant cage on wheels. We were crammed in there tightly, and we could still hear the screams of the dying as the cart took us away and back to Abirad's castle."

Something catches Wise's eye. There's an enormous oak tree to the right of the makeshift cemetery, and beneath it are two large, flat, white stones. Wise draws closer, and when she sees the crude etchings in the stones, she falls upon her knees.

Brock kneels beside her and places a hand upon her back to comfort her as she weeps. She succumbs to racking sobs, and he wraps his arms around her, pressing his head against hers and whispering a gentle "shh" into her ear and rocking her slightly.

Lark moves forward, stopping in front of the two stones. "Meggory," he reads aloud. He looks at the other grave directly next to it. He reads the second name. "Emrys."

Wise nods. "Those were my parents' names," she confirms, her voice strained.

❊ ❊ ❊

Unlike our visits to the other towns, we waste no further time in this place. Anything of use or value has long since been lost or taken, and Wise insists we move as far away from the town as possible before nightfall as she's not keen on remaining close to where her parents perished.

"I've seen enough for five lifetimes," says Wise quietly.

We continue east and come upon another huge expanse of forest. After a while, we find a rather large clearing and set up camp. Despite the cold, Wise sits as far away from the fire as possible. Perhaps she is still recovering from the painful memory of the village being razed. Even well into the night, she still can't seem to fall asleep. Brock snores peacefully at one of her sides, and Lark tosses and turns at her other while Dog stretches out across the kid's feet.

I extricate myself from under the sleeping Scarlet and make my way over to Wise. I sit down across from her but say nothing. Instead, I simply offer my presence so she doesn't feel so alone.

When she speaks, her voice is hoarse from crying and lack of use. "When we were captive at the castle, do you know the one thing that, even in the worst times, kept me going?"

I shake my head and wait for her to continue.

"I spent all that time dreaming of escaping, hoping that, perhaps, someone was missing me. Maybe they were even trying to find me. In the end, they were all false hopes. There is no family to come back to. I just feel so... so lost, Boy."

I think back to what Lark had said to me before, about family being more than blood. "I am truly, truly sorry, Wise... about your parents. But, you *do* have a family. Me, Brock, Old Man, Lark... Even Scarlet, as much as she will probably never admit it.

Dog raises his head and I give him a gentle scratch behind the ears. "Yes, and you, Dog." I reach out my hand and clasp Wise's in my own. "Wise, we all need you, and we never would have made it this far without you. You're the one who gives the rest of us strength. You're the one who will do anything to protect us. You fight for us and take care of us, and we love you for it. *We're* your family."

She considers my words for some time, then gives a small nod of agreement. "I suppose you're right. You *are* all my family. If there's one thing I learned from my parents, it's that we should do everything we can to protect others, and I'll do everything in my power to make sure you're all safe and that Lark makes it home to the king. It's the least I can do for my family."

She beckons for me to draw closer, and we exchange a brief embrace. As I move to return to my area, I see that Brock's eyes are now open, and he silently mouths the words "thank you" to me. He gives Wise a questioning look, and as usual, they seem to be able to communicate without words. She gives a slight nod, and Brock moves his blanket closer to her.

Despite the horrors of the day, she falls asleep peacefully in his arms, dreaming and hoping for better days.

CHAPTER 20

Recent rain has left the road muddy, and soon we're covered from head to toe in muck and grime. Needless to say, it is a welcome sound when we hear the rush of water not far from the main road. Scarlet scouts the area and finds there is a waterfall that feeds into a crystal clear pool. Given the recent cool weather, by all accounts, the water would be uncomfortably chilly to bathe in, but as luck would have it, a small hot spring also contributes to the pool, making the water a manageable temperature.

Given the girls' recent complaints of our stench, the males among us clean up first, and when we've finished, and Lark has his fill of Brock and I chasing him around in the pool and dunking him under the water, we head back to our camp. Scarlet goes next while Wise removes the bandages from her shoulder and inspects the wound beneath. Despite my lack of expertise in such things, it seems to me she's healing very well, and the use of her arm is growing less painful for her.

When Scarlet returns, Wise heads to the pool while the rest of us settle around a small fire for our midday meal. We're all in great spirits, laughing and joking amicably, when the shouting starts.

Brock's eyes widen with panic at the sound of Wise's cries, and he moves faster than I've ever seen him do so before. "Wise!"

Scarlet and I are at his heels with the rest of our party some distance behind us. I hear Dog barking as he gains on me. We make our way as quickly as we can, and when we arrive at the pool, we are startled by what we see.

On the opposite bank from us, a man of immense stature has Wise slung over his shoulder and appears to be trying to carry her off. He is easily one of the tallest men I have ever seen. His brown hair falls to the base of his neck, and his brown eyes are marked with determination as he attempts to thwart Wise's attempts to evade his grasp. Wise strains against him, and despite his enormous muscles, she manages to free herself enough to punch him as hard as she can square in his nose. The living mountain of a man lets out a growl of irritation and reclaims his hold on her, again attempting to make off with her.

"Let me go, you oaf!" shouts Wise, pummeling his back with her fists.

"You're coming with me." His voice is deep and slightly gravelly. He pays no heed to her protests and turns towards the east.

The stranger is exceptionally intimidating. Given his appearance, he has the bearing of a battle-hardened warrior, though he looks to be only a few years older than Quellin, maybe in his mid-twenties. Every inch of exposed skin is covered in scars. Most prominent among these is a grievous looking injury, long since healed, that mars the entirety of the left side of his face, and makes his already terrifying visage even more fearsome. The scar extends from the bottom of his chin to the top of his forehead and just barely misses his eye. There is an enormous greatsword connected to a baldric at his back, and a large dagger at his belt, and I'm sure he's quite adept with both. There is no mistaking it: this is a man who has been bred for battle and forged by the ravages of war.

"Hey! Let her go!" shouts Lark, darting past me. Dog is at his side, and he ferociously barks and growls at the man.

"Lark! Stay back!" yells Wise, fearful for his safety.

Lark freezes in his tracks.

The man's gaze snaps towards us, and he looks more annoyed than anything else. A stream of blood drips from his nose from where Wise hit him, and he wipes it away with the back of his hand. Brock and I already have our weapons unsheathed and move to intercept the brute while Scarlet throws a dagger that just narrowly misses his head and embeds in a tree nearby.

With one arm balancing Wise still slung over his shoulder, he uses his other hand to free his weapon, and I can't help but to be a bit impressed as I've never seen anyone, even the most fearsome of Abirad's guards, wield a blade of such a size with a single hand. This man is easily the strongest I have ever encountered.

"Stay back," he growls. "I have no quarrel with you, and I don't seek to kill children. But if you get in my way, I can't promise I won't hurt you."

"Let her go!" shouts Brock angrily. "If you don't release her, you *will* have a quarrel with me. With all of us."

The man rolls his eyes and readies his weapon, paying no mind to the fact that Wise is still incessantly banging on his back with all her might.

"Be careful, Brock," I warn. "We don't want to accidentally hurt Wise."

Brock moves to close with the giant. He attempts to attack on the side opposite Wise, but the warrior easily knocks his sword away with such force that it immediately disarms Brock, sending his blade skittering across the ground. Another dagger flies through the air just missing the man's left leg, and I can hear Scarlet swear under her breath. I dash forward and swing my blade towards his knees to decrease the risk of hitting Wise in the process. With a slight frown, the man steps on the flat of my blade and pins it to the ground, causing me to fall forward.

"Are we done here?" he asks, his tone one of boredom.

That's when we hear the hum of the singing stones. The stranger hears it, too, and freezes in his tracks.

"By your look, I'm guessing you know what these are," says Old Man loudly.

"Aye. I do," agrees the stranger.

"Then you know what they are capable of. Unhand the girl, and we'll let you leave in peace," promises Old Man.

The man snorts in derision. "I'm more frightened of what will happen if I return without her than being obliterated by your pretty rocks," states the stranger.

"What do you mean?" I demand, then unconsciously take a slight step back when the stranger turns his penetrating gaze upon me.

The man forcefully tosses his sword on the ground and sets Wise upon her feet, but he maintains his grip on her shoulder. When she cries out, he appears startled and seems to suddenly notice the outline of the stitches through her damp shirt. He mutters an apology and holds her by the opposite shoulder.

"I need her to come with me," he says firmly.

"Why?" demands Brock. "What do you want with her?"

The man gives Brock a steely look. "I have reason to believe she's kin to the All-Chieftain."

"All-Chieftain?" A look of recognition crosses Old Man's face. "Ah! You're a Bromus, then?"

The stranger, barely blinking and never once taking his eyes off of us, gives a slight nod. "Aye."

"Bromus?" I look to Old Man questioningly.

"They're a group of clans that answer to no king," he explains. "Instead, they're governed by chieftains, and greatest among them is their All-Chieftain. He is charged with acting as their leader and seeing to the benefit of all the clans." Old Man returns his attention to the warrior before us. "So, you're one of the All-Chieftain's men?"

The man spits upon the ground before him. "I'm my own man... but for now, I work for him, aye."

"Why are you so sure that our friend is related to this All-Chieftain?" asks Scarlet, and I see Wise smile slightly at Scarlet using the term *friend*.

Wordlessly, the warrior turns Wise to face him. He holds her gaze for the briefest of moments, then pulls down the right sleeve of her shirt, exposing the unusual birthmark on the back of her shoulder to us. "Because of *that*," he says firmly.

"It's just a birthmark," responds Wise dismissively.

He gazes down at her, and for a moment, he seems to be studying her, as if looking for something. "All of his direct line bear that mark, including the All-Chieftain himself. It's the mark of the Oak Clan, of whom the All-Chieftain belongs."

"The Oak Clan..." repeats Old Man. "Yes... I've read of them. They have been led by the Oakheart line for many generations. Their leaders are well-respected as fair and reasonable, even among those outside of the Bromus, but they also have a reputation as fierce warriors and brilliant tacticians." Old Man looks to the rest of us. "If this man means to bring us to their leader, then it may be in our best interest to go willingly."

Wise looks up at the stranger defiantly. "Do you often manhandle people who you believe to be related to your All-Chieftain?"

The stranger appears taken aback by her boldness, but his shock quickly shifts to mild amusement. "I've seen a lot of his kin- what's left of them, anyway- since the wars with that bloody sorcerer, and I haven't seen your face around." He lowers his voice and bends down a bit so that his face is eye-level with Wise. "I'd remember it." He picks up his sword from the ground and replaces it in the sheathe on his back.

Wise blushes slightly, unsure of his meaning, but seeming to take it as a compliment. "Fair enough."

"The All-Chieftain had a grandchild... went missing some years ago... a girl," he explains. He cocks his head slightly, continuing to study Wise. "He keeps a drawing of the girl's mother, his daughter, in his war room. Says it reminds him of why he's fighting. She was killed by some of Abirad's men alongside her husband." He pauses for a moment. "I've seen that drawing, and you look so like her that they'd say you could be her, come back from the dead."

"You said some years ago," says Wise quietly. "How long?"

The stranger shrugs. "Hell if I know; I'm not a clan historian."

Wise narrows her eyes at him, and he lets out an exasperated sigh.

"Bloody hell, girl. I don't know! Must have been at least thirteen or so years ago," he responds.

"Thirteen years?" I hear myself repeat.

"Aye. I reckon," he agrees.

I know Wise had been imprisoned for some time before my arrival—Old Man had told me so much— but I never realized exactly how long. Old Man had been right; he would have been a very small child when she was taken, probably half Lark's age.

"You could have just told me all this," states Wise crossly. "It would have spared us both a great deal of aggravation and might have saved you a bloody nose."

His mouth drops open in shock, and I can't believe she is being so forceful with him. The difference in their height is almost laughable. Wise is of average height, and this man is nearly a foot taller than she is, standing halfway between 6 and 7 feet. Yet, somehow, he seems more intimidated by her than she is of him.

"I would have gone with you if you would have just told me your reason. Why didn't you say something before trying to carry me off like some barbarian?" she asks.

The warrior opens his mouth to say something but can't seem to form any words. "I-I hadn't thought of it, all right? Most people aren't too keen on being friendly when I approach them." He gestures to the disfiguring scar on his face.

"Well, I'm not most people," she says as she shoves past him.

"Clearly!" he agrees.

"So, are you going to take me to this All-Chieftain or not?" asks Wise.

His eyes widen in disbelief, and the look of bewilderment on his face is amusing. I almost feel sorry for him. He looks like a dog who has just been scolded by its master and is now tucking its tail between its legs in apology.

He glances towards the rest of us as if asking for some explanation of Wise's fearlessness. I simply shrug in reply, and he gestures for us to follow him.

"Come on then. This way," he mutters.

Wise convinces him to wait long enough for us to collect Horse and our belongings, then we are on our way.

"Nice horse," comments the warrior as he leads us through the forest and towards the Bromus encampment. "Almost as big as mine."

Lark gapes up at him. "Your horse is bigger than this one?" he asks incredulously.

The stranger smirks in amusement. "Aye. But more foul-tempered... like his rider."

Lark frowns slightly and looks up at the gargantuan man. "You don't seem so scary to me."

The warrior stops suddenly and stares down at Lark who evenly matches his gaze without flinching. "Well... That's a first." He almost sounds impressed.

Wise walks next to the stranger, casting an occasional glance up at him. Finally she asks, "What's your name?"

He grunts. "Mostly, they just call me The Cur."

"Isn't a cur another word for a mean dog?" asks Lark.

"Aye," the warrior replies.

"Why do they call you that?" the kid questions.

"On account of my clan," he responds. "The Cur Clan."

Old Man raises an eyebrow questioningly. "I've read up on all the clans, and the Cur Clan is said to be extinct. One book I read said they turned against each other and warred themselves into oblivion."

"That's partly right," agrees the stranger. "There's but one of us left."

"You're the only one left in your clan?" asks Wise, and I

can hear the note of sympathy in her voice.

"Aye," he replies.

"*Aye,*" repeats Lark, doing his best to impersonate the warrior. "Does that mean *yes,* then?"

A slight chuckle escapes the man. "Aye."

"I like that. I'm going to start saying *aye,*" remarks Lark agreeably. "Do all Bromus talk like you?"

"Aye, all that I've met," comes the reply.

"You told me what they call you, but you still haven't told me your name," reminds Wise.

The warrior stops to look at her inquisitively. "Why are you so intent on knowing?"

She shrugs. "Names are important. I don't even know mine. None of us do. That's why I'm called Wise."

The warrior, of course, doesn't seem to comprehend how someone wouldn't know his or her name, and Wise proceeds to recount information of our imprisonment as well as our journey thus far. When she's completed the tale, he looks down at her with a strange mix of emotions present on his face. There is awe, disbelief, and even something that seems akin to sympathy.

He regards her in silence for several moments before speaking a single word. "Albain."

"Albain?" she repeats.

"Aye," he responds simply.

Lark giggles. "*Aye.*"

CHAPTER 21

After a rather lengthy trek, we arrive at the Bromus encampment. Though Albain has been very indulgent and patient with Lark's incessant chattering and endless questions, he seems relieved when we finally get there.

As we pass through the sprawling area of tents, we are the recipients of an innumerable amount of curious stares and frenzied whispers.

"Who are those strangers?"
"Why are they here?"
"The dark haired girl… does she look a wee bit familiar to ye?"

"Where are they heading?"
"The All-Chieftain will want to hear about this."

"We don't host outsiders," Albain mentions to us. "It's no wonder there are gawkers."

As much as we seem to be a source of interest, I overhear just as many mentions of The Cur. It isn't difficult to gather that he seems to be seen as much as an outsider here as we are. If he hears their gossip, he pays it no mind, but I see Wise frown occasionally when she picks up on the harsh tones the others seem to have reserved for him.

"The Cur. What's he up to now?"
"Wish he'd go back wherever he came from."
"He doesn't belong here."
"He's lucky the All-Chieftain finds him useful. Otherwise,

you know he wouldn't be allowed here."

"Beastly man. He looks like hell itself chewed him up and spit him back out."

Eventually, Wise reaches her limit, and she looks up at Albain. There's a deep set frown on her face, and it's a look I know all too well. It's that look she gets when she decides that something is an injustice that must be righted. "If you're correct, and this All-Chieftain *is* my grandfather, I'll be having some words with him about the behavior of his people. I don't much care for their idle gossip."

Albain chuckles slightly, a sound that seems somewhat unnatural from a man such as him. I get the impression getting that giant to abandon his surliness and display any sign of humor is quite a feat, but Wise and Lark already seem to be quite adept at it. "Well, you certainly sound like an heir."

We soon arrive at our destination, one of the largest tents in the area. Outside of it are two large guards, able-bodied looking men dressed in white, linen shirts and blue and green plaid skirts (an item of dress that we learn is common in Bromus culture, even among the men). As we approach, their hands move to their broadswords, but not necessarily in a threatening way. They look fierce enough, though neither of them is anywhere near as large as Albain. One of them is stationed to either side of the opening of the tent, and they look as if they'd make quick work of anyone who sought to enter the tent without their consent.

Albain stops a considerable distance from the tent and is met with inquiring glances from the guards.

"What do you want Cur? And who are these people?" asks one of the guards.

"I've need to see the All-Chieftain," he replies.

One of the guards begins to say something, but before he can utter another word, the flap of the tent parts, and a man with shoulders as broad as a barn steps through. He is barely taller than Wise and wears the same manner of dress as the other Bromus men. However, at his waist is a large, leather pouch decorated with an intricate, silver oak tree. He also wears a silver chain with a pendant that has a similar design. He has deep, blue eyes, and white hair that falls to his shoulders. A thick white beard and moustache, tinged with the slightest hints of red, cover most of his face.

"Cur." The man's voice is deep and stern, and I immediately get the impression he is the type of person whose very presence commands respect. "What's the meaning of this?" As he says it, his eyes scan across our company before settling firmly on Wise. He freezes where he stands, and his complexion blanches, shock evident on his face. He can scarcely force his feet to move, but by degrees, and never taking his eyes off Wise, he slowly comes towards us.

As he approaches, I hear Wise utter a word that is scarcely louder than a breath. "Granda?"

He silently studies Wise, and his eyes travel over her as if looking for something. There is a mixture of excitement and awe present on his face, and I see his large hands begin to tremble slightly. He looks to Albain questioningly.

"Her shoulder. The right," comes his simple reply.

"May I?" The All-Chieftain begins to reach towards Wise, his quivering hands hesitating just inches away from her shoulder.

Wise turns slightly, allowing the man to move the corner of her shirt and expose the tree-shaped mark underneath.

When he sees it, there's a sharp intake of breath, and instantly, the tears begin to well in his eyes. "Y-you must be her. You look just like my Meggie." He steps back slightly, staring at Wise in disbelief. "Eilis?"

At the sound of the name, Wise comes undone, as if devoured by some invisible wave of memory. Her shoulders tremble as she calls out to him. "Granda!"

The All-Chieftain pulls her into a deep embrace, and she buries her head in his neck. "It is you! Eilis! My darling girl!"

They both weep unashamedly, and even the All-Chieftain's guards seeme somewhat touched by the outpouring of emotion that their leader shows at being reunited with his granddaughter.

The Bromus leader fights to speak through his tears. "I knew you were alive! I never gave up hope, Eilis, not even for a moment." He places his hands on her shoulders, and his expression becomes serious as he holds her gaze. "You must know: I never stopped looking for you! I promise you. I never stopped fighting for you!"

"I believe you, Granda," replies Wise sincerely.

"*Granda.* I always hoped I'd hear that word again someday." Reluctantly, he releases her from his grasp, as if terrified that the moment he lets her go she'll simply vanish before his eyes. "Eilis, the moment we heard of the attack on the festival, I led a hundred of my men there. But we were too late. There was not a single survivor. And Meggie..." He takes a breath to steady the tremor in his voice. "I looked at every face we put in a grave, praying you wouldn't be among them, that somehow you escaped. When we found that blasted sorcerer captured some of the folk, I hoped you were among those who still lived. We have fought with all our might against him. We've given Abirad's men hell at every opportunity. We even tried a direct assault on the castle a few years back..."

Something dawns on me. A few years ago, we were all sequestered in our cells for nearly a week. No one was permitted to come or go, work was neglected, and the entirety of the castle seemed to be in a state of chaos. During that time, we heard nothing but constant shouts and loud noises. We were kept in the dark as to what was going on, but it occurs to me that it was likely the assault he is referring to.

"We tried, but we failed," remarks the All-Chieftain sadly. "We lost many men in the attempt. I'm so sorry, my dear girl. I failed you, my love."

She gently places her hands on his cheeks. "Granda, you didn't fail me. You never gave up on me. You could have just assumed I was lost to you forever or dead, but you kept fighting for me."

"It is a miracle you are here, Eilis, and if I died tomorrow, I would die a happy man at seeing you returned to me. Here. Where you belong. How did you come to find us?" he asks.

Wise looks around frantically. "Where's Albain?"

Among the crowd that has gathered, his retreating form towers over the rest. His back is to us and he's making his way from the area.

"Albain?" asks the All-Chieftain, his expression one of confusion. "Oh! You mean The Cur."

Wise frowns. "He has a name, Granda. Albain!"

Albain stops at the sound of his name. He turns to look at us but makes no move to rejoin us.

"Cur!" calls the All-Chieftain. "Er- Albain. You've done a great service for me and all of the Oak Clan. You've returned Eilis, my granddaughter, my heir, to me. What would you have of me in return? Name it, and you shall have it."

Albain glances to Wise, whose face has erupted in an enormous grin as her grandfather places his arm around her shoulders. Albain shakes his head. "I want nothing."

"Surely there must be something!" insists the All-Chieftain.

Albain once again resumes his departure, but as he leaves, I hear him mutter, "I've already claimed my reward."

Wise beckons us forward to meet her grandfather, who introduces himself as Seamus Oakheart. He is more than gracious and thanks us countless times for the part we played in bringing his beloved kin home.

Wise and her grandfather retreat to his tent so that they may have time alone to reconnect. The rest of us go our separate ways. Brock decides to explore the encampment in search of some form of amusement, and Lark, saying that he wants to find Albie (as he has taken to calling Albain- a name I am sure the coarse warrior will certainly love) wanders off with Dog. While I'm not sure it's a grand idea, as his primary guardian is otherwise occupied, Scarlet allows it. Old Man, ever thirsty for knowledge, sets off to find the clan historian.

Scarlet and I decide to take a walk around the area to better acclimate to our new surroundings. Having been personally greeted by the All-Chieftain, everyone is exceptionally friendly towards us. We learn more names than we will ever be able to recall, and every now and again, someone pops out of a tent to offer us a tankard of cider or some delicious smelling food.

We pass a group of children, boys and girls around Lark's age and many even younger, playing in a small meadow that is filled with fragrant, white flowers.

A little girl bounds up to us, her freckled face claimed by an enormous grin. Her red pigtails bounce upon her shoulders as she begins to fall into step with us, skipping next to Scarlet.

"I like your hair," says the little girl. "It looks like mine."

"I like your hair, too," responds Scarlet. She is often so sarcastic and quick-witted that to see her engagements with Lark and other children is truly a treat. She is so kind and gentle towards them.

The little girl hands Scarlet one of the white flowers from the field. "Here. You may wear it. It'll look pretty on you."

"Thank you." Scarlet immediately tucks the flower behind her ear and makes a big deal about displaying it proudly and talking of what a wonderful gift it is.

The girl, pleased with Scarlet's reaction, bounces off again.

My fingers touch the flower before lightly caressing Scarlet's cheek. "Beautiful," I tell her. "Absolutely beautiful."

She blushes. "We can get one for you, too, if you like it so much."

"No, thanks. I'm sure it wouldn't look anywhere near as good on me."

We continue on our walk, and Scarlet comments, "You

know... I could live in a place like this. Everyone is so friendly. But they'd also readily stab anyone who crosses them. This is my kind of people."

On the west side of the camp, near the dining tent, we come upon Brock. He's drinking a mug of cider and is surrounded by five or six Bromus girls. As we pass, I hear him recounting the story of our journey so far, though Scarlet and I both note that in his retelling he adds a few extra battles that never happened for optimal effect.

We are all exhausted and are provided with comfortable lodging where we get some much-needed rest. Wise and Scarlet are given a tent to share, and the rest of us reside in another. After some time, the All-Chieftain summons us to his tent, and we sit down with him to share a meal.

We all gather around his table and are presented with a rather expansive spread. I find myself on one side of Wise while Lark is on the other. The change in Wise's disposition is undeniable. She seems so comfortable and at peace now that she is back with her grandfather and their people.

"So, what should I call you now?" I ask, as I take another huge bite of roasted turkey.

Wise shrugs. "Call me Eilis; call me Wise. It matters not. I'm just glad to be home."

"Eilis is a pretty name," comments Lark, "and since you have a proper name now, we should call you that."

I nod in agreement. "That settles it then."

After our meal, we head back to our respective tents, and on the way, Lark and I pass by Albain who says he's off to find someone to spar with. Lark seizes his hand, and I can tell the warrior is not used to people just coming up and touching him.

"Albie," says Lark.

Albain rolls his eyes. "I do wish you wouldn't keep calling me that." He sighs. "What is it, Lark?"

"I'm very grateful we have somewhere to sleep, but the guards told me that I have to sleep in that tent," he explains, gesturing to the tent he shares with Brock, Old Man, and me.

Albain appears confused. "What's the problem then?

"I don't like being away from Eilis," he says. "I feel safer when she's with me."

Albain kneels beside him so he's closer to the kid's eye level. "I can understand why. She's so fierce she scares even me."

Lark laughs. "Eilis isn't scary. She's the best!"

Albain gestures to his face. "Tell that to my poor nose." He puts a hand on Lark's shoulder. "Look, she's just right over there in the other tent, and I'm sure if you have need of her she'd be with you in an instant, but you've nothing to fear while you're here."

"Because you can protect us now?" questions Lark.

Albain shakes his head. "You don't need me to protect you, Lark. The first time you saw me, when you thought I meant Eilis harm, you faced me down without so much as flinching, and even now, you look me dead in the eye when I talk to you. Not many, even the bravest warriors, can claim to do that. You'll be just fine, boy."

Lark nods in understanding and suddenly wraps his arms around Albain's neck in an unexpected embrace. The latter's eyes widen with shock, and not knowing what to do in such a situation, he looks like an animal caught in a trap. His arms raise up to his sides as if begging for mercy.

Lark releases him, and the minute he lets go, Albain's slight smile is replaced with his usual scowl.

The warrior moves to depart but stops suddenly as he catches sight of Eilis, who had emerged from her tent at some point during this exchange. Given the look of admiration upon her face, she had likely witnessed all of it.

They hold each other's gazes for several moments, and something seems to pass between them before Albain lumbers off into the distance.

CHAPTER 22

Word of Eilis's return spreads like wildfire, and by the time we awake the next morning, it appears as if the encampment has multiplied in size. The entirety of the area is a flurry of activity as people rush to and fro tending to whatever matters they may have. We learn that immediately after her return, messengers had been dispatched to the other clans, and they had all come to pay tribute to the All-Chieftain's heir.

At breakfast, the All-Chieftain is in very good humor as he explains there will be a feast held that evening, and there he will formally claim his granddaughter as his heir.

"I never realized the Bromus clans could unite so quickly," comments Old Man.

"Normally, our people are more spread out across these lands, but we have been planning another campaign against Abirad. We were intending on another frontal assault to the castle in the next few months, so we began rallying our folk to prepare for battle. While some of the clans are still a few weeks' out, several of the closest allies of the Oak Clan, those who are my personal advisors on the war council, will be represented here tonight."

Afterwards, Lark and Dog trot off to play with some of the Bromus children while the rest of us follow the All-Chieftain to his war room, a rather large tent near the rear of the encampment. Once there, we are met by representatives from several of the other clans. Each clan wears their colors proudly displayed on their "kilts" as their skirt-like garments are called, so it makes it at least a bit easier to tell who hails from each clan.

First, we are introduced to Dennan of the Wolf Clan. He is a large, imposing figure, though not quite as tall as Albain. His light brown hair falls in waves upon his shoulders, and he has a deep voice that resonates through the war room. He and the others of his clan have tan skin, and most of them sport a collection of large, tribal tattoos. Dennan himself has a rather large tribal band that takes up most of his left forearm. There is a certain wildness about him and his clan, a certain feral nature that commands attention.

As Dennan inquires about our journey, I find he is one of those rare types of people who one cannot help but to like instantly. He is easygoing and charismatic, and the other Bromus seem to think very highly of his skills as a warrior. He also seems to be a favorite of the All-Chieftain, as the latter insists on Dennan getting to know Eilis, a request that he is all too willing to oblige. He seems quite taken with Eilis, and the two spend quite some time in conversation together.

"While you know you have my affection, I must admit, that Dennan fellow is quite handsome," Scarlet whispers to me.

"I understand the appeal, and I take no offense. He is very likeable," I say. "Don't worry. I'm not like Brock; I promise not to get jealous."

Scarlet pats me on the shoulder. "If you were like Brock, I'd have absolutely no interest in you. By the way, did you notice how sulky he is today?" She gestures to Brock, who is keeping to himself and leaning against a post in the corner of the tent.

"He has seemed a bit off since we got here," I admit.

Next, we meet Magnus, the Chieftain of the Bear Clan, and his son Ragnar. Magnus is a stern, reserved man, but his son is quite a jovial sort. He always seems to have a smile on his broad face. Like the other men of his clan, Ragnar is on the shorter side, but stocky and strong. His hair is of a gold color, and he has the beginnings of a beard that is flecked with shades of red. His bright blue eyes look like liquid sky, and he has an infectious laugh and amiable nature that instantly puts everyone at ease. He also seems to take an interest in Eilis, and spends time entertaining her by playing his lute and sharing his favorite Bromus songs with our group.

We watch as Eilis converses with her grandfather. We, as well as she, know that these introductions are not just about diplomacy, and she does not seem particularly pleased by the All-Chieftain's attempts to present her to the most eligible bachelors among the clans. Eilis has already told me that her grandfather has brought up the need to continue the Oakheart line, and has already mentioned several times that she will need to one day choose a husband and make heirs of her own.

Once again, I see Dennan approach Eilis, and the two speak of topics unheard by the rest of us. Whatever they are discussing, they both laugh at intervals and seem to be enjoying each other's company.

Ragnar, still seated next to us, chuckles to himself. "Well, I suppose I know who my competition is."

Scarlet snorts. "You speak of courtship as if it's some kind of sport."

Ragnar shakes his head. "No, not for me, but Dennan will turn anything into a form of combat. He's a bit rough around the edges, but he's a good man," replies Ragnar.

"So, you plan on courting Eilis?" I ask him.

"To be honest, when my father demanded I come here with him, I wasn't too keen on the idea of being shown about like a prized cow headed for market, but Eilis is quite unlike anyone I've ever met before. I'm of a mind to serve as suitor to her."

Behind us, I hear Brock grumble under his breath.

"So, are you an heir as well?" asks Lark.

"Aye," answers Ragnar. "There's just me and my sister, Pala, and I'm firstborn."

"What about that one?" asks Old Man, gesturing to Dennan.

"Dennan? He's a third son, but they say he's the greatest of the Wolf Clan's warriors. I've seen him fight, and I don't doubt it," replies Ragnar. "The All-Chieftain favors him. In battle, Dennan serves on the vanguard."

"And what about you? You seem quite unlike the rest of the warriors here," comments Scarlet casually. "That is, unless you plan on clobbering your enemies with a lute."

Ragnar laughs loudly, a pleasant sound that seems to bring a smile to everyone around him. "If I could, I would. I'm told I'm an adept fighter, but sometimes one has to rely on diplomacy instead of brute strength to accomplish things. I find it prudent to use both my words and my weapons."

Dennan, a smirk upon his face, saunters up to us. "There's nothing that can't be solved with strength and a bold heart." He puts Ragnar in a headlock and drags his knuckles over Ragnar's hair to muss it up.

Ragnar gives the much larger man a playful shove. "Plenty that can't be solved with fists and steel, Dennan. Just because you haven't found an obstacle you can't smash your way through doesn't mean they don't exist." Ragnar goes back to strumming on his lute.

"That's quite a talent you have," I comment.

"Do you play?" Ragnar asks.

I shake my head. "Not much time for such things at Castle Ciar."

"I suppose not," he replies.

Dennan spits on the ground in disgust. "May the Maker strike that fool sorcerer down where he stands, or at least give me the opportunity to put my axe through his bloody skull."

Ragnar hands me the lute. "Here. I can teach you if you'd like. It's not so hard. Unless you have branches for fingers like Dennan," he teases.

Ragnar is an excellent teacher, and it's not long before I can play a very simple tune. I feel Scarlet's gaze upon me as I play, and I blush slightly at her attentiveness. She must notice because she gives me a wink as I mimic what Ragnar teaches me.

Suddenly, we hear the All-Chieftain's voice. "Eilis, come here, my dear." He crosses the room and suddenly beckons for his granddaughter

She approaches him, and he takes her by the hand and leads her to the back of the tent where a large table is set up to accommodate the members of the war council.

On the back wall of the tent is a beautiful charcoal portrait of a woman who looks remarkably like Eilis.

"Your mother," says the All-Chieftain softly. "I know that she is surely looking down upon us with gladness to see you home again." He presses a kiss to her cheek. "She would be so proud of the young woman that you have become. I promise you, Eilis, we will see her and your father avenged. Emrys was a good man, and he loved my Meggie dearly." The All-Chieftain smiles sadly. "I don't know what you recall of your father, Maker rest his soul, but he wasn't born a Bromus. He was a woodsman from Oak Grove, the same village where he fell. You can imagine, I wasn't too keen on your mother forming a relationship with an outsider, but he proved himself to be worthy of her, and I was honored to welcome him into my family. And he loved you... with all his heart. They both did."

Eilis wraps her arms around her grandfather's broad frame. "In the end, they were both so brave. They cared nothing for their own wellbeing. Instead, they did all they could to save others. We'll see to it that they didn't die in vain. I promise you that, Granda."

* * *

After we meet the representatives from the Fox and Raven Clans, the All-Chieftain leaves us to our own devices. We pass the time in each other's company until the evening when it is time for the feast and something that the Bromus call a Round. Eilis's grandfather was kind enough to locate us some suitable attire for the evening.

I wait for Scarlet outside of the tent that she shares with Eilis, and when she emerges, I feel as if I am looking upon some agent of the divine. Her crimson hair has been freshly brushed, and her skin smells of lavender soap. She wears a long, flowing, green gown that seems to make her hair appear all the redder in the flames of the torches that light the path to the feasting area. I offer her my arm, and she loops hers through mine.

The dining tent has been adorned with all manner of décor depicting the various symbols of the clans that are present. The banner for the Oak Clan, certainly the largest banner of them all, hangs in the center-rear of the tent. To its left is the blue, black, and silver plaid emblazoned with the symbol of the Wolf Clan. To the right of the Oak Clan is the banner for the Bear Clan, a large, white bear head set on the colors of forest green and red. As we enter, the orange, green, and brown banner for the Fox Clan hangs just to our left, and the black and gold of the Raven Clan is to our right.

I scan the crowd for the rest of my companions. Brock, Old Man, and Lark have already claimed a table in the rear of the room, not far from the raised platform upon which are two large, wooden chairs. The All-Chieftain is seated in one of them while Eilis is to his left.

Dog is seated at attention on a bench next to Lark. None of the Bromus take exception to the fact that the canine has decided he is equal to people, even though he occasionally attempts to snag morsels of food from the plates of passersby. Lark rectifies this by taking a large hunk of meat off his own plate and placing it in front of an elated Dog.

Just behind us is a table occupied by only one person. Albain has done away with his travelling clothes and instead wears something akin to the other Bromus men. He wears an off-white linen shirt, and a kilt of a deep red and black tartan. He sits with his arms crossed over his chest, his usual uninviting expression residing upon his face.

Once everyone has assembled, one of the All-Chieftain's

men calls for order, and all eyes turn towards the platform where the All-Chieftain, a beaming smile present on his face, awaits our attention.

"My brothers and sisters, today we are assembled for a most fortuitous reason," begins the All-Chieftain. "We have recently been blessed with the return of my own granddaughter, Eilis Oakheart, and it is with a glad heart that today I shall name her as my heir.

"Many of you had the opportunity to know my Meggie, and you even welcomed her husband, Eilis's father, Emrys, into our clan and our lives. There is no question that the young woman before me has inherited the best qualities of her parents, may the Maker rest them. She has her mother's kindness, beauty, and ferocity, as well as her father's wit and calm. I have no doubt that she will prove to be a great leader when I can no longer serve you as I would need to.

"And so, without further ado…" He reaches around the back of his neck and unclasps the chain of the pendant that bears the Oak Clan symbol. He steps behind Eilis and delicately places it around her neck, fastening the clasp there. "I hereby proclaim Eilis Oakheart of the Oak Clan as the All-Chieftain To Be."

The gathered crowd erupts in resounding cheers, applause, and whistles, and I see Eilis's face redden at the overwhelming amount of attention. After she makes the rounds to thank the clans for their support, she breathlessly seats herself at our table.

Old Man smiles broadly at her. "I've no doubt you'll be an excellent All-Chieftain one day, my dear. While warriors are plentiful among the Bromus, it takes a great mind to set the course for one's people."

"Thankfully, I had a good teacher," responds Eilis smilingly, and she places a chaste kiss upon his cheek.

"Eilis, when you're All-Chieftain, can I be on your war council?" asks Lark.

Eilis gives his hand a squeeze. "I'd be honored to have

you, Lark. I think you'd be the first Prince of Allanon to ever serve in such a role." Eilis scans the assembled masses.

"Who are you looking for?" asks Brock inquisitively.

"Albain," replies Eilis. "I haven't had a chance to thank him for everything."

Brock's demeanor immediately changes. He frowns and seems annoyed by the very mention of the warrior. Perhaps he still holds some grudge against Albain for the manner in which we met him.

Finally, we catch sight of Albain as he makes his way to his seat at the table behind us. He places a heaping plate of food and a large tankard of cider in front of him before sitting down. Eilis rises from her chair and approaches him while the rest of us remain where we are.

Albain raises his eyes to meet hers. "What then? Come to finish me off?" he asks. He gestures to the cut and bruising on his nose then proceeds to take a big swig from his tankard.

"Actually, I wanted to apologize, and to thank you."

He straightens in his seat. "Apologize? I've had worse. And as for your thanks, think nothing of it."

Eilis sits down next to him, and he raises an eyebrow slightly as if he is surprised by her continuing attention. "I think everything of it, and of you. You've done more for me in the past day than anyone has done for me in my entire life, and I sincerely owe you all of my gratitude." She rests her hand on arm, and I see a strange expression play across his features as his eyes flick up to meet her gaze again. "Truly. Thank you, Albain." She pulls her hand away and glances around the rest of the table. "Why are you over here alone?"

"Why shouldn't I be?" comes his reply.

Lark overhears this and takes the opportunity to join them. Scarlet gives me a meaningful look, and soon the rest of us have joined Albain at his table, save for Brock, who instead crosses to one of the tables claimed by some of the Oak Clan. He seats himself next to a girl with pale skin, raven-black hair, and bright blue eyes. I recognize her as one of the girls who had been captivated by his retelling of our journey. I hear him greet her by her name, Molly, and the two begin chatting amiably. Despite this, I see Brock occasionally glance in our direction, as if monitoring the conversation.

"Hi, Albie!" greets Lark.

"Albie?" questions Eilis with a smirk.

Albain drags his hand over his face and shakes his head. "I swear on the Maker, if he keeps calling me that, I'm going to stab myself with my own sword."

Lark thinks this is hilarious and starts giggling like mad. "Albie, you're funny!"

Albain groans.

Lark looks around at all of the banners hanging around the tent as if scanning the area for something. "Albie, where is your banner?"

"I haven't one," responds Albain gruffly.

"Why?" asks Eilis.

"Because I am not counted amongst the clans." His deep voice is tinged with bitterness. "The Cur Clan had a rather poor reputation, thanks in large part to men like my father, and I am merely considered a hired sword of the Oak Clan, more a mercenary than anything else. I hold no place on the war council and simply do as I am bid."

"*I* count you," replies Eilis assuredly.

The All-Chieftain is involved in some conversation with the Chieftain of the Raven Clan. Upon taking notice of the close proximity of Eilis and Albain, he immediately blanches and hurries towards us. Slightly breathless from his sudden burst of speed, he abruptly stops next to our table. "Eilis, why don't you come join our people?" he suggests, with a brief glance towards Albain. "There are still many who wish to meet you."

Eilis seems to consider his request for a moment, as if searching for some hidden meaning. "Granda, I wish to meet them as well, but as you can see, I *am* with our people. Did you not say I am to be All-Chieftain one day?"

"Well, yes, of course," he readily agrees.

"And is not the Cur Clan among our people?" asks Eilis.

The All-Chieftain's face reddens considerably. His lips forms a tight line, and he avoids answering her question.

Albain smirks, clearly pleased by her response.

"As you wish, Eilis," responds the All-Chieftain. He doesn't seem too happy with his granddaughter's decision, but it seems he has already realized she has a penchant for great stubbornness in certain situations and argues no further.

"Hey, Albain. What's a Round?" asks Lark. "Eilis's Granda says there's going to be one after the feast."

Albain snorts. "It's a lot of banging on drums, blowing on pipes, and prancing around like fools in a big circle. That's why it's called a Round."

"So, it's like a dance?" asks Eilis.

"Yes." Albain practically shudders with disgust.

"Don't you dance?" she inquires with interest.

Albain looks horrified. "Never."

"I think it sounds like fun," speaks Scarlet. "You'll dance with me, won't you, Boy?"

I grin widely. "As if you have to ask! Though, I'll probably just step on your feet mostly."

* * *

The All-Chieftain, along with his war council, make their way to the war tent for a brief meeting before they will allow themselves to join in the festivities. After everyone has eaten and has drunk their fill, we meander to the outside of the tent, and the area erupts in the sounds of laughter and music. Drums, bagpipes, tin whistles, and fiddles harmonize to create loud, boisterous music that spurs everyone into motion. I catch sight of Ragnar, his lute in his hands, among the assemblage of musicians.

Old Man nearly gets swept off his feet by a tall, buxom

woman, her light brown hair in a tight bun, and Lark hops about with a cute little girl with pigtails. Dog uses the opportunity to swipe scraps of unattended food off the tables. I catch sight of Brock who has one arm resting against Molly's waist as they dance about.

A large amount of Bromus men converge in our general area. They chat among themselves and frequently glance over in the direction of our group.

Old Man, his face alight with glee, rejoins us and seems to notice the attention as well. "They're here for you, Eilis."

"What do you mean?" she asks.

"Now that you're heir to the All-Chieftain, I'm sure there will be many of them who are interested in courting you," he explains.

Eilis groans. "So Granda keeps reminding me."

"Yet, not a single one of them has approached her," remarks Scarlet.

Old Man nods. "It could be they're intimidated by her position."

I glance across the way and see that Albain is sitting in a wooden chair. His long legs are stretched out before him, and his brawny arms are crossed over his chest. As usual, he looks annoyed and surly about what's happening around him. I take note that everyone who passes near him gives him a wide berth, as if worried he might snap at them at any moment for having too much fun.

Eilis is gazing longingly at the folk who are merrily dancing about in front of us, so I extend my arm to her.

"Do you want to dance, Eilis? I can dance with you," I propose.

Eilis forces a slight smile but seems a bit sad. I see her glance at Brock who is completely engrossed in his conversation with Molly. "No, that's okay, Boy. You should dance with Scarlet."

I hear a slight cough and turn my head to see Albain. He is standing next to Eilis and wordlessly offers her his hand.

She gives him a questioning glance, but he motions with his head to the dancers around him.

"I thought you don't like dancing," she remarks.

"I don't. But you seem to." He pulls her to his feet, and I watch as he awkwardly attempts to dance with her. His movements are clumsy and unyielding, but Eilis manages to coax a small smile from him, and at one point, I even hear laughter.

"May I?" I offer Scarlet my outstretched hand and she readily accepts.

The sound of the music is invigorating, as if waking some slumbering thing within me. I've never danced in my life, but I can feel the steady beat of the drum and the shrill call of the pipes spurring me to movement. Scarlet and I whirl about each other; there is no particular method to our motions save for what our hearts and feet dictate. I am further thrilled by the brief touches of her hand on my arm, her hair as it touches my cheek, and the sound of her laughter as she twirls around me.

I look around at my friends, all enjoying the same merry dance that I am, and it occurs to me then, I don't think any of us have been truly this happy before. It's as if, for a moment, all of the pain and woes of our pasts are forgotten and borne away on the gentle breeze that flows through the camp.

The music changes, and I notice that all those around us seem to be performing the same moves, everyone perfectly synchronized. I watch as Albain effortlessly hoists Eilis into the air for one of the beats, and I nearly drop poor Scarlet as I try to do the same. Eilis is smiling in a way that I've never seen before, and it warms my heart to see her so at ease. Here, among her people, she is truly home.

I glance across the way to see how the others are faring with this particular number. Old Man and his partner have switched positions, and when it is time for the lifts, she lifts him instead, which the Bromus find hilarious. Lark and his pig-tailed friend have abandoned dancing and instead pound on little drums that have been handed to them. Dog, a large turkey bone still clenched between his teeth, is passed out beneath one of the tables.

Finally, I see Brock. He doesn't regard me with even a simple wave as his attention is otherwise commanded. His gaze is locked on Eilis and Albain, and he seems bothered by their laughter and their closeness. Molly bounds up to him and grabs his hand, and with one last look towards Eilis, I see him guide his newfound companion away from the area.

After a few more songs, sweat pours down my face, and I lead Scarlet towards some chairs. I head into the dining tent and return with two cold ciders, presenting one to her and taking the other for myself. I see several large figures heading towards the Round. It seems the war council's meeting has ended. Dennan catches sight of me and approaches us.

"Your first Round, aye?" he asks. "Freedom is a beautiful thing, isn't it?"

I nod emphatically. "I never thought I'd live to see times like these, and if there is one thing I learned from my time at Abirad's castle, it is to cherish what few good moments life offers."

"Aye. That's good advice." Dennan pats me on the shoulder and pulls up a chair beside me. He watches the dancers before us, and his mouth drops open in disbelief. "I never thought I'd live to see the day that the Cur prances about so. It seems the All-Chieftain To Be has brought him to heel. The Cur answers to no one, yet here he is, merrily hopping about. If anyone can tame him, it will be that woman. She seems to bring some much-needed civility to him. In truth, I didn't even know he could speak before today. I just assumed he communicated by growling and snarling at everyone." He chuckles to himself.

"He's been quite kind to us. Well... other than the whole trying to carry off Eilis thing. But he did bring us here," states Scarlet.

We watch as Albain inclines his head toward Eilis so he can hear something she is saying. A smile affects his features, and Dennan shudders.

"Somehow, he's even more terrifying when he smiles." Dennan rises to his feet. "Well, The Cur has had a long enough turn. I'm cutting in."

We watch as he crosses to Eilis and positions himself between her and Albain. The latter appears somewhat annoyed by the intrusion, but I see Eilis give a gentle squeeze to his hand as she says something to him, her words lost to me by the noise that surrounds us.

* * *

Scarlet and I are among the last people to leave the Round, and I decide to walk her back to her tent before returning to my own. My heart thunders in my chest from all the excitement, and I feel half giddy with joy as we walk hand in hand. She presses a lingering kiss to my lips that makes me dizzy with true happiness, and I wrap my arms around her back, pulling her tight against me.

Our tender moment is interrupted by shouting coming from within the tent she shares with Eilis.

"This is ridiculous!" comes Eilis's voice.

Scarlet and I exchange worried glances, and we move to head inside the tent. Brock hangs by the entrance, so we nearly bump into him as we enter, and Eilis stands at the rear of the tent by her cot. Instantly, I can tell we are walking in to a heated argument. Eilis's face is red with anger, and the look she is giving Brock makes me shudder.

"I think you need to keep your distance from him, Wise!" shouts Brock. "You don't know him! Not really!"

"You're just being jealous! You can't endure the fact that someone else should receive my attention!"

Brock shifts uncomfortably. "I-I…"

"What gives you the right? You've made it abundantly clear, time and time again, that you don't share my degree of affection for you." Eilis's voice quavers with emotion. "What gives you the right to covet my attention now and sulk away when it finds a place with someone else?"

"Wise! I-"

"No! I've done nothing but listen to you since we've met! When have you ever cared about what I have to say? You don't get to care about me when it's convenient for you, and to only pay me any mind when you feel you have no other options!"

I squeeze Scarlet's hand. "Should we leave?" I whisper to her.

She shakes her head emphatically. "No, no, no. I want to see this." There is an unsettling note of glee in her voice as she watches Brock get what she likely feels are his just desserts.

Eilis isn't done yet. "This was one of the most important nights of my life, and did you say more than a few words to me? You've barely even spoken to me since we arrived! And don't you think I saw you sneaking off with that girl, Molly, tonight?"

Brock says nothing, his hands stuffed into the pockets of his trousers.

"You almost abandoned us entirely for Jewel. Then, you fancied Scarlet. Now, since we've been here, you carry on with the first girl you come across, and NOT ONCE have you acknowledged how I felt for you!"

Brock's voice comes out in a single, strangled word. "Felt?"

"Felt! I don't want to be your last choice, Brock. I want to be someone's first." Eilis storms towards the flap of the tent, and as she passes, it's as if she is noticing our presence there for the first time. "I-I'm sorry," she apologizes to us as she disappears outside.

Scarlet and I immediately follow after her, intending to ensure that she is okay. In her desperation to get as far away from Brock as possible, Eilis isn't paying attention to where she's going, and she runs smack into an immense shadow. A faint sliver of moonlight reveals the scarred face of Albain.

She looks up at him, and he must recognize the distress in her features as his typical, forbidding expression softens slightly.

Eilis looks up at him apologetically and continues on her way down the path. Albain looks back at us with a questioning gaze, but then he sees Brock emerging from the tent. He seems to have some sudden realization, and the look he gives Brock chills my blood.

Wordlessly, he turns and follows after Eilis.

CHAPTER 23

The entire camp seems to be off to a late start the following morning. Apparently, the merry making took its toll as nearly everybody we come across looks as if they haven't slept for days. Brock and I decide to take a walk around the camp in an attempt to wake up a bit. He looks absolutely exhausted and peers at me through bleary eyes.

"I waited half the night for Wise to return so I could apologize," he explains through yawns. "Eventually, I got so tired waiting that I was forced to give up. You don't think she was with that lout all night do you?"

"Probably," I answer simply.

Brock looks absolutely miserable at my response.

"While you are my friend, and I love you dearly, I tried to warn you this would happen," I tell him. "I'm sure it hasn't escaped your notice that there are plenty of potential suitors vying for her attention. As for Albain… well… it's hard to say. If there is something between them, you certainly won't hear about it from him. However, even that fellow from the Wolf Clan, Dennan, seems to think Albain may have an interest in Eilis."

"Eilis. It still feels wrong to call her that. She's still Wise to me, though sometimes I wonder if she is the same person."

"Well, I can easily answer that for you."

"Oh?"

"She's not," I state flatly. "She *has* changed since we arrived here. For one, while I know she's always been a bit stubborn, but even more so now, she seems much more willing to stand up for what she believes in, as you plainly saw last night."

Brock groans. "As if I could forget. I'm not saying I didn't deserve it. I shouldn't have been carrying on with Molly, but I still can't bring myself to tell Wise... or Eilis, I suppose, how I feel," he admits. "And I don't like that Cur fellow."

"Do you dislike him because of his personality, or do you dislike him because you fear he's competition?"

"Both, I suppose. He's not exactly the most pleasant fellow to be around, and I certainly don't like him around *her*." He sighs heavily. "And now, I'm afraid I can't fix this. You heard what she said last night. It seems she doesn't care for me anymore."

"She'll always care for you, Brock. But she's not just going to sit around and wait for you to come to your senses. She has responsibilities to even more people now, and she can't afford to spend her time pining over you. The Eilis you saw last night realizes that. It's about time you came to terms with it, too. Eventually, you're just going to have to come clean, or simply let it pass."

On the west side of the encampment, we come across a considerable crowd that has gathered to watch warriors from the clans spar against each other. I make my way towards Scarlet, who is leaning against the makeshift fence that is intended to keep the spectators at a safe distance from the combatants.

"Good morning, Boy," she greets happily. "Brock," she says with a hint of disdain in her voice.

"Did Wise make it back okay last night?" he asks.

"Not last night," responds Scarlet with a smirk. "If you mean at dawn this morning, then yes. Albain carried her back to the tent and put her in her cot. I was just waking up when he arrived, and he gave me very firm directions not to wake her because he said she needed rest."

Brock groans loudly. "She was with him all night? Where do you think they went? You don't think she- no, she would never. But him! He seems the sort-"

The first match we witness is an impressive bout between a female warrior who wields a broadsword and shield. The color of her kilt proclaims her to be from the Raven Clan. Her opponent is a man who dual wields shortswords and wears the colors of the Fox Clan. The Bromus are unique in that their female warriors are held in regard equal to that of the male warriors. It is expected for a female Bromus to fight both with and against male warriors. I have no doubt that Eilis will be well-suited for this expectation, as she has proven herself to be particularly adept with an axe and shield.

The warrior from the Raven Clan makes quick work of her opponent, and in the next match, we watch as a man from the Raven Clan closes with Ragnar from the Bear Clan. The former is exceptionally fast and manages to strike frequently and quickly, but when Ragnar does land a blow, each is devastating enough to knock his competitor off his feet. Eventually, Ragnar gains the upper hand and is declared the victor of the match. Afterwards, Scarlet and I congratulate him.

I clap him on his back as he comes to stand next to me. "You weren't joking. You are just as handy with a weapon as your words."

"That was impressive," agrees Scarlet. "Personally, I prefer daggers. Big pieces of metal like that are a bit too clunky for my tastes."

"To each their own," replies Ragnar with a smile. "Any chance you two fancy a round? Not with me, of course. I think Scarlet would make rather quick work of me. There's a fellow from the Fox Clan that favors daggers. He's next, I think." He gestures to the sparring area, and we watch as a tall, lean man with reddish hair and an inordinate amount of freckles bounds into the ring. "Good luck there, Murtagh."

The man with the red hair grins broadly as he unsheathes two daggers from his belt. We watch the match progress. Murtagh clearly has the advantage against his opponent, a massive warrior from the Bear Clan who wields a warhammer.

"I don't understand the skirts," says Brock after a while. "What kind of men wear skirts?"

A deep, gravelly voice responds to Brock's question. "Better men than you."

We turn to see Albain, his sword resting on his shoulder as he prepares for his match.

"And they're called kilts," corrects Ragnar.

"Personally, I kind of want one. They seem liberating," I comment.

Albain snorts in amusement.

"Do you spar often? You seem to have quite a collection of scars," states Brock. I can tell by his tone that he's looking for an argument, and for a moment, I'm afraid that Albain is just going to take off his head with that sword of his. "It seems to me that great warriors would know how to dodge."

"It's difficult to dodge when you're surrounded by twenty men. Perhaps you'd like to show me how it's properly done. I can call more men over here, and you can demonstrate," Albain offers, his voice a low growl.

There's a dangerous look in Albain's eye, and I get the impression that whatever discussion was exchanged between he and Eilis the previous night resulted in him feeling less than favorably towards Brock. Brock's need to irritate the warrior this morning likely isn't helping.

"Or, if you'd like, you can just face me alone. I should be able to make quick enough work of you that my opponent won't be kept waiting." Albain moves closer to Brock, and the latter practically falls over in an attempt to get away from him. Albain laughs to himself as he enters the sparring ring and prepares to fight a rather large, muscular warrior from the Oak Clan.

Cheers erupt around the area as the two warriors begin to move around each other, both of them testing the other's reach and speed. Between the size of Albain's weapon and his rather long arms, it's difficult for his opponent to get close to him, but the Oak Clan's warrior does his best to strike at

Albain. Every time the warrior from the Oak Clan makes a move, his brethren shout cheers of encouragement. Whenever Albain strikes, which is very frequently, silence falls over the crowd. The last of the Cur Clan moves with almost supernatural quickness. He wields his massive blade as effortlessly as if it were a shortsword, and the impact of his blows alone are enough to send his opponent flying through the air or sprawling to the ground. Albain manages to back the man into a corner and slams the flat of his sword hard against the man's side, causing his foe to double over in pain. Albain's opponent yields, and yet another challenger from the Oak Clan volunteers to fight against Albain.

The second warrior is far faster and more skilled than the previous one, but Albain still appears almost bored and unaffected by the lack of a suitable challenge. Still, this combatant is tenacious, and despite Albain clobbering him over and over again, the man simply will not yield. Albain slams the hilt of his sword against the side of the man's head.

Suddenly, I hear Eilis's voice from the back of the crowd. "Well struck, Albain!"

Albain seems momentarily startled and confused by the show of support, but as Eilis joins me and the others at the fence, he fails at suppressing a smirk. He easily finishes off this combatant and two more, before one finally presents a bit of a challenge.

The last of the volunteers from the Oak Clan uses a heavy warhammer, and he manages to land a sound hit against Albain's side. This man isn't afraid to use his fists as well, and he manages to hit Albain hard enough in the head to create a nasty cut on his brow.

By now, Lark has also made his way to the area and bounces up and down on the top of the fence. "Come on, Albie!" he enthusiastically cheers.

The warrior from the Oak Clan laughs loudly. "Albie! Ha!"

Albain lets out a resounding growl and slams his elbow

into the man's jaw. We all hear an audible crack, and Albain's foe collapses to his knees. The man's cries of pain are further exacerbated by the injury to his face.

Albain lowers his voice, and his words come out as more of a snarl than speech. "Say it again, and you won't have a jaw left for me to break."

"Bloody hell, Albie!" calls out Lark as he claps loudly for Albain.

"Lark!" scolds Eilis.

"Sorry, Eilis," mumbles Lark.

Albain chuckles and makes his way over to us. Blood still trickles from the cut on his brow, but he simply wipes it away with the back of his hand. He picks up Lark with one arm and tosses him over his shoulder like he's a sack of flour. This, of course, sends Lark into hysterical fits, and he giggles wildly.

"I'd ask where he picked up such language, but I think I know," remarks Eilis with an accusing look at Albain. Still, she can't seem to bring herself to be cross with him, and there's the faintest hint of a smile upon her lips.

Albain comes to stand next to Eilis, and he redeposits Lark on his feet.

"Thank you for seeing me back last night," says Eilis. "And for... for everything. It was very kind of you."

Ragnar's eyes grow wide with shock at overhearing this comment, and he looks from Albain to Eilis in disbelief.

Albain grunts. "I've been called many things in my life, but kind hasn't been one of them."

"Well, there's a first time for everything," replies Eilis.

"CUR!" shouts a familiar voice.

I look over to see Dennan approach. "Why don't you come face a real warrior? That is, unless you're afraid to look like a fool in front of the All-Chieftain To Be."

Albain responds with a confident smirk. "What's one more body to add to the pile? As you wish, Wolf." He casts a lingering look towards Eilis before reentering the sparring area.

Dennan lands several strikes against Albain before the latter can even swing his enormous sword around. The warrior of the Wolf Clan is exceptionally quick, and he seems to be able to know how Albain is going to move before even he does. Eventually, Albain launches a brutal offense, and his powerful blows begin to be too much for Dennan. Begrudgingly, the latter is forced to yield after a blow to the head renders him unable to stand up straight.

Ragnar hops the fence and crouches next to Dennan who struggles to pull himself into a seated position. "Dennan? Dennan, are you all right?"

Dennan gives a final grunt before falling backwards onto the ground. He groans in pain as some of the other members of the Wolf Clan help to carry him towards the healer's tent.

"I'll be happy to oblige you if you'd ever like another beating, Wolf," speaks Albain as Dennan is carried past us.

Dennan, barely conscious, is able to give him a dark look just before his eyes roll back into his head and he passes out.

Albain glances around the sparring area. "Anyone else?" he asks nonchalantly.

Not a single warrior moves a muscle or raises his or her voice in reply.

"I thought not." Albain rests his greatsword upon his shoulder and starts to head off in the direction of his temporary home, a lone tent on the outskirts of the encampment.

"You should see to that cut," Eilis calls after him.

"Why bother? Won't do my face any favors." He gives a mirthless laugh.

"That wasn't a request," she replies firmly.

Albain freezes in his tracks but does not turn to look at her. Every eye is upon them, and I notice that many of the Bromus now wear tense expressions, and their hands have come to rest upon their weapons as if fearful Albain may lash out at Eilis.

Eilis seems to notice this and appears thoroughly annoyed by their reactions. Without another word, she approaches Albain and seizes his hand in her own. "Look at me."

Albain sighs heavily but does as she commands.

Eilis quickly examines the wound. "You need stitches, but just a few. It needs to be cleaned out as well to prevent infection. I have supplies back at my tent. You're coming with me." She does not drop her hold on his hand, a fact that does not escape the other Bromus, who begin to whisper among themselves.

Albain makes no further objections as Eilis leads him away to tend to his injury.

Next to me, Ragnar looks on in utter confusion. He shakes his head as if doing so will dispel what he is currently seeing. "This is unbelievable. I think I've had my fill of sparring for some time." He turns his attention to me. "What are you up to, Boy? Want to try your hand at the lute again?" he asks.

I can't help but to grin at his suggestion. I have to admit that I feel quite elated to be making friends among the Bromus.

❊ ❊ ❊

Over the next fortnight, more banners can be seen around the encampment. There is the brown and tan of the Falcon Clan and the green and gold of the Snake Clan. Each of them proudly displays their colors outside of the areas of the encampment where they settle. Additionally, each banner also claims a place at the dining tent, as according to Bromus culture, those who break bread are considered allies.

We begin to see less and less of Eilis. At first, she divides her time between tending to her grandfather's directives, keeping us company when she can, and in those rare occasions she has a few moments to herself, choosing to pass them with Albain. The two seem to share some unspoken understanding, and one is rarely seen without the other.

However, Eilis's grandfather doesn't seem very fond of how she spends her time, and he is even less fond of who she is spending it with. Soon the All-Chieftain's requests take up more and more of her time.

It's around then that Old Man brings up journeying to his home again. I know this will be a sore subject for the All-Chieftain. He has already expressed his desire for Eilis to stay with her people, but she has made it very clear that where we go, she goes, and there is still so much at stake. We need to get to Old Man's home in the hopes of claiming some answers, and beyond that, more importantly, we must get Lark home to King Ruden in Vericus.

I spend some of my time in the training yard. There I hone my combat skills under the tutelage of Albain and spar with Dennan, Ragnar, and many of the other Bromus who have gathered at the encampment. While I have come to consider myself half decent with a sword, these new combatants push me to higher levels of skill, and soon, even the All-Chieftain takes notice of my abilities.

"We'll make a proper Bromus of you yet!" he jokes.

However, the majority of my time is passed in the company of Scarlet. We make it a part of every day to walk through the woods and along the banks of the creek. You would think after all the time we spent in forests on our journey that we would have grown tired of such things, but as the camp grows more and more populated, it becomes more difficult to find peace and quiet. Most days are relatively uneventful, and we come and go as we please. However, there are a few happenings that disrupt the strange comfortability that we have settled into.

* * *

One morning, Scarlet and I make our way to the dining tent. Brock and Lark decide to sleep in, and Old Man is gone by the time I wake. Eilis, surely, is off tending to some matter for her grandfather. As we approach the dining tent, we find there's a large crowd of people gathered at the entrance of it. They are whispering among themselves and staring at something inside the tent, but none of them enter.

Suddenly, I hear Albain's heavy footsteps behind me. I can tell from the blood smeared on his shirt and the fact that he's wearing long brown trousers instead of his usual great kilt that he must have just returned from hunting.

"What the bloody hell is everyone gawking at?" he asks irritably.

At the sound of his voice, all the chatter stops, and the crowd begins to part, all of their eyes staring at him as if expecting him to do something. Albain regards them with a mixture of curiosity and annoyance. With a heavy sigh, he walks through them and towards the dining tent.

He stops just short of the opening, and suddenly, I see his fists clench at his side. He lets out a loud growl that chills the blood in my veins, and suddenly his sword is unleashed as he rounds on the crowd.

"Is this some kind of a joke!" he demands angrily.

And that's when I see the source of the commotion.

A new banner hangs in the hall. It is fashioned of black and red plaid and has a silver dog emblazoned in the center. Its mouth hangs open, and its teeth are bared; the craftsmanship makes it appear both fearsome and impressive.

Dennan appears beside me. "Now, now, Cur. Calm yourself or I'll have to put you down." His fingers rest on the handles of the two handaxes that hang from his belt.

Albain spits on the ground at Dennan's feet. "You could try."

Someone must have made the All-Chieftain aware of the commotion, because I see him making his way down the hill, and he does not look pleased. "Cur! What is the meaning of this?" he demands.

Albain looks as if he wants to tear the man's head off his

shoulders. "This is my reward for three years of loyalty? Mockery?"

"What are you talking about?" questions the All-Chieftain.

"That!" Albain gestures to the banner. "You and your clan have made it clear from the beginning that I do not belong among you, and I was only welcome until you had no further use for me. Just last night, you told me it was time for me to move along. Now this?"

Suddenly, I hear a familiar voice. "That was meant to be a pleasant surprise for you. I see I've missed my mark." Eilis appears at the back of the crowd, and everyone turns to stare at her.

It occurs to me then that I have never heard the camp so quiet. It's as if every background sound has been entirely drained from the earth, and the only thing that can be heard is the voices of those who command all of our attention.

Upon seeing Eilis, all the anger drains from Albain's face, and he sheathes his weapon. "Clearly."

"I hope you like it. I'm not particularly skilled at sewing, but I did my best. You'll find another outside your tent."

Albain shakes his head in disbelief, as if trying to make sense of what's happening. "This was *your* doing?" There's a strange hitch in his voice when he questions her. "Why?"

Eilis approaches him, stopping mere inches away from him. "Because it should have been there all along. It's wrong that it wasn't, so I righted the injustice. As you've said, you've served my clan loyally for three years. You've earned the right to be counted among us."

Albain regards her in silence, then gives a slight nod of understanding.

Eilis turns to her grandfather, and her expression sharpens. The ire is clearly present in her features. It's been on very rare occasions that I have ever seen Eilis truly angry, but I can tell, this is going to be one of those situations. However, she is careful to quell her anger in front of the crowd, and each word she utters is quite deliberate. "And Granda, I expect we will discuss what he says about you asking him to leave."

The All-Chieftain lowers his voice. "I just thought it would be in your best interest, given the fact that so many clans will be bringing forth suitors, that you be careful who you associate with. I have tried to keep you otherwise occupied, yet my guards tell me you still find time in the evenings, after everyone else in the whole bloody camp is asleep, to meet with The Cur."

"Albain," corrects Wise. She is quiet for several moments as she contemplates her grandfather's words. "I see. While I love you dearly, Granda, and do treasure your counsel, who I choose to associate with is none of your concern, nor that of any clan or man under the sun, and anyone who thinks otherwise can take it up with me."

Albain appears shocked and impressed by her boldness and he gives a slight bow in appreciation of her defense of him.

Eilis crosses to the scarred warrior. "Why don't you wash up from the hunt and come break your fast with me? We can sit under your new banner." She hooks her arm through his and guides him away from the crowd.

"Well... That was intense," remarks Scarlet casually, and I finally let out a breath I didn't even know I was holding.

* * *

Later that afternoon, I find Eilis sitting outside of her tent as she watches Lark chase Dog around and around in circles.

"Hello, Eilis," I greet as I sit on the bench beside her.

She offers me a half-hearted smile. "So... that was an unnecessary ordeal. I thought I'd present Albain with the banners as a token of my appreciation for all he's done for both me and my clan. Instead, I cause him to nearly skewer a crowd of people and manage to get into a nasty row with my grandfather over my dealings."

"I'm very sorry to hear that," I say sincerely. "So, what came of that conversation?"

"We formed an agreement of sorts. He is very persistent about me entertaining suitors. He's asked that before we leave for Vericus that each clan presents one of their own as a potential suitor."

"Well, I have a feeling that we already know who some of the clans will choose. No doubt, the Wolf Clan will select Dennan, and the Bear Clan will likely choose Ragnar. Both of them seem to be good men," I say in an attempt to cheer her. "Besides, he only said you had to consider them. It's not as if he's forcing you to marry tomorrow. We still have to make our way to Old Man's home before we even leave for Vericus."

"True," concedes Eilis. "The problem is, there's already someone who I've developed feelings for. Very, very strong feelings."

Just then, Albain walks by on his way to my tent to fetch Lark for his morning lessons. Eilis has relented that Lark should be able to train in combat so that he can effectively defend himself, and of course he asked "Albie" if he could be the one to teach him.

I haven't been blind to the stolen glances between Eilis and Albain, the furtive way they touch each other's hands when they think no one is looking, and the way she always seems to be able to defeat the dour expression on his face. To Albain's credit, Eilis never seems happier than when he is around, and while I know her grandfather would never approve of such a union, I realize that Albain is who Eilis is referring to.

"Albain then," I say quietly.

"Yes," she acknowledges. "Is it so obvious?" she asks as she exchanges a brief smile with him.

"I wouldn't say it's obvious, but I've known you long enough to be able to pick up on such things. You seem... happier when you're around him, more at ease. Truthfully, I'm happy for you, Eilis," I tell her. "What about Brock?" I ask.

Eilis shakes her head sadly. "Until a few weeks ago, I foolishly clung to the hope that things might change between us. Unfortunately, Brock has made his feelings very plain. He does not regard me in such a way, and I can't simply keep hoping that he will change his mind."

Part of me wants to tell her of the conversations that Brock and I had regarding that very subject. I want to tell her that he actually loves her, but he's too proud, or scared, or simply foolish to tell her himself. Part of me wants to plead for her to give him the time he needs to come around, and not to give up hope on the idea that they could one day be together.

However, I know it is not my place to say these things, and as much as I care for both Brock and Eilis, I have never seen Eilis happier than when she is with Albain.

"You deserve to have someone who will love you unconditionally, and despite his churlish demeanor and harsh ways with everyone else in the world, Albain has been nothing but kind to us, and he seems to regard you with the utmost respect and kindness. You deserve to be happy, Eilis, and regardless of the path you choose, know that I'll always be here to support you."

"Thank you, Boy." Eilis sighs heavily as she rises to her feet. "I wish Granda would see things that way." Her brown eyes settle on me, and I can't help but to notice the newfound defiance I see in them. "I've spent my entire life answering to the whims of someone else. I'm through with such things. I will never again allow anyone to dictate my life for me."

CHAPTER 24

During our stay in the encampment, Old Man has been busy researching the potential whereabouts of his home. Through hours of research with the clan historian, he finally manages to find a lead to expedite our journey and ensure we aren't blindly wandering around the wilderness for weeks in an attempt to find the place.

"Callow's Hill," Old Man tells me. "As soon as the historian said it, the name sounded familiar to me. It's about two days south of here."

"Are you sure?" I ask him.

"I'm never sure of anything these days, my boy, but I have a very good feeling about it."

"Then, that's good enough for me, Old Man," I say.

Eilis nods her head in agreement. "It's worth a try, isn't it? I feel badly that we've tarried here so long. The fact is, we need to continue on our journey. We need to get to Old Man's home and ensure that Lark is returned to his father in Vericus."

"Fine. I'll go. But I want to pack at least a week's worth of those honeycakes that the Bear Clan makes," speaks Scarlet.

"Scarlet, you heard Old Man. It's only two days away," reminds Brock.

"A... Week's... Worth..." repeats Scarlet firmly.

She really has taken a liking to living among the Bromus, and to be truthful, I know that we will all terribly miss the way of life we have come to enjoy and the people we have met while being in the encampment. Still, I'm cheered by the fact that Eilis has already stated that we are all more than welcome to return to them and to stay however long we like. Honestly, depending how my own journey goes, I could see myself living out my days amongst them.

The All-Chieftain arranges for a group of allied Bromus to accompany us. At first, he insists on at least three dozen men as he is intent on the safe return of his granddaughter, but Old Man reminds him that a larger group would travel more slowly, and it may be wiser to send a smaller, but very capable, group of warriors.

The All-Chieftain reluctantly agrees, and since the camp has been abuzz with word of his decree regarding suitors for his heir, there is no shortage of able-bodied warriors who volunteer to accompany us. In the end, the All-Chieftain selects Dennan, Ragnar, and other members of the Oak, Bear, and Wolf Clans to form our party.

We also decide it would be prudent for Lark to remain behind.

"But why?" Lark doesn't take the news very well and asks the question no less than fifty times.

I sigh in response to his repeated queries. "We told you, Lark. We're going to be leaving for Vericus soon, and you could use all the rest you can get."

"This is because I'm young, isn't it? You know, I can run circles around the lot of you," he says with a frown.

"Lark," speaks Eilis gently. "It's not that. You should get rest while you can. Eat hearty meals, take time to play with your friends and say proper goodbyes to them. It could very well be a difficult journey to Vericus. You should enjoy this time while you can."

Lark looks as if he's going to protest, but when it comes to Eilis, he generally tends to avoid argument, as he knows how committed she is to doing what is in his best interest.

Though he still looks sulky and slightly unconvinced, he begrudgingly acquiesces to our request.

* * *

The day before we are set to leave, there is a gathering in the dining tent to see us off. The clan's cleric gives a blessing for a safe and successful journey, as well as a timely return.

Our group takes up a few tables near the platform where Eilis and her grandfather are sitting. They are speaking of some topic that is making Eilis frown constantly, and I get the feeling that it may be about the suitor decree, which has been a point of contention between the two as of late.

Occasionally, I see her scan the crowd and look disheartened when she does not see what, or I suppose I should say *who*, she desires. Albain has been absent all day, and I know Eilis has been a bit bothered by it, as she told me so much. She had hoped her grandfather would select him for the group that would be dispatched with us, but none of us were very surprised that he wasn't. Since the incident with the banner, the All-Chieftain has spoken to the last of the Cur Clan as little as possible. Since we are to leave the next morning at dawn, Eilis is hoping to say her farewells to Albain before we depart, but as the night wears on, it is looking less and less likely that will happen.

We are just about to tuck in to our desserts when I see Albain's immense form appears at the entrance of the dining tent. Wordlessly, he makes his way to the platform at the front of the room and stops a few feet short of the All-Chieftain. They hold each other's gazes for a few, uncomfortable moments.

Then Albain draws his sword.

Suddenly, the dining tent erupts with gasps and shouts, and there is the sound of dozens of other weapons being drawn. Dennan, along with many other warriors, begin to make their way towards the platform. Albain glances back at them but says nothing.

Instead, he holds his sword in his left hand, unusual considering it is his off-hand. Then, he presses the blade down upon the palm of his sword hand until a steady stream of blood appears. He wipes his hand along the flat of the blade, smearing blood across steel. He steps forward, and the All-Chieftain rises, his hand on the handle of his battleaxe as Albain approaches.

Albain ignores the All-Chieftain completely and sets the bloody blade at Eilis's feet. A hush falls over the entirety of those assembled. I feel as if something significant is happening, but as I'm not very knowledgeable on Bromus culture, I'm at a loss of what is going on.

I look to Old Man questioningly.

"It appears our giant friend there means to take the Bloodsworn Vow," observes Old Man.

"What the hell does that mean?" asks Brock.

Despite the fact we are at a loss for what is going on, Eilis seems to know exactly what's occurring. At first I think that maybe she and Albain have discussed whatever this is before this moment, but given the genuine shock on her face, I somehow doubt it.

The All-Chieftain's face is red with irritation and disbelief, and as Eilis bends to touch the blade, I hear him say her name. "Eilis..."

"Granda," she replies, her brown eyes glancing up to him.

"Are you certain of this? You know what he offers. This is an unbreakable vow," the All-Chieftain's voice tremors with worry.

"I know, Granda." Eilis picks up the sword and holds it out to her grandfather.

The All-Chieftain hesitates, and after several moments of self-deliberation, he drags his fingers along the flat of the blade until they are wet with the warrior's blood, then wipes a bit of the blood on Eilis's face, first the left cheek, then the right.

When the deed is done, Albain kneels in front of Eilis. The All-Chieftain crosses to him. The leader of the Bromus stares down at Albain, which isn't a very great distance given the fact that even kneeling, Albain is exceptionally tall. He looks as if he'd like to put the blade straight through Albain's chest, but instead, he turns the blade so the hilt is pointed towards Albain. Albain reclaims his sword, wipes the rest of the blood away with a cloth he produces from his pocket, then rests his greatsword against his shoulder. He steps onto the platform and takes up a position standing next to Eilis, who has returned to her seat.

Scarlet shakes her head in confusion. "All right, Old Man, start talking. What just happened?"

Old Man clears his throat. "In Bromus culture, a vow is a sacred covenant. They are considered to be unbreakable. Among the most sacred are the Brethren Vow, which is a vow of loyalty taken between allies, the Marriage Vow, which needs no further explanation, and the Bloodsworn Vow, which is what you just witnessed. These three are considered lifelong pledges that cannot be broken, and extend even after one has expired. The Bromus believe so much in the sanctity of these vows that they are observed even in death. It is punishable by execution to break the Brethren Vow. In regards to the Marriage Vow, the Bromus do not believe in divorce, and a widow or widower will never remarry. The Bloodsworn Vow dictates eternal service to the recipient; it is expected that the pledge continues even into the afterlife."

"Why did Albie cut his hand?" asks Lark with concern in his voice. "That looks like it hurts."

"I'm sure it did," agrees Old Man. "The cut is placed on the sword hand for three reasons. First, it signifies the pledge of the person's life and blade to the recipient. Second, until it heals, it can cause significant pain, a sharp reminder of the promise. Third, it leaves a visible scar, so that all who see it know that the person has taken the Bloodsworn Vow and has pledged his or her life and service to another."

Dennan, overhearing our conversation, seats himself at our table. There is a look of annoyance present in his wild features. "It also means that wherever she goes, he follows. Needless to say, it seems The Cur will be accompanying us on our journey tomorrow." He frowns in distaste. "It also means that any potential suitor must defeat Albain in single combat to prove his worth to Eilis. Unfortunately for those like me who seek her hand, even I must admit that Albain is a very capable warrior. It will not be easy to best him, but I certainly will make the attempt."

The rest of the feast passes relatively uneventfully, though I frequently overhear the other Bromus suitors for Eilis voicing their discontentment about this turn of events. At one point, I encounter Ragnar, who is disappointed by the development, but seems to be more understanding of the situation than his brethren.

"I've no desire to continue serving as suitor to the All-Chieftain To Be," he says to me.

"Why not?" I ask. "I thought you fancied Eilis."

"I do. I think the world of her. However, there would be no honor in it," replies Ragnar. "It is obvious where her affections reside, and while I wish it was with me, I am man enough to acknowledge that it's not. Now the other suitors... well, that will be a difficult lesson for them to learn!"

"What will you do?" I ask. "Surely, your father won't be pleased by this."

Ragnar shrugs. "I won't do anything. I'll be presented along with the rest of the suitors, but I know I won't be chosen, and that is fine by me."

* * *

After the feast, Old Man, Brock, Lark, Scarlet, and I make our way back to our tents. When we arrive, we realize that there is another smaller tent to the right of the one that the girls share. Outside of it is the banner of the Cur Clan.

"You have got to be kidding me!" Brock exclaims, his

voice seething with anger. "Why is that there?"

"He's her Bloodsworn now," reminds Old Man. "His job is to see to her protection at every moment. He can't fulfill his duty from the other side of the camp."

"I wonder what other duties he's fulfilling," teases Scarlet. I don't know why she enjoys tormenting Brock so much, but she is quite adept at it.

Her objective is easily completed when her comment incites Brock's anger even further. Swearing under his breath, he stalks into our tent.

Lark's eyes widen. "I haven't heard those words before!" he exclaims.

"Best you not repeat them to Eilis," I advise.

Old Man sighs heavily. "This is sure to feel like an exceedingly long journey. I do hope Brock can contain himself, as I am quite certain Eilis's new Bloodsworn won't hesitate to inflict bodily harm upon him."

"I'll keep an eye on Brock," I assure him. "It's hard to believe we'll be journeying to Callow's Hill tomorrow. Are you excited about returning to your home?" I ask him.

Old Man considers this for a moment. "Recently, I have come to a realization, Boy. Home is many things, but it is not a place," he says as he puts his hand on my shoulder.

It's the hardest lesson I will ever learn.

CHAPTER 25

The following morning, Dennan, Ragnar, Albain, and I prepare our horses for the journey. Albain wasn't joking when he had previously told us of the size of his horse. Despite the fact that Horse is an exceptional example of a strong, well-bred warhorse, he is nearly dwarfed by Albain's mount, a pure black beast with an ornery disposition. Next to me, Dennan checks the saddlebags of his blood bay charger, a far more agreeable steed that doesn't have the penchant for snapping at passersby that Albain's horse has.

"So, that was quite a show last night, Cur," speaks Dennan. The tone of irritation in his voice is obvious.

Albain regards him with little more than a contemptuous glare.

"I never thought I'd see the day when the fearsome Cur pledged his eternal loyalty to anything that didn't offer him gold first," jokes Dennan.

"You can shut your mouth, or I can shut it for you," rasps Albain in his gravelly voice.

Dennan raises his hands in front of him. "I meant no offense. Despite my dislike of your rather loathsome personality, I do have quite high esteem for the All-Chieftain To Be. I'm no fool. I see how she regards your counsel."

Ragnar and I exchange a knowing glance. It is becoming increasingly apparent that Eilis and her Bloodsworn share a special bond, and Ragnar has already confirmed that he no longer has any aspirations of courting Eilis.

Dennan continues. "I know if I am to have any chance

with her, I had better get in your good graces. Perhaps then you'll be more inclined to graciously take the beating I will have to put upon you to win her hand."

Albain snorts with derision.

"You need not worry, Cur," promises Dennan seriously. "As I said, I think very highly of her. I will treat her as if she were the queen herself."

"And that's why she will never choose you," returns Albain sharply. "She doesn't deserve to be treated like a queen."

"We'll see." Dennan laughs and walks off to gather the rest of his weapons.

Ragnar heads back to his tent to gather a few items he forgot, and I find myself completely alone with Albain, something that is unprecedented in our time at the encampment. While I have plenty of interactions with him as he is often around Eilis or Lark, I've never been alone with him, and honestly, even though I know he'd never harm me given my friendship with Eilis, it is a bit unnerving, and I can't help but to be intimidated by him.

It's almost as if he can read my thoughts. "You fear me."

"Yes." I answer honestly.

Albain laughs. "Good. You should."

"That's not what I mean. I don't fear anything you'd do to me, though Maker knows you're certainly capable." I can't help but to glance towards Eilis, who is speaking with Scarlet in front of their tent.

Albain seems to realize my meaning. "I see." He runs a large hand over his horse's mane. "I know that Eilis has likely spoken with you to some degree about me. She says that of all her companions, you are the one she trusts the most and considers the truest of her friends." He closes one of his saddlebags and approaches me. "And it seems you are as protective of her as she is of all of you." He looks over at Eilis, and I can see his grim expression falter the slightest bit, betraying the genuine affection that he has for her. "You need not fear my intentions with her. I'd sooner slit my own throat than let any harm befall her. You have my word on that."

Eilis calls out for him, and he moves to join her, but he pauses to glance back at me. "It's good you care so much for her wellbeing. She said you were a true friend. I believe that now. I'm glad for it, too. If you were anything less than that, I'd kill you."

"Well, I'm glad to keep my life awhile longer," I reply.

Albain laughs and moves to depart.

"Albain," I say.

He pauses in his tracks and regards me silently.

"I have to ask though... Why did you say Eilis doesn't deserve to be treated like a queen? It's fairly obvious how much you care about her... and not just in the way that a warrior cares about his charge."

"You're not wrong," admits Albain, blushing slightly. "I say that *because* I care for her. You see, I've realized something important... something that fool, Dennan, hasn't. She doesn't *want* to be treated like a queen. I don't think she even really *wants* to be All-Chieftain, but her honor will see that she is one, perhaps one of the greatest." I watch as he gives a slight wave to Eilis, and I see the smile that instantly sprouts upon her face.

Albain can't help but to smile slightly himself. "She doesn't want to be anyone's better, Boy. Nor does not want to be anyone's lesser. She wouldn't be content to answer to the whims of a husband who seeks to rule her, but she's also too kind to exert her will over anyone for her own benefit. She doesn't want a master, but she doesn't want to master anyone. She wants to be someone's equal. I can give her that. I *will* give her that."

I watch as he moves to join Eilis, and I see the joy that is shared between them when they are near each other. Albain may be terrifying, but at least he's on our side, and despite what some of the Bromus may think of him, I truly believe he has been nothing but good for Eilis.

Before we depart, Lark comes to see us off. I've never seen him look so miserable, and Dog's large, brown eyes seem to echo the sorrow of his master as he sits next to him.

"Don't worry, Lark," I assure him. "We'll be back soon."

"I'm not worried," responds Lark. "I know you'll be safe. Albie is with you."

I glance over at Albain, and I see something shift in the warrior's stern expression at Lark's show of confidence in him. He dismounts from the hellish beast he calls his horse, and I see him take something from his belongings that he has assembled for the journey. He approaches Lark with it in his hands and kneels in front of him so that he's closer to eye level with him.

When Lark sees the gift, his eyes widen with delight, and an enormous grin overtakes his features. "A sword, Albie! My very own sword! Now I have my own dagger and my own sword! Now I'll truly be prepared for battle!"

Eilis blanches at Lark talking of being battle-ready. She groans loudly. "Why do you people think it's a good idea to give a child weapons?" However, there is no anger in her voice.

Beside me, Scarlet shrugs from atop her dapple grey mare.

"I was given my first sword around the time I started walking," mentions Albain.

"It's a wonder you've survived this long," returns Eilis.

As much as I'm sure that it pains him to agree with anything Albain says, even the All-Chieftain seems to be in favor of the gift. "Eilis, you were far younger than Lark when I gave you your first axe. Do you recall?"

Eilis frowns. "I recall the healer stitching up my hand just after."

The All-Chieftain laughs. "Well, clearly you've gotten better. I've seen you practicing in the sparring ring."

Lark throws his arms around Albain's neck, and the dour warrior smiles in response. "Thank you, Albie! Thank you!"

"Listen here. While I'm gone, you keep practicing what I've shown you," instructs Albain firmly. "Aye?"

"Aye!" agrees Lark.

Albain rises, and I overhear him as he says to Eilis, "Don't worry. I've dulled the blade."

She looks at him thankfully before moving towards Lark, who sticks the weapon through his belt and grins broadly. Suddenly, he darts towards her, wrapping her in an inescapable hug. She places a motherly kiss on his forehead, and I'm reminded once again of the grey-eyed woman from my memories.

"Be good for Granda while I'm gone," she says softly. "We'll be back sooner than you think."

Lark nods obediently. "Aye, I will." He gives her another tight squeeze. "I love you, Eilis."

It's the first time I hear him say it, though I have never doubted that's how he feels for her. Next to me, I hear Scarlet make an odd, strangled sound, and when I look over to her, I see she is fighting back tears.

"I'm not crying!" she shouts to me. "You're crying!"

I can't help but to laugh at her reaction.

Eilis smiles at Lark, and she looks conflicted, as if it pains her to leave him. In truth, it must be difficult for both of them. This is the first time they've been parted since Lark was brought to her cell, and since then their bond has grown incredibly strong. "I love you too, Lark. Now go on. Willa over there seems to be waiting for you." Eilis gestures towards Lark's pigtailed friend.

I watch as he races forward and proudly shows Willa his new sword. Dog happily barks and bounds around the children while the rest of us somewhat reluctantly complete a final check of ours supplies. Once this is done, our party departs the Bromus encampment, and we begin the trek south.

* * *

The first day is, thankfully, quite uneventful. We ride all day and well into the evening until we can scarcely see more than a foot in front of our faces. It is a moonless night, and the pitch blackness seems to swallow everything within it. Dennan scouts ahead and finds a suitable area to make camp for the evening. We settle in a small meadow that he says would be easily defensible should anyone attempt to attack us.

"Mostly, we stand to be accosted by bandits and other ruffians. They're easy enough to kill," explains Dennan.

The Bromus men gather around the fire. Ragnar plays his lute for a bit, and Dennan recounts some of his past battles to anyone who will listen. The men laugh, tell bawdy jokes, and exchange witty banter until they can't sustain their merriment any longer. They cease their enjoyment just in time as I can tell that Albain seems to be losing his patience with their frivolity.

Albain and two of the men from the Wolf Clan take the first watch. I'm having trouble sleeping, so I gingerly remove myself from under Scarlet's slumbering form and seat myself next to Albain, who is sitting with his back against a tree. Eilis sleeps a few feet away from him, and every now and then I see his gaze flick back to her before darting around the area again. We sit in a comfortable silence, and when he gets up periodically to walk the perimeter of our camp, I accompany him.

"I can help with second watch," I offer. "You should get some rest, too."

Albain grunts. "I'm used to going days without sleeping. You learn to adapt when you're on your own."

"So, you've been with the Oak Clan for three years. What did you do before that?" I ask conversationally.

Albain shrugs. "Anything and everything. I've been Clanless for most of my life, so I had to make do for myself."

"How did you end up with the Oak Clan?"

He snorts in amusement. "Dumb luck. I was at an inn

in Harpers Mill when the All-Chieftain was passing through with his men. Found out some idiots were hoping to rob him and his retainers while they slept and slit their throats. That night, after Oakheart and his men had turned in for the night, I took a walk by their rooms. I saw those morons trying to go in. They'd snatched the key from the innkeeper. I painted the halls with their blood. After that, I guess the All-Chieftain thought he owed me and took me on as a hired sword."

"So, you saved his life?"

Albain shrugs. "One way of looking at it. Been with the Oak Clan since then. People know who I am and what I do, and the All-Chieftain is more than happy to use that to his advantage."

Eilis stirs slightly, and her blanket falls from her shoulder. Albain rises and, almost tenderly, pulls the blanket back up and recovers her sleeping form.

* * *

The next day and night pass much the same, and by the third morning, we reach the area known as Callow's Hill. Old Man instantly proclaims that the place appears familiar to him, and we allow him to take the lead.

It seems as if with every step we take forward, Old Man loses more and more of his focus. His gaze becomes vacant, like he's seeing without seeing. We follow Old Man through some dense trees, and suddenly, I see Albain spur his horse onward and towards Old Man. I watch as Albain snatches the reins of Old Man's horse. It's then I notice the cliff. Old Man was so lost in his head that he nearly trotted his horse straight off of it.

Old Man shakes his head, as if awaking from a dream. He looks around blankly as if not sure where he is. He peers out in front of him and notices his horse's hooves almost hang over the edge of the precipice until Albain pulls the mount, and its rider, away from harm.

"Oh... My... But that could have been quite awful." He blinks a few times and shakes his head as if to dispel the fog that has clouded his mind. "Thank you, Albain."

"Think nothing of it," replies Albain gruffly. He stops his horse between mine and Eilis's. "What the bloody hell has gotten into him?"

"He's remembering," remarks Eilis quietly.

"Is that the way of it?" asks Albain curiously.

"It's a little different for everyone," I reply. "But essentially, yes. It's like seeing two things at the same time. You can still see here and now, but it's as if there is another image cast just behind it."

We take a winding path down the side of the cliff, and when we emerge, we find ourselves in a valley. We continue our trek through another dense tract of woods, and eventually, it opens into a vast meadow. At the edge of the meadow, we are all brought to a sudden halt.

Nothing could have prepared us for the sight of Old Man's home.

"Your home is a tower?" asks Brock, the awe clearly present in his voice. "A tower?"

Old Man smiles, and again, I can practically see the memories unlocking within his brain.

"That looks like Abirad's tower at the castle," comments Scarlet. "Far less scary, but still similar."

"Indeed," agrees Old Man.

❊ ❊ ❊

The majority of the Bromus set up a perimeter around the area while Old Man leads Brock, Eilis, Albain, Scarlet, Ragnar, and I towards the tower. The door presents a minor challenge. It has obviously been a long time since Old Man has been there. The heavy, wooden door has swelled, and its hinges have collected a lifetime of rust due to the lack of use. However, peculiarly, the door doesn't even have a handle.

When even Ragnar and Albain collectively cannot manage to pry the door open, and they began contemplating just bashing it in, I see Old Man smile broadly.

"Of course! A warding charm! How clever I was!" He pulls the singing stones from his pocket and presses them against the door. He mutters a few words under his breath and the stones hum louder and glow.

Nothing happens.

He frowns as he rubs the stubble upon his chin. "Hmm... What would I have? Oh, yes!" He repeats the process with the addition of a few more words, and there is a loud, clicking sound as the door opens to allow us passage.

Old Man leads us into the base of the tower which is barren, save for a few, empty chests. Gradually, we make our way up the winding stairs towards the top of the tower. It is very close quarters, and poor Albain has to stoop for most of the ascent upwards. I can hear him mutter the occasional curse under his breath whenever he smacks his head off a low stone.

When we reach the top, we are met with a long hall-way with four doors. The first door is some kind of alchemy room, filled with vials of all different shapes and sizes. There are samples of plants; strange, glowing liquids; shining stones, and odd, dried up bits of various creatures.

Scarlet frowns in disgust as she picks up a small jar of what appears to be eyeballs of toads. "Ugh. Why would you ever need these?"

Old Man shrugs. "If they're here, there must be a use for them."

The next room is a bedroom with a simple bed that appears to have never gotten much use. There is a small chest with a few personal effects that Old Man quickly sorts through. He frowns, clearly not finding what he is looking for. Suddenly, I see his eyes brighten, and he waves Albain over to help him move the bed. Albain does as Old Man asks, and the latter stomps up and down on the floorboards until there is a hollow sound. Much as Brock had done at his old home, Old Man asks Albain to pull some of the boards loose. When the boards are set aside, Old Man reaches into the floor, and he pulls out a long, silver chain. Upon it is a large, blue stone that looks as if it were plucked from a night sky.

The third room looks as if it was simply used for storage and contains nothing of note, but when Old Man opens the door to the final room, his entire body begins to tremble with glee.

"My library! My library! Still here! Just as I left it!" He goes over to one of the shelves and frowns slightly. "Hmm... save for a few rather important volumes that seem to have been spirited away. I suppose I should be thankful he simply didn't have my entire tower destroyed. I wonder if he intended to come back here and use it someday," he muses.

"He?" I ask.

"Oh, yes. Abirad." Old Man scans the books along the shelf and pulls a rather large, leather-bound book. He mutters a few words and uses his knuckles to tap out a distinct rhythm on the front cover of the tome.

A peculiar thing happens. The book shudders, and strange waves of light undulate around it. Suddenly, the tome begins to shrink, and in its place is a smaller, brown book, covered in archaic symbols.

"Always best to hide things in plain sight. Abirad was probably wild with rage when he couldn't find it," says Old Man, clearly pleased with himself.

"And what is *it* exactly?" asks Scarlet.

Old Man is already lost in another thought. He begins to page through the book, and after a few moments, he exclaims. "Of course! That's it!"

The rest of us look to him with questioning gazes.

"The key to our memories! Names! Names are a powerful thing," explains Old Man. "A name is a gift. It marks you as someone loved by another. Therein lies their power. It is also a name that is the greatest key to unlock the mind. Simply knowing one's name is not enough. According to what I read… what I wrote… it must be spoken by someone who knew you as you were, before you lost your memories."

"That's how mine were returned to me," speaks Eilis.

"And mine as well," adds Brock. "When my brother said my name, everything came back to me, as clear as day."

"So, that's it?" I ask. "Someone we knew before just needs to call us by our names."

Old Man shrugs. "It's likely not quite that simple, but it seems to have worked for us already."

"And what if there is no one left?" questions Scarlet quietly. "What if everyone you knew before is dead, or you simply can't find them?"

Old Man shrugs. "I don't know, Scarlet." He frowns slightly, for a moment, once again lost in thought. "Many spells can be undone. Those of us who were imprisoned by Abirad were victim to a very powerful spell. A spell created by a very powerful sorcerer… but not Abirad himself."

"Who then?" questions Eilis. "Who could be more powerful than Abirad? Perhaps he could help us to defeat him."

Old Man responds with a slight smile, tinged with the burden of sorrow. "Unfortunately, he is not what he once was. He, too, lost his name."

Eilis furrows her brow in thought, then her eyes widen and she gapes at Old Man in astonishment. It takes me a few seconds more to catch up.

"You're *him*. You're the sorcerer!" I cry out.

"A what now?" Brock shakes his head in befuddlement.

"I *was*," replies Old Man simply. "More than that, I cannot recall."

"It explains so much. Your knowledge of herbs and healing. The fact you were able to use the singing stones," reasons Eilis aloud.

"It also explains why you were imprisoned," speaks Scarlet. "You were probably a threat to Abirad himself."

Old Man nods in agreement. "That could very well be. To answer your previous question, this, my dear, is my spellbook," he announces smilingly.

"Spell book?" speaks Albain. "What are you on about?"

"So, you created the spell that took our memories?" questions Scarlet.

Abruptly, Brock moves towards Old Man. There is a stiffness in his posture and a rather threatening expression on his face. "Y-you..." His face reddens, and I can see he is struggling to control the rage that seems as if it will boil to the surface at any moment. "You did this!" He seizes Old Man roughly by the front of his collar, and I move to intervene, but Brock gives Old Man a hard shove that sends him backwards into a shelf, causing many of the tomes to fall to the floor.

"All of this! All of it! This is all your fault!" Brock rages. I seize his arm and attempt to drag him off of Old Man, but Brock's strength seems to amplify when he's angry.

Eilis seizes his other arm, and Scarlet pulls her pin from her sleeve.

"Brock, listen, I understand how you feel," speaks Eilis calmly. "We've all lost a great deal, but you *know* Old Man. Whoever he was before, that's not him now."

"I never meant any harm..." mumbles Old Man, his eyes wide with fright. "I swear to you, to all of you, it was never my intention!"

"Then why do it?" demands Brock. "Why even make such a spell?"

Old Man sighs. "I don't know, Brock. I never meant to hurt anyone. In my hubris, I just wanted to see if it could be done... I never would have used it."

"But *someone* did!" Brock releases him, turning away in disgust. "Perhaps you should have thought of that possibility!"

Old Man straightens his clothing and takes a deep

breath. "I can never make up for the damage I've caused," he says, his voice genuinely sorry. "All I can do is try to right this wrong, to bring about some peace from this travesty." He turns to pick up the books that have fallen from the shelf. "Come. We need to keep looking."

Old Man continues to search around the library while the rest of us meander around the room and investigate his belongings. The silence is thick between us, as each of us struggles with what we have learned. As for me, I don't know how to feel. On one hand, like Brock, I am angry for all the time I've lost, all the memories I have yet to regain. In contrast, Old Man has always been a presence in my life, a mentor, a friend, and in many cases, a father figure.

I see the truth in Eilis's words. I dare not judge Old Man for what he once was, as that version of him is someone I have never known. I can only view him as I see him now- a human being who made a truly terrible mistake, a man who desperately wants to fix that mistake, even knowing he will never be able to truly make up for what he has done, whether those evils were his intention or not.

"So... Old Man is a sorcerer," Scarlet whispers to me. "Do you think he could teach me how to turn Brock into a toad?" she asks, a glint of mischief in her eyes.

"You're taking this rather well," I comment.

"As I've told you, it seems most of my life is better left forgotten. I suppose I didn't lose as much as some of the rest of you," she replies, and once again, my heart aches for her.

Albain, his face marked with concern, speaks with Eilis in hushed tones. I see him glance towards Old Man, but she smiles slightly and shakes her head. I can't help but to wonder if he is offering to kill Old Man for his crimes. Somehow, that seems likely.

Appeased by Eilis's response, Albain crosses to the window to ensure the other Bromus are maintaining the perimeter. Suddenly, his eyes widen, and he begins to shout. "South! South! Forces from the south!"

Scarlet and I exchange worried glances and hurry over to another window so we can look out.

We watch helplessly as Albain's warning comes too late. We look out just in time to see the mounted forces of Abirad tearing across the meadow. Within moments, there is a resounding clash, as they fall upon our allies down below.

CHAPTER 26

"How many?" shouts Brock.

"At least fifty by my count." Albain looks to Eilis. "Stay here." He heads towards the door with Brock following after him.

"That's not happening," states Eilis firmly. "Those are my people down there. What kind of All-Chieftain would I be if I remained here while our men are slaughtered? I think not."

Albain doesn't seem very happy with her decision, but he doesn't argue the point any further.

"I need to collect a few more things," says Old Man absentmindedly.

"Well, you'd better hurry," speaks Ragnar with a glance out the window. "It looks like they're coming to set fire to the tower."

Sure enough, I see several mounted soldiers carrying torches aloft, and as Ragnar observed, they are certainly heading our way.

As we hurry out of the library, I glance back at Old Man who is absorbed in his books. I make eye contact with Scarlet, and it's as if she reads my thoughts.

"Go on, Boy. I'll make sure he doesn't forget to leave," she assures me.

I legitimately fear for Old Man's safety. He has a tendency to become scattered as it is, but now that he has been overwhelmed by his memories, I am even more afraid for him. Sadly, I don't doubt he'd still be wholly engrossed in his books even as the tower burns around him.

Barreling down the stairs is far easier than ascending them, and in no time, our feet are back on the soil of the meadow. A brief look around reveals the extent of the carnage. Of the twelve Bromus who accompanied us, excluding Albain, Dennan, and Ragnar, nearly half of them lie dead upon the ground.

Upon exiting the tower, Albain and Brock cut down three soldiers who are trying to ignite Old Man's tower. Several more of Abirad's men have met their ends at the hands of our companions, but the dead among our foes pales in comparison with the impact of our own losses as we have a much smaller force. I see Dennan off to our right; he is surrounded by enemies, and despite his prowess in battle, he seems to be struggling in holding them back. Ragnar immediately runs to his defense while the rest of us break to the left to engage more of Abirad's men.

I draw my sword just in time to parry an incoming blow, and instantly, I feel my heart hammering in my chest as the thrill and terror of battle spurs me into action. In some ways, it's like my labor at Abirad's castle: it is a dance. Slash, slash, thrust. Slash, slash, thrust. The sound of the blade cutting through the air forms a strange rhythm as I connect with foe after foe.

Since arriving at the Bromus encampment, I've had ample time to hone my skills and practice my swordsmanship. The sparring ring has certainly aided me in becoming more confident with the weapon in my hands.

Soon, I find myself near Dennan and Ragnar. The former's axes are covered in the blood of his enemies. A mounted warrior comes thundering towards us, but Ragnar's warhammer knocks him from his saddle, and a second strike shatters the man's skull as he falls. Though we are few in number, against all odds, we are holding our own against the much larger force.

More soldiers advance on our position, and suddenly, I hear the familiar hum of the singing stones. A dagger flies through the air and embeds in the throat of an enemy near me.

A brief glance behind me reveals Scarlet as she charges into the fray. Old Man, his strange words lost in the din of battle, prepares his attack, but an advancing enemy breaks his concentration, and I rush forward to intercept the foe and prevent the sorcerer from being cut down. I sink my sword into the soldier's gut and pull my blade free, allowing Old Man to finish his incantation. I cover my ears just as an immense blast violently expels several enemies across the battlefield where they land in broken, odd angles in a twisted heap.

Across the meadow, my eye catches an immense form, far larger and broader than even Albain, and the blood freezes in my veins.

Though I have never seen the man before, I instantly know him, because even the guards at Abirad's castle only spoke of him in hushed whispers, so fearful were they of this towering behemoth before us. His tell-tale helm, a fearsome thing fashioned in the shape of a bull's head, two large horns protruding from the top, proclaim him to be Tarvus Bullgraden, more commonly know as The Bloody Bull, or simply The Bull. As the stories go, when he's not obliterating enemies with his greatsword, he uses his helm to gore his foes in a display of his bestial nature.

"Bromus!" he shouts, his voice seemingly loud enough to reverberate the ground on which we walk. He utters the words with unbridled hatred, and given what the All-Chieftain had said before about the Bromus attacking Abirad's men at every opportunity, I am not surprised that he does not greet us as friends.

I close with yet another enemy and watch in horror as The Bloody Bull catches sight of Eilis.

The Bloody Bull's voice erupts in a deep bellow. "The girl! She wears the mark of the All-Chieftain! Kill them all! Leave no one alive!"

He charges towards her, his sword held as his side, and the horns of his helm leveled towards her. Eilis, engaged with two other enemies, cannot move to defend herself. I slam my blade through another soldier, and I watch as Albain dispatches his current foe and spins around Eilis to meet The Bloody Bull head on as he comes for the All-Chieftain's heir.

More soldiers, answering the call of their lieutenant, converge on Albain and Eilis. Albain raises his sword to meet that of The Bull, and it becomes a clash between two giants. Eilis struggles to keep the guards off of them, and Dennan, Ragnar, and I begin to cut a swath through the large group of enemies that surrounds us so that we may assist our friends. Suddenly, Brock is beside me. He pulls his sword free from a dying enemy's body, and we fight our way towards Eilis.

Albain and The Bloody Bull exchange blow for blow, and the veteran warriors seem to be an even match. Albain manages to land a solid hit to The Bull's shoulder, but that only seems to enrage the lieutenant more and makes his strikes even stronger. The Bull swings for Albain's head, but the latter deftly dodges the strike. All the while, Albain is careful to keep himself between The Bull and Eilis.

More bodies fall to the ground around us as our group fights its way across the meadow. Suddenly, I see The Bloody Bull raise his enormous, steel boot, slamming it into Albain's stomach and causing the last of the Cur Clan to falter.

In horror, I watch as The Bull's sword plunges into Albain's chest, cutting through his armor as if it were cotton. There is a look of shock and pain on Albain's face, and I realize right away the severity of the strike- it is far too near the place I know his heart to be.

I hear Eilis's heartwrenching scream morph into a vengeful roar, and she throws herself towards The Bull, her axe raised to strike.

But Albain raises his arm to his side and gives her a hard shove that sends her several yards backwards. "No, Eilis!" comes Albain's strangled words. "Stay clear of him!"

But I know the heart of my oldest and dearest friend. She won't stand idly by while someone she cares for is in peril. I watch as she charges forward, heedless of the danger such an action presents.

More enemies close on our position, and again, I hear the familiar hum of the singing stones, followed by an ear-splitting crack, and instantly, five more enemies fall around us.

Albain, the sword protruding from his chest, is forced to his knees, but I watch as his hands seize the blade, the sharp edge cutting through his gloves and causing blood to spill down his arms. The Bloody Bull tries to force the blade deeper into Albain's chest, and the latter cries out in agony. Albain's arms shake as he pushes the blade back towards its wielder, and finally manages to free himself.

Eilis slams her axe into The Bull's side, the strike providing enough distraction to allow Albain to struggle to his feet. The Bull turns to round on her, but she moves with impressive dexterity, landing blow after blow against The Bull, but each barely dents his armor. Finally, she realizes the weak point at the joint of his knee, and she swiftly buries her axe into the back of his leg before pulling it free and hammering it again.

More enemies converge on the position of Albain and Eilis as the rest of us continue to fight our way towards them. Eilis turns her attention to a soldier who hurtles towards her, and one of Dennan's axes cleaves through the air, penetrating the man's armor and sticking in his chest. A dagger flies past my head and finds its mark in the gullet of another enemy while Scarlet vaults over a fallen soldier.

The Bull's leg buckles beneath him, and he starts to fall, just as the rest of us meet the blades of the other soldiers who are overwhelming the position of Albain and Eilis.

Albain charges forward, lowering his shoulder, and slamming it into the chest of The Bull, who collapses backwards, his armor resounding with a tremendous clang as his massive body smashes into the ground. With all that armor, he's like a turtle on his back, and with one swift motion, Albain lifts his sword high above his head and brings it down upon The Bull's neck, severing his head from his body.

Suddenly, Albain collapses to his knees. He begins to cough violently and expels blood onto the ground before him. Eilis rushes forward to aid him just as he begins to slump to the side. She catches him in her arms, doing her best to ease him to the ground, and I hear his labored breathing as he struggles to take in air.

Another earsplitting crack erupts around us, clearing the area of any remaining enemies. A glance around reveals that of our Bromus companions, only Dennan, Ragnar, and two of the members of the Wolf Clan remain, along with Albain who is struggling to survive his wounds.

The smell of burning accosts my senses as the ivy that covers the east side of Old Man's tower catches fire, and within moments, an intense conflagration tears through the area. The flames rapidly spread up the tower and begin to swallow the sorcerer's home.

"Albain! Albain!" Eilis desperately fights to stop the bleeding by pressing her hands against the wound. Blood seeps through at an alarming rate, staining her hands sanguine.

Albain shakes his head sadly, knowing it's pointless to even try. Eilis cradles him in her arms, and I can see the light beginning to disappear from his eyes. He beckons her closer, whispering something into her ear, and she loses any and all composure she has left, completely undone by whatever words he has uttered. I watch as she whispers something back to him, and he smiles up at her, his brief expression of joy soon consumed by pain and sorrow.

I knew she cared for him, but I underestimated the degree, because as she clings to his hand, pleading for him to live, and he looks up at her, his eyes full of adoration, yet his gaze growing weaker by the second, I see it as clear as day.

It's as if we are all frozen, and everyone around me seems to come to understand the truth of it at the same time. I see the realization in the eyes of Dennan and Ragnar as they look upon the couple with sympathetic gazes, and beside me, Scarlet's mournful expression causes me to wrap one of my bruised and bloodied arms around her shoulders and pull her tightly against me. Brock notices it, too, and when Eilis begins to weep anew, I see his own heart break at the sound of her grief.

As Eilis and Albain hold on to each other, we all see it for what it is. It's more than simple affection. It is love. She loves him, and her heart is being torn asunder with such force that I can practically hear its pieces fall. The fallen warrior struggles to maintain his hold on his life, fearful of the prospect of being taken from her before they've even had a chance to fully experience this strange and beautiful blessing that has blossomed between them.

We watch as Albain pulls Eilis down towards him, pressing his lips against hers, in what very well may be both their first and last kiss, bittersweet, as love and passion are tinged with the looming threat of loss.

Old Man comes to stand next to me. His expression is blank, and he seems unaffected by Eilis's sorrow. Suddenly, I see him turn on his heel, and the next thing I know, he's running towards the burning tower.

"Old Man! What are you doing?" I shout after him.

He doesn't even turn to look at me, and his words seem to echo across the meadow. "I can help him, Boy! I can save his life! But I need something first!"

And with that, he rushes into the rapidly growing inferno…

And I follow after him.

CHAPTER 27

As we pass through the doorway of the tower, the air is so hot that it hurts to breathe. While no flames have penetrated the interior on the ground level yet, the spread of them along the outside walls has turned the tower into a giant oven.

"We must hurry!" shouts Old Man over his shoulder. "There is no cure for death, but if Albain can cling to life just a while longer, I can stop it in its tracks!"

We ascend the stairs, and the higher we get, the denser the air becomes. As we pass into the hallway, we see that the fire must have penetrated the storage room through the window as the doorway is engulfed in flames.

I follow Old Man into the alchemy room. It, too, has begun to succumb to the inferno. Along the wall, several jars explode, splinters of glass flying through the air and scattering across the floor. Old Man approaches a chest and strains as he tries to open it.

"Boy! Help me!" he commands.

I do as he bids me, and between the two of us, we manage to pry it open. He quickly sorts through the contents of the chest and haphazardly tosses items out of the way as he searches for what he needs.

Finally, he leaps up, and there is a bottle, filled with a thick, blood-red liquid clutched in his hand. "Come! We need to get out of here."

We sprint back into the hallway, but by now the fire has begun to consume the floorboards there, and the way to the stairs is filled by a wall of flame.

"Is there another way out?" I ask.

"No," replies Old Man gravely. "Towers are designed to minimize routes for intruders. One way in; one way out."

I groan loudly as I push the door open to Old Man's bedroom. I find a large, thick blanket and quickly return to the hallway. I toss the blanket over our heads and shoulders.

"On three," I instruct.

He nods in understanding.

"One... Two... Three!" I shout.

We run through the fire, long, orange tendrils of flame licking fiercely at our legs and any exposed skin. I cry out as the flesh on my right arm begins to blister and burn.

The upper stairway is now filled with smoke, and each breath of air I take scalds my lungs. Old Man and I both begin to cough heavily. We make our way down the stairs as quickly as we can, but debris begins to fall from the upper levels. A large chunk of wood narrowly misses taking off my head, and Old Man is smacked in the shoulder when a loose stone falls.

We are very near the base of the tower, and I can see the doorway that promises freedom and a reprieve from the polluted air and oppressive heat. Our feet hit the stone on the bottom level, and just then, there is a loud, crashing sound that rapidly careens towards us. I glance upward to see a wooden beam fall in front of me...

Right where Old Man is standing.

"Old Man!" I shout.

He is pinned to the ground by the large, heavy piece of beam. It has landed on his left arm and shoulder. The sheer weight of it is likely crushing all the bones therein. I move to pull it off him, and the flaming wood begins to incinerate my palms. I cry out and push through the pain as I struggle with the beam. My head begins to swim, and I feel faint as I continue to be assaulted by the relentless heat and unbreathable air.

Within moments, Dennan's massive form appears in the doorway with Brock right behind him. Between the three of us, we manage to pull up the beam far enough to allow Old

Man to wriggle free. There are fresh burns on his face and neck, and he screams in pain as I help him to his feet.

"Let me." Dennan scoops him up as if he is a child, and Brock helps to support me as I am unsteady on my feet.

Scarlet stands just outside the tower. Her usually aloof expression is replaced with one of intense worry. Upon catching sight of me, she quickly dashes towards me. "Boy!" she calls, and I can hear the panic in her voice.

"I'm all right. I'll be all right," I assure her.

We make our way across the meadow, and as we do, there is a thunderous explosion that rocks the ground beneath our feet.

"My alchemy laboratory," mumbles Old Man.

As we near the place where Eilis still kneels beside her fallen Bloodsworn, she turns her face to me, and I see alarm flash across her features.

"Don't worry about us," I say quickly.

I glance down at Albain, and at first, I think we're too late. There is no color left in his face, his features an ashen death mask. Neither do I see even the slightest rise and fall of his chest.

"Is he-?" I begin to ask.

Dennan shakes his head. "He truly is a warrior; he keeps an iron grip on life." There is a tone of admiration in his voice when he says it.

"He lives, but barely," speaks Eilis softly.

"Barely is enough then," replies Old Man. "Quickly. Put me down next to him," he orders.

"It's a wonder he's still alive," remarks Brock.

Ragnar looks to Eilis. "That's because he has you. He has something worth fighting for... a reason to live."

Old Man pulls the stopper out of the bottle we managed to rescue. He begins to speak in strange words as he pours the dark, crimson liquid into Albain's wound. There is a thick, gurgling sound as the liquid seeps into Albain's chest.

Old Man, still continuing his unusual speech, presses a

hand against Albain's wound. His palm, burned from using the singing stones and further charred within the tower, is enveloped by a bright, white, pulsing light, and we all watch in awe as Albain's bleeding finally stops and the wound begins to close.

I hear Albain take a deep breath. Awestruck by what we have just seen, we all rush forward. The wound still appears quite serious, but the liquid seems to have forced much of the gaping hole back together.

Eilis's features soften with relief as Albain's breathing returns to normal.

It's then that I glance at Old Man. He sways upon his knees, and his features begin to grow lax. He starts to fall, and suddenly I quickly kneel beside him, catching him in my arms as I scream his name.

"Old Man! Old Man!"

"Abirad," speaks Old Man weakly. "He sent them here. He must have... to destroy the tower... so I wouldn't remember. But I remembered enough... not all, but enough."

Scarlet is beside me, her hand placed upon my shoulder in a comforting gesture.

"Tell me what to do!" I plead. "Heal yourself like you did for Albain." I seize the bottle in my hands. The inside is coated in a thick, wet residue, but no liquid remains.

Old Man smiles sadly. "I'm afraid there was only enough for one. He'll be fine now... He'll heal. I'm glad it came in handy. I don't remember exactly who I was, but I do recall I was not well-loved. I remember thinking there was likely to be an occasion during which someone would want to stab me." He laughs mirthlessly. "It's okay... this was my choice. I've accepted this."

Eilis seems to realize what he's saying, and instantly, she is beside me, her heart breaking for the second time today. "Old Man... Why? Why would you-?"

Old Man gives her a weak smile. "All magic comes with a price, Eilis. My wise, wise girl. And I've taken so much from you… from all of you… It's time I give something back."

"You've done enough. You've given us all so much," I argue. "You taught us everything you know, and you took care of us the best you could."

Old Man shakes his head sadly. "That wasn't enough, Boy. I realize how selfish I've been. Brock was right. This has all been my fault. How much evil have I wrought upon the world? It is because of me Abirad reigns supreme. I am not a good man. I doomed Isabel without a second thought, and I put you all at risk by coming here."

"No, no! Don't do this to me, Old Man! You can't do this!" My heart feels as if it is being forcibly torn from my chest as I hold on to him, begging for him to stay.

"I'm sorry, my Boy. I truly am." He looks to his bag where it was hastily discarded upon the ground. "The book. You need to read it. There are answers within. Use it to stop him before he brings about more grief… And the amulet… it's important… though, I don't remember why…" He blinks back tears. "It's my own fault… my own doing." His eyes search for Brock's, and my friend falls to his knees beside me.

"Old Man." I barely recognize my own voice; it sounds like that of a weeping child.

Old Man reaches for my hand, clutching it in his own. "I'm sorry… I'm so, so sorry… Please… forgive me… please…"

He gives me a sad smile, and moments later, there is no strength left in his fingers curled around mine.

With that, he takes his last breath.

CHAPTER 28

There's a spot not far from the remnants of his tower. It is shaded by beautiful willow trees, and even in the crisp fall, there are large, white flowers sprinkled throughout the area, giving it an almost otherworldly elegance.

It's there that we bury him.

I don't know how long we stand there in silence while we all try to process our own grief, but the setting sun reminds us that we need to make camp, and while Albain is stable, he still hasn't woken.

Brock sets to gathering wood for the fire while Scarlet and I attempt to locate our horses, many of which had fled in the fray. I find Albain's mount standing with its hoof upon the crushed skull of an enemy soldier. Apparently, the fool had gotten too close to the beast, and the enormous animal had dispatched him. Scarlet and I are both unable to draw close without being nipped, but Eilis is able to walk right up to the creature. The beast must know his master's love for her. She is able to grab his reins and leads him to our camp.

The remaining Bromus bury their fallen brethren, and the bodies of our foes are piled into a heap and burned, as Dennan points out that the smell of rotting flesh would likely attract wild animals. My second experience smelling burning flesh is far worse than the cauterization of Brock's wound had been. The stench is so awful that several times, I feel myself begin to wretch, and I must excuse myself so that I may vomit in the woods.

After the sun has set, I cry for the first time since I lost my name. Scarlet holds me, whispering soothing words in my ear. I need a few moments to be alone with my thoughts, so I make my way to the edge of our camp. Periodically, the rest of my companions come to check on me. Each one shows sympathy in his or her own way. Brock sits with me in silence for a time. Eventually, he rises and gives my uninjured shoulder a squeeze as he departs. Dennan comes up and offers me a draw from his flask, but I politely decline, and instead he claps me on the back nearly knocking the wind out of my lungs.

Ragnar sits beside me and plays me a song upon his lute. It's a bittersweet number, wrought with grief, yet promising hope.

"That was beautiful," I say quietly.

He places the lute across his lap and looks up at the stars that dot the evening sky. "Your friend... I didn't know him well, but he seemed to be a good man."

"He tried to be."

"That's all any of us can do is try." He puts his hand on my shoulder. "I know this hurts now, and it won't feel better tomorrow, or the next day, or the next. But eventually, you'll find some semblance of peace, and your heart will reclaim its song."

"Thank you, Ragnar."

"I'll leave you to your thoughts, but if you need anything, we're all here for you, Boy." He gives me a reassuring pat on the back, far gentler than Dennan's, before heading back towards the campfire.

I decide to check on Albain. Eilis hasn't left his side other than to take charge of her Bloodsworn's ornery steed, which is tethered on a nearby tree. It glances at me as I walk by, but I give it a wide berth, and it goes back to munching on its apple.

I sit down next to my friend, and for several moments, we sit in silence, neither of us sure what to say or do. Wordlessly, she wraps her arms around me, and I follow suit, draping my good arm around her shoulder. The other is so badly burned that I can scarcely move it without crying out. We sit nestled against each other, two lost children deprived of a dear member of our family, a friend, and a mentor.

"Boy," she says softly. "I love you. I don't think I've said that to you enough... and with all that's happened..." She takes a deep breath to steady the quavering in her voice. "I never got the chance to tell Old Man that, and I very nearly missed the opportunity to tell Albain, so before anything else goes to hell, I just wanted you to know that I love you." She presses a chaste kiss to my cheek.

I rest my head on her shoulder. "I love you, too, Eilis. I know you didn't get the chance to tell Old Man, but I think he knew."

She sighs. "Somehow, I'm not so sure. He was a man who knew so much, but at the same time, so little. He was surely the most intelligent person I've ever met, yet it was worldly things that escaped his notice."

I have to agree with her on that point. "That's all true." I shift slightly to ease the ache in my arm. "Do you remember the first time we met? You and I? They brought me to the yards, and I couldn't stop crying. You came over to me and wrapped me in a big hug, like you're doing now. Then you took me to Old Man. He knelt down beside me, and I remember thinking, who is this strange man with a bird's nest for hair?"

We both laugh at the memory.

"Then he gave me a pastry he nicked from the kitchen." I can practically taste the tartness of the apple and the sweetness of the cinnamon and honey as I recall it. "He told me that things would get worse before they got better, but it would turn out all right in the end. I always believed him. I still do."

Eilis smiles. "The first time I saw him, he was in his cell, playing a game of chess with some pieces he'd made of rocks and sticks he'd collected. I asked him what he was doing, and he pulled the pieces to the door of his cell and told me how to play," she recalls. "The guards would often usher me along after a few minutes, so it took him nearly a month to explain all the rules. Eventually, whenever I passed his cell, he'd already have made his move, and I'd take mine, and the next day, we'd do it all over again until one of us won. It was always him at first, but then I think he may have started to let me win. I actually hated chess," she reveals with a chuckle. "But I loved him."

For a while, we return to our silence, but a thought keeps nagging at my brain. "You know the worst of it?" I ask her.

"What?"

"He died without completely learning who he was. Eilis." I look into her soft, brown eyes, and I fight the urge to cry anew. "What if the same happens to me? What if I die without ever learning who I am?"

She pulls her arms around me tighter. "You won't, Boy. You'll find out who you are, and I promise I'll do everything in my power to help you."

"But what if I don't, Eilis. What if I never know who I am?"

She considers this for a moment. "Then, cherish who you are now. You are one of the strongest, kindest, most wonderful people I've ever met. You are my friend, like a brother to me, and someone I deeply cherish. While I truly hope you learn who you were before, I like you just fine as you are."

"Thank you, Eilis." I glance down at Albain, still unconscious. "I knew it! I knew it was more than just you fancying him." I say smugly. "So, you and tall, dark, and scowly do love each other!" I tease her, changing the subject.

She blushes and rolls her eyes at me. "That's what he whispered to me... before he started to fade. He told me he loved me."

"And you said it back to him, I presume?" I can't help but to grin as she reddens even more. "Truly, I'm happy for you." I glance back to the fire where the rest of our companions are gathered. "I hope Brock can be happy for you, too."

"I loved Brock," confesses Eilis. "But he never felt the

same for me. I suppose in some ways, I'll always love him. I think once you really love someone, you never stop, not completely anyway, but nothing will come of it, and in truth, I'm glad nothing has, because Albain..." She smooths the hair from his forehead. "This is something different entirely. It's as if each one of my breaths echoes his own. Should his cease, I know I'd live on, but I would be forever changed. My heart would be missing; he's claimed it."

"Then a terrible thief I am," comes a deep, gravelly reply.

Eilis and I both jump up in shock, and we see that Albain's eyes are opened. He looks exhausted, but he's awake, and he gives Eilis a slight smile.

"I'm a thief that's been captured and had my own heart stolen from me," he adds.

"Thank the Maker! Albain!" Relief floods her features as she kneels next to him and covers his face in kisses.

"Well, I'm happy to see you, too," he chuckles. "Help me up, will you?"

Between the two of us, we are able to pull him into a sitting position. The rest of our group, signaled by the commotion, quickly joins us, save for Brock, who remains seated by the fire.

"Glad to see you've finally rejoined us," greets Dennan with a grin. "Though you're still ugly."

"And you're still a prick," returns Albain, but his tone is good-natured. He groans as he repositions himself so that he can better look at Eilis. "I'm shite at this Bloodsworn business. You're under my protection less than a sennight, and I go almost getting myself killed."

"Saving my life," Eilis adds. "Surely, Granda can't doubt your loyalty now."

"Bugger him. I'm just glad to see your face again." He raises his hand and caresses her cheek before placing a soft kiss upon her lips. "How long have I been out?" he asks.

"All day and well into night," speaks Scarlet stepping up

beside me.

Suddenly, there is a strange growling noise, and Albain looks down at his stomach.

"I'll grab you something to eat," I offer. "Dennan killed a deer." I rise and go towards the fire to collect some of the still-warm meat from our supper.

I glance over to Brock, but his gaze is firmly fixed on Eilis.

"She looks… happy," he says quietly.

"Brock, that's because she *is* happy," I reply as a tear off a large joint of meat for Albain.

"You tried to warn me, Boy." I can hear the sorrow in his voice, and I see the look of regret in his expression. "You kept trying to tell me that I should confess my feelings to her. Now I fear I'm far too late. The way that they look at each other… There's really something there, Boy."

"Yes, there is. I can tell you that for a fact," I concur. "So, what are you going to do?"

Brock shrugs and sighs heavily. "I-I don't know. I've wronged her so many times… I realize that. Here, I accused Old Man of being thoughtless and selfish, and truly, I am no better. Wise gave me so much: her love, her trust, everything… and all I did was take it. I've been the selfish one. I've brought her so much misery; I want her to be happier. Perhaps, now it's time I follow Old Man's example, and finally do something for her… leave her to her peace, let her claim the happiness she deserves."

I nod in agreement. "I think that would be for the best."

* * *

Later, Eilis goes to grab another blanket for Albain, despite his protests that he's fine.

"Nonsense. You're practically frozen. Boy, would you sit with him for a moment?" she asks me.

Albain rolls his eyes. "As if I need tended like some kind of child."

"Act like one, and I'll treat you like one," Eilis turns and heads off in the direction of Albain's horse.

Albain turns to me, a slight smirk upon his face. "I do enjoy her fire," he remarks. He regards me silently for a few moments. "I am very sorry for your loss, Boy... and the role I played in it. Eilis told me how I came to still be alive now. If not for your Old Man, I surely would have died."

"You've nothing to be sorry for," I assure him. "You saved Eilis's life. She's like a sister to me, and I love her dearly. Had I lost her..."

Albain nods in understanding. "While I am very grateful to the old codger, why would he give his life for mine? We scarcely knew each other."

"He didn't do it for you; he did it for her." I gesture to Eilis who is rummaging through Albain's saddle bags. "Old Man and Eilis were the two prisoners who had been at the castle the longest. He took her under his wing. Even I came along later. Old Man watched over both of us... and he loved us... in his own way."

Albain looks impressed. "He must have been a very selfless man."

Suddenly, I hear Brock's voice behind me. "He was... In the end, he truly was."

CHAPTER 29

It takes us four days to reach the Bromus encampment. Albain is still recovering, and my own wounds impede us as well. When I have difficulty managing Horse's reins, Scarlet swings into the saddle behind me to ensure that I don't fall. Her own dapple grey mare is tied to Ragnar's steed. It is slow progress, but we finally reach the camp.

The scouts must have seen us coming, because as soon as we arrive, nearly the entire camp is waiting for us. Lark comes tearing across the grass with Dog at his heels. Eilis barely has time to dismount before he comes crashing into her with such force that he nearly knocks her off her feet.

"What took you so long?" he cries. "Granda made me tie so many knots in the ropes of the tents that I thought my fingers were going to fall off!"

Eilis's grandfather steps forward. There's a wide grin on his face at seeing his heir return home. "The boy has boundless energy. When running, and playing, and sparring, and riding, and literally anything else under the sun didn't slow him down, I had to find some task to put him to."

Eilis laughs and embraces her grandfather who holds her at an arm's length and looks her over as if to examine if she's still in the same condition as when she left.

"You look no worse for wear," he says. His eyes scan our party, and that's when he realizes the extent of our losses. He ushers us into his tent, and after hearing our story says to Eilis, "I hope you'll excuse me, my dear. I will need to be meeting with the Bear and Wolf Clans."

250

When we emerge from the All-Chieftain's tent, Lark is waiting for us. There's a serious expression on his typically jovial face. "So, are we going to talk about it?" he says frankly.

"What do you mean?" I ask him.

"I'm not blind. I see that Old Man didn't return with you. Did he decide to stay at his home? I'll be cross if he did without saying a proper goodbye." He crosses his arms over his chest, and it's then I notice just how much time he's been spending with Albain. When he does it, he looks almost like the grizzled warrior next to me.

Albain and Eilis exchange a look, and wordlessly, Albain scoops Lark up in one of his enormous arms. He's careful not to hold the kid too near the wound upon his chest, something that is still causing him quite a bit of pain. "Come, Lark. Eilis and I need to speak with you."

When I see the kid later, his eyes are puffy and red. He runs up to me, presses his face into my chest, and wraps his arms around me.

I ruffle his hair, and Scarlet appears next to us, gently stroking his back as he begins to weep.

"I sounded like an arse," he says, his teary words muffled as he cries into my shirt.

I half expect Eilis to come running up to scold him for his language, a word that, doubtless, he has learned from a certain Bloodsworn.

"I didn't mean to say those things! I'm not cross with him! I'm not!" insists the child as he clings to me.

"It's okay, Lark. You didn't know," I say in an attempt to soothe him. "And you were partly right. Old Man did stay home, though it wasn't his choice. It's a beautiful place... and Old Man lived in a tower, a great, enormous tower that practically touched the sky," I tell him. "He was a sorcerer once, but not like Abirad. He was a good man, or at least, he tried to be one." I pull out Old Man's bag and place it at his feet. "These are some of his things. I could use some help sorting through it all. Do you think you could help me?"

Lark nods dutifully, and the two of us sit down on my cot to go through the strange array of belongings that Old Man dumped into his bag. It is an odd assortment of books (some informational and others written in Old Man's hand), loose papers with strange symbols scribbled on them, and various jars, vials, and bottles filled with contents I cannot easily identify.

"Ugh!" exclaims Scarlet in disgust. "He just had to bring the jar of eyeballs!"

"Wow!" breathes Lark, taking it from her hands before she decides to violently toss it as far away from herself as possible.

Scarlet sits next to me. As she pulls it from the bag, her eyes are instantly drawn to the amulet. She holds it aloft and inspects it carefully. "This! This is something!" she exclaims. "This would have sold for a great deal in my old line of work."

"It's just a necklace," remarks Lark.

"Yes, but remember, this belonged to a sorcerer. It's probably magical somehow," theorizes Scarlet.

I recall what Old Man said about the amulet being important, so I tuck it into the pocket of my trousers for safekeeping.

Lark's hand closes on the leather pouch that contains the singing stones. I don't know why I decided to take them, but I somehow felt like he would have wanted me to, and so, after we buried him, I placed them in his bag along with everything else. "Do you think I could keep these?" he asks.

"I think Eilis would have me killed if I let you have those," I reply.

Lark shrugs. "Maybe there's something in all these books that will teach us how to use them."

Scarlet nods in agreement. "He's probably right."

Worried that Lark may get it into his head to try and use the stones, I put those into my other pocket.

For hours, we pore over the books, but it's difficult to decipher Old Man's chicken scratch. In frustration, I put the lot of it aside until I can attack the insurmountable task with a fresh mind. Truthfully, it's difficult sorting through his things. I keep expecting him to appear behind me and start rattling off the contents of the jars and bottles, or to eagerly snatch the book from my hands and wander off to his cot to devour the knowledge that's within.

But, of course, he doesn't, and my heart aches with the memory of him.

❋ ❋ ❋

With the deaths of several of the Bromus during the excursion to the tower, the camp takes on a tone of sorrow, but then, the Chieftain of the Fox Clan reminds the All-Chieftain of his previous promise to entertain suitors for his heir. Soon, the camp is once again a flurry of activity as preparations begin for the Presentation of the Suitors, a formal ceremony that hasn't been held since the All-Chieftain's own great-great grandmother had been the leader of the Bromus.

It's a sennight after our return when we gather in the dining tent for the ceremony. Honestly, I'm glad for the distraction. Lately, my mind and every spare moment has been consumed with going through Old Man's belongings. I miss him more than I can bear sometimes. We spent over seven years in the same cell, and even here, his vacant cot is mere feet away from me. Brock offered to remove it, but sometimes I like to sit there as I'm going through his things. His sheets still smell faintly of peppermint and licorice, two of his favorite treats. When we left the castle, I think his pockets must have been stuffed with them.

I know that Scarlet worries for me, though she doesn't outright say it. She frequently comes to check on me, and I can see the look of concern on her face when she learns I passed yet another night without any sleep. I have also been quite selfish with my time, yet she does not accuse me of neglecting her, and upon occasion, she can even convince me to leave the tent for some fresh air. In these instances, we head to the sparring area to watch our friends compete. Albain oversees Lark's training in combat, and Eilis, as heir to the All-Chieftain, must frequently demonstrate her battle readiness to ensure that her brethren know she is not only mentally strong but a powerful combatant. Other times I set out on my own to find Ragnar plucking at his lute. He helps me to keep my mind off my sorrow by teaching me to play simple songs, and when I manage those well enough, he teaches me more complex pieces.

Still, the moment I return to my tent, the familiar embrace of pain consumes my heart again. I know that this is all part of my grief, and that eventually, I will begin to reclaim some semblance of normalcy, whatever that means in this day and age. But for now, the opportunity to keep my mind otherwise occupied is quite welcome to me.

All of the Bromus are dressed in their finest formal attire, great kilts that have been recently washed and freshened for the occasion. The All-Chieftain has decreed that I, along with my companions, will wear the colors of the Oak Clan, as we have been accepted into his fold by way of our relationships with Eilis.

Lark, twirling here and there, dances around me and giggles as his kilt whirls with him.

Scarlet looks me up and down, and I feel as if I am being closely analyzed. Suddenly, she grins widely. "That's a good look for you," she says.

"Perhaps, but I pale in comparison to you," I reply.

She is wearing a long, blue dress with a shawl fashioned in the colors of the Oak Clan. I take her hand in my own, and we make our way to the ceremony.

As we enter the dining tent, Eilis looks terribly nervous. Her gaze frequently scans the crowd, and eventually, I realize why. Albain is nowhere to be seen. This is odd given his position as her Bloodsworn.

Despite the All-Chieftain being grateful that Albain saved his granddaughter, word of their public display of affection must have reached him as well, and he wasn't too thrilled to hear that his heir had, on at least two occasions, been kissing the last of the Cur Clan.

The ceremony begins, and one by one, the All-Chieftain calls out the name of each clan. As he does so, each clan sends up a potential suitor for Eilis. Eilis nods in polite acknowledgement as each suitor is announced. Suddenly, I see her expression brighten as Albain, dressed in his black and red great kilt, appears in the dining tent.

"And so ends the presentation of the suitors," announces the All-Chieftain hurriedly.

"Granda," begins Eilis. "That is not so. You have not called upon the Cur Clan."

The All-Chieftain groans. "Eilis, as there is only one member of that clan, and he is already your Bloodsworn, I didn't see the point. Surely, he doesn't mean to present himself as a suitor."

Albain makes his way to the front of the tent and steps in line with the rest of the suitors. "You're right. I'll not be presenting myself as a suitor."

Eilis looks absolutely crestfallen, her features plainly expressing her shock and disappointment. "You won't?" she asks.

Albain shakes his head.

The All-Chieftain, in contrast to his granddaughter, could not be more pleased by the announcement. He smiles smugly. "There? You see?"

"I won't chase after her like some dog with a bone," speaks Albain firmly. "She's worth far more that that." He looks to Eilis, who is clearly touched by his words. "I won't court her, and woo her, and put on airs..." He steps onto the platform and deliberately walks past the All-Chieftain without even a fleeting glance. Instead, he kneels in front of Eilis. "I won't do any of those things, because I'm no suitor. However..." He takes her hand in his, and a hush falls over the entirety of the assemblage as we all look on with bated breath to see what will happen next. "If she'll have me... then I'm hers and hers alone."

The entirety of the crowd erupts in shocked whispers, and as I am not very knowledgeable on the ways of the Bromus, I don't immediately realize the significance of what Albain is saying.

Suddenly, Dennan steps backwards, out of line with the rest of the suitors.

The All-Chieftain's eyes are wide with surprise. "Dennan! What are you doing?" the All-Chieftain demands.

"I rescind my offer. I'll not be a suitor for your heir," comes his reply. "It's obvious that The Cur... that Albain, loves your granddaughter. I won't stand between them."

Ragnar, too, takes a step back from the line. "Nor, I."

Finnen, the suitor from the Falcon Clan, nods in agreement. "We've all heard how he saved her from being cut down by The Bloody Bull. It's only right to entertain his request." He, too, steps back from the line.

Merrick of the Raven Clan steps back as well. "He's already taken the Bloodsworn Vow and proven himself true."

One by one, the remaining suitors retract their offers, though the one from the Fox Clan hesitates. Dennan and Ragnar give him a look that would chill the blood in one's veins, and with a heavy sigh, he, too, relents.

The All-Chieftain cannot dispel his disbelief, but even he is forced to acknowledge all Albain has done. "What they say is true enough. You did save her life, and for that, I am eternally grateful. You have also proven your worth to the clans." He looks to Eilis, and in doing so, his stern expression softens. He turns back to Albain and clears his throat. "What then would you ask of me, Albain, since you've already stated you do not wish to serve as a suitor to my granddaughter?"

"I ask nothing of you. I'll ask it of her." Albain tears a piece from the top of his great kilt. It's from a section that sits just over his heart. He crosses to Eilis and places the long scrap of fabric in her outstretched hand. Eilis looks absolutely ecstatic. I've never seen anyone appear so elated to receive a torn scrap of cloth.

The All-Chieftain takes a deep breath and closes his eyes, realizing some significance in the gesture that I still don't comprehend. Suddenly, he provides the context I need. "A betrothal then?"

Next to me, Scarlet spits out her cider, spraying Brock in the side of the face.

"Hey!" exclaims Brock.

She throws a napkin at him before resting her elbows on the table and placing her chin in her hands. "Well, this just got really interesting!"

Albain nods. "I've pledged my life to her once; I'll gladly do it again."

The All-Chieftain is rendered speechless, but when he finally finds his voice, he says something that makes Eilis beam with glee. "I've foolishly tried to put my hand in her affairs, and she has met me with resistance at every turn. I can't say I'm disappointed. She is her mother's daughter, and my heir, after all." The All-Chieftain addresses the rest of the clans. "I'll not make any decision for her. She is my heir, and whatever her will, I hope that you will accept it with my blessing." He returns his attention to Albain. "If you wish for her hand, then ask it of her."

Albain takes Eilis's hand in his, and yet again, I can see the expression of genuine love that passes between them. "Marry me. Or don't. Either way, I'm yours." He presses a kiss to her hand. "Always."

Eilis wraps her arms around his neck and cranes her face upwards as she stands on her tiptoes. Albain tilts his head towards Eilis, and he tenderly presses his lips to hers.

I know her answer before she even says it.

"Yes! Always."

Always is a peculiar word. In that moment, I realize the

gravity it holds. When each of them utters the word, it is as if, truly, a vow has passed between them, and as I look upon Albain and Eilis, I have no doubts it is a promise that will be upheld until the end of their days.

The All-Chieftain beckons them to approach him. He directs them to face each other and joins their hands together. He takes the piece of black and red cloth Albain had given to Eilis and binds their hands together with it, thus solidifying their betrothal.

✳ ✳ ✳

For the rest of the night, the entire camp is alight with joy and festivity. We feast, we dance, and we sit around the fire while we exchange stories and pleasantries. At one point, I see Albain head back into the dining tent to refill his tankard. Brock appears at my side and motions for me to follow him.

"What are you doing, Brock? You're not going to interfere are you?" I ask seriously.

He shakes his head. "No, but just in case Albain gets the idea I am, I need you to be there so he doesn't run me through with that sword of his."

As we approach him, Albain turns to face us, and upon seeing Brock, his expression darkens.

"Hello, Albain," I greet him.

"Boy." He folds his arms across his chest and regards Brock in silence.

Brock clears his throat as he tries to work up the courage to address Albain. "I just wanted to... I want to congratulate you. You're lucky, you know... to have her."

Albain nods. "I know. I'm fortunate that the first person she cared for was an idiot."

"So, she told you... about me?" asks Brock.

Albain snorts. "Of course. We have no secrets. We are to be wed, after all."

"You know I'd never try to come between you two," announces Brock firmly.

Albain laughs. "I know. You'd fail. Furthermore, if you tried, there would be nothing left of you."

Brock instantly pales at the obvious threat. "I-I believe that." He and Albain regard each other in silence for some time. "You really love her, don't you? It took me forever to see her for all she is." He shakes his head, embarrassed by his own foolishness. "When did you know? When did you realize how much she meant to you?"

"Around the time she punched me," replies Albain with a laugh, as he harkens back to the day we met him. "Figured a girl that fearless had more than a few surprises in her. I wasn't wrong. From then, it took only one smile or one kind word from her, and I'd walk through the fires of hell for her. To think that a mighty warrior could be undone in such a way." He chuckles at the thought. "I could withstand any weapon in battle, any foe, but not her."

Brock nods in agreement. "She truly is remarkable. Sadly, I realized it far too late. Promise me something?"

Albain grunts in reply.

Brock's gaze finds Eilis seated between Lark and Scarlet by the fire. "That you'll give her the life she deserves... the love she deserves. Everything that I was too foolish to give her." He extends his hand to Albain in a gesture of friendship.

Albain frowns slightly, as if considering the gesture. Finally, he accepts Brock's handshake to formalize their agreement. "As I promised her... Always."

CHAPTER 30

Once Albain and I are properly healed from our wounds enough to travel, we start making plans for our journey to Allanon. The All-Chieftain has stopped trying to dissuade Eilis from leaving. He seems to begrudgingly accept that there is no way she would be willing to part with Lark before she needs to.

"Very well," the All-Chieftain finally concedes. "I'll send a raven with a message to King Ruden with word of your impending arrival and the reason for your visit. While I certainly wouldn't call him a friend, especially given his unwillingness to intercede in our war against Abirad, we have been allies before, and despite his recent madness, I know he will receive you with my blessing."

"Madness?" asks Lark, his eyes wide.

The All-Chieftain quickly corrects himself. "Er-um... I suppose, madness isn't quite the right word. In his grief, he has become a bit... *eccentric*. He does nothing but mourn in a darkened castle, the shades always drawn to block out the light of the day. That's how it has been for years now. He has been but a shadow of his former self, as I hear it. But don't worry, Lark, or should I say, Prince Trystan?" The All-Chieftain ruffles Lark's hair, and the boy frowns up at him before batting his hand away. "Once he sees you, his heart is sure to warm."

"I doubt it, but I hope you're right," mutters Lark, unconvinced.

Later, as Lark, Scarlet, and I are gathered together to once again go through Old Man's belongings, the kid is sulkier than I've ever seen him. Despite my insistence that he should be excited to meet his father and live in a big castle as a prince, Lark is quite forlorn over our impending departure.

"I don't see why I can't just stay here. I like living with Eilis, and Albain, and Granda," he laments. "And I doubt the king is going to let me see them very much. He'll probably want me to study all the time and become a proper prince. Where is the fun in that? I like riding and swordfighting and all that sport."

"You can still do those things at the castle," I tell him. "Princes can do pretty much whatever they like."

"For example," adds Scarlet, "they can give their friend Scarlet enough gold so that she can buy a little house in the country where she can raise chickens and eat them."

I toss her the roll that I took with me from breakfast. She quickly devours it. We've been so hard at work that we toiled straight through our mid-day meal. With Scarlet's hunger at least somewhat sated, we return to the task of attempting to discern anything useful about Old Man's belongings.

We've been at the task for days and days, and we've barely managed to crack the surface of the contents of his bag. We were able to determine that the small vial of gold liquid is something Old Man developed to bring luck to the user. Scarlet scoffs at that, but when she places a minute dab on her wrist and proceeds to win hand after hand of cards, she tucks the rest of the bottle into her bag for safekeeping.

A while later, Albain and Brock return from the sparring ring. Brock is sporting a large, fresh bruise on his forehead, and Albain is lecturing him about keeping an eye on his enemies at all times.

"If I'd been an actual enemy, I'd have taken off your head," remarks Albain. "Perhaps you should focus more on your enemy's weapon than impressing Molly."

"I can't help it," grumbles Brock. "She kept calling my name. What was I supposed to do? Ignore her?"

Albain looks at him incredulously. "Aye! That's exactly

what you should have done!" He rolls his eyes. "Well, I guess we know the easiest way to defeat you in battle. Just have some tart bat her eyelashes at you, and anyone can just come up and lop your empty head off."

"She's not a tart!" exclaims Brock. "Is she? Albain, is she really a tart?"

Albain laughs and beckons for Lark to come with him. "Come on, boy. Eilis is waiting for us. We thought we'd take you down to the stream to fish for a bit."

Lark's eyes widen with delight. "Really? That would be great!" He bounds towards Albain and takes the immense warrior by the hand. The two of them disappear from the tent to make their way towards the stream that cuts through the forest.

Scarlet shakes her head sadly. "His highness is going to have a very hard time being away from Albain and Eilis. Half the time I forget they're not his actual parents. They act enough like a family."

I nod in agreement. "He'll adjust. It will take him some time, but I'm sure he will love King Ruden just as well."

Brock plops down next to me. "Still at it?"

"Yes, and as usual, getting nowhere," I reply. I absent-mindedly fiddle with the contents of my pocket, one of which is the amulet. I sigh and take it out for about the millionth time today to look at it. "He said this was important, but he couldn't remember why."

"Maybe you should try putting it on," suggests Brock.

Scarlet rolls her eyes. "As if he hasn't done that already."

"Actually... I haven't," I sheepishly confess. "I've been avoiding handling any of this stuff too frequently for fear of what some of it might do. I was hoping the books would shed some light on all this." I hold the amulet aloft. "Scarlet, what if you're right and there is some kind of spell on it?"

Scarlet shrugs. "There's really only one way to find out."

I put the chain of the amulet around my neck and with great anticipation, I wait for something, anything, to happen.

Nothing does, so I breathe a heavy sigh of relief and reach for one of the books, a journal written in Old Man's nearly indecipherable handwriting.

As soon as my fingers close around the journal, my head begins to throb, my breathing quickens, and my thoughts start to swim. I try to turn my head to glance around the room, but my tent, along with my friends, are nowhere to be seen. Instead, I'm in the alchemy room of Old Man's tower.

Before me, there is a man seated at a table. He appears to be fairly young, likely in his mid-twenties, with piercing green eyes and ebony hair. Somehow, he looks familiar to me. It's his eyes in particular, but for some reason, I just can't quite place him.

"Fenustus, I can't simply stand idly by while King Ruden takes our crops and starves our people!" the man shouts.

Fenustus? He's talking to me, but I'm at a loss as to why he addresses me so.

Suddenly, I feel myself sigh heavily and press my fingers to my temple. I run my hand through my hair, but it is long and unruly, definitely not my own. "Sebastian, what you are proposing is open revolt. That kind of defiance does not go unpunished."

The voice that emanates from me is not my own, but it is a voice that I know well. I can see his reflection in the mirror that hands above a table near the bookshelves.

Old Man.

"Fenustus, please!" begs Sebastian.

This man's voice. There is something familiar there as well, but again, its origin is lost upon me. There is nothing truly remarkable about the man. His clothes are stained with dirt and sweat, and there's mud underneath his fingernails and callouses upon his hands. His forearms are well-muscled and his shoulders strong, but the rest of his body is slim and lanky. In fact, he's so thin his ribs practically protrude from beneath his shirt. This is a man who must do a great deal of manual labor. The way he carries himself, he reminds me a bit of Quellin. Perhaps he is a farmer of some sort.

"I don't expect that I won't be punished, or even killed for

it…" replies Sebastian, "…but if it means my family is safe, then so be it!" He clutches my hands, Old Man's hands, in his own. "Please, Fenustus! You must consider it at least. You've seen what's happening! You see the sick and young dying without enough food to allow them to even cling to life. Meanwhile, Ruden turns a blind eye to our plight. He cares not for our suffering! As long as Vericus flourishes, he cares nothing for the cost!"

My feet begin pacing so fervently that it seems as if I will wear a hole in the floorboards. My mind feels clouded, lost in thought, and absentmindedly I begin chewing on his thumbnail, something I'd seen Old Man do when he was truly worried or could not bring an answer to an important question to mind.

"Fenustus!" cries Sebastian.

"Sebastian!" I turn to face him, and I hear the tone of anguished indecision in Old Man's voice. "You know not what you ask of me!"

"Think of all the people you could help!" protests Sebastian passionately.

I sigh heavily, shaking my head as if attempting to dissuade myself from what I'm about to say. "I…I may be able to help."

Sebastian's expression is one of gratitude and relief. "Anything! Anything you can do to help our cause would be welcome."

I cross to a chest and remove a book, the same journal that is currently in my own hands. I open it to a particular page and push it towards the other man.

"What is this?" asks Sebastian in confusion. "Rocks? Singing rocks?"

"Singing stones," comes Old Man's reply.

"Boy! Boy! Ugh! This is all my fault! I told him to put the wretched thing on!" I hear Scarlet's voice screaming into my ear.

"Well, don't touch the thing!" shouts Brock. "What if it's some cursed thing, and it gets us all!"

I shake my head back and forth as if dispelling a strange

dream. I blink my eyes and see Scarlet's worried expression. She throws her arms around me and squeezes me so hard I can't breathe.

"Boy! What the hell just happened?" cries Brock.

"I-I don't know," I reply, unsure of how to articulate what I've just seen.

"Well, obviously it was something. For the past ten minutes you've just been staring into space. We both were yelling and shouting at you and shaking you, and you didn't so much as blink at us," informs Scarlet, concern in her voice.

"I can't... I can't explain it... It was almost like a dream. It kind of felt like... like when I had that memory when I was riding the horse. Only, it wasn't one of *my* memories. It was as if I was seeing everything through Old Man's eyes."

I recount everything to them the best I can; I'm careful not to leave out even the most seemingly insignificant detail out.

"So, who is this Sebastian guy?" questions Scarlet.

"I don't know," I reply. "As I said, he kept begging Old Man to help him. He blamed King Ruden for his people starving and was going to lead some kind of opposition against him."

"A revolt against a king? That sounds like messy business," comments Brock.

I nod. "Old Man seemed very conflicted about helping him, but... the singing stones. He thought of some way to use them to aid Sebastian's cause."

* * *

Brock rounds up Albain and Eilis, and the next thing I know, we're meeting with the All-Chieftain in his tent. Not sure of how this meeting will unfold, we opt to allow Lark to remain frolicking about with his friends. We gather around the table, and I explain everything I saw. All the while, the All-

Chieftain frowns in both concern and confusion.

The Bromus leader turns to one of his guards. "Angus, go fetch Hivolk."

I recognize the name as being that of the Oak Clan's historian. I'd met the man only once before in passing, but Old Man had spoken of him quite frequently since our arrival at the Bromus encampment. He had spent quite a bit of time with him, but beyond discussing Old Man's home, I don't know what they spoke of.

Hivolk is a large man with brawny shoulders and a long, white, braided moustache. There is a certain resemblance between him and the All-Chieftain, and when I inquire after it, Eilis tells me they are cousins.

"You see!" cries Hivolk upon entering the tent. "I told you you'd have need of me someday! Can't solve all your problems by swinging an axe around, Seamus!"

The All-Chieftain groans. "I almost didn't summon you. I knew this would go to your head."

"So," Hivolk sits down to the left of the All-Chieftain. "What can I do for you?"

"Our friend, we called him Old Man," I begin. "He came to see you very often."

"Aye, he did. I was mightily sorry to hear of his passing," replies Hivolk genuinely.

"Hivolk, what did you two talk about when he came to see you?" inquires Eilis.

"Ah, well, he wanted to read the histories I'd written down. Bloody quick reader he was. He practically devoured every book I put in front of him. I'd lend him stacks upon stacks, and he'd have 'em all read by the next day!" relates Hivolk.

I can't help but to smile; books had truly been one of Old Man's greatest pleasures, and I recall how elated he had been every time he returned to our tent with an enormous armload of reading material.

Eilis appears lost in thought for a moment then asks.

"Was there anything in particular he was focused on learning about?"

"Aye. He was particularly interested in the rise of Abirad," relates Hivolk. "Made sense given his imprisonment."

"Did he ever mention someone named Fenustus?" I ask him.

Hivolk rubs his chin in thought. "He didn't, but I've heard the name. Fenustus was the name of that bloody sorcerer who helped to incite the Bread Revolts some years back. Wasn't so much a revolt as a massacre. When King Ruden caught word of that little uprising, he slaughtered anyone who opposed him. If I remember correctly, he decided to make an example of their leaders. Went to a little town called Cynwrig. It was a farming village, but Fenustus and his co-conspirator lived there. King Ruden had the town razed, and his soldiers killed just about everyone who lived there, even the folk who were simply minding their own and had no part of the rebellion."

In that moment, I'm glad that Lark is not with us. The way Hivolk tells it, King Ruden's actions sounded quite a bit heavy handed. To put down an uprising makes sense, but to destroy an entire village and allow innocents to be killed is unfathomable. Lark needs no more reason to fear journeying to Vericus, and such a tale might make him even more wary of the king.

"The entire village? Even..." Eilis can't seem to bring herself to ask the question.

"Aye," replies Hivolk quietly. "Even the women and children. However, that sorcerer, Fenustus, he turned tail when the battle began. His ally lived, but almost all of their supporters died in the failed revolt, so the other man went into hiding just after, and no one has seen hind nor hair of him since."

My companions and I all exchange shocked looks, floored by what we've just heard and for several moments, we are all dumbstruck into silence until I can find my voice again.

"His co-conspirator... What was his name?" I question.

"He was just some foolish farmer who thought he could stand against the crown. Sad, really. Hmm... what was his name?" wonders Hivolk aloud.

"Was it Sebastian?" asks Scarlet. "The man from the memory you saw, Boy."

Hivolk rubs his chin in thought, considering the question for several moments. "Aye... I think it was."

* * *

Afterwards, we set to packing for our departure to Vericus the next day. I hear a slight cough, and when I turn around, Hivolk is standing just inside the flap of my tent.

"Hello there, Boy. I should have come sooner to express my condolences on the passing of your friend. He seemed a good sort," speaks the historian solemnly.

"Thank you. I know he enjoyed your company," I reply.

"It was nice to have someone to talk of the old days with. Seamus finds my company rather tiresome and is always telling me to 'go play with my books.' Stubborn old ox! If it weren't for me, he'd be a piss poor All-Chieftain. I know every detail of the clan dating hundreds of years back! There's not a single All-Chieftain and his or her strategy that I haven't studied. Know what did in All-Chieftain Finley Oakheart?"

I shake my head.

"Rotten berries! You know what's likely to do my cousin in?" He continues when I don't answer. "All that hot air he carries about! If he'd shut his trap long enough to listen for two minutes, he might just learn something!" Hivolk shakes his head disapprovingly. "Anyway, I come to offer my services. I thought I might take a look at that necklace you'd been talking about."

Before we had departed the meeting, Eilis had convinced me it might be prudent to tell Hivolk all I'd seen in Old

Man's memory and how I had come across it. Hivolk had immediately returned to his tent to delve into his books and see what he could find on the matter.

"I'm no sorcerer," says Hivolk, "but I've read up on many, many topics, and perhaps I might be able to shed a little light on things for you."

While I worry over showing the amulet to anyone, especially now knowing it's likely that it is enchanted, if Old Man trusted Hivolk, then I feel compelled to do the same. Plus, as one of Eilis's kin, that gives him an extra vote of confidence from me. I show him the amulet, but he doesn't take it from my hands. Rather, he inspects it from a reasonable distance as it dangles from the chain in my hand.

"Have you tried to do it again?" he asks.

"Why would I ever do that? The first time was unnerving enough," I tell him.

"To ensure it wasn't some random coincidence. It happened when you touched his journal, didn't it? Try it again."

Reluctantly, I place the chain around my neck. I take a deep breath and take Old Man's journal from the bag. I prepare myself to again be swept away into one of his memories.

Nothing.

"Feel anything?" asks Hivolk.

"No," I say, almost disappointed.

"Maybe it only works once. Go on then. Try something else that belonged to him," he suggests.

My hand closes on the jar of eyeballs.

I'm standing in the alchemy room. There's a dead toad in front of me, and the sharp knife to my left tells me it didn't die of natural causes.

"Ugh. I'm getting sick of toad leg soup, but I won't let this creature have died in vain. So long as I need more of these, it looks like that's all I'll be eating." The voice is coming from me, but a glance at the long, slender fingers and the smell of peppermint tell me that I am Old Man again.

"At it again, Fenustus?" comes another voice from the door-way.

It's Sebastian, but slightly younger this time. He appears to be in his late teens, and he carries a large bag slung over his shoulder.

"Ah! Sebastian! How fortunate! I was just going to try my hand at brewing a luck potion. Would you like to watch?"

Sebastian's eyes light with glee and he hurries forward, dropping the back on a nearby table. "Do you even have to ask?"

"How's your Da then?" I hear Old Man ask.

Sebastian's features are tinged with sorrow. "Still sick. Doctor says he's not got long left, but I know my Da. He's still got plenty of fight left in him."

"I have always thought well of your father. When I first set up my tower here, the locals weren't exactly running to greet me with open arms, but your Da was a good man. He said I had a right to settle anywhere I wished, just as long as I didn't make the whole village smell like brimstone with my alchemy."

I move to a small cauldron and dump in a third of the jar of toad eyeballs. Then I add an assortment of other vials and bottles. The liquid begins to simmer then progress to a rapid boil, and when there is a bright flash of yellow light, Old Man declares it is done.

"Will it work, Fenustus? Do you really think it can bring luck to someone?" questions Sebastian.

My eyes drift to the bag. "What's in the bag?"

"Sweet rolls made with anise. They taste like licorice," Sebastian explains. "Mum said you like them. And she sent you a bit of peppermint tea, too, with her thanks for sending that potion to ease Da's pain."

"Then, yes. It must be working already!" laughs Old Man. He takes a roll from the bag and chews off a big bite. I have to admit, it tastes pretty good!

Sebastian stares into the cauldron. "This is all fascinating! I wish I had a mind for such things!"

"Well, with enough anise rolls and peppermint tea, I might be persuaded to take on an apprentice," says Old Man.

Sebastian laughs and rises to leave. "No, but thank you all the same. I think my place is on the farm, like my Da, and my Granda, and his Da before him."

"Oy! Boy! Snap out of it, will you?"

Two large, beefy hands shake me back and forth, and a moment later, Hivolk's worried face comes into focus. "Oy, was that it then?" he asks. "You just blanked out there for a bit. I was starting to get worried!"

"Yes," I reply. "Another memory."

"I see." Hivolk seats himself on Brock's cot, and the entire thing sinks under his heavy weight. "Phylactery."

"Bless you," I say.

"No, no, Boy. That pretty necklace you got there. I think it's a phylactery of sorts. Some sorcerers learn more in their lifetimes than they can ever remember, so they store their memories in phylacteries. Frees up room in their heads I guess. Then, when they need them, they wear the phylacteries to get their memories back. This one seems to be tied to certain objects. Whenever you touch something that belonged to your Old Man, you're likely to get something from it."

My heart begins to thunder in my chest. It sounds absolutely insane, but it's just the type of insane that makes sense when it comes to Old Man.

When Hivolk takes his leave, and I'm left to my own devices, I put the amulet back in my pocket and sit on Old Man's bed. I can still taste the sweet anise roll on my tongue and smell the strong aroma of peppermint tea, and for one bittersweet moment, it's as if he's right there with me.

CHAPTER 31

The next day, just before dawn, we gather in the dining tent for a final meal before we leave the Bromus encampment. While most of us are eager to make our way to Vericus, Lark is simply inconsolable.

"I don't want to leave, Dog!" cries Lark, tears streaming down his face. "Why can't he come, Albie?"

Albain sighs and lets Lark press his face, runny nose and all, into the warrior's chest as he weeps. "It's as I said, Lark. We don't know what we are going to encounter on the road, and we have to go by horse to get to Vericus as quickly as we can. Dog wouldn't be able to keep up, and I don't think he'd enjoy being bumped about on a saddle all day."

"Don't worry, young man. I'll take good care of Dog, for you," promises the All-Chieftain. "I'll even let him sleep on my bed, eat all the meat he could ever want, and chase sticks until his heart's content."

"And as soon as you get settled in to the castle, Albain and I will personally bring him to you," adds Eilis.

Lark sniffles but nods his head. He grabs a few pieces of bacon from his plate and goes over to Dog who is busy investigating the contents of a large bowl of bread pudding precariously balanced on the edge of a table.

Albain frowns as he looks down at his shirt. There is a large, wet imprint that looks a lot like Lark's face there. Albain groans, but Eilis places a kiss on his cheek and takes his hand in her own.

"Thank you, Albain. You're so good with him," she remarks.

Albain smirks. "If all it takes for me to get you kissing on me like that is to let Lark use my shirt like a handkerchief, then I'll be sure to pinch him as much as possible on the way to Vericus," he teases.

The All-Chieftain rolls his eyes. "Excuse me. I think I need to go be sick somewhere." He rises from our table and makes his way to the table claimed by the Wolf Clan.

"So, how long do you think it will take us to get there?" asks Brock.

Albain shrugs. "A fortnight. If we can push through by moonlight each night, maybe less."

"Ugh," groans Scarlet. "I was just starting to get used to not having to hear Brock's incessant snoring."

Brock narrows his eyes at her. "Ah, Scarlet. I'd say I've been missing your constant cruelty, but truthfully, I don't think I've missed it all that much."

"Please. You know that you live for my derision," replies Scarlet, sticking her tongue out at him.

He throws a grape at her, and she catches it in her mouth, chewing as loudly and obnoxiously as possible.

Albain sighs and looks to Eilis. "This is going to be a long trip isn't it? I'll be amazed if the lot of them make it there in one piece."

* * *

We gather our belongings, pack our saddlebags with provisions, and check the fastenings on our saddles. The All-Chieftain ensured we are outfitted with the finest weapons and armor that the Bromus can provide, which are all of excellent craftsmanship.

A large portion of the encampment comes to see us off, and Ragnar seeks me out to personally bid me farewell.

"Here," he says as he hands me his lute. "So you can keep

practicing."

"Ragnar..." I look down at the instrument he has gifted to me. In his hands, it creates the most beautiful music; in mine, it is only passable. "I couldn't."

"You can, and you will. Even in my darkest times, it is the melodies of this lute that have brought me back from the brink of sorrow. I have others, but this... this was the first one I ever held, as it was the first for you."

He pulls me into a strong embrace and claps me on my back. I truly hope that I have the opportunity to visit the Bromus again as I know I'll miss his easy laugh and relaxed demeanor.

Albain, clad in his black battle armor, helps Eilis to triple check our provisions.

"I see you've decided to quit your pretty skirt again, much like last time we traveled. I suppose kilts don't provide much leg protection, do they?" jokes Brock.

"Bugger off, Brock or you'll need greater protection for your face when I decide I've seen enough of it," retorts Albain with a smirk.

While I can't say that they've become friends, they have been spending quite a bit of time at the sparring ring. Brock finally seems to have realized he's not the greatest fighter on the planet, and he could stand to learn something from more experienced warriors. While Albain is a rough teacher, he is an effective one, and Brock seems to have improved under his instruction.

"Albain. A word, if I may." The All-Chieftain beckons the last of the Cur Clan to him and the two seem to engage in a short, but very serious discussion, likely about the continued safety of the All-Chieftain's heir. After some time, the leader of the Oakheart Clan seems appeased by Albain's responses and gives him an awkward pat on the shoulder before dismissing him.

Albain shakes his head in amusement. He gives Eilis a slight smile as he passes her. The latter approaches her grandfather, and the old man pulls her into a strong embrace.

"Hurry home, love. I've lost too much time with you already. I won't spare another minute more than is necessary," says the All-Chieftain. "You stay close to that Bloodsworn of yours. I'm still not overly fond of him, but I know he'll do his duty for you and that no harm will befall you while he draws breath."

"I love you, Granda. I'll be back as quick as I can," she promises. Eilis kisses her grandfather's cheek and gives him one final embrace before making her way towards her horse.

Lark solemnly trudges up to the All-Chieftain. Dog looks almost as sorrowful as Lark. His shaggy, black head is bowed, and his tail droops pitifully.

"Go to Granda, Dog," commands Lark, and the beast reluctantly obeys. He seats himself beside the All-Chieftain but stares up at Lark miserably. Lark kneels next to Dog and scratches him behind the ears and under his chin. "You be good for Granda, all right? I'll see you again soon. Stop stealing Willa's stockings and burying them in the pig pens. It's not nice, and it makes her all fussy." I can see him bite his lip to keep from crying. He rises and throws his arms around the All-Chieftain. "Goodbye, Granda."

The All-Chieftain chuckles. "Called Granda by the Prince of Allanon. I never in a million years would have dreamed such a thing. You take care of yourself, young man, and if you ever have need of us, you need only send word to me, and I'll have every clan of the Bromus at your doorstep quick as I can."

The rest of us bid farewell to the All-Chieftain, Ragnar, Dennan, Hivolk, and the rest of the friends we've made. When the sun finally rises, bringing dawn in its autumnal splendor, we turn our horses west towards Vericus.

❊ ❊ ❊

We make good time on our journey, and a sennight passes before I decide to try my luck with the amulet again. Albain and Brock keep watch over our camp while Lark, Eilis, and Scarlet slumber. Scarlet stirs when I move to rise, and she looks at me with a questioning gaze when she sees me pull the amulet out of my pocket.

"Boy, what are you doing?" she asks, a tone of worry in her voice.

"I thought I might..."

"Fine, but let me join you in case anything odd happens," she states firmly.

"You mean, odder than seeing Old Man's memories through a magical necklace?" I jest.

"Fair point," she concedes as she pulls herself into a sitting position next to me. "So, what are you going to try?"

Without hesitation, I pull out Old Man's spellbook.

Scarlet's look of concern doesn't go unnoticed by me. "Are you sure that's a good idea?"

"No, but it might be able to give us some answers."

I take a deep breath and slip the chain of the amulet around my neck.

Immediately, I am barraged by an inordinate amount of swirling images of varying degrees of acuity. There are so many that I can't focus on just one, and with a cry, I pull the chain over my head and drop it on the ground next to me. I feel dizzy and overwhelmed, and my head throbs as if it's just been squeezed in a vice.

Albain and Brock, their swords drawn, are standing on either side of me.

"We thought you saw something," says Brock.

"I did... too much. Just not out there," I reply, gesturing to the woods around us.

"Maybe just try one page," Scarlet suggests.

I nod, randomly opening to something in the back of the book, a page scrawled with Old Man's indecipherable handwriting.

I'm standing in the meadow outside of the tower. There are singing stones clutched in my outstretched hand, and a look to my left reveals that I'm not alone. Sebastian stands next to me. He looks older again, much like the first time I saw him. He no longer wears the stained clothes of a farmer, but long, dark blue robes much like Old Man's. However, something has drastically changed in his expression. His gaze is vacant, void of all emotion.

"I'm sorry, old friend, truly I am," apologizes Old Man, his voice filled with regret. "But there was no other way. Your vengeance has claimed too many lives, and I cannot, in good conscience let you go on any further in this course."

Sebastian does not respond in any way; it's as if his mind is somewhere else entirely.

Old Man continues. "I understand why you felt you had to do this. Emily was a good girl, an innocent girl, who did not deserve the fate this cruel life wrought upon her, but how many souls have you taken in revenge for her death, and how many more will suffer? Yes... it had to be done." Old Man sounds as if he's attempting to convince himself that whatever action he took was justifiable, and the sinking feeling in my stomach tells me that something awful has happened to poor Sebastian.

Suddenly, Sebastian blinks his eyes and looks at me in confusion. "Who are you? Where am I?"

CHAPTER 32

"No. It can't be. Old Man wouldn't..." Eilis shakes her head in disbelief. I can see that she is struggling with the information I have just given her.

Next to me, Brock leans against a tree. There is disappointment in his expression, but I can't say that I see surprise there. "Perhaps, Old Man wouldn't, but we don't know what he was like when he was this Fenustus."

Scarlet nods in agreement. "He already admitted he was the one who came up with the memory spell. Wouldn't it make sense that he tried to use it?"

Honestly, it's something that I am still having difficulty accepting as well, but Scarlet is right. In fact, her logic mirrors my own. My old friend not only created the spell that robbed me, and so many others, of our memories, but he also used it on someone, someone who he had once considered a friend. This poor Sebastian fellow likely never even saw it coming.

My relating of this memory to my companions creates a dark cloud over our day. We ride in silence, each of us aggrieved to learn of Old Man's transgression.

* * *

As we move closer to Vericus, the villages become more populated, unlike the ghost towns that we'd seen on the first part of our journey. So great is our melancholy in the wake of the revelation about Old Man's past that we fairly jump at the chance for distraction. When we pass through a rather large village, and Lark spots a food stall selling fresh caramels, he manages to convince Albain it wouldn't be a bad idea to stop for a bit. Honestly, the warrior resists at first, until the smell of roasted chestnuts catches his nose, then suddenly he needs no further persuasion.

We browse our way from stall to stall and examine the finery, bits, and baubles each artisan has to offer. When Eilis spots the bookshop, she practically sprints through the door, and Albain begrudgingly follows after her. The rest of us make our way there and meander through the stacks as Eilis darts from here to there coveting each book she takes in her hands.

Scarlet catches sight of Albain as he attempts to obscure something in his hands. It's a small, red, leather-bound volume that looks miniature in his large palms. "I didn't take you for a great lover of poetry, Albain," teases Scarlet.

"I'm not," he says gruffly. "I think it's horseshite, but Eilis favors it." He holds the book out to me so that I may look it over. "Do you think she would like this?"

"I think she'd like just about anything that came from you," I tell him.

Albain represses the urge to smile at the sentiment and makes his way towards the shopkeeper to purchase it.

Lark stares out of the large window at the front of the store. His gaze is fixed on the commotion in the main square. "What's going on out there?"

"Oh! They're setting up for the festival," the shop-keeper explains. "Used to be a magnificent one in Vericus, but the king put a stop to that once the queen passed and Prince Trystan vanished. We don't celebrate peace with Blackwood anymore, obviously, so we had to look for some other excuse to celebrate. Now we have the Vigil Festival. It's a celebration of faith in the thought that Prince Trystan is alive and well and will return to Allanon one day."

I see Lark shift uncomfortably. "Well, that's a pleasant thought."

We head towards the town square where even more

vendors have assembled. There is a flower seller with a cart that contains a vast array of beautiful flowers. It's this that draws Scarlet's attention. She and I make our way there while the rest of our companions amuse themselves by watching a firebreather.

Scarlet's pale, trembling hand reaches out towards a single, red rose, absolutely perfect in its splendor. Each part of it immaculately formed, its color is vibrant, and the feel of its petals is soft to the touch.

"It's beautiful," I comment.

Scarlet doesn't respond to me right away, but several moments later, when she turns to face me, I notice the tears in her eyes.

"Scarlet?" She must hear the worry in my voice. "What is it?"

"A memory," she says quietly, taking my hand in hers. "A single red rose on a pauper's grave. My mother's grave." She takes a deep breath in an attempt to steady her nerves and dispel the sorrow that threatens to consume her.

"Scarlet... I'm so sorry," I say, taking her other hand in my own.

"Why? It's not your fault she died," she replies. "When she passed, we had nothing... so a local priest arranged for her burial at a church cemetery. There was no marker. Each day, I placed a rose upon her grave, so I could always find it. Roses were her favorite, and she loved the color red. She said it reminded her of me. Roses are beautiful, and she said I was beautiful, too."

I don't know what to do to ease the ache in her heart, but despite the sadness of such a memory, I know that it must be a powerful one. I fish around in my pocket and produce a coin, which I hand to the flower seller. I pick up the rose and pass it to Scarlet.

"She's right. They are beautiful," I agree. "But roses are also strong. I remember seeing some back at the castle. Even in winter, there were some that forced their way through the snow. Others carried thorns, sharp enough to make those who would do them harm draw back. Roses also bring joy to people. I know that it brought me great joy to see them, thriving even in the unforgiving cold. "You've more in common with a rose than just its beauty."

Her blue eyes look up at me as I pull her into a tender embrace. "Thank you, Boy."

* * *

Despite Lark's pleas that we should stay at an inn, Albain, ever wary, urges us to remain in the woods.

"The more people there are, the more likely there is to be trouble," he says gravely.

So, we make our camp some distance from the town. Scarlet nestles against me, but I do not hear the slowed, rhythmic pattern of her breaths that I know indicates she is sleeping.

"You should rest," I tell her.

"I can't sleep," comes her reply.

"Shall I have Eilis tell you a story then? That always seems to help Lark fall asleep," I suggest jokingly.

Right on cue, Lark snores loudly.

"See? It works," I say.

"*You* could tell me a story," she replies with a slight smile.

"I don't know any," I confess. "I heard Dennan and Ragnar telling some bawdy jokes about women they'd met in taverns, but I doubt that will help you sleep."

"Then make a story up," she recommends.

"All right then. Once there was this boy... named Boy... and he lived in this awful castle with his friends. Then one day, this amazing, red-haired girl, a living wonder, nearly stabbed his friend with a pin."

Scarlet laughs, and she begins to feel more at ease as I

continue my story. Around the time I get to the apple orchard at Quellin's farm, I notice she's fallen asleep.

Suddenly, I hear a gravelly voice not far from me. "And then what happened?"

"Albain, how much of that did you hear?" comes my startled response.

He shrugs. "Enough. Well, go on then."

"They kissed beneath the apple trees, and she stole his heart, and he knew that he loved her and would forever." I gaze down at the sleeping girl in my arms.

Albain grins and shakes his head in amusement. "That sounds like something right out of Eilis's bloody poetry book."

"Did she like it?" I ask.

He groans. "Loved it. Loved it so much she proceeded to make me read some of them aloud for her. Kindness is its own punishment sometimes."

* * *

The following morning, I awake to Lark's face mere inches from my own.

"Boy?"

"Lark!" I shout, startled.

"Do you have any of Old Man's peppermints left?" he asks.

Scarlet stirs beside me. "Lark, isn't it a bit early for peppermints? Eilis will take a fit if you ruin your breakfast."

Lark's gaze darts to the left, then to the right, as if looking to see if anyone else is listening. "Eilis doesn't have to find out," he whispers conspiratorially.

"I appreciate your spirit of mischief and hereby condone this poor decision," announces Scarlet formally. "Boy?"

I chuckle and point to Old Man's bag. "Go on then. They're in the little pocket on the front. But don't touch anything else, and if Eilis finds out, I'll say you coerced me."

As soon as Lark scurries off, Scarlet presses a tender kiss to my lips.

"What was that for?" I ask.

"Does there have to be a reason?" she asks coyly.

I shake my head. "No. I just want to know what I did to warrant it so I can do it again!"

She swats me playfully on the shoulder. We wrap our arms around each other and rest comfortably together. We both end up falling back asleep. When I wake again, I rise from the ground and stretch my arms over my head.

Suddenly, I notice something amiss. One of my pockets feels a bit too light. I check for the singing stones, and they are still there, safely kept in their little pouch. However, the amulet is missing.

"Scarlet!" I cry. "Wake up! The amulet is gone. It must have fallen out of my pocket."

Scarlet snaps to attention, and together with Eilis and Brock we begin to search the camp.

"Any chance it fell out in town?" asks Brock.

"No. I had it last night here, at camp," I reply.

Eilis frowns. "Where is Lark? He's being far too quiet."

Albain gestures to the edge of our camp where Lark is facing the woods and humming to himself as he happily munches on a handful of peppermints. "He's been over there reading for a bit. He wasn't asking me a million questions, so I figured I'd leave him well enough alone."

That's when I see the glint of something silver around Lark's neck, and I recognize the book he is currently reading.

"Lark! What are you doing?" I shout, panicked. I hurry over to him with the rest of my companions close behind me.

Just as I thought, he's wearing the amulet, and in his hands is Old Man's spellbook. Lark looks up at us innocently.

"Do you know Old Man made a spell to instantly send messages over long distances?" he informs us. "Brilliant, isn't it?"

Eilis snatches the book away from him, and I hastily reclaim the amulet from around his neck.

"I think I'd like to try sending a message to Granda to let him know we're all right," says Lark. "Maybe I can send one to Dog, too."

"Lark, why did you take these things from Boy? You could have been hurt." The worry is clearly present in Eilis's features. "We don't truly know how any of these things work."

"I do now," he replies simply.

We all stare at him in confusion.

"Aye. With the spellbook, each spell is a memory," he casually informs us, "and if you watch closely, you can see how Old Man does the spell."

We are all suffering from a shock-induced silence until Scarlet manages to speak up.

"How many pages did it take you to figure that out?" she asks.

"Five," replies Lark. "I saw the message one three spells back, but I liked it so much I decided to read through it again. Once you hear Old Man say the words, it's easy enough to remember."

"Lark, what do you mean?" I inquire. "What words?"

"It's how the book words. If you touch the page on the left, that's the spell. Old Man says the words, and it either works or it doesn't. Each page on the right is another of Old Man's memories. It shows if the spell was successful or not. The one Boy touched before must have been a page on the right." He turns to Scarlet. "Hey, Scarlet."

"Hmm?" Like the rest of us, she seems intrigued by where this conversation is headed.

"I saw a spell that you'd like," he mentions gleefully. "I can make Brock think he's a squirrel rummaging for nuts. Want to see?"

Scarlet's eyes widen with delight. "Ye-"

"No!" the rest of us shout in unison.

"I figured out how it all works," says Lark with pride in

his voice. "If you give me the book back, I can-"

"Lark, what you did was dangerous," states Eilis firmly. "You must promise me that you won't do it again."

Lark doesn't seem very pleased with this response. In fact, I see his brow furrow and his face redden, then he does something I never thought he'd do.

"No!" he shouts at Eilis, taking us all aback. "You're not my mum, Eilis! And you can't always tell me what to do!"

Eilis's mouth drops open in shock, a hurt expression stained upon her face. "Lark... I-"

Albain frowns down at the kid. "Now, you listen here. You'll not talk to Eilis like that. After everything she's done for you-"

Eilis puts her hand on Albain's arm. "It's all right, Albain," she says quietly. "He's not incorrect."

But Lark isn't done yet. Apparently, this has been building for quite some time, and he's decided to expel all of his anger in one, fell swoop.

"The whole lot of you are always telling me what to do!" he shouts. "You're not my bloody parents!" He rounds on Eilis. "I *had* a mum! She died! I was there when it happened! I saw her! She had gold hair and blue eyes like me! And she always smelled of strawberries!"

"So, he remembers his mother, Queen Fiona," says Brock quietly.

"It seems that way," returns Scarlet with a frown.

Lark glares at me. "And you!"

"Me?" I squeak. I know I shouldn't be intimidated by him, but the little goblin is terrifying when he's angry.

"Why should you be the only one to get to see Old Man?" he demands angrily. "I miss him, too, you know! And you're hogging him all to yourself!" He turns to Brock. "And you! You're self-centered and stupid!"

"Hey! I'm working on all that!" protests Brock loudly.

"And you!" He looks to Scarlet next. "You're... you're..." He seems to be struggling to think of something worth shouting at her for. "Your hair is too bloody red, and you're too bloody beautiful!"

Scarlet grins. "You really think so?"

Lark ignores her question. "None of you are perfect! Far from it! So next time you tell me what to do, you can just go bugger off!" Lark's rage turns into tears, and he takes off further into the forest.

Eilis looks absolutely heartbroken and dumbstruck, and I feel awful for her. She's only ever tried to help Lark, and his words were said in such a spiteful way that surely grieves her. The tears begin to well in her brown eyes, and Albain pulls her into his arms.

"I'll go after him," offers Scarlet. "His criticism of me was more of a compliment after all."

Albain gives Scarlet a slight nod, and she heads off in the direction that Lark went.

"Eilis, you were right," concedes Albain. "I need to learn to bite my tongue. I can see that now. The boy is all *bloody this* and *bloody that* and *bugger off*. I'll take the blame for all that."

Eilis looks up at him. She still appears upset, but he has managed to coax a slight smile from her.

"Ah! It's a shade of a smile, but I'll take it," says Albain gently. "Don't worry, love. He just needed to get it all of his chest. Everything will be fine."

"It was never my intention to... I've only tried to protect him," Eilis says, and I can hear another sob building in her voice.

"I know," soothes Albain, softly pressing a kiss to the top of her head.

"He made a fair point," I say. "I need to talk to him."

I head off in the direction that I saw Lark and Scarlet go. When I find them, they're sitting on a fallen log, and Lark is weeping uncontrollably. When he catches sight of me, he buries his face in his hands.

"I shouldn't have said those things. I shouldn't have said it to them!" he cries wretchedly. "I've begged and begged to stay with Eilis and Albain, and now they probably hate me! I wish they *were* my real parents. Then I could stay with them always! But now they'll be cross with me, and they probably won't even want me around anymore!"

Scarlet wraps her arms around the kid, and he presses his face into her shoulder. "They could never stay cross with you, Lark," she tells him. "They love you, as do we all. And of course they want you around! They were only worried for you!"

Lark nods miserably. "I know. I'm an absolute twit."

"No, you're not," I speak. "You were just frustrated. I understand you just wanted to help, but you have to do so wisely. Eilis was right; you could have been hurt."

"I know," sighs Lark. "Eilis is always right." He rises to his feet and begins pacing frantically. "And now I've gone and upset her. I'm sorry I yelled at her. I'm sorry I yelled at all of you. I know it was wrong."

"It's partly my fault," I reply. "I know that you miss Old Man, too. I should have paid more attention to that."

"I've been a right arse," mumbles Lark.

"So, you know what you have to do then?" poses Scarlet.

Lark nods, and we follow him back to the camp.

Eilis's back is to him when he approaches her. Her face is buried in Albain's chest, and the giant is whispering soothingly into her ear. Lark's gaze is firmly fixed on his feet, as if they're the most interesting thing in the world. He seems to deliberate for a moment, then he reaches over and pulls at her sleeve to get her attention. As soon as she turns to him, I see his lip quiver, and he falls apart all over again.

In one, fluid motion, Eilis pulls him in to a comforting embrace as she whispers apologies and comforting words in his ear. Lark is undone.

"I'm sorry, Eilis! So, so sorry!" He begins to ramble through his sobs. "I shouldn't have said those awful things! I love you so much, and I don't want you to stop taking care of me! I don't want to leave you and Albie! I want to live with the Bromus! I'm scared to go to the castle! Everything will change!"

"You're right," agrees Albain. "Things will change, but the one thing that won't change is how much we care about you."

"Lark, we love you," adds Eilis. "And just because we may be parted doesn't mean we'll love you any less. And you know that you will always have a place with us."

"Promise me," says Lark firmly. "Promise me you mean it, all of it, no matter what."

"Aye, we promise," replies Albain.

Eilis nods in agreement. "No matter what."

CHAPTER 33

"It's... it's beautiful," breathes Scarlet.

She's managed to express the simple sentiment that has left us all breathless for the last several moments. Far in the distance, we catch our first glimpse of Vericus and Elidure Castle, an impressive stone edifice with immense towers that seem to stretch into the sky, scraping its fingertips against the clouds themselves. It's situated atop a rather steep incline, likely to give it a favorable vantage against anyone foolish enough to attack its very well-fortified walls.

"How much farther?" asks Brock.

Albain shrugs. "Two days at most, I reckon. Less if the weather cooperates. Smells of rain. We'll want to ride hard to avoid it."

We do as he suggests, but despite our best efforts, we are caught in a relentless deluge of pounding rain. The water is so plentiful and rapid that we can scarcely navigate our horses down the road.

It's nearly evening when we come upon the small town of Rhode. In fact, I nearly run my horse right into the simple sign because I can't see more than a few inches in front of my face.

"Albain, can't we find an inn and stay here for the night?" begs Lark through chattering teeth.

We're all soaked and frozen to our bones. The biting chill of the air nips at our exposed skin as if to serve as a poignant reminder of the fact that soon autumn will give way to the unforgiving winter.

I can barely make out Albain's scowl through the unending smattering of rain. He drags one of his large hands across his face in a fruitless attempt to clear his eyes of water.

"Come on, Albain," adds Scarlet. "We're close enough to Vericus now. What harm could it do to stay for the night?"

Reluctantly, Albain concedes, and we manage to make our way towards a large inn attached to a tavern. We find the stables and quickly dismount from our horses. My fingers are so numb with cold that I can barely tether my horse to its post.

"I'll finish up here with the horses and get our belongings. The rest of you head inside the tavern. Go warm yourselves by the fire," directs Albain. "I'll find the innkeeper and get us some rooms for the night."

"I'll help you," offers Eilis.

The rest of us thankfully make our way into the inn where we are met by a young serving girl who urges us to seat ourselves by the fire while she gathers steaming mugs of hot, mulled cider.

Scarlet sits next to me on a bench. She holds her hands out before her, warming them close to the fire. She's shivering with cold, and I'd offer her my cloak, but that's as soaked as every other inch of me and likely won't do her much good.

Despite my shivering body and chattering teeth, I'm careful not to draw too close to the fire. Ever since the raging inferno that consumed Old Man's tower and scarred my arm, being too near open flames makes my skin prickle and my stomach knot. I wrap my arms around myself a bit tighter to stave off the chill.

Thankfully, the serving girl soon reappears with the cider and offers to fetch us some hearty beef stew to warm our bodies and fill our bellies.

"I'll be back straightaway with that," promises the girl. She moves toward the kitchen, but a rather drunken patron at a nearby table seizes her by the arm.

He's a large, obnoxiously loud man surrounded by seven

equally rowdy companions. "Oy! Catherine, was it? How about you grab us another round, poppet!" He slams his tankard on the table and shoves it towards her.

"Of course, sir. It will be just a moment," says the serving girl quickly.

He releases his hold on her arm, but as he does so, he gives her a hard smack upon her buttocks which causes his entire table to erupt in laughter. The girl's face reddens in embarrassment, and she scurries off to the kitchen.

"What a horse's arse," mutters Brock. "Bunch of loud fools."

The serving girl, Catherine, hurries back to our table with a heaping tray. She gives us each a bowl of stew before heading over to the table of drunks, who nearly knock the tray from her hand in an attempt to grab their pints.

The same man as before reaches out a beefy hand to seize her by the waist. He pulls her into his lap, despite her impassioned pleas for him to release her.

"Please, sir! As you can see, we are very busy this evening! I have many patrons to tend to!" cries Catherine as she attempts to wriggle free from his grasp.

"I'm the only patron you need tend to, girl. How about you just stay put here, and I'll show you what you can tend to for me?" He laughs loudly, and the rest of the men at the table boisterously whoop in amusement at his boldness.

"Please, sir!" she pleads, again attempting to flee from his grasp.

The man pulls her back towards him again. "Rast. You can call me Rast, girly. Would you like to know why? Because I'm likely to be your first and your Rast. Once you've tumbled with me, you'll never want another!" He howls in laughter, and his fellows follow suit.

"That's it. I've had just about enough of this nonsense." Brock, a look of disgust upon his face, rises from his chair.

"Brock, what are you doing?" asks Lark worriedly.

"That poor girl has suffered enough of their stupidity,"

returns Brock. "I'm putting an end to this." He makes his way over to the table of drunkards.

"What do you want?" grumbles the loudmouth when he takes notice of Brock.

"You heard the girl. She has work to do, and you're keeping her from it," speaks Brock firmly.

"Don't worry. You can have a go at her soon as me and my men finish up." Rast takes a large swig from his pint. Once again, Catherine tries to break free, but he's not about to let her go yet.

"I think it's time you take your hands off of her." I watch as Brock meaningfully places his hand on the sword at his side.

"Is that right?" asks Rast, his eyes sparkling with glee. "Drummond."

He turns to one of his fellows who rises from the table and comes to stand in front of Brock. This Drummond fellow is tall and broad with a mean look in his eyes. Rast's lackey gives Brock a hard shove, but moving Brock when he doesn't want to be moved is about as simple as getting a mountain to roll over.

"Be on your way, boy," threatens Drummond in a low growl.

"Tell your friend to let go of the girl, and I'll do just that," replies Brock as he fearlessly meets the man's hard gaze.

I see Rast shake his head, and the next thing I know, Drummond pulls back his fist and aims for Brock's face. Brock is faster and deftly dodges out of the way. He brings his knee up and slams it into the man's gut. Drummond doubles over, and Brock punches him hard in the side of the head, sending him tumbling to the floor.

Scarlet and I are on our feet at the same time. We move to either side of Brock just as Rast violently shoves Catherine to the ground and draws his weapon. Lark helps the girl up, and she scurries off to the kitchen and away from the impending violence. The other men at the table draw their weapons as Rast comes to stand in front of Brock.

292

"Big mistake, boy," growls Rast.

He gives a slight nod of his head, and his men charge forward to close with us. Brock and I quickly unsheathe our swords, and Scarlet pulls one of her daggers.

Suddenly, there's an earsplitting crack and three of the men are violently knocked from their feet. I whirl around toward the origin of the sound and see Lark with his hands outstretched before him, his fingers encompassed by a faint glow.

The book. It's the only explanation for it. He must have learned one of Old Man's spells somehow!

"You've got to be kidding me!" laughs Rast. "Boys, look what we have here!"

Suddenly, the door to the tavern slams open with force, and Albain and Eilis appear in the threshold. Both of them already have their weapons drawn, and when the rest of the patrons see them, every voice in the entire tavern goes silent; even the faintest sounds instantly evaporate from the room as everyone freezes in their tracks.

Albain quickly assesses the situation and moves towards us, and that's when I hear Rast's men begin to fearfully whisper among themselves.

"Do you see that scar? I think that's The Cur," comes a trembling voice.

"The Bromus warrior? They say the devil himself would yield to him," comments another.

"What the bloody hell is he doing here? Thought he was working for the Oak Clan now," says a third.

Rast grins in amusement. "Ah! The Cur! I remember you. Never forget a face that ugly. You did some work for my boss a few years back."

Albain glances at each one of us as to ensure we are okay. Satisfied we haven't been harmed, his gaze locks onto Rast. "Aye. What of it?"

"That job should have gone to me and my men. Would

have been a fair bit of gold in it, even split eight ways. We was told our services weren't needed. Boss said you'd do the job well enough on your own."

"Aye," responds Albain flatly. There's an edge of annoyance in his voice, and I can tell he doesn't have much patience for this fool. "So, you're mercenaries then? You work for Hollis in Gold Mill?"

Rast nods and grins, showing a mouthful of rotting, crooked teeth. "For days, Hollis flapped his gums saying how the fearsome Cur had done the task of eight men. Impressive." He rubs his double chin with a greasy hand. "Given our shared history, how about a proposition?" suggests Rast.

Albain tilts his head slightly in response. I somehow doubt he cares a whit for anything this man would suggest, but we're all rather curious to see where this is going.

"That one," Rast gestures to Brock. "Thought it was wise to interfere in our sport. But that one," he points towards Lark. "That's the one we're interested in. The little caster there bears a rather uncanny resemblance to a boy has a hefty bounty on 'im."

"Bounty? Of what sort?" questions Albain.

"That bloody sorcerer up north wants 'im. Alive," explains Rast. "Though he never said nothin' about takin' no fingers off. He injured my men there, so he stands to learn a lesson or two before we turn 'im over. How about you help me take 'im, and I'll split the coin with you"

Without a reply, Albain moves protectively in front of Lark.

Rast seems to find this hilarious. "This is too much! You runnin' protection for other freaks now? Want to be sorcerers and their meddlesome friends?"

Lark grabs Albain's forearm. "I'm sorry, Albie. They were being cruel to that girl. Brock was just trying to help, and that man attacked him." He gestures to that Drummond fellow who has reclaimed his seat and is nursing a bloody nose. "I-I remembered some of the words from the book. I just- I just reacted."

"Albie?" Rast laughs uproariously "The rabid dog has a name!"

Albain stares at him unflinchingly, and suddenly the tension in the room becomes palpable with the threat of further violence in the air. "Call me that again, and I promise you, I'll run you through with your own, pretty blade.

"Fair enough. Perhaps you'd like to reconsider my offer," states Rast. He and the rest of his men simultaneously take a step towards Lark and Albain.

Eilis comes forward and touches Albain's arm. "Albain, let's get out of here. You were right. We shouldn't have stopped here. Let's continue on."

Rast chuckles in amusement. "Look at that. The Clanless Cur found himself a master... or maybe a bitch to give him some mongrel pups. How much you pay for her, Cur? Must have taken all the gold in Allanon to find yourself a whore willing to look past that mug of yours. She's a might step up from the ones in Gold Mill, in't she?"

Albain moves his head from one side to the other, causing his neck to crack loudly. His expression is impassive, almost bored, as he readies his sword. "Eilis, you and the others, go wait for me in the stables."

"Albain, no," responds Eilis firmly. "I'll not leave you."

"That's right," I agree. "We can help."

"You'll be of more help if I don't have to divide my attention my watching over all of you," responds Albain. He speaks to Eilis without taking his eyes off of Rast for even a second. "Eilis, go now, love. I'll be along in a moment. I don't want Lark to see this next bit."

Reluctantly, we follow his directions. Brock looks as if he intends to stay and watch, but I grab him by the sleeve and practically drag him out behind me.

As we exit, there's a loud commotion inside. There are sounds of men crying out in pain, glass breaking, tables and chairs being smashed, and the heavy thumps of bodies hitting the floor. We make our way to the stables and reluctantly begin to ready our horses so we can hopefully find a cave or some other shelter in the woods to make our camp for the night. It's still raining, but it's not nearly as bad as it was prior to our arrival in the town. However, the cold has become more severe. I shudder slightly as I finish preparing my horse.

When Albain returns, he's covered in blood, though it appears to be that of others. The rain instantly begins to wash the crimson liquid away, leaving trails of red streaming off his coal black armor. He comes to stand next to his foul-tempered steed. "I told you towns were a bad idea. The more people, the more trouble." Albain's eyes flick to Lark. "Don't worry. He'll not bother you again."

"Those men said there was a bounty on me," speaks Lark fearfully. "What if more come for me?"

"Let them come," returns Albain gruffly. "They'll meet the same end as that fool in there. His fellows seemed perfectly content to pretend he didn't exist in the end, especially after a few more of them decided to try my patience. I cleared them all out anyway; I wasn't about to take any chances. Take a moment to collect yourselves, then we'd best be on our way."

Eilis reaches up her hand and tucks a clump of his long, dark hair behind one of his ears. "Albain, are you hurt?"

He shakes his head in reply.

"You've a cut just there." Eilis takes out a handkerchief and gently presses it to a cut on his lip. Save for this small blemish, he looks entirely uninjured.

Something flickers in his eyes, and the next thing I know he's captured Eilis in an embrace and is moving his lips, cut and all, against hers.

Lark groans loudly and looks thoroughly embarrassed by the both of them. "This again!"

Albain grins down at Eilis. "That's a better balm than your scrap of cloth there."

Eilis swats him on his shoulder. "You're incorrigible, Albain."

Lark sighs in exasperation. "I swear you two will use any

excuse to gum at each other." This isn't the first time he's made such a complaint on our journey. Thankfully, Scarlet and I are a bit more discreet in our affections and don't have to endure his criticisms about such displays.

"Just wait until you take an interest in girls," teases Albain.

"Not bloody likely!" cries Lark in protest.

Albain gives him a sharp look.

Lark sighs at the reminder to correct his poor language. "I meant, not likely."

"I'm not an expert on royals," begins Scarlet, "but Lark, as a prince, you probably won't have much choice on that matter. King Ruden will expect you to marry and have heirs to continue your line."

Albain smirks. "And I'll follow you around groaning and grumbling every time I see you snogging." He pulls Eilis hard against him, kissing her again until they're both breathless.

I can't help but to chuckle knowing he probably did it for equal parts pleasure and to irk Lark.

We mount our horses and depart the stables, but suddenly, a female form appears in front of us.

"Wait!" It's Catherine, the serving girl from the tavern.

"Are you all right?" asks Brock concernedly.

"Quite well, thanks to you and your friends," she replies, a smile of relief present on her features. "Look, I know I've cost you a night of warmth from the cold. Please! Let me repay your kindness."

"That won't be necessary," replies Brock.

"I insist! My home is on the outskirts of town, about half an hour's ride," relates Catherine. "It's not much, but we have a barn. Haven't used it in a few years, since my father can't tend animals anymore, but it's warm and dry. It's yours for the night. And I can make you a good, home cooked meal. Will be better than venturing around in the cold and darkness. You can leave at first light."

We exchange glances, but eventually, we all just look to Albain since our previous deviation from his plan resulted in the chaos at the tavern. Lark looks up at him pleadingly, and the warrior sighs heavily.

"Very well," Albain agrees. "We appreciate your kindness and are of a mind to take you up on your offer."

"Fantastic!" Catherine collects her mount, an old draft horse, from the stables, and we follow her down the main road.

Albain whistles to himself as we progress, seemingly unbothered by the events that recently unfolded.

"You're in an awfully good mood for someone who just killed eight men," observes Scarlet. "If I didn't know any better, I'd say you enjoyed yourself in there."

Albain shrugs. "I suppose so. I'd be lying if I said it didn't bring me some satisfaction to shut Rast's whore mouth."

It's easy to forget how dangerous Albain truly is. Despite his love for Eilis and his regard for the rest of us, it's clear to see that he is not someone to be trifled with.

"I'm just glad he's on our side," mutters Brock to me.

"Rast is... *was*... the worst sort of mercenary," continues Albain. "He used to frequent the brothels in Gold Mill. Liked to take his pleasure in the form of young girls... very young girls."

"That's disgusting!" remarks Scarlet in horror.

"I'd like to say I'm surprised, but I'm not," speaks Catherine quietly. "Rast and men like him are becoming more common by the day. Not to speak ill of the king, but he turns a blind eye to the plight of the common folk. I hear Vericus is well-protected. As far as everywhere else... there are people out there who are even far worse than Rast. Quite frankly, I'm glad to know he's gone for good."

"That man seemed to imply you'd spent some time at the brothels. Just how much time did you pass there, Albain?" jokes Brock.

Albain reddens slightly, and an unsettling quiet falls over him. Finally he finds his voice. "I took a job for Hollis, and he was so pleased with my work, he decided to send me what he called *a bonus*. I was staying in some fleabag inn in Gold Mill, and this girl showed up at my door..."

We all listen silently, and though Eilis has her eyes on the road ahead of us, I can see the tension in her body language as she hangs onto every word Albain utters.

"She looked up at me, and I could see the disgust she felt. Her face went all white... Looked half frightened to death... as if she had seen some monstrous beast. Didn't take me long to realize that was what she saw when she looked at me." Albain glances over to Eilis who meets his gaze. His expression softens, and there's a tone in his voice that is almost pleading. "I never let her past the threshold. I tossed her a few gold pieces. Told her to make up some story... tell everyone she saw how cruel and awful I'd been. Then I sent her on her way... *untouched*. Never had to worry about whores banging on my door again."

"So, you didn't even— " Brock abruptly ends his question after Scarlet elbows him hard in the ribs. "Ouch! It's a legitimate question!"

"What do you think *untouched* means?" asks Scarlet in exasperation. "I think you're touched... touched in the head. I swear, you were born with an empty space where your brain should be."

Albain halts his horse in its tracks, putting a brief pause to all of our progress. He grabs the reins of Eilis's horse, pulling it, and Eilis, closer to him. He reaches out a hand to caress her cheek and speaks softly to her. "You needn't worry, Eilis. You claim to know the kind of man I am, and I swear on my life, I never touched her or any other."

"Albain, I wouldn't fault you even if you had. It would be foolish of me to assume you haven't had lovers before me," replies Eilis.

It would be a reasonable assumption. Albain is nine years her senior, and in his pursuit of work, he has travelled long distances and seen so much of Allanon. Surely, he could not have passed all of his time in solitude.

"But *I haven't*," emphasizes Albain, his eyes firmly focused on those of Eilis. "I've never... I've never taken a lover. Any fool can kiss a woman. Any fool can lay with a woman. It takes far greater courage for a man to open his chest and lay his heart at her feet, a bravery I didn't know until I met you."

I can't help but to glance towards Scarlet, who is watching these proceedings with rapt attention. I would gladly lay my heart at her feet.

I see Brock shake his head in disbelief, and I can guess the reason why. At Castle Ciar, we had frequently heard the sniggering jests of the guards as they bragged of their conquests with women, as if the number they bedded was some badge of honor. They proudly touted their manliness in such ways. Even Brock's attentions have always seemed to be seized by whatever fleeting interest he has at the time, and he has been known to joke about how many girls he has kissed and how many fawn over him.

Yet, here is Albain, who in my eyes, is every measure a man, admitting he has never partaken in such things for sport. It reinforces what, in my heart, I have always known, but perhaps Brock needs to hear: kissing and bedding is pointless without love.

"It's the greatest things in life that take the most courage, Albain, and you have more courage than anyone I have ever known." Eilis reaches forward and lovingly pushes back the hair that hangs over the scarred side of his face. "To go through all that you have, but to still be so strong, you have my admiration, my love."

Albain takes her hand in his and places it over his heart. "My whole life, all I've cared about is surviving. Didn't really leave much time for anything else, and I certainly wouldn't risk making whoresons. My father made a few bastards. But his whores had an unfortunate habit of falling down stairs or showing up half conscious and battered black and blue. There may have been others, but I haven't come across them."

"So, you might have brothers and sisters?" asks Lark excitedly.

"For their sake, I hope not," says Albain. "My clan was a blight on the earth. I always thought the Cur Clan would die with me."

Eilis gently caresses the ravaged side of his face. "The world would be a far better place if there were more men like you."

"As I am now, perhaps... Not as I was... I've done... terrible things." He averts his eyes in shame, but she places her fingertips on his chin and gently raises his face upwards so he can look her in the eyes again.

"And it's obvious you regret them," reasons Eilis.

"Aye, much of it, I do. I don't regret doing what I had to, but I regret that I didn't try harder to find another path. Eilis... I've never told another soul except you that I loved them, save for my mother, rest her soul, and I certainly have never been Bloodsworn or betrothed to anyone neither. There will never be another." There's the slightest tremble in his voice, and I can sense the sincerity and emotion when he says it.

"You needn't prove your loyalty to me, Albain. You've done so time and time again," replies Eilis gently.

There's a fragility in his expression, as if he's somehow afraid that she'll suddenly find cause to reject him. "All the same, I need you to know, I'm all for you, and only you."

"I know, Albain. It's all right," she assures him. She reclaims the reins from his hand, her fingers lingering for a moment on his own. "I don't care about who you *were*, Albain. I didn't fall in love with *The Cur*. I fell in love with *you*. I care about who I know you to be. Despite the things you may have done, I think no less of you." She smirks slightly, the faintest glimmer of mischief passing over her lips. "And while you say that you thought the Cur Clan would die with you, I hope I can dissuade you. You aren't entirely opposed to the idea of children, are you? Someday... I think I'd like a *very large* family."

Albain's face takes on a ghostly pallor, and he looks as if he's about to fall from his horse. Suddenly, he clears his throat and collects himself. "Er-uh... I've never really given much thought to... to a family."

"Well, you're soon to be a married man. Best you start thinking about it now. You heard Granda, after all. I'll be needing heirs." Eilis gives him a wink and moves her horse forward.

Albain looks after her with an expression of wonder and admiration. "Bloody hell! As if I could love that woman any more!"

We resume our ride with Brock and Catherine still at the front of our group. They're engaged in some conversation that is lost to my ears, but they both smile and laugh occasionally at something the other has said. The rest of us ride in silence for some time, until Lark, who has been strangely quiet, speaks up.

"Albie... Have you ever killed someone who didn't deserve it?" asks Lark timidly.

"Despite my reputation, I'm not overly fond of taking lives. But Rast, he had it coming," says Albain. "His men weren't much better. I did the world a favor by killing them. Besides, it felt good to stretch my muscles a bit."

"You didn't answer my question," comments Lark quietly.

Albain looks almost ashamed as he slowly nods his head in response. "Honestly, I was hoping to avoid answering. Aye, Lark. As I've said, I've done many things I'm not proud of. I've spilled a fair bit of innocent blood, too, I'm sure. I did what I thought I had to do to get by. I'd no loyalty to anyone but myself; I followed the coin most of my life- didn't ask questions for the cause of the killing."

Lark's eyes widen in disbelief. "That's awful."

Scarlet clears her throat. "Sometimes we must do things we're not proud of... in order to survive."

I reach across the space between us and give her hand a gentle squeeze. I recall our discussions regarding her past, and my heart hurts for her. Despite the brief glimpses into her old life that she has given me, I know there is still a great deal that she keeps to herself.

Albain nods in agreement. "Aye. That's the truth of it. I'm not a good man, Lark, and I've never proclaimed myself to be one. But, I'll try to be a better man than I was. For her." He gestures towards Eilis who rides next to him.

She's been quietly listening to the conversation, and she smiles slightly at his words.

He looks to her, his voice suddenly taking on a tone of sincerity. "I'm more sinner than saint, but I'll be the sort of husband you can be proud of; I'll not disappoint you."

"I'm already proud of you, Albain. We all have our pasts," says Eilis, "but they don't define our futures. I would never judge you for your transgressions, my love. Whether you choose to believe it or not, you are a good man."

I look to Scarlet and notice a strange expression delicately painted across her features. She appears lost in thought, as if finding her own meaning in such words.

"That's a relief," returns Albain. "There are likely to be plenty more transgressions before I draw my last."

CHAPTER 34

After such an eventful evening, Catherine's home is a welcome sight. It is a small cottage, only large enough for her and her father, but it is well-maintained and comfortable. When we enter, there's a blazing fire in the hearth that spills light and warmth through the quaint common area. Her father is seated just in front of it, and when he hears the door open, he turns slightly.

It's then that I notice his eyes. They are a strange, milky white, completely glazed over.

"Ah! Catherine! I was beginning to worry for you!" he calls to his daughter.

Catherine beckons for us to enter, and as we do, her father's expression turns to one of confusion.

"Who is that with you there?" he asks. His eyes are fixed on me, but I know he doesn't see me in the slightest.

"Friends," she replies. "Travelers who are on their way to Vericus. There wasn't enough room at the inn, and I offered for them to stay in the barn. Father, they helped me a great deal tonight. There was a fellow there who gave me a bit of trouble. He had too much to drink and was bothering the other patrons. These folks were kind enough to see him on his way."

Lark frowns. "Don't you mean he-"

Brock claps his hand over Lark's mouth and shakes his head at the kid.

"Trouble?" Her father's expression turns to one of concern. "Catherine, I don't like the sound of that. If people are giving you trouble at the tavern, perhaps you should find some other employment. Perhaps as a seamstress?"

Catherine shakes her head at us and silently points towards a pile of half-finished sewing projects. She quickly changes the subject. "Are you hungry, father? I thought I would make us a nice chicken and vegetable soup with some fresh bread."

"That would be fantastic my girl." He shivers slightly and wraps his blanket more tightly around his shoulders. "Awfully chilly tonight. Why don't you have your friends come and warm by the fire? If they've been travelling in this nonsense they're probably half frozen!"

We gratefully huddle around the hearth to warm ourselves. Catherine's father introduces himself as John Hammish and proceeds to tell us all about his work as a farmer before he lost his vision. He's a kind and friendly man, and within the hour, he has us all laughing and feeling quite at ease. We pass the time talking of trivial things, and a short time later, Catherine has placed a considerable sum of food on the table. There's piping hot chicken soup, freshly baked bread, fruits, vegetables from their garden, cheese, and a small pumpkin tart.

Catherine warms some cider for us and offers to fetch Albain a wineskin of a sweet, red grape wine she says she makes herself or a brandy her father favors.

Albain thanks her but declines. Instead, he reaches across the table and refills a tall, dented, metal tankard with mulled cider. I don't know why it occurs to me, but it comes to my mind that I've never seen him drink anything but cider or water. Even when we were journeying with Dennan, Albain would refuse the former's offer to share his flask of honeymeade with him.

Lark is sitting across from me, and as he reaches for another thick slice of bread, I notice the raw skin upon his hands. His palms are red and blistered, and he winces slightly when he picks up his spoon again.

"Lark," I breathe. "What happened to your hands?"

"Oh..." He quickly places his hands in his lap beneath the table. "I... uh..."

I think about what Old Man had said once before. *All magic comes with a price.*

"Come with me," beckons Eilis. She leads Lark over to where we have stacked our belongings and begins to sort through various vials and salves for something to use on his hands.

"Is he all right? Do you need my help?" asks Albain.

"No, no. I've got him. Thank you, Albain," replies Eilis.

"So, what brings you to Vericus?" asks John.

"Visiting some friends who live in the city," replies Albain.

"Ah! I do miss my trips to Vericus. Used to make the trek twice a month. Made rather good coin selling our produce and the clothes my wife used to make. If you get a chance, be sure to visit the little toy shop in the square. Your son will probably enjoy it!"

"Son?" asks Albain in confusion.

"The young lad with the injured hands," clarifies John.

"Aye... *Da*," replies Lark waggishly.

"You might find something there for your missus, too," suggests John.

Eilis chuckles at this, but more so at the implication that John has surmised they are a married couple travelling with their young child and some friends.

"You see, when you've no sight, you come to rely on other senses," explains John. "You've a gruff way about you. But, when you speak to the woman with the kind voice, your own voice softens. That tells me you care for her. And the child... when he speaks to you, there's a tone of affection there as well."

"That's impressive," I comment.

"What can you tell of me?" asks Brock.

"That you've been no more than two feet from my

daughter since you arrived. Any time I hear your voice, it comes from the same direction as where she is," replies John.

Scarlet laughs wildly at Brock's reddening expression, and Catherine's coy smile indicates she isn't adverse to the idea that Brock is paying so much mind to her.

"I can learn many things through hearing," continues John. "For example, I know my daughter understated what happened at the tavern. I could hear the slight tremble in her voice when she spoke of it, and she's not in the habit of bringing strangers home, so you all must have helped her far more than she let on."

Lark and Eilis rejoin us at the table, and John inclines his head slightly towards Lark. "I'd also wager that one of you is a caster of some sort."

Lark sucks in his breath in surprise.

"Or at the very least, dabbles in it. Magic has a very distinct smell. I'd caution you about using it too openly. There are many who fear such things," informs John. "Casters are rare. Some places, they kill them on sight. Others, they're worshipped. Round these parts, they make folks a bit jumpy. Catherine tells me there's been rumors from the north about a sorcerer snatching people up and working them to death, for what purpose I know not."

After supper, Brock offers to help Catherine clear the table and tidy up. Scarlet and I make our way to the barn while John shows Lark some coin tricks, and Albain teaches Eilis how to play a card game with a deck of cards he had brought with him.

The rain has picked up again, but luckily, the barn isn't very far from the house. Scarlet and I each carry an armload of blankets that Catherine had gathered up for our use. As there haven't been animals there for quite some time, the barn is immaculately clean and provides a great deal of warmth and protection from the cold and wetness outside.

Within the barn, there are a few large pens, and there is a ladder that leads to the loft above. Since Scarlet and I arrived first, we have our pick of places to bed down for the night, so we take a few of the blankets and climb the ladder to the loft for a bit of privacy.

Scarlet had been fairly quiet at supper, so I'd been hoping to have some time alone to speak with her.

"Are you okay?" I ask her.

She tucks her bright, red hair behind her ear and rests her chin on her palm. "I'm fine, Boy."

"You're awful at lying, you know that? When you do it, your ears get just about as red as your hair," I tease her.

She snorts in amusement, but moments later, her expression once again becomes thoughtful.

"Scarlet?"

She sighs heavily. "It's just... I was thinking... About Albain and Eilis... How quick she was to overlook all he had done in his past... even the parts that weren't so grand."

"And you're afraid you'll be judged for yours?" I guess.

She nods, and a look of shame affects her pretty features. "Boy... I did... I did something awful. Something unforgivable."

"What?" I ask, genuinely intrigued. I don't want to press her too much, as I know it is difficult for her to speak of her past, but if something is bothering her this much, I want to do what I can to help her and assuage her fears.

"That's just it... I don't remember exactly. Not yet. Maybe not ever. All I recall is this inescapable feeling of guilt. It's as if the burden of the sin still bears down on me every day."

"I wouldn't be too hard on yourself, Scarlet... especially if you don't even know why you're feeling this way."

When she looks up at me, I can see the tears beginning to well in the corners of her eyes, and it takes me aback. Scarlet is one of the most mentally strong people I know, but for a moment, she looks absolutely broken, vulnerable, and fearful.

I sit down next to her and wrap my arms around her shoulders then pull her against my chest.

"What if it's something truly horrible? I already know I was a thief. Who's to say I didn't do far worse?" she asks.

"Then you did something worse. You can't change what's already happened," I tell her. "It's as Eilis said. We all have pasts. I know so little of mine, but I'm sure I wasn't a perfect person either. No matter what you may have done, it won't make me love you any less."

Scarlet freezes, her eyes wide with shock. "You... you... *what*?"

I realize the words that have slipped from my lips, and in that moment, I must make a decision: to somehow obscure what I just said or to tell her what's truly in my heart.

I take a deep breath and clasp her hands in my own. "You heard me, Scarlet. *I love you.* I love how smart and bold you are. I love your wit and your grace. I love how you try to act so impassive, when it's so plain how much you care for others. You know, if you're not careful, everyone is bound to catch on to the fact that you actually like them," I joke.

She laughs, a delightful sound that causes my heart to flutter in my chest. If I could only hear one sound for the rest of my life, it would be that.

Suddenly, her pale pink lips come crashing into mine, and I'm overcome with a rush of powerful emotion. Her delicate fingers loop through my hair, pulling me closer towards her, and my own hand trembles slightly as it comes to rest on the side of her hip. She pulls away from me for the slightest moment, and though she hasn't said it, I can plainly see the love I bear for her reflected back at me. She kisses me again, her hands roving across my shoulders and coming to rest at the small of my back, and I can feel the entirety of my body shudder at her touch.

Suddenly, we hear conversation outside the barn, and moments later, the large door opens. Reluctantly, we untangle ourselves from each other. I run my hands over my hair to smooth it back down, and Scarlet inhales deeply to steady her breath and vanquish the crimson blush that has formed upon her cheeks.

I listen as our companions sort through their belongings and ready their sleeping areas for the evening.

"Boy!" Lark calls out. "Can I have a peppermint? I ate all my dinner."

"Fine, but you're on rationing," I tell him. "We're almost out." I peek my head over the ledge and see Albain and Eilis settling in next to each other and Lark staring up the ladder at me. "Where's Brock?" I ask.

Scarlet scoots over beside me to glance down below.

"Jawing with Catherine and her father," replies Albain.

"Well, they seem to be getting on well," I say.

I toss Lark his peppermint, and he winces when he catches it in his hands. He grimaces as he inspects his palms. "Albie, do you think they'll scar?" he asks, displaying his hands for the warrior to see.

"If you're lucky," returns Albain. "Some women apparently find that sort of thing attractive." He gives Eilis a mischievous look, and I watch as her hand moves to stroke the deep ravine that mars his face.

"Is that true, Scarlet?" asks Lark curiously.

Scarlet shifts next to me so she can better see Lark. "Why are you asking *me*?"

"Boy has scars, too. Do you like them? You obviously find him plenty attractive," reasons Lark. "When we came in, you two were looking at each other all funny, and your faces were all red. Then you got that embarrassed look Eilis gets when I catch her and Albie necking in the woods. So, you two must have been kissing or something. Honestly, I think I'm going to be sick with all this pawing at each other going on." He begins to make exaggerated vomiting sounds. After his little performance, he peers up at us with an impish grin upon his face.

"I knew it didn't take that long to collect firewood!" I call down to Albain and Eilis in mock accusation.

Albain laughs loudly, and Eilis gives him a playful

shove.

Eilis blushes uncontrollably. "I told you we need to be more careful, Albain."

"Well, Scarlet? Am I handsome with my scars?" I ask her, showing her my burned arm. In truth, while it certainly isn't the most pleasant thing to look at, I'm simply glad it isn't worse.

She rolls her eyes. "Yes, Lark. Scarred or not, I like Boy just fine."

Lark unrolls his blanket and glances over to Albain. "How *did* you get your scar, Albie?"

"Lark, I'm not sure that's an appropriate topic," speaks Eilis softly with an apologetic glance to Albain.

"What scar?" asks Albain flatly. It's easy to tell from his tone that he's being sarcastic.

"You know which one, Albie," returns the kid.

"It's not a tale for children, Lark." Albain's voice becomes solemn, and I see Eilis hold him tighter. Something tells me she already knows the answer to Lark's question, and I get the feeling it must have been something truly awful due to Albain's sudden change in demeanor.

"I bet you got it in a big battle!" Lark guesses. "You probably killed 50 men with one hand tied behind your back while hopping on one leg just to prove that you could."

Albain snorts in amusement. "You're partly right. It was a battle... of sorts. And as I said, it's not a tale for children, especially this late at night. Get your rest. You'll be needing it for the morning."

Soon, I hear the soft sounds of Albain snoring. I poke my head over the ladder. I doubt the warrior has had a decent night's rest since we began our journey to Vericus, but he must feel safe enough here to not post a watch. Anyway, he seems to be quite a light sleeper, so if there were any trouble, I'm certain he'd be up quickly. Eilis is nestled against him with her head resting on his chest and her arm draped over his stomach.

In the dim light, I can see that Lark is still wide awake. It seems we are the only two who are. Scarlet fell asleep almost as soon as her head hit the floor.

I listen to the sound of the rain pinging off the side of the barn and thudding against the soft ground outside. I give a heavy sigh, and moments later, a blonde head of hair and shining, blue eyes peeks up over the top of the ladder.

"I can't sleep," whispers Lark.

I pat the floor next to me, and Lark scurries over to sit beside me. His eyes glance over to my bag.

"I told you, Lark. You're on rationing with those peppermints," I remind him.

"No, it's not that."

The book. He wants to get his hands on the spellbook and amulet again, I'm sure.

I frown as I realize his desire. "I don't think that's a good idea. I'm sure Eilis likely talked to you at length about using the words in that book."

"Aye, but... If I tell you something, you promise not to make a big deal about it?" he asks.

I offer him my pinkie finger, and he wraps his own around mine and gives it a little shake.

"I won't lie... it hurt my hands, but... I rather liked it... saying the words. Somehow it just felt... it felt right. I felt so bold and powerful," he confides.

"Lark, that may not be such a good thing," I tell him.

"Yes, but, the words helped us. They could probably help lots of people. What if there's a spell in there that may help us to get our memories back? Don't you want to know more about that grey-eyed woman? The one who looks like you? And what about her?" He gestures to Scarlet who is still sleeping soundly. "Don't you want to at least *try* if it can help her?"

I consider this for several moments. I'm already cursing myself for entertaining the idea, but the kid's words do ring with truth. While I am happy that my friends have managed to reclaim so much of their old lives, I admit to feeling the slightest pang of jealousy that I still know so little of my own. I do want to know more about my past, and if there is anything that I can do to help Scarlet, I'll certainly try.

"Fine. But if Eilis is cross about this, I'm going to tell her plainly it was all your idea," I threaten.

He grins broadly and drags my bag to rest between us. I take out the spellbook and amulet, placing them on the floor before us. I move to put the amulet on, but Lark stops me.

"Boy… That's an awfully long chain. What if it's possible for two of us to get to see? Maybe if we're both wearing it…" he suggests.

"Lark, I'm not sure that's a great idea."

"Isn't it at least worth trying? Just to see if it can be done? Besides, Albie always says two sets of eyes are better than one, at least that's what he says when he takes me out hunting for food. He says I have sharp eyes. Maybe with both of us watching, we might see things we otherwise could miss."

"It may not even work," I reason. "I don't know much about how any of this comes to pass, so don't be disappointed if nothing happens."

He grins like mad at my willing cooperation. He sits as close to me as he possibly can. I loop the chain over both of our heads and place the spellbook on my lap.

"Let's try the last page," I suggest.

He nods in agreement, and I open the book. As I do so, I see Old Man's familiar scribblings, but then there are a few blank pages, and finally, a large tear, as if one of the pages was ripped out.

"A page was torn out," I observe with a frown. "Why do you think that was?"

We both touch the tear, and instantly, I find myself back at Old Man's tower.

My eyes, or I should say, Old Man's eyes rapidly dart around the room as if searching for something. My heart is thundering in my chest, and I feel a sense of panic and dread.

There are heavy footsteps coming up the stairs, and this just makes my pulse quicken further.

"Fenustus!"

I recognize the voice instantly. It sounds like Sebastian, and his tone is one of intense anger. I recall the last memory I saw and how he had been robbed of his name.

"Fenustus! Come out and face me, you coward! Or are you too ashamed to admit your fault! What kind of monster robs a man of who he is?"

The footsteps are drawing closer, and I cross to the chest at the foot of the bed. Quickly, I begin rummaging through the contents. Old Man seems to be intently searching for something specific.

"Fenustus! Your bloody spell wore off! I bet you weren't anticipating that! You wanted me to forget! You wanted me to forget what you did! How you ran off like a coward when we needed you most! When *I* needed you most!"

The sinking feeling in my stomach tells me that Old Man must be feeling terribly guilty about something.

"Ruden is a killer!" shouts Sebastian. "He turned a blind eye to those he swore to protect! He let the poor starve, and when we opposed him, he cut us down where we stood! And you! The moment things became difficult, you turned tail and ran! You bloody coward! You ran back here while they massacred those who rallied to oppose Ruden's tyranny! You abandoned everything! Our cause! Our people! Me! You left as my fellows, my friends, innocents were slaughtered by Ruden's soldiers! You left as Emily..." I hear Sebastian's voice crack noticeably. "as Emily..." His words fail him, and he is unable to finish the thought. "You ran as they set fire to our homes and drove their blades through good folk, kind folk, better folk than you!"

Suddenly, the bedroom door shudders violently. Old Man begins to mutter a few words under his breath. He stretches his hands out towards the door, and there is a faint glowing light that envelops his palms and stretches across his fingertips. The light *quickly intensifies. His palms begin to itch slightly then burn. The air around him begins to waver, and as I look from left to right, a glimmering sheen affects the area around me. Old Man reaches his fingertips out, and when he touches the strange rippling, his fingers are met with solid resistance. It seems to be a forcefield of some sort.*

He reaches back into the chest and finally produces what he's been looking for.

The amulet.

He quickly and quietly moves the bed. He mutters a few more words under his breath, and several planks pull themselves upward from the floor to produce a small opening. Another word from old man sets the planks stacking themselves neatly upon the floor. Old Man produces a folded sheet of paper with a torn edge and a bit of charcoal from his pocket and writes a message in his messy scrawl.

Hide this quickly! *it reads.*

"Fenustus! Face me!" screams Sebastian. The door violently shudders again.

"You can't do this, Sebastian!" calls Old Man. "I understand your ire towards King Ruden, truly I do. I hate him as much as the next person. What he's done is unforgivable, but the path you walk is a dark one that is sure to bring nothing but infinite tragedy and sorrow. I cannot condone it any further. Sebastian..." His voice is pleading as he attempts to reason with his old friend. "I understand your feelings, but to target the queen... to bring misfortune to his heir ... What has the queen done? What has the young prince done to deserve such treatment? Would you really move upon an innocent child? Why, that would make you no better than Ruden himself!"

"He deserves everything he gets!" shrieks Sebastian. "And if I have to destroy those who are closest to him to deliver justice upon him, then so be it!"

Again, the door quakes from a powerful force. "I have to admit, Fenustus... I'm impressed with the strength of your warding spell, but I can feel it weakening! My own magic has grown too strong for you!"

Old Man begins to mutter more, strange words, and the

amulet starts to glow brightly. He casts a final glance back at the door and takes a deep breath. The amulet pulses and begins to burn painfully in his grasp. I, too, feel its heat and fight the urge to throw it upon the ground. Old Man's eyes close briefly, and when he re-opens them, it's as if he's awaking from a dream or peering through fog. In confusion, Old Man looks down at the amulet in his hand, then the paper clutched in his other. He quickly reads the words as the door nearly buckles with force.

He scrambles to the hole in the floor, deposits the amulet inside, and tears up the scrap of paper. He quickly replaces the floor-boards and repositions the bed.

The door is violently torn from its hinges and explodes inward, sending large chunks of wood and much finer splinters scattering across the ground.

A tall, thin form dressed in a black, hooded cloak steps into the room. Immediately, my gaze is drawn to his piercing green eyes, alight with fury and hatred. It's Sebastian, but not as he was before. His black hair is longer, his features sharper, and he has grown a short, well-kept beard. His expression speaks of barely contained rage, and the look he gives Old Man makes the older sorcerer tremble with fright. With age, Sebastian has matured into a familiar figure, one that I recognize all too well.

Abirad.

"Fenustus!"

Old Man's feet shift, and I feel him tilt his head slightly, inquiringly. "Who?"

There is a look of confusion, then sudden understanding, as Sebastian... as Abirad... seems to realize what has happened.

"You fool. What have you done? What? You thought that by taking your own memories you might keep your secrets from me?" he laughs bitterly, and the sound sends a jolt of terror through my heart. "There are worse things than death... In fact... death is far too good for you, **old friend**."

It's Lark's hysterical screams that snap me out of the

strange, twilight state of the memory. I nearly break the chain of the amulet in an attempt to quickly get it off of us, and the moment the kid is freed, he scrambles away from me. Tears stream down his face, and he balls himself up on the floor.

Scarlet, awakened by his frantic cries, stirs behind me.

"Lark!" I hear Eilis shout from down below, and within in instant, Albain appears at the top of the ladder.

"Lark!" He crosses the distance in a single stride and kneels beside the child, scooping him up into his arms and pulling him tightly against him. "Lark." His deep voice takes on a soothing tone as he gently rocks him back and forth.

Eilis scrambles up the ladder and joins them while Scarlet comes to sit next to me. She glances from me to Lark, her expression questioning as she searches for the cause of this nighttime outburst.

Eilis whispers comfortingly to Lark, and within seconds, he begins to relax. His whimpers become more sporadic, and he buries his face into Albain's chest. Albain looks up at me, his eyes pained with worry.

"What the bloody hell happened!" he demands.

"Lark had an idea…" I say quietly. "We… we both wore the amulet. There was a page torn from the book. We touched it."

With a firm expression, Albain holds out his hand. His eyes glance towards the amulet still clasped in my fingers. Without argument, I toss it to him, and he holds it with merely a fingertip, as if it is some cold, dead thing or some awful creation not to be trusted. Eilis takes it from him and tucks it into her pocket.

"I think that's enough of that for the night," growls Albain, and I can't help but to feel a bit guilty, as if I'm a child being scolded for some foolishness. Still holding Lark to his chest, he swiftly slides down the ladder. I can hear him below as he continues to comfort the kid.

"Boy, what happened?" asks Eilis in confusion.

So, I tell them. I tell them everything, sparing not even

the smallest detail of what I can recall.

"Suddenly seeing Abirad would certainly give me cause to take a fit," reasons Scarlet. "Probably scared poor Lark half to death."

Eilis's hand trails to her pocket. She takes out the amulet and replaces it in Old Man's bag. "Albain's right. I think it best if we let the amulet alone, at least until we get to Vericus. Lark has already injured himself using the words. Maybe there's someone in the capital, someone like Old Man, who might be able to help us to use it more responsibly. There's no telling what more could be found in the book. We don't want to inadvertently do something we can't undo."

I nod my head in agreement.

Eilis makes her way down the ladder, and some time later, when I dare to peek back down at them to see how Lark is faring, I see the boy is fast asleep. He is nestled between Eilis and Albain, both of whom have a protective arm wrapped around him as they slumber.

Scarlet and I sit in silence. Our hands are joined, and our fingers are entwined. I don't know how long we stay that way, but the rain dies down, and the sky begins to grow lighter in its absence. It's around that time that we hear the barn door slowly creak open, and Brock finally beds down for the night. Scarlet falls asleep on my arm, but I struggle to claim any rest, as all I can see when I try to is a pair of piercing green eyes and a menacing expression that declares its wearer has malice on his mind.

CHAPTER 35

I'm awakened by the first rays of sunlight streaming through the window. I can see my breath as I exhale, the chill in the air still damp from the relentless torrent of rain the day before. Scarlet, her head still resting on my shoulder, stirs slightly.

"Morning," I mumble, as I place a kiss on the top of her head.

She buries her face in my arm. "Ergarhargum."

Apparently, she's not quite ready to wake up.

I stand, stretching to my full height, my neck cracking slightly. I peer down the ladder. Eilis is folding her blanket while Lark still sleeps soundly.

I glance towards Old Man's bag, still on the floor where it had been left the night before. I cross to it and warily take out the amulet, letting the cool metal and heavy weight of the jewels rest in my hand. My mind is encumbered with the memory we released the night before. I think of all the things Sebastian—no, Abirad— accused Old Man of. He wasn't wrong. Old Man had shown cowardice before. I can't say I'm surprised by such a revelation. Old Man had allowed Isabel to take the fall for his own ambitions and greed. Had he not lamented his foolishness mere moments before his death?

However, something else nags at the back of my mind.

Emily.

Who was this Emily? This was the second memory in which she had been mentioned, and there are only a few things I can surmise from what I've seen. Whoever she was, she must have meant a great deal to Abirad. Additionally, it is quite apparent now that she was killed, likely during the Bread Riots. Even Old Man's voice was tinged with sadness when he spoke of her. Abirad clearly blamed the failure of the peasants' revolt on Old Man. He also blamed him for the death of Emily.

I reflect on what I've learned of Abirad, the cruel sorcerer who oppressed thousands of people including myself. He was a merciless slavemaster who robbed us of our lives and didn't seem to care whether we lived or died.

However, it has become clear to me that he wasn't always that way. He used to be… normal. He was a simple farmboy with an ailing father and a struggling mother. He saw Old Man as a friend and mentor, much like I and the rest of my companions did. He wanted to bring about a better existence for the poor and unfortunate, people like himself who he felt were being mistreated by King Ruden.

And he failed…

Miserably.

And perhaps when Sebastian failed, perhaps when he was seemingly betrayed by his own friend, maybe that was the moment Sebastian vanished and was replaced by Abirad.

Furthermore, the more I learn about King Ruden through Old Man's memories, the more I understand Lark's reluctance to return to him. Yes, the king may very well be his father, but just what kind of man are we entrusting his safety and wellbeing to?

The barn door opens, and Albain steps in. "Horses are ready," he announces.

Eilis kneels beside Lark and gently shakes his shoulder. "Lark. Come, now. It's time to wake up."

A few moments later, Brock enters the barn. "Catherine made breakfast."

My mouth starts watering, and my stomach grumbles loudly at the promise of food. We've had dried rations, fruit, and bread on our journey from the Bromus encampment, but I can still practically taste the belly-filling home cooked meal from the previous night, and the prospect of more of that is exciting.

Once we are all up and moving, we join Catherine and John for breakfast. There are heaps of biscuits, thick brown gravy with sausage, mounds of bacon, sliced apples with cinnamon and honey, and late season berry tarts. After we've eaten our fill, we say our goodbyes to John, and Catherine comes to see us off.

She stands next to Brock who looks towards the rising sun ruefully, as if he's not quite ready to move on. As he told me over breakfast, he and Catherine stayed up practically all night talking about all manner of things, and he seems quite taken with her.

"Thank you again... for your help at the tavern," Catherine tells us, but I see the way her gaze lingers upon Brock. "I've packed you all some provisions for the last bit of your journey. It's not much, but there are some honeycakes and some bread I baked this morning." She holds a small, burlap bag out to Brock who gratefully takes it from her hands and places it in one of his saddlebags.

"Thank you, Catherine, for hosting us last evening. It was exceptionally kind of you," I say to her.

"I wish you success on your business in Vericus. Brock said you are journeying there on an urgent matter," she replies as she tucks a stray strand of blonde hair behind her ear. "Perhaps, you can all come back and visit sometime. Hopefully, it will be far less eventful."

"We'll plan on it," promises Brock. "Despite the excitement of last evening, I rather like it here."

Scarlet and I exchange a knowing look. The coy smiles and obvious gazes between Brock and Catherine tell me that he will very likely keep that promise. At first, he looks as if he might kiss her, but I see him hesitate then glance towards Albain. The warrior doesn't seem to notice as in that moment all of his attention is claimed by Eilis. She's looking up at him with a look of pure joy, and Albain has abandoned his surliness for the time being. Instead, he presses a gentle, lingering kiss to her lips. Then he says something that instantly brings a smile to the face of his betrothed before clasping both of her hands in his own. Despite all of the hardships they have endured in their lives, there is no denying the happiness that radiates from both of them whenever they are near each other and the obvious degree of the love they share.

Brock seems to contemplate something for a moment, then he takes one of Catherine's hands in his own and whispers something in her ear. She smiles broadly as she nods enthusiastically, and Brock grins in return before parting from her.

❊ ❊ ❊

We mount our horses and head back towards the main road. With each hoofbeat, we are borne closer and closer to Vericus. Elidure Castle, the immense fortress that is King Ruden's home, soon to be Lark's home, grows even larger as we near our destination.

We make excellent time, and when we make camp for the evening, Albain announces that we should be able to reach the city by the following afternoon.

Lark seats himself next to the fire. He wraps his arms around his knees and morosely stares into the flames. Truly, he wears the most forlorn expression I've ever seen. I know that he should be happy to be returning home to his father and the life that was taken from him, but at the same time, I understand his grief. We have come to rely on each other so much, especially since our departure from Abirad's castle, and Eilis and Albain have treated him as their own. It must be difficult for him to cope with the idea that, though we have all promised to stay a while so he can acclimate to his new life, our days of travelling about as a group will soon be ending.

I sit down next to him. It's the first chance we've really gotten to speak together since the incident with the amulet.

"Lark, I'm sorry about last night."

He glances over at me and raises one of his pale, blonde eyebrows. "Why?"

"Because it obviously upset you."

"Don't apologize, Boy. It was my idea. And... despite all... all that... It was a *good* idea." He grins broadly. "I *was* right after all. It worked."

"Yes, you were right."

"Boy..."

"Hm?"

"I'm going to miss you," he says quietly, his voice barely a whisper. I can see that he's fighting back the tears that are welling in his eyes and threatening to spill forth at any moment.

I wrap my arms around him and pull him into a strong embrace. "I'll miss you too, Lark. But it will be all right. We'll see each other plenty. After all, I don't have the slightest idea about how to reclaim my own memories. Hopefully, Eilis is correct, and we can find someone to help us with the book. Maybe there will be some way to undo the spell. But that will probably take a while, so I may be able to stay in Vericus for quite some time"

"There has to be a way," responds Lark thoughtfully. "Sebastian... Abirad... got his memories back somehow."

* * *

The next day, we ride as swiftly as we can. We push our horses to their limits and skip our midday meal to ensure that we reach the exterior walls of the city before sunset. When we arrive, it is truly an incredible sight to behold.

"Wow..." breathes Brock. "It's even larger than I thought it would be. You could fit a thousand of my villages in the walls of Vericus."

We make our way through the main gate and dismount

from our horses. The entirety of Vericus seems to be in a flurry of activity. People dash about on all manner of business and pleasure. Heavily armed city guards patrol the area and keep watch for the slightest sign of trouble. A few of them cast wary glances at Albain, but none of them are bold enough to approach him. Children merrily play in the streets while their parents tend to buying produce for their evening meals or haggling with the butcher over the price of a pig or chicken.

"The castle isn't far from here. We should be able to reach it within the hour," announces Albain.

"No!" cries Lark.

Startled by his outburst, we all turn to look at him.

"Can't we... can't we just wait until the morning?" he begs, his blue eyes pleading.

"Lark, we really should get you to the castle as soon as possible," I tell him. "I know you're worried, but don't you want to go home? Don't you want to get your memories back?"

Lark looks torn, and his gaze oscillates between all of us and the great castle in the distance. "My memories will still be there in the morning. I just want to be Lark for one more day...before I must be someone else. Please?" He makes eye contact with each one of us, and there's not a soul among us who can muster the resolve to refuse his simple request. "Please... Can we go to the castle in the morning?"

Eilis, lost in thought for a moment, bites her lip. She seems to be warring within herself, and it occurs to me she's likely just as reluctant to part from Lark as he is to part from her. "Perhaps... perhaps we can do as Lark asks. It's been such a difficult journey since we left Castle Ciar."

I nod in agreement. "Why not? It will give us more time together."

"Yeah, before the prince here needs to resume his royal responsibilities, like prancing about in fancy clothes and learning not to feed Dog from the table," Brock jokes.

Lark sticks his tongue out at Brock and grabs Albain's hand.

"Please, Albie? Just a while longer."

I see Albain's expression soften as he looks down at Lark. He kneels before him, still towering over the boy. "You really want to see this ugly mug any longer than you have to?" he teases.

Lark throws his arms around the warrior's neck, and Albain scoops him up in one arm, using his free hand to lead his mount towards the stables.

We find the inn not far from there. This time, we all enter the inn as a group as Albain is unwilling to take his eyes off of us for even an instant. He plunks a few pieces of gold into the innkeeper's hand, and we take a short time to rest before venturing out to explore the city.

Scarlet and I walk hand in hand while Brock trails just behind us. In front of us, Lark merrily skips between Albain and Eilis. Even here in the safety of the walled city, Albain's eyes dart about watchfully; the warrior is ever vigilant for potential trouble.

As we progress even further down the road, the crowds become denser and denser. However, most people give us a wide berth. Albain is a rather imposing figure, and when people see him coming, they quickly scramble to get out of his way. We stop at a stall that sells finely made cowls, and Scarlet begins to look through the wares.

While we wait, I occasionally hear hushed whispers of the word *"Cur,"* and I overhear a little boy ask his mother, *"Mum, what's wrong with that man's face?"*

Albain must hear it, too, because I see his expression sour, and he shifts uncomfortably as we await Scarlet to finish.

I see Eilis reach her hand up to touch his face, and she lovingly caresses the scarred side with her outstretched fingers. "This face is perfect," she says softly. "This is the face I'll awake to for the rest of my days."

Albain's glower is instantly swept away at the genuine love within her words, and he bends down to press a kiss to her lips before offering her his arm and guiding her down the street. The rest of us follow for a ways before our groups comes to linger by a food stand selling fresh, caramel dipped apples. Brock readily purchases one and munches on it as we move along.

When we encounter another very large crowd of people, Albain extends his hand to Lark. "Keep a hold on me, boy. Too easy to get lost in a place like this."

Lark accepts it then reaches his other hand out for Eilis, who takes it in her own. "Boy is very smart," he says. "He and Scarlet have been holding hands this whole time."

Brock snickers, and I quickly stop in my tracks, causing him to nearly trip as he attempts to avoid running into me.

Simply being in the city has lifted all of our spirits, save for Scarlet, who is strangely quiet, her gaze distant and her attention divided as we go from stall to stall and inspect every craft and ware imaginable.

We find the toy store that John alluded to, and Lark eagerly rushes about, touching every doll, marble, puzzle, and any other source of amusement. Finally, he sets his eyes on a handful of small, carved, wooden figurines. He proudly displays them to us: a large dog with bared teeth, a slightly smaller one with a serene expression, and a tiny pup.

"Look, Albie! This one with the teeth looks like the one on your sigil. This one here is like Eilis, because she always seems so calm. This pup here is like me because you always used to say that I followed you around like a lost pup."

Albain laughs at the memory. "Aye, that's true."

Lark reluctantly goes to set them back on the shelf, but Albain swiftly snatches them from his hands and readily pays the shopkeeper for them. He gives them back to Lark who elatedly bounces from foot to foot in his joy.

We move on to another stall where a weaponsmith is selling well-made blades, and Scarlet finds another dagger to add to her growing collection.

"Don't you have enough of those?" asks Brock warily.

"You can never have enough daggers," replies Scarlet.

"It's always nice to have variety when you're deciding how to best stab someone." She points to one of the knives set upon the display. "This one looks like the ones the Bromus use when they're gutting deer. I presume it would work on a human, too, if need be."

There is a look of abject horror on Brock's face, and Scarlet giggles to herself as she inquires after the price of the rather well-made dagger with a slightly curved edge. Moments later, she's tucking it into the back of her waistband, should she have need of it in the immediate future.

"You play a dangerous game, Boy," Brock whispers to me. "You best not ever have a reason to make her angry. I'd fear for your life if you did."

"You know she only says those things to get a reaction out of you," I point out helpfully.

"Well, it works. I'm bloody terrified of that girl!" exclaims Brock.

Another stand yields all manner of treats: pastries, candies, chocolates, caramels, and any other sweet item one could possibly fathom.

I grab a small, paper bag and fill it to the brim with white and red peppermint candies. I pay for them and hand the entire bag over to Lark, whose face erupts in a look of unbridled glee.

He wraps his free arm around my waist and gives me a firm hug. "Thank you, Boy!"

"What's with your obsession with peppermints lately, Lark?" asks Brock curiously.

Lark's broad smile falters slightly. "They remind me of Old Man... he always smelled of them. He used to offer them to me, but I never much cared for the taste. But now... now I find that I like them very much." He pops one into his mouth and offers some to me and Scarlet. They're sweet and leave a cool, refreshing flavor long after they've dissolved.

We reach the central part of the square. This is the busiest section of the city that we've encountered so far. People hurry to and fro on their afternoon errands. Performers such as firebreathers and puppeteers command the attention of large portions of the crowds. Beggars line the outer part of the square in the hopes that some gentle soul will grant them some small measure of coin. However, the most impressive feature of the square is an ornate fountain that seems to draw the attention of every eye that beholds it. It is finely crafted with exquisite details. Within it is a massive carving of a beautiful woman carrying a jug of water in the crook of her arm, her other hand held out towards us. The expression on her face is one of peace and contentment, and a large, circular pool of water, a few feet deep, surrounds her on all sides.

My gaze is commanded by this piece, and no matter how hard I try to, I just can't seem to tear my eyes away. There is something strangely familiar about the fountain, and I can begin to feel the strange sensation of a memory washing over me.

I'm sitting on the edge of the fountain, and the grey-eyed woman is sitting next to me. She holds a shiny, silver coin in her hand. She closes her eyes, appearing to be thinking hard, then presses the coin to her lips before tossing it into the pool of the fountain.

She reaches into her coinpurse and extracts another silver coin. She places it in the palm of my small, child hands and gestures to the pool. "Go on, love. Do as I did. Make a wish."

I repeat the same actions I saw her take before gleefully dropping the coin into the fountain.

"Boy? Are you all right?" asks Scarlet, giving my hand a gentle squeeze.

I nod numbly. "Yeah... I just... I just... I've been here before." My body trembles with emotion, and my pulse races with excitement. "Scarlet... she was here. The grey-eyed woman. A long time ago, she sat just there on the edge of the fountain. Do you think…" My heart begins to thunder in my chest with such force that I'm certain it will burst forth at any moment, and a mixture of hopeful optimism and trepidation overtakes me. "Do you think she could still be here somewhere? What if she lives here in the city?"

"Boy, if she's here, we'll find her," assures Scarlet. She wraps her arms around me, pulling me close, and the comforting smell of lavender emanating from her alabaster skin soothes me and quiets the flood of emotion that threatens to consume me.

"Boy, if you've had one memory here, there could be a chance you'll have others. Maybe we should explore this area a bit more. Maybe it will bring something else back to you," suggests Eilis helpfully.

"That's a fair point," agrees Brock.

We spend some time milling about the main square in the hopes that it may bring to mind some other memory for me, but to no avail. After a while, we make our way down one of the connecting streets. We browse through a few stalls that offer thick scarves and heavy cloaks for the coming winter.

As we make our way down the road, I see Albain's expression become grim, and I notice that his hand comes to rest on the dagger sheathed at his belt.

"Albain. What is it?" asks Eilis quietly.

"We're being followed," he replies in a hushed voice. "Pickpocket has been trailing us since the square."

"What pickpocket?" I question. I almost turn to look behind us but suddenly think better of it. If we are being followed, it seems it would be unwise to draw attention to the fact that we are aware.

"The one posing as a blind beggar," relates Albain.

"I saw him," says Lark. "You mean that poor man isn't really blind?"

Albain shakes his head. "I've seen plenty of blind men and many a beggar. Blind men don't watch for coinpurses as folk pass by, and beggars don't carry jeweled daggers."

"Why do you think he's following us?" inquires Brock, a note of concern in his voice.

"I doubt he'd be fool enough to try and rob us. You'll find most aren't willing to come too near me on their own accord. As you've seen, I have a bit of a reputation. I'm not sure what he's playing at," replies Albain with a frown.

"So, what are we going to do?" asks Scarlet.

"There's an alley up ahead. He's following a considerable distance behind us. When we turn the corner, you all slowly keep walking," directs Albain. "I'll duck into a doorway and wait for him to pass. When he does, I'll find out what he wants."

Albain gestures for us to walk down an alley to the right, and after we do, we follow his instructions. A few moments later, there is a loud *"Oof!"* followed by a thump. When we turn, we see that Albain has snatched our pursuer by the collar of his robes and slammed him against the stone wall of a building. Albain's other hand holds a dagger against the man's throat.

We make our way back towards Albain but keep a reasonable distance away. A few other folks meander down the alley, but when they see what's going on, they either quickly scurry away or avert their eyes and pretend they don't see anything.

At first glance, the man looks like any other beggar, but the longer I gaze upon him, the more I begin to notice. Albain was right. The dagger hidden beneath his dust brown cloak is jeweled, his leather boots are only lightly worn, and his pale hands look as if they've never done an honest day's work. His icy blue eyes are apparently working just fine as he stares up at Albain in stark terror. His knees tremble slightly, and his pale skin seems to grow paler by the second.

"Who are you? And why were you following us?" growls Albain threateningly.

The man lets out a strangled cry and begins to plead

passionately. "Please! Please! I meant no harm! Just let me go! I promise I won't bother you again!"

Albain is quickly losing his patience. "Answer the damn questions!" he demands through clenched teeth.

"I-I I thought I saw-" His panicked eyes search out our group, and when they lock on their intended target, I see him relax slightly.

"Keep talking, or I really will make you a blind beggar." Albain moves the dagger to the man's cheek, just near his left eye.

"Rose! Rose!" His desperate shouts resound through the alleyway, and it's then that I realize he is speaking directly to Scarlet.

Scarlet stands frozen to the spot. Her piercing blue eyes look hollow and vacant, and for a moment, I think she must be experiencing a memory. She makes no move and utters not a word for several moments. Suddenly, she frowns, a look of disappointment on her face, and she slowly shakes her head. "Sir, I don't know who you think I am, but that's not my name."

The man struggles against Albain's grasp, but the warrior holds him fast, not allowing him to move even an inch towards us.

"My hood! My hood!" he says to Albain. "Please! Let me take it down! Perhaps she'll recognize me then!"

Albain gives Scarlet a questioning glance. She simply shrugs in reply, and with a heavy sigh, the warrior releases the beggar imposter. However, Albain keeps his dagger at the ready, just in case the man would do anything he disapproves of.

Never taking his eyes off Scarlet, the man removes the hood of his cloak, revealing shocks of bright, red hair. "There now. You see? It's me. It's your Uncle Fenton. Fenton Hall. You remember me, darling, don't you?" There's a tone of desperation in his voice.

Scarlet shakes her head again. "No. I'm sorry. You must have me confused with someone else."

"No, no, no. You've your mother's look about you. Rhea. She was my sister. Your mum. Maker rest her soul." The man, Fenton, attempts to move towards us, but Albain bars his way.

"You'll keep your distance if you know what's good for you," he warns. "The girl says she doesn't remember you."

"Rose!" Fenton's voice is desperate and pleading. "Please, please! It's me! Your dear old uncle! You've been gone so long I thought you dead! And now here you are! There's no mistaking you! You have your mother's eyes, and the same red hair as her, and as me!" He reaches up and tugs at a clump of his own hair as if to demonstrate the resemblance.

I turn to Scarlet, taking her hands in my own. "Are you sure, Scarlet? He called you Rose. Perhaps that's why you remembered the roses. And he is... well... you said that in one of your memories you saw a man who taught you to steal. He seems to fit the part."

Scarlet's expression becomes one of instant aggravation. It's a look I've never earned from her before, and I can't say I'm fond of it. I feel as if those ice blue eyes are skewering me with unseen daggers. "So, since I may have been trained to be a thief, then I must be related to every cutpurse in Allanon?"

"I-I-I didn't mean-" I stammer.

Scarlet sighs heavily and returns her attention to the stranger. "Sir, I am truly sorry, but I don't know you."

Albain glances from Scarlet to Fenton. He frowns slightly before roughly seizing the latter by his upper arm. "Be on with you then, and if I see you skulking about around us again, you won't have to *pretend* to be blind anymore." Albain gives him a shove back towards the square, and the man scurries away as quickly as his legs can carry him.

* * *

We make our way back to the square and move a little further past the fountain. We pass another small alleyway, and when we do, I feel the hair on the back of my neck stand on edge, and a shiver shoots up my spine causing me to tremble slightly. I freeze in my tracks, my gaze drifting down the narrow alleyway to my right.

"Boy?" Scarlet tugs on my sleeve. "Boy, are you all right? You've gone all pale."

"I... I need to..." As I step towards the alley, I am accosted by brief flashes of memory.

A hooded figure juggles three, small crystal balls, deftly moving them from hand to hand. I laugh wildly, thoroughly amused by the trick. The person's face is completely obscured by a black cloak, but the hands that protrude from the sleeves are small, pale, and childlike. The figure moves towards the alleyway and beckons for me to follow.

I glance back towards the fountain where a tall, broad shouldered man has his back to me. I cannot make out his face, and he doesn't see me turn away and follow the figure with the crystal balls.

As I laughingly follow the other child into the alleyway, large, rough hands seize my shoulders, and a black covering falls over my head, shutting out all light.

I begin to panic and try to call out and struggle against my captors. A hand clamps down over my mouth to silence my cries.

"Hurry!" comes a male voice. "We need to get him to that bloody sorcerer."

Suddenly, I feel a sharp pain in the back of my head, and I begin to fall.

"Boy?" Scarlet is tugging at my sleeve. "Boy!"

I shake my head and return to the present, a time in which a beautiful girl with enthralling eyes and bright, red hair calls out to me with worry in her voice.

"It was another memory," I say quietly. "I think... I think it may have been when I was taken to Abirad." I am keenly aware of the tremble in my voice as I relate this.

Scarlet clasps my hand in her own. "Boy, you're shaking."

The others have their eyes upon me, worry the prominent emotion displayed in their expressions.

"Boy, maybe we should head back to the inn for the night," suggests Brock. "It's getting late. We can return to this place in the morning. After you've had time to sort through what you saw."

"Aye," agrees Albain. "I think we've all had enough excitement for the night."

* * *

We make our way back to the inn and enjoy a hearty supper of roasted rabbit, smashed potatoes, vegetables, brown bread with fresh butter, and some sweet drink made with cooled black tea, orange slices, lemon, and honey. We pass the time laughing, sharing stories, and reminiscing of our times together, but our joy is tempered by the bittersweet note of Lark's impending departure. The following morning, we will make our journey to the castle, and with hope, Lark will be reunited with his father, King Ruden.

Lark stares down at his full plate of food. It's obvious that his nerves are interfering with his appetite. It's strange that anything should stay on his plate longer than a few minutes; he usually inhales his food as quickly as Brock does.

"Lark," says Eilis gently. "You've barely touched your food."

Lark sighs and moves closer to Eilis on the bench. He rests his head on her shoulder, and I can see the tears welling in his eyes. "I know, Eilis. It's just... I'm really going to miss... I'm going to miss all of this... All of you."

"We can remain in Vericus for a while," I remind him. "After all, if there's any chance that the grey- eyed woman could be

334

here, I want to do all that I can to find her."

"Yeah, Lark. It's as we promised," concurs Brock. "It's not like we'll just drop you at the castle and leave you there forever."

"Aye," agrees Albain. "Don't fret so much over it, boy. We're not saying our goodbyes just yet." He puts a long arm around Lark, and his hand comes to rest on Eilis's shoulder. The pair of them look down at the aggrieved boy and continue to reassure him that all will be well.

Once we have eaten and drunk our fill, we prepare to turn in for the evening. We climb the main stairs and easily locate our lodgings. Unfortunately, there weren't any rooms left that were large enough to accommodate our whole group, so Albain, Eilis, and Lark take the room on the right, and Brock, Scarlet, and I take the one on the left.

We are all exhausted, so we lay down to sleep for the night. Moments later, Brock is snoring loudly. Scarlet rests next to me, but her mind seems elsewhere.

"Are you okay, Scarlet? You've been so quiet this evening... ever since that man approached us. Again, I sincerely apologize for my comment. I meant no offense." I've said it no less than ten times, and despite her assurances that everything is all right between us, I still feel terrible about it.

"It's fine, Boy," she says again. "It's just been a very long day, and I'm very tired."

"I understand. Good night, Scarlet." I move to press a kiss to her lips, but she turns her head at the last moment, and instead I kiss her cheek.

I feel awful, but I'm at a loss as to what I can do to quiet her discontentment. I wait to hear the rhythmic pattern of her breathing, but her bright, blue eyes still glint in the moonlight long after my own grow heavy with sleep.

Later, I would come to wonder if, perhaps, she was waiting for me to succumb to slumber.

I don't feel it when she carefully extricates herself from

under my arm.

I don't hear her gather her belongings.

I don't see her pause in the doorway, perhaps stilled by a moment of regret for what she feels she must do.

I don't know when she crosses to the stable, mounts her horse, and rides out of my life.

CHAPTER 36

When I awake early the next morning, I become painfully aware of Scarlet's absence. At first, I assume that she headed downstairs to join Albain, Eilis, and Lark for breakfast, as Brock is still snoring loudly across the room.

But then I find the simple scrap of paper upon the small table near the hearth.

There are but two words written in Scarlet's script:

I'm sorry.

Suddenly, I notice that her belongings are gone; her bag, stuffed with the few sparse items she's collected along our journey, is nowhere to be found. My heart aches with dread, and panic seizes me. Without even pulling on my boots, I bolt down the stairs and nearly knock over a rather large man who is making his way up the stairs. I barrel past Albain, Eilis, and Lark who glance at me inquisitively over their breakfast.

My feet carry me to the stable, and the sinking feeling in my stomach reaches a new level of pain as I see that her dapple grey mare is gone. My companions suddenly appear behind me, and I see the look of realization on their faces as they comprehend the reason for my alarm and hasty exit from the inn.

"Boy? Where's Scarlet gone?" asks Lark.

Wordlessly, I reach into my pocket, and with a trembling hand, I hold the note out to Eilis for her and Albain to read.

"Sorry? What does she have to be sorry for?" wonders Eilis aloud.

"All of her stuff is gone," I mumble despondently. "I don't even know when she left."

Albain growls under his breath. "It was that bloody beggar yesterday. I'd bet every coin I have on it. I knew something wasn't right with all that. She said she didn't know him, but I've learned to spot a lie over my years, and something in her look didn't sit right with me. She knew him; I'm certain of it." Albain turns to me, and there is regret reflected in his eyes. "I'm sorry, Boy. I should have said something. I wanted to believe her when she said she didn't remember that piece of scum, but her expression said otherwise."

"Do you think she went to him?" I ask. "Perhaps we can track him down."

Albain seems to ponder something for a moment then says, "Lark, follow Boy back inside and head back to his room. Lock the door, and don't open it for anyone except me. Eilis and I are going to go see what we can find out about where Scarlet was headed. I'll also ask around about this Fenton Hall and where we might find him."

Lark and I head back inside while Albain and Eilis set off to seek out answers. I sit on my bed and Lark sits cross-legged beside me. He puts his small hand upon my shoulder in an effort to comfort me.

"It will be all right, Boy. Albie and Eilis will be back soon, and Scarlet will be with them," he says in an attempt to cheer me.

Soon, Brock stirs, and when I relate all that he's missed, he looks at me with sympathy in his eyes. "I'm sure that wherever she's gone, she'll be back soon. She wouldn't just up and leave permanently without saying goodbye, would she? Maybe she's just gone somewhere to clear her head."

I want to believe him, but the ache in my heart loudly protests otherwise.

* * *

It's nearly two hours later when I hear Albain's heavy footsteps just outside the room. There's a single knock on the door followed by his familiar, deep, gravelly voice. "It's me."

I quickly unlock the door, and Albain steps inside. The look in his eyes tells me he does not return with glad tidings. Eilis steps in after him, and her expression is equally bleak.

"I did some asking around. Stable boy said she rode out just after midnight. Left the main gates and was headed to the west," he reports.

"Midnight? That was nearly eight hours ago. She could be anywhere by now!" There's an edge to my voice, and I feel Eilis give a gentle squeeze to my shoulder.

"I inquired after Fenton Hall as well. No surprises there. He's a thief and a gambler. He owes money to half of Allanon," Albain explains. "Innkeeper said he had a sister named Rhea, as he told us. She died some years ago. She had a little girl. Pretty little thing with bright red hair and blue eyes. Way the innkeeper tells it, when the girl's mum died, Fenton took to using the kid in his cons. Then she just disappeared one day. Fenton didn't seem too worried about it, and when people asked after her, he pretended not to know who they were talking about."

"Maybe we should seek out this Fenton guy," suggests Brock.

"Already ahead of you," responds Albain. "He lives in a hovel in the northwest part of town. Nothing but slums. Fairly sure every crook in Vericus lives in those parts. Neighbor said he never came home last night."

"Is there any chance he took her?" I ask worriedly.

Albain shakes his head. "Stable boy said she was alone when she left. Spoke with some guards at the gates, too. They said the same."

"Well, let's follow her!" cries Lark, rising to his feet.

"You know how to track, Albie. We can't just leave her alone out there. She could get into trouble!"

"Something tells me Scarlet can take care of herself just fine," assures Albain. "I also think she doesn't want to be found just now." He turns to me. "I'm sorry, Boy. There are far too many horses that have come and gone down that road. Other than just following the road northwest, there's not much more we can do just now to track her down, and she's got hours and hours upon us. Perhaps we can set out to look for her after we get Lark to the castle."

Lark's face instantly pales, and a miserable expression comes to reside upon his face. "Oh... right."

"I know that you're worried, Boy, but we'll find her," promises Eilis.

I nod, but my hope is growing weaker by the second. I knew something was amiss the previous evening, and I curse myself for not doing more to assuage whatever it was that troubled her mind. Now she is gone, and I have no way of knowing for sure where she is headed or why she left.

❋ ❋ ❋

A heavy cloud of grief pervades over the rest of our morning. Scarlet's absence coupled with Lark's impending departure rob us of both good humor and conversation. In silence, we gather our belongings. I tuck Scarlet's note into my bag. I don't know why I keep it as it serves as a reminder of one of the worst days of my life in memory. I would sooner take days of floggings and endless backbreaking labor under Abirad's command than the eviscerating sorrow that causes my stomach to ache and tears at my heart. I berate myself incessantly, convinced it must have been because of something I said or did, and that makes the endless pain terrorize me even more fervently.

We collect our horses from the stable and follow Albain

on the road that leads to Elidure Castle. It is exceptionally frigid, and every breath we take leaves a puff of smoke in the air. My lungs ache with the chill, and I pull my cloak more tightly around me. My thoughts drift to Scarlet. Thankfully, the Bromus had supplied us with warm traveling cloaks, but I worry for her, alone and cold somewhere.

Lark barely says a word the entire time, despite all of our efforts to cheer him. His expression is devoid of all semblances of excitement or joy. Rather, he looks as if he is dreading what is to come.

"It's okay, Lark. You'll see your father soon. You'll have a family, a home, and more peppermints than you could ever eat in a lifetime," says Brock in an attempt to lighten the kid's mood.

"I already have a family," replies Lark glumly. "And living with the Bromus is far better than staying in some stuffy, old castle."

"Lark, I know this must be difficult for you; it is a big change. But I think you will come to be happy here," speaks Eilis comfortingly.

Lark simply frowns in reply, and with every step we draw closer to the castle, he looks more and more distressed.

Much as Albain predicted, it takes about an hour on horseback to get to the castle from the inn. We leave our horses at the outer stables and make our way on foot across the stone bridge and up to the main gate.

When we arrive, we are met by several heavily armed guards, clad in chainmail armor and wearing surcoats of blue emblazoned with the gold lion that serves as the symbol of King Ruden Elidure and his line. Eilis relates the reason for our visit, and one of the guards hurries off to fetch the Captain of the Guard.

An imposing man clad in golden armor arrives at the gate and begins to scrutinize us under his suspicious gaze. He casts several nervous glances at Albain, who glowers down at him in irritation.

"State your business at the castle," demands the Captain of the Guard.

"My name is Eilis Oakheart of the Oak Clan. My grandfather, the All-Chieftain, sent a raven ahead with word of our arrival," explains Eilis. "We need to speak with the king. It is on an exceedingly urgent matter."

"Yes, his majesty told us that Seamus Oakheart was sending a small party here," replies the Captain of the Guard. "But we can't just let anyone traipse into the castle. You could very well be here under false pretenses. Have you any proof of your identities?"

I almost want to laugh. Proof of our identities? Lark and I still haven't the slightest idea who we really are, though with luck, Lark will be reclaiming his name soon enough.

Eilis reaches into her bag and presents a handwritten letter bearing the seal of the All-Chieftain that reiterates our reason for visiting the castle. She gives it to the Captain of the Guard who scarcely looks at it and remains unconvinced.

"Letters can be forged," he returns.

Eilis sighs and reaches for the medallion around her neck. She holds it out for the guard to see. "Here. This is my grandfather's."

The Captain looks slightly more convinced but is still reluctant to let us in.

Albain looks like he is on the verge of reaching one of his long arms through the gate and strangling the Captain of the Guard, but surprisingly, it's Eilis who loses her temper first.

Eilis seizes one of the bars of the gate in her hand. "We are cold, we are exhausted, and we have been through hell and back to get here." Her voice is quivering with barely repressed rage. "Now open the bloody gates or so help me, I will make my own way through and truly give you proof of who I am!"

We all stare at her, our mouths agape, save for Albain who looks upon her with admiration.

"I love you so bloody much," he tells her, and I see the rage begin to dissipate from her features.

The Captain of the Guard frowns slightly. "Well, you certainly sound like Seamus Oakheart." He turns to his men, and they talk among themselves for several moments.

Lark stands beside me and shifts nervously from foot to foot.

I put my hand upon his shoulder. "It's okay, Lark. They just want to be sure we are who we say we are," I reassure him.

Several of the guards glance back in our direction, and I hear the Captain of the guard whisper, "This could very well be legitimate. He looks like *her*."

After a while, the Captain of the Guard gives the order for the gate to be opened. We are ushered inside the gate, and he leads us towards the main doors of the castle. "I've had word sent to his majesty. He will meet with you in the throne room."

We follow him through the doors and down a long, broad corridor that is ornately decorated with golden sconces, oil paintings, and tapestries that depict events of interest in the history of the Elidure line.

When we reach the end of the hallway, the Captain of the Guard says, "I'll go in to announce you. Wait just outside the doors." He heads towards the throne room and disappears within.

We reach the enormous red and gold double doors that lead into the throne room, and Lark comes to a halt, unable to will himself to travel even another step forward.

"I-I can't," he whimpers. His lip trembles, and the tears begin to well in his eyes. "Take me back to the camp, Eilis. Please!" His voice is pleading and so filled with terror that my own heart aches for him. "Take me back! I can't do this! I'm not- I'm not brave enough!"

Eilis pulls him into her arms. "Lark, you are one of the bravest people I know. Look how far you've come."

"Lark, you have nothing to be afraid of. You're home now," says Brock. "Just through those doors is your father."

We hear several sets of footsteps within the throne room,

and suddenly, the enormous doors begin to move, pulled open by two heavily armed guards.

Lark simply stares into expansive room. At the very end of it is an enormous throne, and upon it is seated the silhouette of a man, one whose features we cannot make out from where we stand.

Albain kneels before Lark "It's all right to cry, boy. If I saw my father again, I'd be trembling in my boots, too. This is no small thing for you. But he's just a man of flesh and bone like any other. You've nothing to fear. We're right here with you." He presses his forehead against Lark's as the kid takes several deep breaths to steady himself. "There now. There." The warrior rises to his feet. "On your word."

Lark takes another deep breath and slowly begins to walk into the throne room. "I-I'm ready."

The rest of us fall into step around him. Black curtains cover every window, so very little light graces the place save for the torches and sconces that line the walls. It is obvious the darkness of the place mirrors the king's mourning for his deceased wife and vanished son.

As we draw closer, the king's features slowly begin to materialize. A tall, broad-shouldered man is seated upon the throne. His hair falls to his shoulders in waves of reddish brown, and he is dressed in a black doublet with matching black pants and boots. Yes, this is certainly a man in mourning. There is an enormous gold crown, adorned with blue and white jewels atop his head. Beyond the most obvious details, I can't make out much of his face in the dim light.

The Captain of the Guard stands to the left of the throne, and I see him whisper something into the king's ear. We come to a stop some distance from the throne, and I find myself standing behind Lark. A heavy silence fills the entirety of the cavernous room as we await some acknowledgment from the king. For quite some time, he neither speaks nor moves, but eventually, we see him rise from his throne and slowly make his way towards us.

"Can it… Can it truly be you?" His deep baritone resonates through the room. Even with the simplest of words, it possesses a certain commanding quality.

At the sound of his voice, my stomach begins to churn with nervous anticipation, and my palms sweat profusely.

His face comes into view, revealing a thick, reddish brown beard, and as he gazes upon us, his sapphire blue eyes are wide with disbelief.

"My boy! My boy!" Without warning, he rushes forward, his arms outstretched before him.

But he doesn't approach Lark.

In fact, he pushes past him as if he doesn't see him at all.

Instead, he finds his way to me.

Two, strong arms wrap around me, gathering me in a warm and familiar embrace. Somehow, it feels right. It feels like home.

"My boy!" His voice, thick with emotion, breaks apart as he succumbs to sobs.

He doesn't call me Boy; he calls me *my boy*.

"It's you!" he cries. "Girard was right! You look just like her! There's no mistaking it! My boy!"

His lips are near my ear when he utters the word.

"Trystan!"

With this final revelation, my knees buckle beneath me and a deluge of tears pours down my cheeks in endless rivers as a flood of memories washes over me, causing me to cry out.

My mother, Queen Fiona, the woman with the grey eyes sings to me and twirls me in the air.

She watches me ride upon a white pony as the Master of the Horse leads me around the courtyard.

I wake up crying in the middle of the night, stirred by some nightmare, and she instantly appears in the threshold of my room, drawing me into a warm embrace that seems to stop the terror in its tracks.

She offers me a blueberry tart, and I devour it. It's sweet as it hits my tongue, and it leaves a smear of purplish liquid upon my lips that causes her to laugh uproariously and dab at my mouth with a white napkin.

But it's not just her.
My father is there, too.

My father, King Ruden, bouncing me on his lap as he tells me tales of the kings of old.

He offers me a wooden sword and watches as I attack a hapless straw-stuffed man in the training yard.

He places his heavy hand on my shoulder and speaks comfortingly to me as we stand in a room made of stone. Before us is the tomb where my mother has been laid to rest, her beautiful grey eyes forever closed. I struggle with this memory because he tells me she is gone, but I cannot remember how or why.

More and more memories accost my mind, and among them is one that I have seen before.

A hooded figure juggles three, small, crystal balls, deftly moving them from hand to hand. I laugh wildly, thoroughly amused by the trick. The person's face is completely obscured by a black cloak, but the hands that protrude from the sleeves are small, pale, and childlike. The figure moves towards the alleyway and beckons for me to follow.

I glance back towards the fountain where a tall, broad shouldered man has his back to me.

My father.

He doesn't see me turn away and laughingly follow the other child into the alleyway. Suddenly, large, rough hands seize my shoulders, and a black covering falls over my head, shutting out all light.

I begin to panic and try to call out and struggle against my captors. A hand clamps down over my mouth to silence my cries.

"Hurry!" comes a male voice. "We need to get him to that bloody sorcerer."

Suddenly, I feel a sharp pain in the back of my head, and I begin to fall.

As I hit the ground, my vision swims, and I reach up to my face, grasping at the bag that obscures it. I start to pull it off of my head, and when I do, there is a pair of piercing blue eyes gazing down upon me. It's the figure that I followed into the alleyway, but now the hood of her cloak rests on her narrow shoulders, and waves of red form the tresses of her hair.

Scarlet.

"He's still awake! Hit him again!" comes the male voice from before. "Put more of your arm into it this time! The little bugger was scarcely dazed by the last one!"

Scarlet stares down at me, her eyes wide with panic and her expression one of regret. "Uncle! Don't! You'll hurt him! You said you wouldn't hurt him!"

A large hand shoves her roughly, and she tumbles to the floor.

There's another sharp pain, and all fades to black.

My eyes begin to refocus, and I find myself in the throne room, gazing into the eyes of the King of Allanon, my father. His arms are fastened firmly around me, as if he is afraid if he relinquishes his hold on me even slightly that I will simply deliquesce before his eyes, and once again, he will be left alone to mourn for his wife and son.

Tearfully, he kisses my forehead and reaches forward to hold my cheeks in his hands as he looks upon me with unbridled joy and relief. "Trystan... My boy..."

I don't know for how long we cling to each other, but when we reluctantly part, neither of us can command any words to our lips. We simply gaze upon one another, tears still unabashedly falling from our eyes and making the wooden floors slick with a salty ocean of loss and reclamation.

Tentatively, Eilis steps towards me. "Boy? Are you... are you okay?" she asks. Her hand comes to rest upon my shoulder, and her voice is filled with worry. "Is he... is his majesty correct? Are... are you..."

I feel numb and exhilarated at the same time. It is a strange contradiction that I can't quite seem to readily dispel.

I clutch her hands in my own, and my voice trembles terribly with the answer to her unfinished question. "Trystan. *My name is Trystan.*"

CHAPTER 37

My companions are stunned into silence. Each of them stares at me with mouths agape and bewilderment in their eyes.

All except for Lark.

The poor kid looks as if he'd like to simply melt into the floor. It's then that I feel heartily sorry for him. All this time, we had been operating under the belief that he was Prince Trystan. He had prepared himself time and time again for his departure from our company, begging us to let him stay. All of that emotional turmoil served no purpose. In fact, he should look relieved.

But he doesn't.

His face is pale and sweat teems from his brow as his hands tremble at his sides.

Perhaps it is because we had ensured him that all would be well once he was reunited with King Ruden. We had told him- even I had personally told him- that he would soon reclaim his memories.

But that isn't the way of it.

"I-I don't understand," says Eilis, shaking her head in confusion. "How is it possible? According to everything we read, Prince Trystan disappeared on his second birthday. By all accounts you should be Lark's age!"

"Blessed born on the Day of Mercy," speaks King Ruden quietly. "The Day of Mercy occurs only every four years. Trystan was born, four years later, we celebrated what was considered his 'first' birthday. Four years after that, we celebrated what was his 'second' birthday. That was the last day I saw my son… until today. It's been seven years… seven painfully long years."

"Ughhhh." Eilis buries her face in her hands. "Of course! My name should have been Fool, because that is what I was. I was so consumed by the idea that Lark was the missing prince that I overlooked such a significant detail."

"It was an honest mistake, Eilis," I console her. "It is a very irregular circumstance. Even Old Man didn't account for it." I make my way to where Lark is standing. His gaze is fixated on the ground before him, and though I see him tense slightly as I approach, he does not raise his eyes to meet mine. "I'm sorry, Lark. Despite your anxiety over coming here, you must be very disappointed to be without your memories still."

Lark looks up at me, his blue eyes weeping pools of sky. "I'm sorry."

"Sorry? What do you have to be sorry for?" I question.

Before he can answer, I feel my father's heavy hand on my shoulder. "Come, Trystan. We have much to discuss." He beckons the Captain of the Guard, Girard, to approach.

Girard hurries forward and bows deeply before me. "Prince Trystan, my sincerest apologies for delaying you at the gate." He rises, but still keeps his gaze averted and pointed towards the floor. "Over the years, many impostors have come forward to try and claim your identity. We have thwarted them at every attempt, but because of this, we have had to be very cautious when anyone claimed to be you."

My father's face reddens considerably, and he looks as if he is about to unleash hellfire and fury upon the Captain of the Guard. "Girard, you foolish-"

"No harm done," I assure Girard. "I understand you were simply doing your job. Please don't be too angry with him, father. I'm sure he was only trying to fulfill his role in protecting you."

My father considers this for a moment, but I can tell

from his body language and the continuing redness in his features that he is still seething. "Girard, why don't you make yourself useful and see that the prince's companions are made comfortable? I wish to speak to my son privately."

"As you wish, your majesty." Girard beckons for my friends to follow him, and they are led from the throne room.

"Come, Trystan. Let us speak just the two of us," offers my father.

I follow him out of the throne room and down the main corridor to the west wing of the castle where we make our way to the expansive library. Next to the gardens, this was always my mother's favorite place in the castle.

My mother.

Queen Fiona.

Dearly departed and laid to rest in the royal tombs among my ancestors.

I had always believed, always hoped with all my heart, that I would be reunited with the grey-eyed woman. While I am beyond grateful to have reclaimed my memories, my heart aches at the idea that the one vestige of my former life, the one person I had managed to preserve in my mind, is no more. The pain is just as poignant as it was seven years ago when I learned of her sudden passing.

When we enter the library, there is a roaring fire burning in the hearth, and the entirety of the room bears the distinct aroma that can only be created by the pages of old books. Like most of the castle, the immense windows are covered in shrouds of black, and my father orders his servants to uncover them, allowing the light and warmth of the sun to illuminate every corner of the immense room.

We seat ourselves by the fire, and for several moments we can do little more than to stare at each other in awkward silence. So much has happened since our parting that neither of us seems to know where to begin.

Finally, I take a deep breath, and I tell him everything.

Being abducted in the square during the Festival of Mercy.

Arriving at Castle Ciar as Abirad's prisoner.

The loss of my memories, and how my mother was the only aspect of my former life that I could recall.

Laboring in the courtyard of Castle Ciar. I even show him the scars that mar my back from the frequent floggings.

How I came to know and travel with my companions.

Living among the Bromus.

Even though it pains me, I also describe the loss of Old Man and the origin of the burn scars that cover my arm.

However, I do not tell him that my departed friend was truly Fenustus, the mage who had helped to spur citizens against the crown during the Bread Riots. Nor do I tell him of the amulet and spellbook for fear that he may remove them from my possession.

Finally, I tell him of Scarlet, the girl who has captured my heart, of her recent disappearance, and my desire to find her again.

My father listens quietly, every now and then interjecting with a question or comment, and when my tale is done, he wordlessly stares into the fire as he processes all I have told him. Finally, he reaches out and places his hand on my shoulder.

"Trystan, my son, I will never be able to make amends for the injustice you have suffered on my part. I believed you may have been taken to Blackwood, and so, the majority of my searches for you have been done discretely through men I paid well to track down your whereabouts. Obviously, none of them were able to give me the information I desired, and most of them were executed for their incompetence. Eventually, I accepted the thought you must be gone forever, dead... and that I was condemned to be an heirless king, robbed of a wife, a queen, and my only child. I ceased the searches nearly four years ago as I was convinced no more could be done."

Four years ago? Eilis's grandfather never stopped looking for her; he never stopped fighting in the hopes he would one day see her again. However, my father, separated from me for only half the time Eilis was parted from her kin, resolved that I was dead, and simply stopped searching. I try to understand how difficult it must have been for him in such a situation, but at the same time, I cannot fight the flash of anger that jolts through my body.

He pauses to collect himself, fighting back the tears that threaten to spill forth. He clears his throat and continues. "I must admit... when I received the message from the old Oakheart, I thought he'd finally gone mad or was perpetrating some ruse. The whole idea seemed farfetched. My son, taken by some sorcerer and hidden away for nearly half his life."

"As I understand it from my time in the Bromus encampment, Abirad had long been viewed as a threat," I reply. "Why would it be so surprising that he was capable of such cruelty?"

My father leans back in his chair. "By the Bromus he was viewed as a menace, but not so much by me. The first rumblings of a sorcerer in the north began about 15 years ago. At first, I faultily assumed it was the same fool mage who had tried to act against me in the Peasants' Revolt."

The Bread Riots.

"Soon after, old Oakheart's granddaughter went missing. He swore up and down it was the fault of that Abirad fellow. The Bromus started rallying support in the ambition of attacking the mage's stronghold."

"So, did you ever join their cause? Did you *ever* try to free those he imprisoned?" There's an edge to my voice that I hadn't intended, and the accusatory tone therein does not escape my notice.

My father appears a bit taken aback by my meaning then shakes his head slowly. "No. I believed that acting against the sorcerer was not in the best interest of Allanon. Had I known you were among his prisoners, it would have been a different story, but in truth, his presence was a boon to me."

"How so?"

"The Bromus have long been a thorn in my side. I resolved to let them fight their battles on their own. Either way, the outcome would benefit me. If the Bromus prevailed, the sorcerer would be dispatched, and that is one less charlatan in the world. If the sorcerer somehow prevailed, the Bromus would be cowed, and perhaps those that remained would finally swear fealty to the crown."

My father must notice the obvious shock present on my face, and he frowns slightly at my reaction. "Don't be deceived, Trystan," he warns me. "Despite your camaraderie with the All-Chieftain's heir, the Bromus are dangerous. Any group who refuses to bend the knee to the king are little more than rebels. They are a liability."

"But the All-Chieftain mentioned you fought alongside each other in the past," I point out.

"I have allied with the Bromus upon occasion, but only out of necessity," returns my father. "In this situation, I thought it best to wait and see who emerged victorious. Unfortunately, neither side decimated the other."

"Father..." I am stunned into silence. I think back on my childhood; I never recalled him being so cruel and callous. Perhaps it was my mother's death or my sudden disappearance that hardened his heart, but this is not the same man that I remember.

"Trystan." He holds my gaze with his own. "While I am grateful the Bromus helped you through a very difficult time, I would suggest that once your friends leave, you should cut ties with them. It would be unwise for the public to think the Bromus have the ear of the prince through the All-Chieftain's heir. And that bodyguard of hers, The Cur- I recognized him on sight- has a reputation, and not a pleasant one. Until he fell in with Oakheart, he was a mercenary of the worst sort; it was said he'd kill anyone for the right amount of coin."

I think of all the kindness that the All-Chieftain and his people, Eilis's people, have shown me, and as much as I want to argue against my father, I feel as if I would gain more progress trying to convince a pig to fly. It is obvious he bears no love for the Bromus and sees them as a threat, even more of a threat than Abirad.

"What will you do now... about Abirad?" I inquire. "Now that you know how dangerous he is, surely you will move on him."

"I will bide my time. Make no mistake, he will pay for what he did to you, but I do not fear him. Sorcerers are skilled frauds; their 'powers' are little more than smoke and mirrors. They are men, like any other, and bleed just as men do. As I've said, I've dealt with sorcerers before. They are weak-willed cowards. During the Peasants' Revolt, at the sight of my soldiers, one fled from the battlefield and was never seen again."

I know he speaks of Old Man, and there is a painful twinge in my chest as I recall his final act of selflessness.

My father continues. "In my grief, I even called upon one to heal your mother when she fell ill. He failed, of course, and before I could have him executed, he fled. Casters have no true power save for that which our foolish belief grants them. This Abirad is no threat to my crown. Furthermore, in some ways, he's done the kingdom a service."

I feel my blood begin to boil. As much as I love my father, I am shocked by the degree of his ignorance. While there is some pity in my heart for Sebastian, who lost so much and fought so hard to secure a better life for the peasantry, Abirad is the man who robbed me of my past and nearly stripped me of a future. He is the man who imprisoned thousands of innocent people over the years and forced them to work as slaves, punishing them for even the simplest acts of defiance. To hear my father regard his actions as anything other than vile incenses me.

"I can see you are angry with me, Trystan. Believe me when I say I do not laud the actions he took against you, but he did manage to address a problem that has plagued the kingdom for nearly two decades. While it is not common knowledge here in Vericus, the entirety of the kingdom has been suffering from food shortages. When the sorcerer took a portion of the population to his labor camp, that relieved some of the burden."

Again, I am reminded of Old Man's memories and the cause of the Bread Riots. I remember how vehemently Abirad had spoken of my father, blaming him for poverty, starvation, and death. While I do not claim to know how to be a king, I like to think that I do know how to be a decent person, and in my estimation, a good ruler does not let his people starve to the point that they feel forced to revolt against him.

I don't know how to reconcile the man who sits before me with the father who exists in my memory. When I was young, my greatest ambition was to one day be like him, a man who I believed to be strong, wise, and compassionate, a man who I believed to be a beloved ruler, a brilliant strategist, and an honorable person. Now, there's a war in my mind as I try to make sense of who he really is. I love him; he's my father and that cannot be changed, but at the same time, a feeling of deep disappointment consumes me. How could he turn a blind eye to the happenings in his kingdom? How could he allow his people to suffer, a sorcerer to reign unchallenged, allies to be betrayed, and a son abandoned to his fate?

Eventually, my father's steward, a man named Sorrel, comes to collect him for some urgent business.

"Where is Nigel, father?" I ask, recalling the name of the previous steward, a kind, older gentleman who always kept sweets in his pocket for me and humored me with card games and hide-and-seek when I had no one else to play with.

"He failed to fulfill the duties ascribed to him, so he was... retired," replies my father with a meaningful look at Sorrel.

Sorrel shifts uncomfortably, and I can guess that the fate of his predecessor was not a pleasant one.

Unfortunately, I am beginning to notice a rather disturbing trend. Whenever someone displeases my father or does not live up to his expectations, his punishments seem excessively cruel. The All-Chieftain had corrected himself when he mentioned the king had shown signs of madness. Perhaps he was not incorrect in his assumption.

For the rest of the day, I am hurried about on this task or that. My room is just as I left it, even down to the small, stuffed bear that rests upon the enormous, four poster bed. A servant hurries in to clear the closet of old garments, and a tailor is sent in to see that I am measured for proper attire befitting a prince. Until such can be made, I am given three chests full of clothing made from the finest materials in all of Allanon. A barber comes in and trims my hair to what my father views as a respectable length; no longer does it fall across my forehead and ears. After him, an armorer and a weaponsmith arrive to present me with their goods, and the royal jeweler comes soon after to fit me for a crown.

That evening, I dine alone with my father, and he rambles on and on about how far behind I am in my training to become the next King of Allanon. He vows to rectify this situation and tells me he has already secured me a tutor and a combat trainer who will be working with me the following morning.

I inquire after the whereabouts of my companions and am told that they have been given suitable lodging close to the guard barracks.

"Will they be joining us for dinner?" I ask.

My father laughs uproariously, but he does not answer.

From what I can recall, guests of the royal family were always given the best possible apartments and treated with warmth and hospitality when my mother was alive. However, it is obvious that my father's suspicion of the Bromus has rendered him a very poor host.

* * *

After dinner, I say goodnight to my father and make my way to my chambers. I wait for what seems like an eternity for the drowsiness to take me, but it never comes. In truth, this is the first night I've spent alone in a room in seven years, and the silence seems unnatural. I open the main door to my apartments and make my way into the hall where I find there are six guards stationed outside of my room and the immediate area.

One of them is Girard. "Your highness," he greets me. "Do you have need of something?"

"The bed is too soft and the room too quiet. Truthfully, I just want to pass the rest of the evening with my friends," I tell him.

Girard shifts nervously and glances down the hallway as if worried the king will show up at any instant to fly into a rage. "I don't know if that is a wise idea, your majesty."

"Don't worry, Girard. If my father takes exception to it, I'll tell him that I threatened to execute you if you refused me. Is that not his way?" I mumble moodily.

He does not attempt to correct me. "At least allow me to escort you to their quarters."

I give him a nod, and we move through the hallway in silence. My father has long since fallen asleep, but Girard still looks a bit anxious when we move past his room. It is a considerable trek to the wing where the guard barracks is contained. It lacks the ostentatious décor and finery proudly displayed throughout the rest of the castle and is distinctly colder in temperature. Finally, we arrive at the doors of two relatively small rooms near the guard barracks.

I can hear loud snoring coming from the one on the left and recognize the abrasive sound as coming from Brock. I sigh in amusement but do not wake him. Instead, I knock on the door at the right.

Girard reaches to his belt and takes a key to unlock the door.

"What's this?" I ask incredulously. "You've locked them in? For what purpose? They are guests, not prisoners!"

Girard appears embarrassed. "King's orders," he mutters. "I'll be right here, your majesty. Just call out if you have need of me," directs Girard, and he takes up a post near the door of the room.

When I open the door, I find that my friends are staying in a rather spartan room scarcely larger than the cells in the dungeons. There is a small fireplace by which Albain crouches as he attempts to coax a more suitable fire from the pitiful looking one that currently burns. There are two small beds, and from the size of them, I guess that Eilis and Albain are either about to be very cramped for the evening or that the latter may have to simply stretch out on the worn floorboards. The room is clean but drafty and lacks any degree of the comforts found in my own chambers.

As I enter the room, three sets of eyes immediately settle upon me. I can tell that I must have walked in on a rather intense discussion as Lark's entire face goes white as a ghost when he sees me.

"I'm so very, very sorry about all this," I say as I make my way towards them. "I had no idea you would be treated this way. Believe me, I would not have this done. You are my friends, and you are being treated in a way far less than you deserve. Unfortunately, my father seems to have some very strong opinions about the Bromus."

Albain looks as if he wants to say something, but Eilis puts her hand on his arm, and he takes a deep breath. I can tell by his expression that he is not pleased with the situation, but he likely bites his tongue out of regard for our friendship. "It's no fault of yours, Boy... er... your highness. It's always been the way of the Elidure line. They tolerate us well enough when they have need of us, but otherwise, the king has made it plain he is not overly fond of us. Honestly, I'm used to such treatment, but I don't condone Eilis or Lark being so disrespected."

"I am sorry," I apologize again. "This is ridiculous! He has you locked in here like a bunch of barn animals! I'll speak with my father first thing in the morning to see that you receive more comfortable quarters."

"If I truly wanted to be out of this room, there's not a soul in this castle who could stop me," replies Albain, a touch of bitterness in his tone. "And don't bother. We'll rest here for this evening, but we intend to be on our way at first light."

"So soon?" I ask, my voice breaking slightly.

Eilis rises and moves to clasp my hand, as she has hundreds of times before, but as she reaches out her fingers, she stays them, unsure of whether she should or not.

In reply, I reach forward and take her hand in my own. "This changes nothing, Eilis. Whether I'm prince or not, I'm still the same Boy you have always known."

I glance over at Lark who refuses to make eye contact with me. Instead, he looks down at his hands folded in his lap. It's obvious that something has been troubling him, and I intend to find out what I can do to alleviate his worries.

"Lark, are you all right?" I inquire.

"Lark," speaks Eilis gently. "Tell him."

Lark shakes his head emphatically. "No, Eilis, please no! He'll be so cross!" Lark bites his lip, and I can see that his entire form is trembling with fear.

"Tell me what?" I question curiously. Lark has been acting more peculiar than usual ever since we arrived in Vericus, and I can only guess that it must have something to do with what he needs to tell me.

Albain puts his hand on the kid's shoulder. "Lark, go on now. You have nothing to fear."

For several moments he says nothing while an agonized expression mirrors the war currently raging in his mind. Reluctantly, he looks up at me, and I can see that his blue eyes are brimming with tears. "Prince Trystan, I haven't been honest with you... with any of you."

I move across the room and plop down on the bed next to him. "What do you mean?"

"I know who I am... I've known for some time." This should be excellent news, but he says it so miserably that it catches me off guard.

"Lark, that's wonderful!" I say in an attempt to cheer him.

"It's not though... not really," he mutters.

Albain puts his enormous hand on Lark's shoulder. "Go on,

Lark. You've nothing to fear. We're right here with you. Tell him your name."

Lark takes a deep breath and tears his gaze away from me, unable to look me in the eyes any further. "Sebastian. My name is Sebastian."

I am overwhelmed by a sudden wave of realization. Yet, while I understand his meaning, my addled mind is hesitant to acknowledge the gravity of what he is saying. Still, there is no denying it, and piece by piece everything clicks into place.

I realize why Lark was kept apart from the rest of the prisoners.

I know why he was treated so differently.

The only thing I can't figure out is why he was eventually sent to live among us.

The idea seems so surreal, and I have to say it aloud to confirm its truth to my own ears. "You're his son... Sebastian's... Abirad's..."

Lark nods and buries his head in his hands. He weeps quietly, and when he pulls his hands away, his eyes are red and puffy, and tears pour down his face and drip off his pointed chin onto his dark blue shirt. "I've had my memories taken more times than I can count, and eventually, my father always started to feel guilty and would return my name to me. But this time... when I made him angry, when I made him shout the words, the spell didn't work, so he had to find some other clever way to punish me."

"That's why you were sent to the yards," I finish for him.

Lark draws in a ragged breath. "Yes. Harding said he couldn't stand to see me suffer anymore. Honestly, he was never fond of the way the prisoners were treated, but if he would have done something about it, Abirad would have had him killed or just wiped his memory, too. He promised he would find some way to help me. He was the one who told me to work next to you, Boy. He said I should get to know you. Then he convinced Abirad I should be placed with Eilis, as she was sure to look after me because everyone knew her to be kind."

I look to Eilis and she smiles slightly at this sentiment.

"Abirad wanted to teach me a lesson," continues Lark. "But I'd be of no use to him if I was completely broken. When Eilis started with her theory about who I was, Harding told me to go along with it. He said I'd already met the real prince, Boy, and that if we could get him back to King Ruden, maybe the king would be convinced to rule again and stop Abirad for good. Harding made me swear to keep who I was a secret. He said if you all found out, you'd likely turn me out... or far worse. I wouldn't have blamed you for it." Lark rises from his place beside me and begins to pace in front of the small, grimy window at the rear of the room. "But I tell you what's worse: keeping it all inside... lying every day to people, good people, who care about me... or did. You're back where you need to be, Prince Trystan, and I'm ready to go where I need to be."

"Where's that?" I ask in confusion.

"The dungeon," he answers simply. "Because of my awful, traitor father."

We all sit in silence, and I know that the others await some reaction from me, as if Lark's fragile fate hangs in the balance. "I'm not going to see you sent to the dungeons, Lark."

Lark looks shocked, as if he's just been spared from a beheading in what should be the final moments of his life. He lets out the deep breath he had been holding.

"I wish you would have told us sooner," I tell him, "but I understand why you didn't. Lark, it's important we keep this information between us," I insist. "Now that my father knows how I was treated by Abirad, he's biding his time until he can take revenge on him. He can't know you're Abirad's son. You've nothing to fear from me. As I said, I understand."

Lark nods numbly, and he still looks aggrieved. He glances nervously from Eilis to Albain.

"What's wrong, Lark?" I ask him. "Something still troubles you."

Lark leaps up and throws his arms around Eilis, clinging to

her as if hanging on for dear life. "Please… Please! Can I stay with you? You promised! You said to matter what!" There's a desperation to his frantic pleas. "Do you remember, Eilis? You said no matter what!"

"Aye, we did," agrees Albain, "and a Bromus never goes back on a promise."

"Lark, you've nothing to fear," adds Eilis. "As we've said, you will always have a place with us."

"What about Granda?" questions Lark fretfully as he resumes sitting next to me. "Once he knows who I really am, he'll probably hate me."

"Granda knows who you really are, Lark. You're a kind, wonderful boy who has done nothing to earn anything less than our affection. As for the origin of your birth, we'll explain it to him," soothes Eilis. "Granda will understand."

Lark is appeased by their responses, but something still seems to nag at his conscience.

"What is it, boy?" questions Albain.

"My father… he will still try to come for me." There is abject terror in his voice when he says it, as if simply mentioning Abirad will cause him to materialize before us.

Albain snorts. "Let him try."

Despite more assurances from all of us that everything will work out, Lark can't seem to shake the malaise that has ensnared him.

Finally, Albain sits on the other side of Lark, and I feel the shoddy bed creak under the added weight. "Lark, do you still want to know how I got this scar?" He gestures to his ravaged face.

Tentatively, Lark nods a reply.

Albain glances to Eilis who comes to stand beside him and rests her hand on his shoulder. "My father… he wasn't a good man either. My mother died when I was young, and after she passed, it completely broke my father. He had always been a bit of a hard man, and heavy-handed, but she had managed to keep him in check and had a calming effect on him."

"Like Eilis can calm you down?" offers Lark.

Albain nods and smiles up at Eilis. "Aye. You're right about that. Anyway, my father took to drinking. If he was awake, there was a bottle or flask attached to his lips. It always put him in a piss poor mood, and I can't tell you how many times I had to help him home by half carrying and half dragging him from whatever brothel, tavern, or ditch he happened to pass out in."

Suddenly, I see a flash of pain in Albain's brown eyes, and he takes a moment to compose himself before he continues his story. "One night, he had been drinking Rot Ale, a particularly nasty concoction they make down south. Strong stuff; puts the devil in folk when they drink it. Needless to say, it had quite an effect on my father. Made him even meaner than usual, and when I helped him home, he was raging at me for some trivial thing or another."

Albain pauses, his face simultaneously displaying anger and something akin to remorse. "When we got home, he decided for whatever reason I needed a good arse kicking, so I took a few good shots from him, but when he picked up the wine bottle and started waving it at me, I shoved him away from me. This made him angry, and he smashed the end of the bottle on the table."

The warrior rests his elbows on his knees and clasps his hands in front of him, resting his chin on his knuckles. He draws in a ragged breath, and I know this memory must be difficult for him to recount. "I remember the feel of the glass scraping against my bone. I remember my back hitting the table in our common room as he drove the edge further into my face, all the while, cursing the day I was born and telling me I was a waste of air. I remember the sour smell of wine on his breath. I remember grabbing the knife on the table and jamming it into his throat, and the sick gurgling sound he made after as he gasped for breath. It was my first kill... not on a battlefield, but in my own home."

Lark's eyes widen, and we are all stricken by a sudden

silence, save for Eilis, who Albain must have told before this night. She whispers something comforting in his ear, and I see his expression soften as he gazes up at her with love and adoration in his eyes.

"Albie, how old were you...when you had to kill your father?" Lark asks quietly.

"I was 14," he replies.

"In the time I've known you, I've never once seen you drink ale or wine," I observe. "Is that why?"

Albain nods. "Aye. The very smell of it turns my stomach, and even if it didn't, I wouldn't dare pass a drop over my lips. I'll tell you the truth of it. I fear no man nor death itself. I fear only three things in this life. First, that I'd ever lose this woman beside me. She's the only one I've ever loved, and the only one I'll ever love, of that I'm sure. I'd sooner brave the fires of hell than to ever part from her."

Eilis wraps her arms around his shoulders and hugs him tightly before placing a kiss on his cheek causing Albain to smile slightly.

He continues, gazing meaningfully into Lark's eyes. "The second is that I'd ever fail my family should I be so blessed with one. I remember the disappointment I bore for my father, and no wife nor child of mine should ever be made to feel such. But last, is perhaps my greatest fear... that I should somehow come to be a man like *him*. I would sooner die than let that happen." He places a hand on Lark's shoulder. "But that's the thing of it. At the end of the day, at least a part of our fate is in our hands. We can choose to take a different path from our fathers."

I know that Albain shared his story for the sake of Lark in the hopes of proving to the kid that his father's sins are not his own, but honestly, his words bring comfort to me as well. I am struggling with how to justify my own father's actions, and it occurs to me, there is no justification. He may be my father, and he may be the king, but that does not necessarily mean he is a good or just person.

"Lark, I'm telling you all this for a reason," explains Albain. "King or peasant. Sorcerer or slave. Who our fathers are does not define us. We must strive to be better than them, and if I ever do have my own son, I hope he will be better than me, as well."

* * *

The following morning, just as the sun begins to cast its first rays over the city of Vericus, I gather with my friends to see them off on their departure. My father, surrounded by a dozen of his personal guards, stands some distance behind me as I say my farewells to my companions. Brock, too, says his goodbyes. As he is not a Bromus, and I have spoken so highly of him and how he saved my life, my father has agreed to allow him to remain with me in the castle, and even offered him the position of my personal bodyguard, once he is formally trained for such a task.

I stand in front of the enormous, Bromus warrior who I have come to regard as both a protector and great friend. I extend my hand to Albain, who accepts it and gives it single shake.

"Safe travels, Albain," I say to him. "I'd ask you to promise to take good care of them..." I glance to Eilis and Lark. "...but I know you will."

"On my life," he assures me, placing his fist over his heart.

Suddenly, he pulls me forward for a quick but firm embrace. I hear the drawing of dozens of weapons, and when I look back, my father's guards are at the ready. The king raises his hand to stay them, but my father maintains a steely gaze upon Albain, as if hoping that he will act out of turn and give my father some excuse to act against him.

Albain releases me as he rolls his eyes. "Ruden can bugger off. He's no king of mine," he mutters. "You're a good man,

Trystan. Don't let others change that in you. Remember what I said: let us all be better men than our fathers."

I glance back at my father, then return my attention to Albain. "I'll be the same Boy I've always been."

"I'll hold you to that," replies Albain. He grabs the reins of his horse and swings one of his long legs over the beast's back before settling into his saddle.

Next, I stop in front of Lark and ruffle his blonde hair, causing him to giggle.

"You know, I've always hated when you do that... but I think I'm going to miss it," he tells me. He glances towards my father and his men, as if afraid to draw any nearer to me for fear they might use their weapons on him.

I take the initiative and pull him into a hug. "Be good, Lark."

Lark smiles sadly. "I hope to be. I'll miss you."

"I'll miss you, too, kid. But we can write to each other, and when things calm down a bit, perhaps I can come visit." Even as I say the words, I doubt their truth, but it is enough to make Lark smile, albeit momentarily. "Lark, before you go... there's something I need to ask you."

He looks up at me inquisitively.

"I know you might not want to talk about it, but... the girl that was mentioned in the memory... Emily. Do you know who she was?"

Lark shrugs. "I honestly don't know. He never mentioned her to me, but the way he spoke of her in the memory... she must have been pretty important to him."

It couldn't have been Lark's mother as he was born several years after the Bread Riots. I can't help but to let out an involuntary sigh. We still haven't figured out the extent of Abirad's ambitions, and the lack of such knowledge makes him even more dangerous.

Brock helps Lark into the saddle of his strawberry roan horse, a fitting mount for a child who still grieves for a mother who loved strawberries. I see so much of myself in him: deprived of a mother's care and left to the impulses of a difficult father. Though our origins may be different, at least a part of our journey is the same.

Finally, I find myself staring into Eilis's big, brown eyes, deep pools of kindness that have always brought me hope in even the darkest of times. I hand her Old Man's bag.

"Keep it safe, Eilis. I don't trust I will be able to do much in the way of finding a caster here, as I've told you my father's feeling on them. Perhaps you will have better luck," I tell her.

She nods in agreement. "I intend on meeting with Hivolk as soon as I arrive home. Perhaps he knows someone who can help or can at least point me in the right direction."

"Does it still feel odd to say that?" I ask her. "*Home.*"

"At first. Now it just feels right. I pray that you will come to have the same feeling when you think of your own home."

"I hope you're right, but I'm beginning to doubt it."

She eyes me with concern. "Remember, Trystan, there's not a place in this world I wouldn't go to get to you if you needed me." She lowers her voice to a conspiratorial whisper. "Even if it means storming the bloody walls of Vericus to do it."

I can't help but to laugh. "Albain has definitely had an effect on you."

She looks over at her Bloodsworn, her betrothed, and smiles, and the mountainous warrior responds in kind. "That he has."

"Old Man once told me that home is not a place. I think I'm finally beginning to understand what he meant."

Eilis considers this for a moment. "I suppose that makes sense. The Bromus never remain in one place. When we say home, it's not really a physical location; it's who we share our lives with." Eilis glances back to Albain and Lark. "Wherever they are is my home,"

"I'm not sure what I'm going to do without you, Eilis."

"You'll never be without me. If you ever have need of me, say the word, and I'll be there. It doesn't matter how many roles I have as heir, one of my greatest gifts is to be your friend.

That will never change."

"What a pair we are. You heir to the All-Chieftain, and me the Prince of Allanon. Old Man is surely laughing somewhere," I say.

"He'd be proud of you, you know," replies Eilis. "He thought the world of you."

"And of you," I return. I wrap my arms around her, and we hold onto each other for several minutes. I don't want to let her go as I'm terrified of parting with my truest friend. "I love you, Eilis. You'll make a fine All-Chieftain one day. The Bromus are fortunate to have someone as wise and kindhearted as you. Take care of yourself... and the others."

"I love you, too, Trystan. Until we meet again, *Boy*..."

Suddenly, I hear my father loudly clear his throat, as if wordlessly scolding me for impropriety. Eilis and I reluctantly pull apart, and I move to stand next to Brock.

Eilis mounts her horse, and she, Albain, and Lark turn their steeds towards the gates of Vericus.

In that moment, if I'd known it could very well be the last time I'd see them, I would have made it a point to thank Albain for his wisdom and express my respect and admiration for him.

I would have held on to Eilis, my oldest and dearest friend, all the longer.

I would have reassured Lark a million times that all would be set right and that his future was promising.

But instead, with a heavy heart, I watch them disappear into the horizon.

EPILOGUE

Immediately following the departure of my friends, I undertake the grueling process of becoming fit to rule in my father's eyes. I spend most of my days listening to my father lecture me regarding what is proper behavior for a prince. We spend hours discussing how to spot liars, how to quell revolts, and how to punish those who challenge the laws of the land. All the while, I can't help but to think there must be far more to it than what he tells me. Never am I given a lesson on how to be just and reasonable, how to mediate disagreements, or how to forge alliances. Never does he teach me how ensure my subjects are well cared for, or how to address potential threats posed by outside countries or enemies within our borders. I know that these are the things that are most important, yet these topics are neglected during my father's discourses.

Other than that, I spend much of my time studying with my personal tutor, Galius, who may legitimately be 110 years old, or in the training yards refining my skills in combat with Tobias, a grizzled, veteran warrior who has cumulatively spent more years on the field of battle than I have been alive.

When I don't have anywhere specific that I need to be, I spend a great deal of my time in the library or in my chambers. With every passing day, my father's behavior seems to grow more erratic. His paranoia soon convinces him that I'm going to be spirited away again, so he has me sequestered in my room for lengthy periods of time while the guards search every inch of the castle for potential threats to my safety. During these times, I try to distract myself by practicing the lute that Ragnar gave me or attempting to teach Brock to play chess. He's not fond of the game, but he humors me by feigning interest.

❋ ❋ ❋

A few weeks after my arrival to Vericus, winter descends upon the capital with the full force of its unyielding nature. From the windows of my chambers, I watch the changing scenery and observe how the deep snows overpower the grounds and the way the ice clings to the windows. I also see the change in the people as well. It is a harsh and unforgiving landscape, and the people of the city begin to fall to the icy clutches that diminish the food supply and make simply existing an insurmountable task.

Some of the townsfolk begin to linger at the gates. Their dirty clothing is threadbare, and their bare feet are pressed against the frigid snow. Their chattering lips are blue with cold as they huddle against each other for warmth. Gaunt faces are turned towards the castle, and lean bodies with protruding ribs quake as blustery gusts of wind tear through the grounds. I have known hunger from my days at Castle Ciar, and I can practically see their empty bellies growing hollower by the second. All the while, wagon after wagon laden with food stores from the surrounding towns arrives at the castle, keeping our larders overflowing with food. Soon, the townsfolk at the gates begin to protest, begging for aid for their starving children, ill elders, and the rest of their shivering, underprivileged kin.

It's the coldest evening of the year when the soldiers are dispatched from the castle. I am awoken from a fitful sleep by the screams. When I look out the window, the snow is painted with blood and littered with fallen bodies. I see their horrified faces and hear their anguished cries as they are cut down where they stand. A few of them flee but are chased down by the guards and made to pay with their lives for what my father perceives as disobedience

The next day, freshly fallen snow has covered all traces of the incident. It's as if nothing happened, and for a moment, I wonder if perhaps it was the product of some awful nightmare. However, when I ask Girard about it, his face goes pale and he mutters "King's orders" under his breath before making a hasty exit.

After that, I notice that any passing townsfolk give the road to the castle a wide berth and do not even dare to glance towards the castle.

I wish for all the world I could do something or say something that would change my father's course, but most days I feel like little more than a glorified prisoner. I'm not allowed to leave the castle, and even walking around the grounds, I am under heavy guard. My only reprieve is at night when the guards remain outside my chambers. This was a matter of conflict between my father and me, but I was able to convince him to simply let Brock remain with me in an adjoining room. While my friend's snoring can be unbearable, it's far more comforting than the silence that I would be otherwise left to.

There is also loneliness, a deep, permeating loneliness that I cannot seem to shake. While I was imprisoned, I always had Old Man or my other companions to bring some semblance of cheer to my mind. At first, I receive regular correspondence from Eilis. In fact, my only knowledge of the world outside of Vericus comes to me through Eilis's messages. It's how I learn that survivors of Castle Ciar, including Harding and Isabel, showed up at the Bromus camp. It's how I learn that the Bromus lead an assault on Castle Ciar, but they found the place to be little more than a tomb. It had been abandoned by Abirad and those loyal to him for many months. While most of the prisoners escaped, there were those who were too old or sick to flee, and they were left in their cells where they starved and succumbed to slow and painful deaths. The bodies from the conflict between the two factions of guards were still where they had fallen, and when the Bromus found them, they were little more than piles of bones and rusted armor.

But suddenly, Eilis's letters stop, and I began to fear something awful has happened to her or that she simply has forgotten about me in her growing duties as heir to the All-Chieftain.

* * *

It is a few months later when I realize my father has abandoned his promise to me. Upon seeing how heartbroken I was in the wake of Scarlet's absence and the departure of my friends, he had vowed to do all he could to bring Scarlet back to Vericus.

I can't bear the smell or taste of apple. The very thought of it once brought butterflies to my stomach, but now those delicate creatures have been crushed by the stones that weigh down the pit of my gut when I think of her.

Once again, I ask him if there have been any further leads regarding where she may have gone.

Finally, my father sighs in exasperation and says, "Trystan, it is time you abandon this foolishness. The girl is gone... for good... and you're better off without her."

I quickly rise from my chair, nearly knocking it over in the process. "What? How can you say that, father? You promised me you would find her!"

He crosses his arms over his chest, a measure I have come to learn means that nothing I say or do will sway him. "Trystan, you must let her go. You said before that her uncle is Fenton Hall. That man has been in and out of our dungeons his entire life. If not for the fact he's occasionally useful, I would have had him executed years ago. If she's kin to him, she's not the sort you should be taking up with. It's best if you cease searching for her, son."

My heart thunders in my chest with both grief and indignation, and without another word, I excuse myself from his presence, and make it a point to say as little as possible to him for the next sennight.

* * *

Some time later, it's Brock who uncovers my father's second betrayal. It is in the spring, and I am sitting in my chamber and reading from a book about military formations and tactics when he enters the room.

"Your highness," he begins and bows before me.

"Brock, I've told you time and time again, you're like a brother to me. It's just Trystan to you," I correct him for likely the millionth time.

"Trystan? Your father says otherwise," comes his curt reply.

"Brock..."

"First names are for equals, and we both know I am not equal to you," replies Brock. Instantly, I can tell that something is troubling him, something beyond formalities.

"Brock, what's truly bothering you?"

Brock sighs heavily then crosses to the door to ensure that it is properly closed. He beckons for me to join him on the far side of the room and lowers his voice to a whisper. "The king threatened me with the dungeons if I told you, but I have to, Trystan... Eilis never stopped writing to you."

My heart leaps in my chest at the acknowledgment that my oldest friend has not truly forgotten me, but its wings are pierced, and it sinks into my stomach when I realize the implication. "Then... why have I not been receiving her messages?"

Brock averts his gaze, unable to make eye contact with me. "Her messages are being destroyed before you can see them. It's been going on for months now. One almost got through last week, so today, your father called me in and made me agree to intercept any I find before you can get them. I would never do that, but I told him I would to appease him."

The devastation I feel at my father's orders pains me more than I can express. For several moments, Brock and I sit in unhappy silence, until finally I say, "Brock, I need your help. Send a message to Eilis at once. Tell her what has happened. Let her know that any future messages should be sent directly to you. Read the messages and report them to me. Be sure to destroy the papers themselves so my father remains unaware of them. If anyone inquires as to why you are receiving so many messages of late, tell them you have decided to arrange a marriage between yourself and Catherine for next year."

Brock blushes considerably as the thought of a betrothal with Catherine likely isn't foreign to him. He has already been corresponding with her regularly, so an increase in messages in anticipation of a wedding would be a reasonable assumption

Soon after, Eilis sends word that those loyal to Abirad are amassing their forces on the border, and their numbers are being bolstered by soldiers from the neighboring country of Evinster and Talvair mercenaries. Sometime later, the All-Chieftain himself personally scrawls a message that he sends to Brock so that it may reach me.

While I bear no love for your father, you will always be held in my highest regard. Call upon us, and the Bromus will answer. We'll ensure you have a kingdom left to rule.

* * *

One night at dinner, I overhear my father discussing the possibility that Abirad's forces will move against Allanon.

His general, Matthias Kearney is an enormous man who looks more like a wall than a human being. Next to Albain, he is probably one of the most fearsome warriors in all of Allanon. As a result, the look of consternation on his typically impassive face causes me to be immediately concerned. "Your highness, every day Abirad and his forces grow bolder. Even now his allies encroach upon our borders, and there is word that Abirad himself and his soldiers intend to make their way towards Vericus. If we don't put them in check now-"

My father seems unconcerned and loudly boasts, "Let them come then! The walls of Vericus have never been breached. Stop bothering me with these inconsequential matters. The prince will be 17 this autumn. While the Festival of Mercy is still banned given our relations with Blackwood, I wish to host a most memorable celebration for him!"

I offer a weak smile, but in reality, I want to sink into the floor from the embarrassment brought upon me by his foolishness.

"But your highness, we've received word from the All-Chieftain-" Matthias is abruptly cut off by my father's venomous words.

My father reaches forward, his hand moving faster than lightning, and roughly seizes Matthias by the front of his armor. "*All-Chieftain*? Are my own people now lauding Seamus Oakheart with his self-serving titles? The old Oakheart is more a threat to Allanon than that fool sorcerer." He gives Matthias a rough shove backwards. "Don't be a fool, Matthias."

"But the All- er... Oakheart offers the aid of the Bromus to fortify our borders and to protect Allanon," persists Matthias. "Perhaps we should-"

"Do you now fancy yourself King of Allanon, Matthias? I AM YOUR KING!" my father roars. "We don't need the aid of the Bromus! Now cease your incessant stupidity!" my father shouts irately. "Get out of my sight, or I'll see that your traitor head is put upon a pike!"

Matthias quickly takes his leave of us, and as he passes

me, I give him a sympathetic look. He has an impeccable reputation as a soldier, and he is known throughout the kingdom as a brilliant tactician. It is disheartening that my father is so quick to disregard his advice.

It is even worse when the general's predictions are correct. Reports begin to pour in regarding Abirad's numbers, and even my father must acknowledge that they dwarf our own. When Abirad's soldiers begin to lay waste to the outer cities of Allanon and move in towards Vericus, my father very begrudgingly calls upon the All-Chieftain for his aid. It is agreed that the Bromus will lead an assault against Abirad's forces to give us time to muster as many troops as possible.

* * *

Soon, it is summer, and the unrelenting sun beats down on the sparring ring as I manage to land a few clean hits against Tobias, my sword ringing against his armor.

"I've been meaning to ask you for quite some time. Who was your trainer before me?" He asks, obviously impressed with my skill. "You fight like a Bromus!"

I'm not sure if it's a compliment or an insult given my father's stance on the Bromus. He grins broadly, so I assume it is the former.

"I've met Old Oakheart, and that's not his style," he comments as he tosses me a skin filled with cool water. He draws the back of his gauntlet across his forehead to wipe away the sweat from his brow.

I take a long drink from the waterskin. "A man named Albain. He's arguably their greatest warrior."

Tobias scratches his beard and pushes a handful of shaggy, gray hair out of his eyes. He always seems to be in good humor, and he's one of the few people in the castle I can claim to enjoy the company of. "Never heard of him."

I consider this for a moment. "Many call him The Cur on

account he's the last of the Cur Clan."

In surprise, he expels a stream of water from his mouth. He sputters for a moment then says, "Now that's a name I know. Not a warrior worth his salt who hasn't heard of him. I'd be reluctant to take him on, even if I was in my prime. He must have been a good teacher."

"He was," I agree.

The conversation makes my heart ache terribly, and I'm poignantly reminded of how much I miss them. I miss all of them. I miss talking with Eilis about anything and everything, and the way she always knows exactly what to say to put my mind at ease. I miss Albain's gruffness and the protectiveness he has shown over all of us in our makeshift family of misfits. I miss Lark's mischief and even the thousands of questions he asks a day. Most of all, I miss Scarlet. I miss her smile and her shining blue eyes. I miss her voice and the light touch of her hand upon my arm. I miss waking to her in the morning and going to sleep every night with her resting upon my shoulder.

Tobias and I shoulder our weapons and he heads off towards the barracks while I make my way to my quarters to wash up before my midday meal.

After thoroughly cleaning my face and changing into fresh garments, I plop down on my bed, and my mind begins to wander to Scarlet.

There is a soft knock on my door, and Brock enters. His face is pale and his eyes are wild with worry.

Instantly, I spring up from my bed and rush towards him. "Brock, what is it? Is it about the weapon?"

One of Eilis's letters had alluded to a weapon Abirad may have in his possession. It was referenced in one of the papers Old Man took from his tower and hastily stuffed in his bag. During our time apart, Eilis managed to track down a caster named Mara and her apprentice and granddaughter, Fray. They have been staying with the Bromus and assisting Eilis in deciphering Old Man's journals and uncovering more about the nature of the amulet. While gathering information, they stumbled upon the designs for the weapon. Apparently, that was why Abirad required the singing stones. Eilis had expressed fear that the sorcerer may have successfully built the weapon and could be planning to turn it on his enemies, namely us.

"I just received word from Eilis. Some of the Bromus doubled back to Castle Ciar to see if they could find any trace of it, but there was nothing."

"Damn it!" I can't contain my frustration, and I have to take a moment to try to collect myself before I press him any further on the matter. "Where else could he have it? He spent years acquiring all those stones, and the more there are in one place, the louder the noise they would produce. They should be simple to locate."

"That's just it," replies Brock anxiously. "Old Man had a spell that could mask their music, so they could be hidden in plain sight and no one would be the wiser. If he had the spell, there's a good chance his apprentice, Abirad, may know of it, too."

"What more does Eilis say?"

"She thinks we should evacuate the city," relates Brock. "The All-Chieftain sent word to your father suggesting the same, but I bet you can guess his response."

"I can only imagine."

"He started raving about how the Bromus are just fear-mongering so that we'll leave the city, and the Bromus themselves can take Vericus unopposed."

"What foolishness!" Furiously, I begin to pace the room. I am once again disappointed by my father's ambivalence to the wellbeing of his people. "How are they faring? Eilis, Albain, Lark? Are they alright? What of the All-Chieftain?"

Brock's expression falters at my question. "Lark is safely tucked away and under heavy protection in the main Bromus encampment. The Bromus continue to hold the line... but..."

"Brock..." I grasp his arm.

"Their losses have been great. Eilis is and Albain are all

right. She's already developing quite a reputation as a strong leader and fierce warrior, and no enemy can harm her with Albain by her side. The All-Chieftain stands strong, but so many have fallen."

His reluctance to look me in the eye tells me that he has something awful to say, but I'm at a loss as to what it can be. He takes a deep breath. "However... Ragnar..."

As soon as he utters the name of the heir of the Bear Clan, my legs grow weak beneath me. During our time with the Bromus, I had come to regard him as a friend, and the expression on Brock's face tells me all I need to know before he even finishes the thought.

"He and his father both fell in battle," reveals Brock with a tremor in his voice. "His sister, Pala, isn't much older than Lark. She stands to become the next Chieftain of the Bear Clan."

The news burdens my heart, and I am compelled to take a seat in one of the plush, high-backed armchairs in my bedroom. I think of Ragnar's amiable nature and the way he tried to comfort me after Old Man's passing. I think of the kindness he showed me while we were at the encampment, and the beautiful songs he played on his lute, one of which holds a place of honor in my chambers. Since I've been in Vericus, I've used it many times to dispel the melancholy that so frequently affects me. I practice the melodies Ragnar taught me, and in those moments, I find some solace here.

"I'm sorry, Trystan. I know you thought well of him," apologizes Brock. "Some of the Bromus forces are falling back to support Vericus, in case the lines break. Eilis and Albain themselves will lead some of the allied Bromus to a short distance outside our walls. They should be in position within the hour."

"And what does my father say of this?"

Brock rolls his eye, and a heavy sigh escapes his lips. "He says it's not necessary."

"I need to do something about this," I say, rising to my

feet and making my way towards the door. "I need to try to talk some sense into my father."

"Good luck," mutters Brock, falling into step behind me.

We quickly make our way to the throne room, where we find my father loudly shouting at Girard. The Captain of the Guard looks relieved when we enter, as if our presence will be enough to grant him some respite from the king's ire.

My father grins broadly at me as I approach. "Ah! Trystan! I was just about to summon you! I'd like to speak with you about the plans for your birthday next month."

"Father, I-"

People say that in times of tragedy, the world comes to a halt, as if that moment is temporarily frozen in time, and you can see the fell shadow of impending sorrow and loss with perfect clarity.

The sound comes from far beneath us and resounds with such a deafening pitch that it causes everyone in the room to cover their ears with their cupped hands. Even then, it remains unbearable. Somehow, the sound is familiar to me, and with horror, I realize the unmistakable tone of singing stones. I drop to my knees in pain, my teeth chattering and my cries of agony drowned out by the sharp roar that fills the entirety of the throne room. Suddenly, Brock is next to me and pulling me to my feet. My father has fallen from his throne and writhes upon the floor as he holds his ears in an attempt to drown out the sound. Girard half drags and half carries him towards the door as the other guards run forward to assist us.

Suddenly, the sound peaks in a terrifying crescendo, and an immense explosion rocks the throne room, knocking everyone therein off their feet. Sconces and torches fall from the walls, catching the long curtains and banners on fire. The enormous chandeliers suspended from the ceiling come crashing to the ground, narrowly missing my father and Girard as they scramble to their feet. The windows explode with a violent shatter, sending splinters and large shards of glass scattering across the floor.

Once again, Brock rights me on my feet. We try to make our way to the main doors, but one of the stone columns that supports the ceiling of the throne room begins to collapse. I can't get out of the way fast enough, and suddenly, I feel Brock give a sharp push to my back that sends me sprawling forward out of the path of the pillar's destruction. I glance back and see one of Brock's hands and one of his boots sticking out of an immense pile of rubble.

My hearing has been temporarily damaged, so I cannot hear myself scream as I dodge the falling beams and fiery banners that plummet to the floor around me. I try to make my way back to Brock, but Girard appears next to me. Blood pours from a rather severe wound in his head. He throws me over his shoulder and makes his way for the door. His first duty is to the safety and wellbeing of my father, and it is then I realize why he tries to carry me away instead.

There, in the center of the room where my father's throne once stood, is a massive beam that became dislodged from the ceiling. It must have cracked and broken on the way down because half of it has decimated the seat of power, and the other has pinned my father to the ground. His eyes are vacant and blood pools around his head and drips from his open mouth.

I feel Girard stumble as a large chunk of stone slams into the back of his knee, causing him to pitch forward. We both topple to the ground just as another beam falls from the ceiling above us.

The door is nearly fifteen yards from where I have fallen, and despite the pain that accosts every inch of my body, I roll to my stomach and attempt to drag myself forward. I don't make it very far before the smoke burns my lungs, causing me to cough and choke, and my eyes to feel heavy.

Then there is darkness.

I don't know for how long.

I see only the briefest flashes of what occurs around me.

I hear shouting and one of the doors to the throne room explodes inwards, kicked in by a familiar and imposing figure.

Suddenly, I hear Eilis's voice in my ear. "Trystan! Trystan! Albain! Come help me!"

I feel my body borne upwards by strong arms.

"The king is gone," comes another voice. *Harding?*

Then comes Dennan, his deep voice calling out across the room. "I've found Brock."

There is the frantic sound of many hands digging, discarding large pieces of rock upon the ground.

"Is he-?" asks Eilis, her voice heavy with emotion.

* * *

My dreams are filled with the sharp, acrid smell of smoke and the heat of flames. I am haunted by the vision of my father's broken body and lifeless eyes, and the few parts of Brock that are not buried under a mountain of rubble. I will my eyes to open and my body to move, but I fail miserably at both of these tasks.

Occasionally, I hear voices around me and feel the gentle touch of a healer's hands and the binding of many wounds.

"It was all right under the castle," comes Albain's grave voice. "Old tunnels beneath the dungeons. The castle took the worst of it, but the entire city is in ruins."

"What of Abirad's conspirator?" *Eilis.*

"We tracked down Fenton Hall and have him in custody."

"How long do you think he'd been smuggling the stones into the capital at Abirad's behest?" That voice is the All-Chieftain.

The voices fade, and when I hear them again, they are little more than hushed whispers, and some of the low mur-

muring gives way to the sounds of weeping. I want so desperately to wake up fully, to hop up from the makeshift bed upon which I lay and assure my friends that I will be all right.

But in a way, it's easier to let the sleep overtake me. When I'm asleep, there's no pain. No dead mother. No dead father. No ruined kingdom. Maybe if I can just let go instead of trying to stay, I can see the grey-eyed woman again and find some peace.

It's then that I hear her voice, a soft whisper in my ear that cuts through the darkness that has nearly claimed me.

Scarlet.

"Fight. Fight, Boy. Come back to me." Something soft and warm brushes against my lips, and I smell lavender and taste apple.

A tremor runs through my body as every part of me is desperate to awake from its slumber and seek out her comfort. If she's truly here, if it isn't some torturous dream, then there is hope left. There is a girl I love, a girl who I feared might be lost to me forever, an incredible young woman who came back to me, even though she was likely afraid I would hate her or reject her given her part in my kidnapping.

"He'll be okay, won't he, Scarlet?" *Lark.*

"That boy is a fighter," comes Albain's voice. "He won't be taken so easily."

"He *is* a fighter. He always has been, and he always will be," Eilis agrees. "He's strong. He'll pull through."

Only Brock is missing, and I wish for all the world I could know his fate in that instant.

My friends, the family I have chosen, surround me, believing that I will return to them again, and despite the fact it would be easier to simply succumb to the darkness, I know that Scarlet is right.

I *must* fight.

My friends, my family, need me.

My people need me.

My kingdom needs me.

Vericus, the symbol of Allanon's power, sits in ruins, little more than smoldering piles of rock and ash. The people will need a strong leader to unite them, to heal the wounds my father has inflicted upon his subjects. I won't be like him and turn my back on them. Despite all I have lost in my relatively short life, how many more citizens have lost everything?

Abirad must be held accountable for his crimes, the full extent of which seems to grow by the day.

I feel the light touch of Scarlet's fingers as she smooths the hair from my forehead. "Trystan."

As much as it pains me, both in body and spirit, I call upon every measure of strength I can, and I open my eyes, prepared to face a world of ashes.

To be continued in Book 2 of *The Stolen Heir Series*.

A World of Ashes

ACKNOWLEDGMENTS

I began *A Gift of Name* six or seven years ago, and it has undergone a massive transformation from its earliest form. Along the way, I encountered innumerable obstacles, but despite shelving it multiple times, I always believed it would one day turn into something beautiful.

I certainly could not have done this alone.

I'd like to thank my incredible editor, Sara Stevenson, who laughed, cried, and raged with me as the story began to take shape. When I struggled with how to proceed with certain parts of the story or the development of certain characters, I was always able to count on Sara as a voice of reason. She may be the only other person on the planet who loves these characters to the degree that I do!

I'd like to again thank Sara, along with Cortney Leister and Marceline "Mac" Locklyre, my co-founders of Writers 4 A Purpose. Their support has been unparalleled during this journey.

Chris Shearer may legitimately be some kind of art wizard. His skill with creating the covers for this series is absolutely awe-inspiring, and I can't thank him enough for his work on this project.

During the creation of this series, I have been immeasurably blessed with excellent test readers. Thank you to Elizabeth, Emma, Ryley, Tyler, Austin, Sarah, and Lizzie. Additionally, my gratitude to Olivia, whose feedback was indispensable during this process.

Gaven, there is a reason that I chose you as the recipient of the dedication. Without your early encouragement and your belief in the possibility of this story, this series would have never come to fruition. You have my eternal gratitude, respect, and admiration.

Thank you to my students (past, present, and future) who continue to inspire me to practice what I preach in regards to writing.

All of my love and gratitude to my family and friends, who endured countless ramblings and rantings about the progression of this story, and without whose unconditional love and support, this piece would have never seen the light of day.

Bryan, you deserve a medal for enduring having to listen to me talk about this book all the time. You've patiently sacrificed and frequently woke up to an empty bed while I toiled away during all hours of the night. Ben, you're still far too young to read Mommy's book, but one day, I hope you do, and I hope that you are proud of me and that you love the story I have told. I love you both with all my heart, always.

Last, but certainly not least, thank you to the readers. My goal all along has never been to achieve fame or make money. The only thing I have ever wanted is to tell a story that people will love, and I hope these characters and this tale have found their ways into your hearts.

ABOUT THE AUTHOR

Val Cates is a teacher, author, and one of the founding members of Writers 4 A Purpose, an organization founded by writers who are committed to giving back to their communities through writing. In addition, Val hosts a series of videos on social media that is geared towards inspiring fellow writers.

Val is an equal opportunity writer. She does not confine herself to a specific genre, format, or audience. She appreciates all of these things for the uniqueness they offer.

For more information and to follow Val's work, visit

www.valcates.com

Made in the USA
Middletown, DE
21 June 2019